Battle of

"You aren't going to run off alone again," he warned.

"I think you're forgetting something, McIntire. I'm the boss here and I'll give the orders."

He closed the distance between them, grabbing her shoulders when he reached her. "Do you want to prove that?"

"Yes!" she bit out hatefully.

The lips that covered hers were relentless, devouring. Her mind screamed at her to resist. . . .

Praise for Summer Rose
By Bonnie K. Winn:

"Superb . . . a spicy, sensuous story with touches of humor that will touch your heart . . . You won't be able to put it down!"   —*Affaire de Coeur*

"An enjoyable clash of wills . . . exccllent."
—*Romantic Times*

"Excitement is at a high level . . . heartwarming."
—*Rendezvous*

Diamond Wildflower Romance

A breathtaking line of searing romance novels . . . where destiny meets desire in the untamed fury of the American West.

Diamond Books by Bonnie K. Winn

SUMMER ROSE
RECKLESS WIND

RECKLESS WIND

BONNIE K. WINN

DIAMOND BOOKS, NEW YORK

This book is a Diamond original edition,
and has never been previously published.

RECKLESS WIND

A Diamond Book / published by arrangement with
the author

PRINTING HISTORY
Diamond edition / June 1993

ISBN: 1-55773-902-1

Diamond Books are published by The Berkley Publishing Group,
200 Madison Avenue, New York, NY 10016.
The name "DIAMOND" and its logo
are trademarks belonging to Charter Communications, Inc.

PRINTED IN THE UNITED STATES OF AMERICA

10 9 8 7 6 5 4 3 2 1

To my parents. I love you.

Acknowledgments

Webster defines support as helping, sustaining, defending, comforting, and promoting. I define support as Howard. Thank you, my love.

To my editor, Judith Stern, and my agent, Jane Jordan Browne. You are the best.

Far as the eye could reach, the long and dusty roadway of the cowboys lay silent . . . Here was a riot of animal intensity of life, a mutiny of physical man, the last outbreak of innate savagery and primitive man against the day of shackles and subjugation. The men of that rude day lived vehemently. The earth is trampled over their bold hearts, and they have gone back into the earth, the air, the sky, and the wildflowers.

—Emerson Hough, *The Story of the Cowboy* (1897)

Chapter
1

Wyoming Territory,
1870

He certainly wasn't the groom she'd always pictured. Long, blackish hair hung over the face buried in the stale bedding of the cell's cot, while seemingly yards of body hunched into the inadequate space. When he snorted in his sleep, she was glad his features remained hidden.

Turning to the territorial marshal, she focused instead on the huge key that dangled from a round holder.

"You're sure he was only locked up for being drunk?" Jem Whitaker asked doubtfully, her brown eyes assessing the prone man's form.

"Yep. That and breakin' two of the saloon's best poker tables."

"Mean, is he?"

The marshal shrugged. "No more'n most. Just had a snoot full."

"Why didn't he pay his fine?" she persisted, wondering if the hidden face was pitted with smallpox, marred by broken teeth, or possibly worse.

"He wasn't in a talking mood last night, and neither was I. You want to get him out or not?"

Jem hesitated only for a moment. "Yes." She paused again. "I do."

While she counted out the money to pay the stranger's fine, she signaled to her companion, Pete Johnson, a sturdy-looking man with rather unremarkable features. He vanished through the doorway, and before the marshal had opened the cell, Pete had returned with a wagon.

"Don't 'spect he's gonna wake up on his own," the marshal observed.

Jem nodded to her companion, who hoisted the inert cowboy's form over his shoulder and walked solidly toward the door.

"What's his name?" Jem asked, her eyes following his long form.

"McIntire. Reese McIntire."

The marshal swung the cell door shut. The clanking pierced Jem's heart for a moment, then she swallowed and started forward. The ranch was a long, hard ride from town. She hadn't time for foolish whimsy.

"His pony's out back," the marshal added.

Nodding to the marshal, Jem walked outside and noted that Pete had already retrieved McIntire's horse and tied it to the back of the wagon. Climbing into the wagon seat, she deliberately ignored Pete's compelling stare.

"You sure about this, Jem?"

Not trusting her voice, she nodded. With a sigh he snapped the reins and began the ride home. She refused to look any further at the man in the wagon bed, though it did cross her mind occasionally that he might be bruised beyond repair from the jostling. But then, the good Lord protected drunks and fools, didn't He? Considering what she'd just done, Jem wasn't sure.

The house seemed interminably quiet as Jem paced the confines of her father's study. How long could the man sleep? Not able to bear looking at him, she'd rushed into the house before Pete could dump him out of the wagon. Now she wondered if perhaps more was wrong with the man than drunkenness. Why hadn't she checked better, more thoroughly?

Hearing the front door slam, she jumped as though it had been a gunshot. Because stories travel, gossip flies! her mind mocked. Remembering her father's habit of downing a whiskey when times were bad, she sloshed a fair portion in a tumbler and tossed down the contents. Choking, she tried not to gag on the fiery concoction.

With perspiration breaking out on her forehead, she tried to catch her breath when a loud knock on the study door startled her.

"Jem?" Pete poked his head around the doorway. His eyes widened when he saw her gasping and trying to swallow. "He's awake."

She quickly put the tumbler on the desk. "Good."

"Maybe not. He wants to know who the hell shanghaied him."

"Did you tell him?"

"Yeah. He didn't seem real impressed."

Jem smiled humorlessly. "I guess you'd better bring him here."

Pete shook his head in denial. "I don't think so."

She frowned in question.

"He's already in the barn, looking after his horse. Wants to make sure his pony's all right before he comes and beats the hell out of whoever the boss is."

Jem strummed her fingers against the desktop and then met Pete's eyes. "Let me handle this."

He didn't answer, but discreetly followed her out of the house, and Jem knew he wouldn't be far from the fray. Girding her courage, she covered the distance to the barn. Dusk had settled in the summer day. The twin peaks of the mountains were gilded by the crimson edges of the setting sun. Entering the barn, she smelled the flare of sulfur and was relieved to see the spreading light of a kerosene lamp. The tall cowhand holding the lamp seemed considerably less pleased, however. His face was shaded both by the shadows of the barn and the brim of his wide Stetson. "What do you want?" he bit out.

Jem cocked her head and studied the man a moment. "You," she replied.

He turned his back in dismissal and bent down to examine his pony. "You'll have to get in line."

Jem bit her lips to still the sudden urge to laugh. He sounded madder than hell. When she'd worked out her plan, it had seemed very well thought out, logical, calm. The man who so carefully ran his hands over the paint's forelegs didn't sound as though he'd agree.

"You married to the fellow who shanghaied me?" McIntire asked abruptly.

Jem thought a moment, then answered truthfully, "No."

"Good thing. I aim to beat next Sunday out of him." Apparently satisfied with the horse's condition, he stood up. There *were* yards and yards of him, Jem realized. He was a tall one. She swallowed, wishing her plan hadn't been so impersonal. So necessary.

"You want to lead me to him?" he asked.

"That won't be possible."

"Hell, it won't. I aim—"

"Yes, I know—to beat next . . ." She cleared her throat. "You see, I brought you here."

"You? You just said you weren't mar—"

"I'm not," she interrupted hastily.

"Then what the hell's going on?"

"This is my ranch, Mr. McIntire, and you were brought here under my orders."

"Why?"

This wasn't going at all as she'd planned. She'd envisioned calmly explaining the situation while seated behind the forbidding desk of her father's study. In control. It was difficult to feel anything but intimidated by the man's presence. He was so—large—even in the vast space of the barn.

"I have a request to make of you."

"You got a funny way of asking, lady."

"Well, it's a rather unusual request."

"Most people do their asking before they drag a body halfway across the territory. To my way of thinking, the answer's no."

"But you don't know the question!"

"I don't have to. Whatever it is, I'm not doing it."

"Aren't you even the least bit curious?"

He turned back to the pony, patting its sturdy haunches. "Nope."

"Do you mind if I ask you anyway?"

McIntire never stopped his movements, throwing the blanket over the horse's back and smoothing it out. He shrugged. Apparently she would have to use dynamite to shake his composure. Then dynamite it was.

"Mr. McIntire, will you marry me?"

Chapter 2

It was better to be sitting behind the solid barrier of her father's desk. Not that Jem was sure she was truly in control.

"That's one hell of a request, lady. Why marriage?"

"I told you. My father was blacklisted at the time he was killed. Cattle were stolen from every ranch in the area. Everyone was hit, and hit hard. Since whoever actually rustled the cattle left before we could prove Pa was innocent—"

"You're blacklisted, too," he finished for her.

"Which means I can't drive my cattle to market with the other trail bosses, I can't get any hands to work the cattle. . . ."

"Why not sell out?"

"I'll bury the last head of beef myself before I lose my father's land."

"What if your father really was behind the rustling?" Reese watched her carefully for signs of anger or guilt. Instead she raised gravely saddened eyes.

"I don't necessarily expect you to believe his innocence. It's enough that I do. What I want from you hasn't anything to do with feelings."

Reese's steel-blue gaze slid over Jem's shapeless duster and frowsy oversized trousers. She was brown from the top of her weather-beaten hat to the tips of her scuffed boots. He couldn't tell what she was hiding beneath the ugly garb, other than what seemed to be an overly tall, skinny frame. Lord, she had to be at least thirty from the look of her. Good thing she wasn't talking physical. Hell, it had been a while since he'd set his eyes on a good-lookin' woman, but at least he remembered what one ought to look like.

"Why not marry that big ape who threw me in the back of the wagon?"

Jem glanced up sharply. "How do you know it was Pete?"

"No offense, ma'am, but I don't expect you picked me up and tossed me in that wagon. There ain't more than half a dozen people on the whole ranch. He's the only one who's strong enough and young enough. He can't be much past forty-five. The rest of the 'boys' look like they've been put out to pasture."

She paused, weighing her words carefully. "They're old hands who worked for my father and my grandfather before him. They'll be here as long as the Bar-W is. Pete's married to our housekeeper. He's one of the few hands who stayed out of loyalty."

"Guess it wouldn't do to pay back that loyalty by stealing him from his wife."

Jem didn't spare him a smile. She'd obviously chosen a man so far from herself in values that she might as well have picked the murderer in the adjoining cell. Nevertheless she needed him. And time was of the essence. She had to add her cattle to the trail that was heading out early in the week, which gave her three days to get married, establish McIntire as the new "boss," and hire enough hands to get the beef on its way to market.

Her words were frosty. "No, it wouldn't."

Reese sighed inwardly. This was no molasses-dipped cookie. She was probably tougher than the harsh mountains dominating the landscape. He pitied the man who married her for real.

"Why should I rescue you?" he finally asked, sauntering over to the cedar-lined wall, negligently studying the

7

etched drawing of the Bar-W spread, neatly detailed, largely impressive.

"I don't think 'rescue' is the key word here, Mr. McIntire. I'm ready to offer you a business proposition. Straight out and legal."

He turned away from the wall to face her. "What would that be?"

"You agree to marry me, add the McIntire name to the Bar-W, and remain married to me for one year until we complete the army contract."

"What do I get out of this deal?"

"Three thousand dollars in gold."

He'd figured money was in her plans, but he'd never dreamed . . . He was a top-notch rider and drew near thirty-five dollars a month. The money she was talking about was better'n five years' wages. He thought of his slow-growing poke of money and his dream of what he'd do with it when it was saved. Money she was talking about would shave at least four years off that time.

"And after the year?"

Her facial muscles remained still, her eyes deadly calm. "You keep your end of the bargain, you ride out of here a free man."

A free man with all the money he needed to build the life he wanted. He turned to the tall, wide window at the rear of the study. The last of the sinking sun surrendered the remainder of its rays in a breathtaking display of orange illuminating the purple edges of the ragged mountain peaks. But all McIntire saw was his future. One year as Mr. Jem Whitaker or five years of busting his tail to scrape together the money he needed.

"How much of this marriage stuff is gonna be for real?" he asked awkwardly. He supposed he could bed her, but the prospect of getting paid to . . .

Her voice was cold. He could swear she'd stripped every emotion from it. If she had any emotions, that is.

"We must appear to the other ranchers as a normal married couple. I'll expect you to attend dances, barn raisings, and such with me as my husband. If the other ranchers don't believe you, the deal's off. The only reason for this marriage is to get the Bar-W off the blacklist. If you don't succeed in making that happen, you don't get paid."

"Any other conditions, ma'am?"

"This marriage is a business deal, that's all."

"Yes, boss."

He expected her to react to that at least. But, if anything, she only grew paler. "I'm glad you see how it's going to be."

"What's your first order, ma'am?"

She glanced down at the ledger book spread out on the desk. As she closed the book quietly her body clearly signaled dismissal. "I'd suggest you get cleaned up."

"Any special reason?"

"You have a wedding to attend, Mr. McIntire. Yours."

McIntire straightened up, unconsciously awaiting his sentence. "And when will that be, ma'am?"

"Tomorrow, Mr. McIntire."

He forgot to swallow. Not even twenty-four hours of freedom left. Strange, this deal was supposed to provide freedom, not take it away. Mindlessly he turned away from her, heading toward the doorway.

"Don't be late, Mr. McIntire. Our deal starts at sunrise."

Unconsciously he glanced back out the window. The last of the sun had disappeared behind the massive range of mountains. Sunk. Just like he was.

The guests started to arrive close after daybreak. Pete had posted a notice at the town meeting hall, and better than half the people in the territory had seen it and shown up. Of course, word of mouth was a powerful tool in a land conspicuously lacking in social events. A wedding, even a blacklisted Whitaker's wedding, was a draw no one could resist.

McIntire stubbed another hand-rolled cigarette butt into the dirt with the heel of his boot. The ground was littered with over a dozen more. He'd smoked and thought through the night, and both proved bitter. Pride was harder to swallow than he'd imagined. But no matter how hard he chewed on it, he couldn't deny that he wanted the stake Jem Whitaker could provide. There was even less doubt that the sooner he had the money, the more likely he was to succeed. Someone else was bound to grab onto his idea before he could finance the operation, and he'd be out. Beaten again.

Watching the wagons continuing to roll in, he stifled an audible curse. Hell, she hadn't told him she'd invited the whole territory. The unfamiliar string tie that replaced his customary bandanna felt like a noose. Reclining against the bunkhouse wall, he started and jerked around when an unfamiliar hand closed over his shoulder.

"Hold on, fella. Just came to tell you breakfast was ready. Figured you might need something to fill you up."

Reese studied Pete's face, wondering what the other man thought of him, a man willing to marry for money. It was an unfamiliar sensation. And not a pleasant one.

"Not too hungry," Reese replied, staring out at the gathering wagons.

"Can't say as I blame you."

Reese glanced at the older man in surprise. He'd expected undying loyalty to the mistress of the house.

"Best I can remember, I had cold feet myself."

Cold, hell. It was way past freezing in the middle of a North Dakota winter.

"There's a hell of a lot of people here. I thought folks around here knew the old man was a rustler."

"The 'old man' didn't have a chance to prove himself one way or another. Not everybody believed he was guilty."

"Just enough to keep you blacklisted."

"Yep." Pete watched the growing cluster of people. "Rest of 'em probably came out of curiosity."

"Can't believe Jem landed herself a man?"

Pete's eyes were far-reaching, and their sharpness

grazed Reese's consciousness. "Mebbe. Then mebbe it was to look you over."

Reese glanced away. His job was to make sure folks believed he was Jem's husband, not plant the seeds of suspicion. "You know when the"—he paused slightly, clearing his throat before continuing—"doings are supposed to begin?"

Pete's eyebrows rose in surprise. Reese almost flushed at the shock written on the other man's face. Hell of a thing for him to be asking when his own wedding was.

"I 'spect you ought to mosey up to the big house," Pete answered finally. "You'll be moving your stuff there today anyway."

Not waiting for an answer, Pete left him. Moving to the big house, eh? Well, that was sure something to find out from one of the hands. Straightening up, he drew a deep breath and turned toward the imposing structure. *Happy wedding day, McIntire. You're gonna be earning every penny.*

Jem tucked the required scrap of blue satin in her garter, trying to smile at the gaggle of women who surrounded her. Their invasion was as welcome as a blizzard in spring. But much like the irksome frock she wore, it was necessary. She wouldn't convince her neighbors she'd really married McIntire if they didn't witness it for themselves. The thought of McIntire made her wince, and the headache growing between her brows blossomed. But it was almost welcome. The pain distracted her from the cause of her headache.

"No flowers," Abigail Fairchild bemoaned.

"What did you expect? English tea roses?" chided Lorraine.

"She scarcely looks like a bride in that ... dress," chimed in Beatrice.

Jem glanced down at the serviceable dress. It had been more than adequate for the few social occasions she attended.

11

"It does need something," Abigail commented. She cocked her head critically to one side, walking in a complete circle around Jem.

"Maybe in her hair," Lorraine suggested, taking a stance next to Abigail. Beatrice and Mary stared at Jem as well.

Jem wanted very badly to tell them she wasn't a steer on a Kansas City auction block, but decided it wouldn't suit her purpose. Resolutely she stared ahead while the women fussed over the plain cotton dress.

"Don't you have anything, um, fancier?"

Jem unconsciously focused on the cedar chest wedged at the end of her bed. Lorraine followed Jem's eyes and pounced on the chest. Opening it wide, she squealed in delight.

"These things are gorgeous. Why—"

"They were my mother's," Jem answered quietly, the old pain rising. So many memories they hadn't shared together. What would her mother think of her daughter on her wedding day, selling herself to save the ranch?

Abigail's gentle voice filled the room. "They're lovely, Jem. Don't you think your mother would have wanted you to wear something of hers today?"

That had never occurred to Jem. The delicate items in the chest belonged to another time, another set of memories.

Abigail held up a satin dress of pale ivory. "This would be perfect."

Jem hesitated. An unexpected longing surfaced. She remembered in years past holding the beautiful clothes in front of her, pirouetting before the mirror. But the image in the mirror always stopped her. Barnyard fowl dressed like a peacock.

Abigail brought the dress close. "Why don't you just slip it on? If it doesn't suit you, you can change back."

Lorraine muttered something incomprehensible into the depths of the trunk. Jem doubted her words were complimentary. Beatrice and Mary fussed while Lorraine emptied the cedar chest.

12

Shimmying out of her plain cotton dress, Jem stepped into the cold satin skirt and pulled the bodice up. She started to release the fabric to push away the unaccustomed garment, but Abigail's hand stayed her.

"Let's just see how it looks fastened up." Abigail worked the intricate row of buttons, finally fastening the last one. Jem started to turn toward the cheval glass, but Abigail guided her instead toward the dressing table in the alcove off the main portion of the room.

"Lorraine's right. We need something in your hair."

Before Jem could protest, Abigail seated her at the dressing table and picked up the brush. She unwound the knot of hair Jem had hastily pinned up. Long, sure strokes brought the glistening highlights of Jem's honey-blond hair to the surface.

"What about this?" Lorraine had discovered a bow of lace and ribbon and held it up like a trophy.

"Perfect," Abigail answered before Jem could. "And could someone find the curling iron and heat it, please?"

Lorraine shrugged and continued digging while Beatrice and Mary searched for a curling iron. Jem tried to twist toward the mirror, but Abigail gently yet insistently held her head firmly in place.

Soon the smoking of the curling iron filled the room. Jem squirmed as Abigail continued her styling. Finally she finished shaping Jem's hair, attaching the bow and allowing the ribbons of satin and velvet to trail against the golden tresses of curls.

Abigail stood back and critically surveyed the finished effect. "No jewelry," she muttered.

"She'll be getting a ring today," Lorraine piped in.

Jem started. She'd completely forgotten about rings. "We haven't had a chance to buy our rings yet. They'll have to come in on the next shipment."

"He's an eager one—couldn't even wait for the rings to get here," Lorraine mocked. Abigail tried to shush Lorraine with a glance, but the other woman turned her head aside and whispered to Beatrice, "Wherever do you suppose Jem dug him up? I know I never heard his name before yesterday."

Jem, who had heard every word, wanted to respond that she'd dug him up in the nearest cemetery, but that would hardly endear her to the women. She hated how their foolish opinions mattered now. But they did. Their husbands could still keep the Bar-W blacklisted. Beatrice's hissing whisper reached Jem's ears as well.

"I don't know. The only reason I came to this wedding is 'cause I had to see with my own eyes that she'd really snagged a man. Who'd have believed it?"

Jem's cheeks suddenly turned crimson. She wanted to hold her head high with pride, but there was scarce little to be proud of these days.

"What about this?" Lorraine held up a gold locket, which hung from a delicate chain.

"No!" Jem hadn't realized her outburst was so strident. "I mean, it belonged to my mother. I can't—"

Abigail's gentle voice interrupted as she scooped the locket from Lorraine's outstretched hand. "It can be a symbol until your rings arrive. Two hearts now one."

The pain intensified. Once in her life Jem had thought that was truly possible, had thought she'd found that special man. But now he was gone, and she knew no other such man existed. Especially one she had bought for a lion's share of gold.

But Abigail had slipped the delicate chain around her neck, fastening the locket in place. Jem's hand automatically reached for the ornament.

"Your mother would have been so proud," Abigail murmured. Hot tears clogged Jem's throat. Nothing could have touched her more.

"Now it's time to look," Abigail announced, turning Jem to the cheval glass in the corner of the room.

Jem stopped short, shock waves ricocheting through her body. The stranger in the mirror looked as surprised as she felt.

Lorraine untangled herself from the trunk and turned to her with a gasp. "Is that you, Jem?"

"I'm not sure." Only the eyes were familiar. Abigail had used Spanish papers to bring out the color in her lips, while a delicate rouge rested on her cheeks. Soft curls framed her face, and long ribbons rested between strands of gleaming gold hair. And the dress. Her hand automatically rose to cover the exposed flesh. Never had so much of her skin shown before. She opened her mouth to protest when the gold of her locket winked in the mirror.

Jem thought of the portrait of her mother, painted while wearing this very gown and locket. Her mother's exquisite black hair, ivory skin, and intensely blue eyes had not been passed down to her daughter. Jem favored her father in every possible way. But standing in front of the mirror, Jem could see some resemblance. Something that claimed she was Camille Whitaker's daughter. And in that moment she couldn't bear to remove the locket. McIntire need never know the significance of the heart. She doubted he would ever wonder.

Turning to Abigail and Lorraine, Jem gathered her flailing courage. "I believe I'm ready."

Abigail smiled at her gently. "Yes, I think you are."

Lorraine, Beatrice, and Mary led the procession, chattering without pause. Abigail held her own counsel. As they reached the head of the stairs she reached for Jem's hand. "It will be a new life, Jem. Be happy."

Happy. The word buzzed through her mind as Jem descended the stairs, her eyes registering the shock on several faces, Pete's included. But the one face that should have been registering some reaction was nowhere to be seen.

"You look plumb beautiful, Jem."

"You been into the punch already this morning, Pete?" Her voice was shaky, and she tried desperately to control it.

"Nope." He leaned closer. "Don't get worried. McIntire's outside. Said he had to get something."

15

Relief whooshed through her. McIntire might not be her choice for a husband, but not only was she desperate, she had no desire to be humiliated in front of everyone in the countryside.

When McIntire entered the room, fiddling with something he held behind his back, Jem watched his every move. He'd apparently taken her advice. Clean shaven except for a newly trimmed mustache, hair combed neatly, he didn't look like the dazed man who'd stumbled from her study the night before.

When he glanced up, however, disbelief set in. Jem couldn't decide who was more shocked—McIntire at her transformed appearance, or herself at the realization that cleaned up and sober, Reese McIntire was one of the most attractive men she'd set eyes on.

Last night, hung over and mad, he'd seemed almost menacing and certainly older. But the uncompromising blue eyes that now stared at her were set in a handsome face, free of lines. Thick, stubby eyelashes shadowed hollow cheeks pronounced even more by the contrast of his jutting jawline. His full lower lip edged out past the draping of the mustache across his mouth. His ebony-colored hair curled down his neck, but it was clean and shiny. Uncomfortably she realized he couldn't be more than thirty-five or so.

Jem sent up a silent prayer of relief when Pete, obviously recognizing their mutual state of immobility, stepped in and called the group together.

"Reverend, you out there?"

The crowd glanced around at one another, breaking into conversation as the old preacher creaked forward. The interruption allowed Jem and McIntire to regain some composure.

Reverend Filcher took his stance at the front of the large drawing room, and the bride and groom hesitantly moved forward to join him. They stood awkwardly in front of him, neither speaking.

"Well?" he finally bellowed. Being hard of hearing, he assumed everyone else was, too.

Jem and McIntire stared at him.

"Ain't you gonna hold hands?"

They stared at one another in dismay. Before he took her hand, McIntire pulled the hidden item from behind his back. It was a bouquet of evening primrose. Obviously painstakingly picked, for the delicate wildflower blossoms grew only in the foothills of the mountains. This early in spring they weren't easy to locate. Jem stared silently as he clasped a large strong hand over hers. She wondered whose hand trembled the most.

The old familiar words began. Jem tried to concentrate on them, knowing her response would be forthcoming. Instead she found herself focusing on the unexpected feelings caused by the hand holding hers. Points of warm, cool, and hot tripped up and down her arms, as though her skin had taken on a life of its own. She wondered dumbly if she'd ever realized she could experience so many sensations from one touch.

But then the words she'd dreaded the most arrived. "Do you, Jem Whitaker, take this man . . . until death do you part?"

Her lips opened, then closed. She swallowed, glanced at the minister, and then dared a glance at the man she would pledge to marry. He stared back at her solemnly. This was a vow not only with him, she reminded herself. She was undertaking a vow with God as well. Forcing the thought aside, she managed to speak.

"I do."

She wondered if the surprise in his eyes matched her own. But in moments he repeated the same words.

Then the final words bound them together. "I now pronounce you man and wife."

Silence along with an overwhelming sense of expectation filled the room until Reverend Filcher's voice boomed out, "Well, ain't you gonna kiss her?"

Twin pairs of dismayed eyes met, hers in uncertainty,

17

his in hesitation. They strained awkwardly toward one another an inch at a time, their bodies stiffer than store-window mannequins. Feeling foolish and ungainly, Jem hadn't the scarcest idea what to do next. Before she had to decide, Reese's face moved closer. Tipping her chin up, he angled his head toward hers, their lips meeting in unexpected discovery. The brief moment encapsulated feelings Jem could scarcely discern as a ragged jolt of awareness rippled through her unsuspecting body. Before she could begin to even wonder at the sensations, the room exploded in sound and movement.

They were surrounded by boisterous well-wishers. In western fashion, Reese was welcomed as though he'd lived in their part of the country forever. Hearty slaps on the back were accompanied by shots of whiskey and good-hearted congratulations. He had no taint associated with him, no reason to be shunned.

The women, caught in the magical moment, surrounded Jem with equal excitement, casting aside any previous stigma she'd borne. Now that she was no longer a Whitaker, she'd been accepted again. Jem, who had never fit into their circle, felt like a homesteader at a cattle auction. But she responded to their giggles and squeals of delight with grace.

"I declare, Jem, I don't believe I've ever seen you look so"—Mabel Deems began, then paused—"lovely," she ended on a note of wonder.

Jem glanced up to thank Mabel when her eyes met Reese's. It seemed his eyes held the same expression of wonder.

Feeling a flush of heat suffuse her cheeks, Jem glanced away in unexpected shyness. She'd always met every situation, every problem, head-on. Indecision was a unique experience.

When Reese started to move toward her, Jem felt an unexpected flutter of nerves. But before he could come any closer, he was drawn up in the revelry the cowhands had in store for him. Before Jem could determine if the change in her feelings could possibly be described as disappointment, she was swept up by the same high spirits of the women in the room.

The rugs were rolled back and the furniture carried from its normal resting places to line the walls of the room. A fiddle and harmonica soon filled the air with lilting music. The loud thumping of boots against the wooden floors overwhelmed the gentle hiss of skirts as they swooshed about that same floor. Bourbon punch flowed as rapidly as the currents of the Snake River.

Jem, as the belle of the evening, was asked to dance by every man from age twelve to eighty. Her feet, encased in unfamiliar dancing slippers, ached with the effort, but not nearly as much as her face from the smile she was forced to keep in place. She was in Pete's arms when she unconsciously glanced around for her new husband.

"He's in good hands," Pete drawled.

Jem flushed. "Just trying to make sure all the guests are having a good time."

"Uh-huh."

Knowing she hadn't fooled her old friend, Jem discarded that tack. "So, where is he?"

"Getting good'n drunk."

Jem digested the information, not sure whether it boded well.

"What do you think of him, Pete?"

"I 'spect it's a little late to be worrying about that now."

Knowing he was right, Jem merely followed his lead around the dance floor.

As the day and eventually the night wore on, the crowd grew louder, more unruly. Jem tried to keep track of Reese's whereabouts, but the fun-loving cowboys kept him well supplied with whiskey and good-natured taunts.

Knowing many of her guests would be staying the night, Jem felt the pit of her stomach tighten. Reese McIntire now had the legal right to move into her room. And into her bed.

Chapter
3

Reese felt the fur lining his mouth and lifted his head to seek out a pitcher of water. Waves of pain assaulted his head when he moved it. He'd been hung over before, to be sure, but never so painfully. He'd drunk everything put in front of him last night, something he rarely did. The last time had landed him in jail. This time he had landed in Jem Whitaker's bed.

At that thought he bolted upright and searched the confines of the bedroom. There was no sign of his not-so-blushing bride. The tidy room was hard to distinguish as belonging either to male or female. Glancing at the dent in the pillow resting next to his own, he knew he'd had some company during the night. But beyond that he drew a blank.

He remembered seeing Jem in the ivory satin dress, and his surprise at how she'd looked. Who'd have ever dreamed the brown wren was actually female?

When he'd seen her, he was glad for the custom of having any guests who lived far away stay the night. He knew in order for Jem's plan to work, she would need to appear truly wedded, and overnight guests would question why the newlyweds weren't sharing a room. But, as the whiskey and bourbon punch flowed, Reese had lost sight of his bride. He wasn't even sure how he'd gotten to his room or, for that matter, how he'd known which one to inhabit.

Holding his hands to his aching head, Reese decided it was time to find out. Pouring cool water from the pitcher into the washbowl, he dunked his head, feeling somewhat refreshed. Finding a razor and strop lying neatly next to the pitcher, he located a mug of soap and lathered his face. Peering into the mirror above the washstand, he glanced with disgust at the bleary, red-rimmed eyes that stared back at him.

After shaving, Reese wiped his face dry, tossed the towel down, pulled on his shirt, and buttoned it before opening the door. He paused, tucked in his shirttail, and glanced back at the room. Then a thought hit him. He felt as though no particular personality inhabited the room. It contained nothing that spoke of the person who slept there, dreamed there.

Making his way down the stairs, he heard voices from the dining room. A few stragglers from the night before remained, but most of the guests had long since departed. Cattle wouldn't wait while their owners socialized. Reese greeted those he remembered, searching out Jem. But she was nowhere in sight.

"Good morning."

Reese tried to ease a name from his aching head. Oh, yes, Abigail. The quiet one. "Morning, ma'am."

She poured a cup of steaming black coffee, and he dove into it gratefully.

"The wedding was quite lovely, Mr. McIntire."

"Reese," he responded automatically, glancing up to catch her gentle smile.

"Reese, then. I'm so pleased for Jem."

"Um." He swallowed more of the robust brew, wondering if his head was going to stay attached to his shoulders.

"She hasn't allowed herself much happiness, you know, even before her father's death."

Reese raised his head slowly to study Abigail's expression.

"But of course you know that. You're the man who won Jem's heart."

Reese stared into Abigail's huge blue eyes and sweet smile and realized the woman truly believed her words.

"You'll have to tell me how you and Jem met," Abigail continued.

Reese choked on the burning coffee. "Right." His scrambled brain searched for some sort of answer. Finding none, he shoved back his chair and escaped, refusing Abigail's offer of breakfast.

He walked to the front porch, his eyes picking out a few riders near the corral, but no one familiar. Turning away, he spotted Pete near the breaking corral. Ambling toward him, Reese breathed in the clean air, appreciating the lay of the land. The site for the house had been wisely chosen—nestled between the ragged peaks of the mountains, encased by gently sloping foothills that beckoned to the adventurer.

Pete turned as Reese approached. His expression gave away little, but his eyes asked a thousand questions.

"Morning, Pete."

"Reese."

The brevity of the exchange was something both were accustomed to. But Reese had a need to know. And he figured Pete was the one with the answers.

"That was some wingding last night," Reese offered.

"Yep."

Pete wasn't tripping over himself to offer more. The ache in Reese's head throbbed more fiercely.

"I had a might more to drink than I reckoned on."

"Can't remember nothin', I 'spect."

Reese drew a breath, started to deny Pete's words, then nodded.

"You were havin' a helluva time till you passed out."

"Passed out?"

"Yep. Drug you up to bed, and you never even moved."

That registered with Reese. If what Pete said was true, it hadn't been the wedding night Reese had imagined.

"Guess that didn't go over too well with Jem."

Pete shrugged without offering a comment.

"Don't suppose you know where she is this morning?"

Pete reacted with surprise. "You had more to drink than I realized."

Reese's face reflected silent confusion.

"She's over there." Pete pointed in the direction of the riders Reese had noticed earlier. "Workin' the stock. You were starin' right at her."

So he was. Reese blinked and looked again. Pete was right. He must have had a lot more to drink than he'd realized. Last night Jem had seemed so, so . . . Almost beautiful. Today she wore her customary baggy, brown trousers and flapping duster, topped by a well-creased brown hat that shaded her face. Had he been so liquored up he'd just imagined how she'd looked the night before?

As though he'd willed her to ride in his direction, she trotted her horse forward to the corral. Reining in the tall stallion, Jem peered down at him.

"It's about time you were up and about. Make no mistake, McIntire. If these cattle don't make it to market, you don't get paid."

Reese stiffened suddenly. He'd been a hired hand for a lot of years, but like every cowpoke on the range, he'd never taken orders from a woman. Especially one who was now supposed to be his wife.

He opened his mouth to tell her to take her orders and her crazy idea of a marriage to the devil. Before he could issue the words, she pulled her horse around, gaiting the powerful beast in place, speaking at the same time.

"We've got six thousand head of cattle to move out, and the trail boss won't wait for us. You'd better get over there, McIntire."

Reese moved forward to protest when Pete's arm came down strongly on his shoulder, holding him in place. Reese started to shrug off his hold when Jem turned back again, this time a bit hesitantly.

"It's important, McIntire. If they don't accept you, they

23

don't accept the cattle." Before he could answer, Jem dug her heels into the mount's flanks.

"She sure as hell has a sweet way of askin'," Reese muttered, his eyes unconsciously following the trail of dust she left behind.

"Jem don't know sweet. But then, you knew that when you signed on."

So he had. He'd sold his soul for a promise of gold, and Pete was right. He had a job to do, and Jem was the boss, bitter as that was to swallow.

"Where do I go meet this trail master?"

"Over to the Lazy H, northwest a piece."

Reese nodded and started to turn away.

"Don't be too hard on her. She don't know any other way to be."

Letting out a sigh, Reese supposed Pete might be right. Didn't make taking her orders any easier, though.

"I'll ride over there with you, show you the spread after I get some mending up to Della."

"Della?"

"My wife."

"I remember meetin' and dancin' with a lot of women last night, but I don't recollect dancin' with your wife."

"Be surprised if you did. My wife's crippled. Hasn't walked in ten years."

Reese's jaw sagged. Jem had said Pete's wife was their housekeeper. If she and Pete had stayed on with the Whitakers for ten years, unable to carry their load, that meant Jem . . .

Reese stared long and hard at the retreating dust of Jem's trail. This was the harsh taskmaster? A woman who paid a housekeeper who hadn't been able to walk for ten years?

Shaking his still-aching head, Reese turned back to the stable with reluctant steps. Jem was turning out to be harder to figure than a game of two-fisted poker in a dark saloon.

* * *

Jem slid off her horse and slapped the dust from her trousers. It was nearing sundown, but she didn't spare the dazzling display of crimson and magenta even a second glance.

She wondered what awaited her inside. Would McIntire be lounging in the study, more interested in her supply of bourbon than the fate of her cattle? Or had he packed himself back off to where he'd come from?

She'd seen his expression as his eyes traveled over her that morning. He looked as though he'd seen buffalo chips that were more appealing. She reached up automatically to remove her hat and try to repair her flattened, windblown hair, but as quickly stayed the action.

This was not a love match. It was a business deal. True, she had been gratified to see the uncloaked admiration in his eyes when she'd appeared in the ivory satin gown. But she was no peacock. She was Jem Whitaker. No, make that Jem McIntire.

But she was still as sensible as the day before. She'd not pretend to be something she wasn't. Her hand strayed involuntarily to the locket hidden beneath her rough chambray shirt. The metal was cold to the touch. She swallowed again, dreading to enter her own home.

A figure emerged from the growing shadows, and Jem braced herself. But the voice didn't belong to Reese.

"Miz Whitaker?"

Jem let out a sigh of relief. The familiar voice belonged to Grady Orton, her former assistant foreman. "Grady?"

"Yes'm." He took the hat from his head and held it out respectfully.

Jem's gaze traveled over Grady's nondescript features and unreadable dark eyes. "What are you doing round these parts? I thought you and Charles—"

Orton shrugged and interrupted. "I like it best here, ma'am. This was my home."

"I can understand that. Why don't you stay around,

Grady? We'll be hiring more hands in the next day or so."

Orton ran a hand over his lank, dark hair. "Thank you, ma'am. I'd be mighty obliged."

"Head on over to the bunkhouse and get a good meal. Supper ought to be ready about now."

His smile flashed in the growing twilight. "I was hoping maybe it would be."

Jem managed a smile in return as she watched the cowhand leave. If Orton was here, did that mean Charles Sawyer wasn't far behind? Before she could complete the thought, the door was flung open.

"Jem! I'm glad you're back." Abigail's voice washed over her. Jem had completely forgotten about her guests. She thought they'd all be gone by now.

"Supper's just about ready. I'm afraid I've been quite a pest. But I was in the mood to bake."

Jim simply stared. She'd never been at ease with other women and their seemingly mindless chatter. Even as a girl she'd avoided the simpering company of other females, preferring riding and roping to clothes and embroidery.

Although they were contemporaries, Jem had shunned Abigail's friendship as well. But the other woman had always gone out of her way to make Jem feel comfortable.

Abigail apparently misinterpreted Jem's look of dismay. She came down the steps in a rush. "I don't mean to impose. I know you want some time alone with your new husband. . . ."

Jem cleared her throat, struggling for a reply.

"And honestly I wouldn't still be here if Michael had returned to take me home."

Abigail's husband Michael hadn't been able to stay and attend the wedding. His foreman had broken his leg the week before, and he had to prepare for the cattle drive only days away.

26

When Jem didn't speak, Abigail rushed on, "I'm truly sorry. I . . ."

Jem finally found her voice. "No, I'm glad you're here." As she issued the words Jem realized they were true. It would ease the awkwardness, the strain she knew was in store. "Is Reese inside?"

Abigail looked puzzled. "He hasn't been back since breakfast."

Maybe he'd headed to the hills after all.

Jem started to turn back to the corral. "I'd better find Pete and—"

"He hasn't been back, either."

Absorbing this, Jem reluctantly followed Abigail up the steps.

Once inside, Abigail started toward the kitchen. "I'll get you something to drink while you're changing."

"Changing?"

"After you clean up, of course." Abigail stopped, turned, and glanced back at Jem. "Reese will be home soon. I'm sure you'll want to freshen up."

Jem, who had always eaten, shared a game of cards with her father, and then bathed quickly before collapsing into bed, looked dumbstruck.

Abigail drew closer, her voice soft. "Now that you're a bride, these things are important, Jem."

Belligerence surfaced. "I'm not going to twist myself into something I'm not for anybody."

"No one's suggesting you should, Jem. After all, you're the woman Reese fell in love with."

Abigail's words were more effective than a dash of cold water. Jem glanced down at her dusty trousers. With a slow movement she reached up to remove her hat, shaking loose the matted tresses that clung to her head.

"I'll have some water brought up." Abigail's voice was gentle, understanding.

Jem swung the hair away from her face, and the movement caused the locket to sway slightly. Turning toward the stairs, she stopped a moment, the right words difficult to dredge up and even harder to utter. "Thanks, Abigail. I know I haven't been very friendly in the past . . ."

"You've been a busy woman, Jem. Running a ranch—"

"Even before . . ."

"Before we had little to bring us together. Now that you're married, there will be quiltings, taffy pulls—"

"Me? At a quilting?"

"While Reese is at the turkey trot, of course. You know you'll be joining other married couples, participating in their activities."

"I expected to go to barn raisings and such, but I never thought about quiltings and . . ."

"There will be differences, Jem. But in time I think you'll enjoy them. Perhaps not the way you enjoy ranching, but in a different way."

Jem felt the knot in her stomach grow. She had never considered that simply taking McIntire's name would be enough. She'd known that they'd have to attend activities, but to appear married at every social occasion! Thank the heavens she and her neighbors were too far apart to meet often. Still . . . To make matters worse, she didn't know one end of a quilting hoop from the other. Her step was heavy as she turned toward the stairwell.

"Jem?" Abigail's voice was hesitant. "No one wants you to change who you are."

"Not much." Jem couldn't keep the bitter irony from her voice.

"Think of what you've accomplished, running a ranch on your own. And before that, defying everyone all your life to be the person you want to be. How many women can say that?"

"How many would want to?"

"I would."

Jem's eyes flew open in shock. Sweet Abigail with her gentle feminine ways? Ways that were foreign to Jem and for that reason admired even more. Abigail possessed the decorum and loveliness Jem's mother had. When she found her voice, it was little better than a squeak. "You?"

"Yes, me. Do you think I'd have the courage or the ability to run a ranch alone? If anything ever happened to Michael, I'd be helpless. You don't have to depend on anyone else." Abigail's eyes shone with admiration before she turned away. "Now, why don't you go on up? I'm sure I brought some bath salts along. I'll be up in a minute."

Bath salts! But after Jem had been soaking in the warm, scented water, she did feel considerably better. Her freshly washed hair dried in soft waves, and even though the water had begun to cool, Jem resisted leaving the unaccustomed luxury. Usually she bathed quickly in tepid water, staying in only long enough to get clean. Reluctantly she rose from the tub and dried herself with the thick towels Abigail had thoughtfully provided. Never having had women friends, Jem was surprised to find Abigail surprisingly insightful, not witless and annoying.

As Jem turned to the chifforobe still she did not reach for one of the few dresses hanging there. Instead she chose a pair of breeches. When her hand moved to select a shirt, she paused, glancing down the rack. Rather than the rough cambric of every day, she chose a soft ivory linen. Refusing to think anymore about her clothing, she jammed the trousers on and quickly buttoned up the shirt.

When she glanced in the mirror, however, she was disconcerted. Here was the everyday Jem, but instead of hair pinned hastily in a knot, long waves of gold, fragrant from Abigail's shampoo, billowed over her shoulders. Hesitantly she reached for her brush, pulling the boar's-hair bristles through the long strands. Softened by Abigail's rosewater soap, her hair parted easily, falling into orderly waves. She reached automatically for the hairpins stored next to the hairkeeper.

Her hand paused as she glanced once again in the mirror. Knowing she could never live up to the beauty her mother had been, Jem had deliberately chosen to disregard her appearance. But it wasn't as though she'd never dreamed of being lovely. Leaning forward a bit more, she felt the locket sway against her skin. She backed away from the hairpins and the cheval glass. Swallowing a lump that threatened to fill her throat, Jem left her orderly room and walked down the stairs. She had a stranger to confront, and she was scarcely comforted when she remembered that stranger was her husband.

Chapter 4

The front door opened, then slammed heartily. Jem ceased the constant pacing that had kept her occupied while Abigail quietly stitched on some sort of tapestry. Jem glanced over at the other woman's calm countenance, wondering at Abigail's endless patience. Jem wanted action and answers, and both were far too late in coming to suit her. Hearing the heavy thud of Reese's boots, she turned in the direction of the doorway.

"Reese," Abigail greeted him quietly.

"Ma'am."

Jem met his glance. "Mc . . ." She could hardly call him McIntire with Abigail present. "Reese." Was that a flicker of victory in his eyes? Annoyed, she matched his expression, and a smile broke over his features. Jem leaned forward impatiently. Instead of trying to stare the man down, she needed to find out the fate of her cattle. "Did you speak to the trail boss?"

"Yep."

"And?" Jem wished Abigail weren't present so she could remind Reese who was the boss. Apparently he'd already considered that aspect as he turned to Abigail.

"Sherry, ma'am?" Reese uncorked the decanter and carefully filled the glass.

"Jem?"

Rigidly she shook her head in refusal and watched as he ambled over to Abigail and handed her the drink.

31

With great care he pulled the stopper from the bourbon, her father's twenty-year-old stock, and poured a tumbler full. Easing himself into the leather chair that had also been her father's, he took a leisurely sip. When he raised his head, he was careful to smile at both Abigail and Jem in turn.

"What was that you were asking about, my dear?"

"The cattle," she gritted out between clenched teeth. *My dear, be damned.*

"Ah, yes, the cattle." He sipped again, and Jem wondered if she could suppress the urge to yank the glass out of his hand and demand to know what had happened.

"It seems the herd was already larger than the trail boss was willing to handle."

Jem's face fell. She had counted on the acceptance of those cattle. She'd even married McIntire to ensure that acceptance. Splaying her fingers, Jem allowed them to hide her shock.

"Good thing we had a talk."

Jem lifted her eyes slowly.

"Seems he liked what I had to say."

"Are you trying to tell me in your own strange way that he did accept the cattle?"

Reese tilted his head back, not to savor the drink he took, but the moment. "Yep."

"That's wonderful!" Abigail burst out.

Dazed, Jem stared between the two of them. Abigail's impulsive response should have been her own. Instead she watched as Abigail coaxed a reluctant smile from Reese.

"However did you convince him, Reese?" Abigail's eyes were filled with admiration while Jem's roved over the planes of his face.

"Told him I'd ridden with Sheridan at the battle of Cedar Creek. Seems he'd heard tell of our outfit."

Who hadn't? Jem reappraised Reese's features. Sheridan's troops were one of the most celebrated and decorated of the Civil War. What kind of man was Reese McIntire?

But Abigail's response was both quicker and more verbal. "I didn't know we had such a hero in our midst. And both of you too modest to tell anyone."

Reese and Jem's eyes turned rapidly toward one another. They were strangers, and each moment, each newly discovered fact, emphasized how much so.

"You must be starving!" Abigail suddenly exclaimed.

It hadn't occurred to Jem that Reese might be hungry or tired. While Abigail's full skirts swooshed out of the room Jem searched his face. Weary lines etched around his mouth, and his eyes bespoke the long night and even longer day.

"So you did it, McIntire."

"Yep."

The thanks refused to move past her lips. "You look done in."

He swallowed a hearty slug of bourbon. "I am."

"A good night's rest should cure that."

His hand paused midair, the glass clenched tightly. Tonight they were both sober and aware of the bed to be shared. Before she could recall her errant words, Abigail returned.

"Come on, you two. Dinner's warm."

When they reached the dining room, both Jem and Reese stared quizzically at the table set with only two places.

"But what about you?"

"I told you I wasn't here to interfere. I have a lovely tray upstairs. Now, enjoy."

"No!" Jem and Reese's voices chorused out together.

"I won't hear a word of it. See you in the morning." She waved cheerily and disappeared up the stairs.

Turning to each other in dismay, they awkwardly settled in at the table that Abigail had so painstakingly prepared. Soft candlelight glowed on the polished wood. Jem stared at the fragrant balsam pine boughs that lay bowed against lace runners while early-blooming hibiscus filled her mother's crystal vase.

The hearty beef lay on her mother's finest platter, but

neither of them reached for it. At the end of the table stood an elaborately decorated cake, its spun-sugar frosting gleaming in the candlelight. The significance of the smaller version of a wedding cake was not lost on Jem. Any appetite she might have maintained disappeared.

Reese, however, averted his face from the confection and speared a thick slice of meat. Jem automatically handed him the accompanying side dishes, the thud of the china and the clink of the silverware providing the only sounds in the room. Unable to stop herself, Jem watched each forkful of food journey to Reese's mouth, remembering the feel of his lips against hers during their brief wedding kiss. A weakness invaded her already unsettled insides, and she stared at the flickering candlelight, wondering what this moment might have been like had it truly been a wedding supper.

The shadows danced over Reese's face, hiding the stubble and lines of weariness. But even they couldn't hide the well-carved planes of his handsome face, the piercing blue of his eyes. She was surprised at the extent of her curiosity about the man. What else lurked beneath his concealing features? But she felt much too awkward to ask, and after he'd eaten his fill, silence descended on the room in a thick cloud.

"I don't quite know how to put this, boss, but if I don't hit some clean straw pretty soon, I'm gonna fall asleep in my plate."

It was the moment Jem had been dreading all evening. But Abigail was still under the roof, and for the past twenty-four hours they had been legally married. Resolutely she shoved away from the table and stood, her boots scraping the floor.

Each footfall echoed on the stairwell, and Jem felt ridiculously like Marie Antoinette on her way to the guillotine. Glancing around at Reese's set face, she reminded herself that the French queen had not been forced to sleep with her executioner.

Reaching the bedroom, Jem's hand paused on the doorknob before turning it. With a confidence she didn't feel, she strode forward, then stopped abruptly. *Now what?*

Her eyes riveted on McIntire's saddlebags casually looped over the back of a chair. She swallowed nervously and averted her eyes. Striding to the chifforobe, she pulled open the door.

"You can put your, er, things in here," she started.

He stared into the depths of the door she'd carelessly flung open. Wondering at his fascination, she turned to look. Her nightgown and wrapper were in full display. Cheeks flaming, she slammed the door shut. "I'm sure you're too tired to worry about unpacking now."

Sinking to the edge of the bed, he grunted a sardonic reply. "Yeah, right."

Daring a glance at him, she saw his words didn't match the expression in his eyes. She stood stock-still as he raised one foot up and began tugging at his boot. When it slipped off, he glanced up at her, a corner of his mouth lifting sardonically. "You plannin' to keep standin' there and watch?"

Jem opened and shut her mouth, looked in every direction possible before moving awkwardly toward the chifforobe. Trying to appear nonchalant, she opened the door, took out her nightclothes, and pushed the door closed as she turned around. Glancing up, she encountered Reese's amused smile as he watched her hold the same garments she'd tried to hide moments before.

"I'll just . . ." She cleared her throat. "I'll be, that is, change . . ."

Reese's smile mocked her as she fled to the alcove at the side of the room. She silently damned all the fates for putting her in this ridiculous position. Shakily she unfastened buttons, quickly shed her garments, and even more quickly pulled on the concealing gown.

Drawing up her courage, Jem stepped back into the room. But her steps froze when her gaze riveted on McIntire's denims and shirt slung carelessly alongside his saddlebags.

He couldn't very well sleep fully clothed, she chided herself. Her movements slowed, and when she finally reached the bed, she gently eased her weight onto the mattress. Just as quietly she placed the lamp on the marble nightstand. Trying to ease under the comforter without dislodging it, Jem ever so carefully positioned herself on the far edge of the mattress. McIntire's face was buried in the pillow, and he presented only his back to her. He neither spoke nor moved. With exquisite care she raised up and blew out the lamp.

Darkness closed in about her in a way Jem had never been aware of before. The moon insistently forced its gentle beams through the curtains, outlining the room in muted tones of gray. She picked out objects in the dark— the sturdy highboy and practical dresser—and her eyes skipped over them with familiarity. Then she found herself staring at McIntire's boots as though they were weapons. They stood sturdily next to the chair that held his clothes. Staring at them reminded her even more fully of the unclothed body lying next to hers.

A tiny squeak of the bedsprings nearly made her bolt upright. Scarcely breathing, she heard a soft sigh and realized McIntire had only stirred. She couldn't quench the memory of their wedding kiss. Her fingers slid over her lips, touching, remembering. As she did, the unaccustomed weight on the bed shifted abruptly. Holding herself stiff and still, she clung to the edge of the mattress with the desperation of a lone survivor clutching the mast of a sinking ship.

Chapter 5

Entering the kitchen, Jem kept to the sideboard, her back facing Della. One glance told her that Mary, Della's helper, was nowhere in sight.

"Morning, Jem." Della's voice was cheerful, perhaps a bit more than it needed to be. "Sleep well?"

There was no mistaking the undertone in her question. Jem gripped a steaming cup of coffee and turned to her inquisitor, trying to quell her nervous stomach.

"Aren't we just full of questions this morning?"

"My, my. Sounds like somebody got up on the wrong side of the bed. Or could it be she laid down on the—"

"Don't you have breakfast to serve or something?" Jem asked irritably.

"As a matter of fact I was just waiting for the lovebirds to come down so I could serve rosette-shaped waffles and jam."

Jem gazed at the cast-iron pans that held fluffy scrambled eggs and crisp bacon. Their sturdy appearance held little resemblance to rosettes and jam. "Rosettes? I think you need to work on your technique."

Della controlled the laughter brimming beneath her voice. "Better me than you two. I thought you wouldn't be up for hours."

Jem laid her cup on the table with a distinctive thump and headed for the backdoor.

"Don't tell me you're not waiting for"—Della paused dramatically—"him?"

Jem slammed her hat on her head, but not before she heard the full mirth in Della's voice. "Now, don't go away mad, Jem. Eat a good breakfast. After all, you'll need your strength."

"Very amusing, Della. Too bad I was so *young* when you and Pete got married. Looks like I missed out on so much fun."

"You got me there, youngster." Della placed a worn hand to her face. "Do I look as old as I really am?"

Immediately remorseful, Jem tossed aside Della's earlier teasing as she traced a path back to her side. Fifteen years older than Jem, Della was still a very attractive woman. Jem's voice was light as she answered, "As a matter of fact, I believe I heard someone at the wedding ask Pete if he'd robbed the cradle when he married you."

Della flushed becomingly. "You did not!"

"I'm not going to say one more word. You're obviously fishing for compliments. With a territory full of men more than willing to give them to you, I refuse to enlarge your ego."

Della smiled softly. "You're sweet to say so." She glanced down at her useless legs. "Very sweet."

Jem crouched beside Della's rattan wheelchair until they were eye level. "I wouldn't say so if it weren't true."

Della's smile reached her eyes, then she took Jem's hand. "Is everything all right?"

Knowing what Della referred to, Jem answered honestly. "Very all right. He fell asleep."

"Asleep?" Della mouthed the word.

"Guess I got all worked up for nothing." Not to mention feeling like a fool after McIntire had merely turned in his sleep and then remained motionless while she'd gotten a stiff neck from clinging to the edge of the bed.

"He won't always be tired and recovering from a hangover," Della cautioned.

"Hmm," Jem answered noncommittally. From all counts,

McIntire was interested in only one thing, the money he planned to collect.

Jem stood up and turned toward the backdoor.

"Jem?" Della's voice was unusually low.

"Yes?"

"Will you watch out for Pete? I'm awfully worried about him." She paused, concern etched in her face. "He was dead tired last night."

Jem's mind flashed back to a month earlier when Pete had collapsed. He swore it was just the heat, even though it was pushing a point even to claim it was fully spring yet, but Doc Riley said it was likely Pete's heart and that he needed to slow down. Pete had dusted himself off, said it was all bullshit, and kept on working just as he always had.

"I'll see to it he doesn't overdo anything."

"Don't let on I told you!"

"I won't, Della. He wouldn't listen to me either if he knew why I was checking up on him."

Della smiled bravely, but Jem could see the worry she couldn't contain. Jem didn't intend to let anything happen to Pete. He and Della were like family, and she couldn't imagine life without either of them.

"Jem, your breakfast . . ."

"Not today, Della. I'd sooner eat tree bark than rosettes!"

The worry fell away a bit from Della's brow, and she even managed a smile as Jem escaped.

Between Reese and now her new concern about Pete, Jem's stomach felt like it was lurching to the rhythm of a ship during a storm. Still she couldn't stop herself from searching the corral area. Ready to turn away, she spotted her quarry. Grady Orton was ambling across the space that separated the bunkhouse from the barn.

"Grady!" she called.

He turned in surprise and then schooled his features as he returned the greeting and headed her way. "Miz Whitaker."

"Did you get a good meal and a bunk?" she questioned.

"Yes'm. Thank you."

"Like I said, we'll be hiring on soon. You just got a head start." She paused, not quite certain how to continue. "So, how've you been, Grady?"

"Fine, ma'am." He shrugged as he spoke, a habit Jem remembered.

"Did you and Charles find the kind of ranch you were hoping for?"

"Not exactly. Me and him didn't wind up at the same place."

"Oh." Jem couldn't keep the disappointment from her voice.

"Was there anything else you needed, ma'am? I thought I'd take a look at that corral railing. Looks like it could use some mending."

Jem smiled at his industriousness. "No, that's all, Grady. Glad to have you back."

"Thank you, ma'am. It feels right good being home."

Jem led her horse away and, after mounting the beast, gaited him backward to watch Grady. Maybe things were going in the right direction after all. It was a positive sign that Grady Orton had returned. As she thought of the insurmountable task ahead it was comforting to know she had allies for the job.

As the day wore on, Jem kept checking on Pete. Glancing through the harsh swirls of high-flying dirt, she saw that he was working even harder than usual. It was time to get him to take a break, even if it made him madder than hell.

Reining in near him, she had to shout to be heard over the milling cattle and the yells of nearby riders.

"Time to get the chuck wagon out here, Pete."

He nodded in agreement and started to holler at one of the hands nearby.

"No, you go, Pete."

"I got more'n I can handle here, Jem. Just send—"

"I want you to go. Della wasn't herself this morning.

You'd better check on her while you're seeing to the chuck wagon."

The hesitation flickered across Pete's face, his loyalties obviously torn.

Reese watched their exchange, first in disbelief and then in growing anger. With precious little help, Jem was going to send their best man to fetch the chuck wagon so that he could check on his wife? Not that Reese didn't feel for the older man—his wife being crippled—but sweet Jesus, it would take every man's sweat to get these beef headed out.

He couldn't complain about Jem's contribution. Hell, she was a better cowhand than most men he'd ridden with. But she was still acting like a damn fool female, sending Pete on an errand any of the lesser hands could handle.

Angrily Reese whipped his horse about, cutting out the unbranded cows and heading them toward the roaring bonfire. His nostrils twitched at the smell of burning hide and scorched hair, but years of doing the chore had all but numbed him to the odor. Jem rode close by, dogging a group of unmarked beef, and he had to wonder, looks aside, how a female tolerated all this. And why? When her father was alive, there'd been money and no scarcity of hands to do the work. Why then had Jem chosen to put herself in those blasted trousers to do a man's work?

Leaning in close, Jem rode with the expertise of a rider born to the saddle who'd done little else in her life. 'Course riders were born, not made, he knew that. Grudgingly Reese had to admit she was good. Better than good. And for some unknown reason, it irked the hell out of him. When she shouted an order at a nearby cowhand, the reason clarified. He'd resigned himself to taking orders in exchange for the money Jem had offered, but he hadn't counted on her being a working boss. He'd figured the orders would be filtered down through Pete. Spending the day in the grit and muscle-grinding work with her had drastically altered that conception.

Keeping to his section of the herd, Reese waited until

the others had eaten their fill before heading toward the cook wagon. He accepted a steaming plate of beef, beans, and corn bread, then hunkered down near the rear wheel of the wagon, hoping to escape some of the dust that painted the air and permeated even the food he was eating.

Pushing his Stetson back on his forehead, he glanced at the sun directly overhead. It was only noon, and he'd been in the saddle for better than eight hours. Turning his attention back to his plate, he acknowledged that it was easier to concentrate on the food rather than the aching of his muscles.

He sensed a movement beside him and turned aside, watching Jem accept a similar plate of food. Hesitating only a moment, she laid her plate down and picked up two tin cups of steaming coffee. He peered at her frowsy silhouette as she silently handed him one of the hot cups of coffee. Accepting the tin cup, he watched as she turned back to get her plate and then joined him on the ground.

"Thanks." Reese's voice was slightly muffled by the corn bread he washed down with the bitter, black brew.

Jem nodded, her attention focused on the plate she held. Reese was surprised at the gesture. Would she bring coffee to any other cowhand? Married to him or not, she was still the owner, and where he'd worked before, owners didn't serve cowhands.

He watched silently as Jem pushed her own hat back, allowing more of her face to show. Staring at her tanned face, he saw her eyelashes sweep down as they shadowed her eyes. He hadn't remembered that they framed her eyes so distinctly. When she looked up, however, she appeared every bit as tired as he felt. The fact that she'd risen even earlier than he had bit into him. He wasn't used to being bested by a woman. Watching her eat quickly, Reese sensed she wasn't planning on slowing down. He wondered if she had iron girders instead of feelings.

"Think we'll make it, boss?"

Jem's eyebrows rose only slightly. "Of course."

Of course. As though there was no doubt. But then,

maybe with Jem there wasn't. "You always this sure about everything?"

He thought he saw a moment's doubt cross her face, but the hesitation was so brief he guessed he must have imagined it.

Jem searched his face for hidden meanings. "Why? Something you think I did wrong?"

"I don't know if wrong's the word I'm looking for. Stupid or maybe *female* might be a better way to describe it."

He watched the slow rise of color in her face and wondered what it would take to send her into a full-fledged rage.

"You want to tell me exactly what you're talking about?"

"Sending Pete to get the chuck wagon when even a kid could take care of the chore. I'll grant you his wife might need checking up on, but now's not the time to go soft. One of the old guys back at the ranch could have seen about her."

The silence stretched out for a moment. "You through?"

He nodded.

"I have work to do and I don't have time to sit here and listen to you whine. I have a damned good reason for everything I do, which is none of your concern. Try to remember who's boss here, McIntire. If I decide to send Pete to tat doilies, I will." With that, she dumped the rest of her uneaten food in the slop bucket, slammed her plate in the wreck pan on the chuck wagon, and retrieved her horse. Without a backward glance, she rode off in the direction she'd come.

Reese glanced down at the steam still swirling up from his cup of coffee. The burr under her saddle must have been lodged near a foot deep. One thing was for sure, out on the range she was never going to let him forget who was boss. Maybe it was time to try for new territory. Their bedroom ought to be a good place to begin.

* * *

Della wheeled herself to the table, reaching awkwardly for the chopping board that was just out of her reach. Pete's strong hand reached past her, easily grasping the wooden block. At the same time he plucked the knife from his wife's hand. Picking up an onion from a nearby basket, he began chopping it expertly.

"Eighteen hours in the saddle wasn't enough work for you?" she chided.

"Nope, just gettin' my second wind." But he paused a moment, taking time to nuzzle her soft cheek and pass a hand over her thick mane of black hair.

She luxuriated in the feel of him, wishing she could convince him to take it easy, knowing he never would.

"You ought to slow down."

Ignoring her comment, he asked, "What're we cookin'?" while sliding the sliced onion off the board and into a waiting bowl.

She smiled, a bit of pixie shining through. "Pecan pie."

"Pecan pie? Then why are we chopping onions?"

The twinkle in her blue eyes intensified. "I don't know, dear. Why are we?"

He glanced sheepishly at the knife he held.

"Still say you're not tired, cowboy?"

He cocked his head a moment, considering. "Mebbe, just a mite."

She took his callused hand in her own. "I hope not too tired."

He squatted down beside her chair, his gray eyes steady, his heart full. "Never too tired for you."

"Then I think the pecan pie can wait until tomorrow," she answered softly.

"I think it'll have to." Rising, he scooped her up and headed up the back stairs, not using the dumbwaiter the Whitakers had installed after Della's accident.

Their quiet murmurs barely trickled back down the staircase, but Reese still felt much like a hack at a peep show. He hadn't meant to spy, or even to overhear. He had stepped into the pantry off the kitchen to find something to eat before Pete had come to the kitchen. Once their conversation had begun, he'd been too embarrassed to announce his presence.

Thoughtfully he polished an apple against his denims, thinking of Pete and Della's loving exchange. When he had come home, he'd purposely avoided the dinner table until Jem had finished her dinner and made her way upstairs. Automatically his eyes strayed up toward the stairs that led to Jem's bedroom. No longer having an appetite, he tossed the apple into the barrel that rested inside the pantry and started toward the staircase. It was time to conquer that unknown territory. Now.

The floorboards creaked ominously beneath Reese's heavy boots as he made his way up the stairs, determination clear in every purposeful step. He barely paused at the door, thought of knocking, decided against it, and entered the room. Much like a Viking warrior standing at the bow of his ship, Reese surveyed the room. Dim light from the lamp flickered over the well-made furniture and over the massive bed that was piled high with soft bedding. And Jem.

He strode up to the four-poster bed and stopped just as abruptly. Under the lamplight, Jem was outlined clearly. Her eyes were closed, and her even breathing indicated that she was asleep. His gaze washed over the long lashes that lay feathered over her cheekbones. Her lips were parted slightly as the air from her breath escaped. Allowing his eyes to roam farther, he saw that her hand was flung up into the long strands of blond hair. Her movement had pulled the coverlet down, revealing the modest gown she wore. Despite the gown's utilitarian design, the shape of her breasts was emphasized as they rose with the even pace of her breathing.

Mesmerized, he stared for a moment, his hand starting to move forward hesitantly. But no sooner did he reach out than he drew back. Instead he pulled his gaze upward until he saw the shadows beneath her eyes. The vulnerability she never allowed to show was etched starkly on her weary features. Even as he watched, a small sigh escaped as she stirred restlessly. Without thinking, he placed his hand gently on her brow, smoothing back the hair from her forehead. She settled at his touch, and he allowed his hand to linger in the long tresses that spilled across her pillow.

The belligerence seeped out of him. He felt a sudden shame at the direction of his thoughts when he'd entered the room. Easing away from her, he pulled off his boots and socks and then stripped off his shirt and denims. He climbed in the bed carefully, making certain not to disturb her. Resolutely he started to turn his back toward hers when suddenly she turned in his direction, flinging one hand over him. Face-to-face, he found it difficult to turn away. Her breathing, still even, indicated her state of sleep.

He reminded himself of that fact as he felt her hand resting on his hip. Seeing the softness in her face, he merely sighed in resignation and slid his arm beneath her head, cradling it. As he did, a bit of gold winked from between her breasts. Fingering the locket briefly, he laid it gently back in place. Some conquering warrior, he thought with disgust. Staring in the darkness that shrouded the room, he wondered again at their misbegotten bargain.

Chapter
6

"You knew I had to be the one to hire the hands. Isn't that one of the reasons you brought me here?" Reese demanded.

Jem glared at him in exasperation. They'd argued over the issue for nearly a week. Of course he was right, which irritated her that much more. "It was part of the reason," she hedged.

"You're damned lucky we got the herd over to the trail boss in time with only a few hands. But we can't keep on going without more help."

"I know that," she bit back, thinking of the bone-crunching weariness of moving the herd, grateful that part of the job was behind them.

"You got to get it through that ornery head of yours. The men aren't gonna sign up to work for you."

Defeat tasted like a prickly-pear cactus she was trying to force down. She knew men wouldn't take orders from a woman boss. The fact that she'd been a Whitaker only made it worse. "So, which ones looked like they had a lick of sense?"

Reese's eyebrows rose. She might not like that he was right, but at least she wasn't going to fight to the death over the issue.

He named a few, and she nodded, recognizing their names, knowing them to be good men. He listed a few more, ending with Boyd Harris.

"Boyd Harris?" she asked in disbelief. "Are you crazy?"

He met her expression evenly, refusing to give an inch. He was fully aware of Boyd's reputation, but he'd also ridden with the man, served in the army with him. When word got out that Reese was running the Bar-W, Boyd had sought him out, hoping for work. Reese had never believed the unproven rumors about Boyd and knew he was no thief, certain that if there'd been any truth to the charges, Boyd would have been convicted at the time. Far as he was concerned, Boyd Harris was the best man of the lot. "I know him and I want him working for me."

"Well, I refuse to consider it."

Reese's eyes simmered with controlled anger. "Refuse?"

"You heard me. I won't have someone like him at the Bar-W. There are plenty of good men available. Grady Orton's looking for work. He's been staying at the bunkhouse for a few days, making himself useful."

It was Reese's turn to look amazed. "Grady Orton? I talked to that piece of scum. I wouldn't let him ride drag during a sandstorm."

"He was a very capable assistant foreman and he'd make an excellent foreman. Charles thought very highly of him."

Reese noticed the way her voice had softened imperceptibly when she said Charles's name. "Charles?"

"Sawyer. He was our foreman."

Reese wondered if he'd imagined the pause in Jem's voice. Charles Sawyer. Why did that name sound familiar?

"I don't want Orton," Reese stated flatly.

"And I don't want Boyd Harris."

"Then you've got a problem, don't you?"

"Me?" Jem's eyes narrowed. "Why do I have a problem?"

"From where I'm sitting, it looks like unless we come to an agreement, you won't get any hands hired."

They squared off across the breakfast table. The crisp

48

bacon, fried eggs, and biscuits lay untasted; the coffee cooled.

Reese's voice washed over Jem like a frigid rain. "And no hands, no contract."

A red haze clouded Jem's vision as anger and frustration threatened to overwhelm her. They had one year to fill the army contract. One year to know whether they'd prosper or fail. It was galling to know that the Bar-W's survival depended on the smirking man seated across from her. She couldn't deny that she'd created this situation herself. "Do I need to remind you that your own financial reward depends on filling the contract?"

"No. I remember just fine." Reese stood up and crossed to the sideboard. Jem forced herself to refrain from noticing his lithe movements or the material that strained across his muscled back as he reached toward the coffeepot. He turned, staring down at her, placing her at a disadvantage. "But I'm not the one with the most to lose."

The blood drained from Jem's face. It would mean far more than losing the ranch, the land. Too many people were depending on her: Pete, Della, Mary, the old retired hands. They'd all be without a home.

"Think about it." He drained the cup and replaced it on the sideboard. As he walked out of the room Jem doubted she could do little else.

The door knocker sounded throughout the house, and Jem rubbed her throbbing temples. Her argument with Reese had left her frustrated and, worse, without a solution. She heard Della's voice brighten in pleasure and then heard another feminine voice. While she wondered who the visitor was, she also hoped they wouldn't bother her.

The distinctive creak of Della's rattan wheelchair neared the study door. "Company, Jem." Standing behind Della was Abigail Fairchild. Just what she needed. A living, breathing reminder of everything she coveted and didn't have.

"Have I come at a bad time?"

Jem rose and stepped from behind the desk, forcing her face into a smile of welcome. "Abigail."

"I hope I haven't disturbed you, but I wanted to bring you this in person."

Jem stared at the ivory-colored rectangular envelope in Abigail's hand with foreboding. She hoped it wasn't what she thought it was.

Abigail's words dispelled that notion. "We're having a social Saturday night. It will be a perfect time for everyone to get to know Reese."

Just perfect. "It's a really busy time—" Jem started to protest.

"I know. But . . ." Abigail seemed to hesitate. "Could we sit for just a moment, Jem?"

Embarrassed, Jem realized she hadn't even offered Abigail a chair. "Certainly."

After they were seated, Abigail looked away for a moment and then back at Jem. "It's just that everyone seems so curious about Reese."

Jem opened her mouth to object and then promptly snapped it shut.

"That's why I thought it would be nice to have this social. People can get to know him, to know . . ." Abigail's voice trailed away while Jem completed her unspoken thought. *To know Jem hadn't just married him for convenience.*

So people were already questioning their marriage. This wouldn't do at all. The next year was crucial, cattle had to be shipped, and blast it, hands had to be hired.

"I hope you don't think badly of me, Jem." Abigail's face was earnest, her china-blue eyes full of concern. Jem took stock of the woman and felt a growing gratitude. She'd been nothing but kind, and this gesture, too, was generous.

"I appreciate your concern. Not many others care."

Abigail's expression cleared, some of the doubt leaving her eyes. "You just haven't allowed many people to get close enough to care, Jem. But that will come in time, too."

Embarrassed, Jem turned away.

Abigail rushed on. "I do think you'll have a fine time, Jem. I've planned some of the newest parlor games. Even Michael thinks they sound fun."

Jem smiled weakly. Parlor games. She would have more luck trying to run down a steer without a horse. "Oh, well . . ."

"I'm so pleased that you'll be there and that you're not upset with me."

Words stuck in Jem's throat. She wanted to acknowledge Abigail's friendly overture, but she hadn't any experience at it. But before the moment became awkward, Abigail patted her hand and started to rise.

"Now I must be on my way. I know how busy you are. We'll see you at the social." Abigail tugged at her flawless white gloves, the ribbons on her hat bobbing as she ducked her head forward, allowing a few of her golden curls to escape. "It won't be too dressy. Just Sunday best." Jem glanced self-consciously at her trousers, remembering the lean rack of dresses in her chifforobe. "If you'd like to get together before then, I have some new patterns."

Jem, who'd never held a needle and thread before in her life, stood mute.

"But if you're too busy . . ."

"I appreciate the offer, Abigail. I'm sure I'll find something to wear."

As she ushered Abigail to the door Jem realized the other woman had been kind in letting her know what was appropriate to wear to the social. But as she closed the door behind her Jem realized life as a married woman was becoming increasingly difficult.

The familiar rattle of Della's chair sounded behind her.

"I thought only city folks had socials. Out here we have get-togethers." When Jem didn't answer, Della sought to fill the silence, realizing Abigail's visit had upset her.

"Don't worry. I can run up something for you to wear. When is it, Saturday night?"

Jem nodded absently, staring out the window.

"Don't fret about it, Jem. I have some material in my trunk. I'll get started on it this afternoon."

Jem dredged up a smile for Della's benefit. At the moment her wardrobe was the least of her problems. Appearing in public with her husband was the biggest.

Chapter
7

Saturday night arrived far too soon. Jem and Reese had spent the last two days arguing over the hiring of both Boyd Harris and Grady Orton, and still nothing had been resolved. Since Jem had installed Orton in the bunkhouse, Reese had allowed Boyd Harris the same privilege. Both men were in residence, waiting.

The star-dappled night had a rapt audience as Jem and Reese both stared into the inky depths rather than look at one another as their wagon bounced its way toward the Fairchild home. Jem didn't know which would be more damaging to their reputation—staying home and avoiding the others or showing up and letting them see the true condition of their marriage.

In keeping with her lighthearted nature, Abigail had hung cleverly crafted paper lanterns from the wide veranda. Their candles winked out a welcome as Reese reined in the horses and set the brake. The stillness of the night surrounded them, broken only by the snorting of the horses as they settled.

Jem turned to him finally. "You know how important tonight is, how we act . . ." Her voice trailed off. Of course he knew, which was why, no doubt, he'd baited her all day.

"Important enough for you to realize we should hire Boyd Harris instead of Grady Orton?"

Jem glared at him in reply.

"Guess not. Well, this should be a long night."

He stepped from the wagon, but Jem didn't wait for him to cross to her side and help her down. Unassisted, she awkwardly clambered down, smoothing the unfamiliar taffeta of the gown Della had hastily constructed. Glancing up, she encountered Reese's mocking eyes. It was apparent from his expression that he'd caught her ungainly maneuver.

She tried to dismiss the mounting flush heating her cheeks as she strode forward. Reese moved in step beside her, sardonically offering her his arm. Disdaining the gesture, she walked ahead, ignoring the amusement on his face.

Abigail opened the door within moments of their knock. The room was alive with people. It seemed everyone in the territory had put in an appearance. Quickly Abigail drew them in and stayed close by as she introduced Reese to the sea of unfamiliar faces. Some he remembered from the wedding, others were a blur. Abigail hovered protectively, covering awkward moments, easing the tension.

Jem released a sigh of relief. So far, so good. Reese was behaving, she felt a little less like a prize beef at auction, and the evening wasn't turning out as badly as she'd anticipated.

But even as her breath began to ease Abigail clapped her hands together. "It's time!"

Jem looked about in confusion. *Time for what?*

Her question was answered too quickly. Games. Swallowing her discomfort, Jem joined the others in selecting a chair and placing it in a circle. But it wasn't as difficult as she'd thought it would be. The first game, Black Cap and Red Cap, was fairly easy. It was a word game, and all she had to remember was some silly phrasing and the colors of the caps. She breathed a sigh of relief at its end, wondering why anyone would choose to spend their time with such mindless frivolity, but glad she hadn't embarrassed herself.

The next game was announced: I Love My Love. Feeling a sudden panic, she slanted a glance at Reese, who looked equally uncomfortable as the rules were explained.

Michael's deep brown eyes twinkled as he turned to Abigail. "I'd like to go first." Abigail's expression matched his as he turned to her. "I love my love with an A, because she's affectionate, ageless, because her name is Abigail. I would give her an amethyst, priceless works of art, and all my love."

"You forfeit," one woman chortled. "Love doesn't start with an A."

"She's worth the forfeit," Michael murmured, his dark head close to Abigail's fair one.

Jem felt a growing itch at the base of the unaccustomed collar cloaking her neck. What words would she use to describe Reese? Renegade, rapscallion? But, glancing up, she met his eyes and realized he was in the same quandary. With a sinking feeling, she acknowledged that she had hardly inspired any kind feelings either.

The other players took turns, laughing at some of the absurd descriptions, sighing aloud at some of the more romantic revelations.

The moment she'd dreaded arrived. It was her turn. Nervously she stood. "I . . ." she began. Saying she loved him might be more difficult than dreaming up the other adjectives. She started over, mentally blocking the words as she spoke. "I love my love with an R because he's . . ." She cleared her throat. "Because he's . . ."

Abigail's soft voice drifted across the room. "Newly-weds always have the most difficult time, there's just too much to choose from."

Certainly, Abigail, that's my problem. Clearing her throat again, Jem started again. "Because he rides well." She paused again. Daring a glance at Reese, she saw that his eyes flickered a bit in surprise at the compliment. She started again, unable to resist a little jab. "He's not repulsive." Laughter tittered through the room, and she noticed that the tips of Reese's ears had reddened. She relaxed a bit and finished in a rush. "I would give him a red-shouldered hawk because they are both rebels." Grateful she was through, Jem sank back to her chair.

"Forfeit," the same woman announced with glee.

"Forfeit? Why? I—"

"You forgot to say your love's name." So she had. A sudden memory of her true love stabbed her painfully. Why couldn't he be sitting beside her? There wouldn't have been enough words to describe her feelings for him. Glancing away from Reese, Jem tried to smile as he stood.

His deep baritone echoed through the room as he began. "I love my love with a J because she doesn't jabber and she's not jealous." He looked down for a moment, and the pause lengthened. "I would give her a jewel . . ." Jem glanced up in surprise. His voice continued quietly, ". . . and joy. Her name is Jem."

He sat down, and Jem's eyes locked with his. He'd just given her what she'd asked for. At the soft clapping of hands about them, she realized he'd convinced the others of a true affection.

Jem wished she could recall her own taunt. It seemed mean and very small. Before she could ruminate further, they broke into romp games and were separated as they played Hiss and Clap and Quakers' Meeting. Jem tried to fit in as they played the games, still feeling awkward and ill at ease.

Abigail announced that the last game would be Rule of Contrary, and Jem gave silent thanks, relieved to see the evening end. Reese was caught and received a forfeit also. The game ended, and Jem looked around for her cloak, ready to bolt out the door. She hoped this social thing wasn't something they'd have to do very often.

But even as she planned her escape Michael's deep voice boomed out, "Time for forfeits." Jem blinked and looked up. She thought forfeits meant you lost. Whatever was coming next?

"Reese and Jem, you have a double forfeit." Michael's voice was teasing as he drew them forward. Jem tried to hang back, but Michael was insistent. "Not to worry. You two will enjoy this one." He whipped out two bandannas and proceeded to blindfold them. "Mack, your fiddle."

Unable to see, Jem jumped as the fiddle screeched to life, then lilted into a waltz tune. "Your forfeit is the Blind Man's Waltz." They both stood stock still, and Michael continued. "You have to dance one waltz blindfolded." He leaned closer, lowering his voice to a conspiratorial whisper. "Have fun."

Jem felt Reese's hands hesitantly grope toward her, trying to find her waist. Instead his hand grazed her breast, and he stopped still as though he'd touched a red-hot poker. They both heard a few hoots from the others as he moved his hand down, locating her waist. They clasped hands, and Reese drew their bodies closer. Jem swallowed a thickening lump in her throat as her breasts pushed into Reese's chest.

His voice sounded unnaturally deep as he muttered into her ear, "Do I have everything right?"

She tried to answer, but the words stuck in her throat. The feel of his body against hers was setting off an explosion, the likes of which she'd never imagined. Unable to see, all she could do was feel. And feel she did. Long lengths of sinewy frame pressed against her. As tall as most men, she'd never been held by one who towered over her, making her seem small in comparison.

Placing a tentative hand toward his waist, she realized she'd touched his hip instead. Sliding her hand upward, she lingered on the journey, startled by her thoughts as her fingers finally found his waist. Her breath shortened, her chest filling as he fit their hips together and began the movements of the waltz. They made a small turn, then bumped into a wall. Instinctively Reese pulled her close to prevent a fall. As he did, her breasts crushed into his chest while her legs met his.

From a distance Jem could hear the hoots of the others, but her body compelled her to ignore them. Fire was rushing through her blood, journeying to every sensitive cell in her body.

Reese's voice was even hoarser, more strained. "You all right?" She nodded, unable to speak. He must have felt her movement, since he, too, couldn't see.

Righting them, he attempted to navigate the room, trying to remember the placement of the furniture. Instead all he could remember was the feel of Jem's body as she fit close to him, the hardened tips of her breasts as they'd grazed his chest, the softness of the one breast in his hand. . . .

The crash shouldn't have been unexpected, but as they toppled over, Reese tried to catch Jem as he pulled the blindfold off. Instead they both landed on the rolled-up rug that had tripped them. He flung off his blindfold completely and quickly yanked Jem's off also.

Then he paused, startled at the expression in her eyes. His mouth dry, he realized what position they were in. Lying atop her, his body touched her as close as it possibly could fully clothed. The pulse at the base of her throat beat raggedly, and her chest rose with the accelerated effort. And her eyes. Like a startled doe, she gazed at him, the dawning awareness visible.

He searched those eyes, wondering what kind of woman this was, this woman who was his wife in name only. The beat of their bodies signaled a different message, one neither could ignore.

"All right, you two."

Startled, they turned toward the others, who laughed merrily.

Good-natured taunts of "newlyweds" rang through the room as Reese eased off Jem and helped her stand.

Lorraine tweaked Jem's cheek. "You two are just too precious for words." The men responded to Reese with a lot of good-natured backslapping and jabs. Jem stood still amid their revelry.

Abigail moved close to her side. "No need to be embarrassed, Jem. We were all newlyweds once."

Jem stared at Abigail, realizing the other woman thought she was speechless with mortification. In fact, she was right, but not the kind of mortification Abigail meant. Jem knew she'd felt more passion in those moments in Reese's arms than she had in anyone else's. How was that possible? She'd known true love once, but it had been sweet, chaste. Never had she felt hot and mindless. If they hadn't been in the middle of someone's living room . . .

Gazing over Abigail's head, Jem met Reese's eyes. No doubt or retreat was written there. They'd just crossed a line, and Jem knew there was little chance it would ever be redrawn.

Chapter
8

"If you didn't want to have this social, why did you agree?" Della's voice washed over Jem's fractured nerves.

"Because." Jem unclenched her teeth and softened her voice. "I told you, I didn't have any choice. While we were leaving, everyone was discussing where the next social would be, someone suggested the Bar-W, and ..." Jem's voice trailed off. Caught up in the intoxication of Reese's body close to hers, her mind simply hadn't functioned.

"You've been acting funny ever since last Saturday night. Want to tell me what happened?"

Jem stared out the study window. "Where do you suppose Charles is?"

Della's mouth turned downward at the mention of Charles Sawyer. As far as she was concerned, he'd done Jem a huge favor by leaving.

"If you knew, what good would it do?"

"Probably none." Jem fingered the curtains at the window again. "I know you and Pa didn't approve of his courting. But just because he was our foreman ..."

"It didn't have anything to do with him being the foreman," Della stated flatly.

"Maybe not to you, but it did to Pa."

Della didn't try to pretend she had read James Whitaker's mind, so she kept her own counsel. But foremen didn't marry owners' daughters. It was the code of the land, and James Whitaker had known and respected that code. Suddenly Della's eyes narrowed.

"Why are you wondering about Charles now?"

Jem fiddled with the curtain again, remembering her first beau, the only man who'd ever treated her like a woman instead of a freak. "No special reason."

"Hmpft."

Jem turned as Della wheeled toward the other end of the study and left the room, her implication clear. Jem had been snappish and contrary all week, and it was a wonder Della hadn't confronted her earlier about her behavior. But Jem's broken promise had mocked her since the night of the social.

She'd never told anyone about her vow to wait for Charles and marry him when he returned. Instead she had chosen to put the Bar-W first and marry Reese. She knew that Pete and Della thought she should forget about Charles, pretend he meant nothing. Jem touched the locket at her throat, remembering just how much he had meant to her, which made her feelings about Reese that much more confusing.

She'd spent the week dodging him, waiting until she was certain he was asleep before climbing into bed, arising before he was awake. A few nights she'd simply curled up on the uncomfortable settee in her father's study and grabbed what little sleep she'd managed to claim since Saturday night. When they had encountered one another, all they'd done was argue over who to hire. The true reason behind their tension remained unspoken, untouched.

Hearing the distinctive clatter of Reese's boots on the hard oak floor, Jem pressed a hand to her forehead and willed her thoughts to settle.

He approached the desk and spoke abruptly. "You planning to waste the whole day away in here?"

"I'm—"

"I know what you're doing. Frittering away the day when we've got decisions that need to be made."

"I don't account to you for my actions, McIntire. Or did you forget who's—"

"How could I forget with you reminding me every minute of the day? Well, boss, it's time you made up your mind. I need an assistant foreman. That is, unless you plan to cancel the contract."

Jem's stomach twisted in a familiar knot. She hated the fact that Reese had outmaneuvered her at every given chance. Even playing his part so well at the social had irked her. It was what she'd wanted, but he'd managed it in such a way that her own actions had appeared irresponsible and worse, petty. Even when he did the right thing, it angered her.

His next words took her by complete surprise. "I'm making Pete the foreman. Don't know why he wasn't before."

"But—"

"You going to argue about your own man? Isn't there anything you don't want to fight about?"

Silenced, Jem considered telling Reese about Pete's health. But perhaps as foreman he would take on less of the physical work. She wondered in surprise why she hadn't thought of the solution herself. *Because no one can take Charles Sawyer's place!* She had persistently fought any action that would erase Charles's stamp on the Bar-W.

Straightening up, she met Reese's gaze. "Pete will make an excellent foreman." She turned her attention back to the ledgers in front of her. "Was there anything else?"

"Yes, Your Majesty." Her head jerked upright at both his words and his tone. "You know damn well there is. I want to settle on the hands."

"As far as I'm concerned, it is settled."

Reese strode behind the desk, just short of yanking her up from the chair. Intimidated, she pushed the chair back and rose, adroitly stepping to the other side of the desk, putting as much distance between them as possible.

His voice was unrelenting. "Nothing's settled. Don't

forget. I can just as well go out and fire everyone I've already hired."

Jem's face paled. While she hadn't minded playing a mental game of tug-of-war with him, she had no intention of endangering the Bar-W. "You wouldn't dare."

"Don't test me, boss. You might not like what happens."

Jem gritted her teeth and stared at him across the small expanse that separated them. The way he said the word "boss" sent a silent but potent message. Her reaction to him the week before had shown their positions could be reversed—quite literally.

Watching her chest heave with repressed emotion, Reese remembered the feel of her against him, the crush of her breast in his hand. He had watched and waited all week, his temper becoming nastier every day. And the fact that it had, irked the hell out of him. Why was he getting so wrought up over a woman who resembled a brown wren, one he couldn't even pick out from the male hands when they were riding? Why did he want to stride around that desk and pull her to the floor with him and . . .

Refusing to think further, he slammed his hat on the desk. He felt a moment of satisfaction in watching her jump slightly, although she took great pains to conceal the action. It was as though she'd read his thoughts.

"Right now we've got to decide about the bull."

Stupefied, she stared at him, unable to digest his words. His thoughts had translated themselves to her clearly. Too clearly.

Reese's voice was impatient. "Wisner's bull. Got to decide whether it's the one we want and if it's worth the money." As abruptly as Reese had slammed his hat down, he picked it up again and started to stride out of the room. She hadn't moved, instead only staring after him. "You coming or not?"

Jem shook her head a bit to clear it. Still her voice emerged as little better than a croak. "Of course." Starting forward, she was surprised that her legs seemed almost too weak to proceed. She stared down at her offending legs when Reese's voice belted back into the room, "We don't have all day!"

Wobbling forward, she reached the entry leading to the front door. She turned to pluck her hat from the hall tree and stopped, her arm outstretched. Next to the oak armoire hung a mirror. Glimpsing the flush of her face, the expression in her eyes, she halted her movements. This was not the Jem Whitaker she knew. The image in the mirror mocked her. No, now she was Jem McIntire.

The horses ate up the ground between the Bar-W and the Wisner ranch. Glancing aside at Jem, Reese watched her movements, her natural grace on the animal. She still wore the frowsy duster, but today her breeches were different. His eyes narrowed, trying to figure out what had changed.

It hit him as he stared at her legs. These breeches were tight-fitting rather than baggy. They encased her endlessly long legs like gloves. His eyes traveled upward to the waistline she had cinched with a woven leather belt. Taking stock, he realized those legs were as long as some men's. He wondered in a flash what they looked like without the heavy denim covering them. As suddenly he wished his thoughts hadn't taken that direction.

She was still as ornery and unfeminine as the day they'd met. Putting on a dress twice hadn't changed that. A cougar didn't turn into a house cat by coming down the mountain.

Spying the Wisner ranch in the distance, Reese urged his horse to go faster. He saw a moment's flicker of surprise on Jem's face before she, too, prodded her horse on. The sooner they got this over with the better.

Greetings exchanged, they all got down to the serious business at hand. Clambering up on the corral railing, Jem and Reese stared at the pawing beast. Proud, undaunted, the bull challenged them as he trotted across the expanse of the corral.

"Don't like being cooped up in there," Hank Wisner

commented unnecessarily. Head erect, nostrils flaring, the bull pawed once again at the ground.

Jem watched Reese examine the animal, assessing its qualities. As she gazed at Reese she had the uncanny sensation of comparing him with the bull trapped in the pen— both proud, stubborn, but ultimately trapped. Their loss of dignity was the supreme outrage. Instead of studying the animal they'd come to judge, she watched Reese's concentration, his sense of determination.

"Do you like him?" Reese asked.

"What's your opinion?" she countered.

His face started to contort into a mask of exasperation until he realized she was serious. Quietly she waited as his eyes roved the beast again. "I think we should buy him."

Turning to Hank Wisner, Jem retrieved some of Reese's self-respect. "Mr. McIntire would like to buy the bull. If you'll make the arrangements with him, I'd like to look at the other stock."

She turned before she could see Reese's jaw sag in amazement. By the time he'd worked out a price for the bull and they were set to leave, he seemed to have regained his equilibrium.

After they were out of Wisner's line of vision, he pulled her horse over, reining the impatient stallion. "Why?"

Jem sensed she would lose the upper hand with him if she told him. Deep inside she knew the final insult would be to let him know that she realized his loss of pride. So she answered instead, "You're going to earn your money, McIntire. This year isn't going to be a free ride."

He searched her face, trying to fathom the depths concealed beneath her benign calm. Instead of answering, he released the reins of her horse, and the stallion bolted. Controlling the beast easily, Jem set off across the wild grass. Reese watched the flying hooves of a horse few men could conquer and wondered at the woman who could.

Dismounting, Reese led the paint into the barn, his voice soothing as he talked to the horse. "Here you go, boy." The leather creaked as Reese uncinched and removed the saddle. After taking off the blanket, Reese began grooming the pony. Although there were now enough hands that Reese could direct someone to groom the horse, he had no intention of delegating the chore.

He picked up a handful of clean straw, rubbing away the sweat until the horse was dry. Reese's voice soothed the pony as he walked him to the trough. "Come on, boy. A cool drink'll go down good." Waiting until the horse had his fill, Reese listened to the other sounds of the night. Crickets sang to the hoot owl while the intermittent sound of the horse lapping its water permeated the night air. Reese breathed in the sweet air as he watched the moon outline the jagged peaks of the mountains.

He had to admit the Bar-W was one hell of a spread. Working the stock, he'd ridden the ridges and covered the long plateaus of the range. Never staying at a place long enough to feel anything other than gratitude to be off and free again, he'd never wondered what had lain within a ranch's borders, only what had stretched beyond their confines. The paint whinnied, catching his attention.

"Want me to get on with it, don't you, boy? Then you get your oats." The horse whinnied in reply, rubbing his nose against Reese's shoulder. Reese chuckled and led the horse back into the barn. Reaching up, he grabbed the currycomb and began the long combing process.

"Ah, Danny, we've come a long way, haven't we?" The horse turned its long neck toward Reese as though not wanting to miss a word of their conversation. Reese continued the circling motions with the comb, surprised at how calm he felt. While Jem had him in knots, the land had exactly the opposite effect. He'd been running from one thing or another all his life. It was an unsettling feeling not to be seeking the next border, not restlessly watching for the next job.

The horse stood patiently while Reese finished with the comb and then picked up a dandy brush to continue the grooming. Reese spoke to the animal in a low voice.

"She's something, Danny. Not quite sure what yet." Long, sure strokes brushed through the horse's mane as Reese continued talking. "Name's Jem. Funny sort of name, don't you think?" Danny flicked his tail, and Reese kept on brushing and talking. "If she was smart, she'd sell out instead of risking everything. Hell, she figures on me sticking around for a year. A year, Danny. You know we haven't stayed anyplace that long in . . ." Reese paused. "In so long I can't remember when." His thoughts traveled back to a time when he hadn't been on the move, when he'd had a family, a place to call home.

It had never been much, but he had belonged there. His father had died when he was thirteen. The oldest of five children, Reese had quit school to go to work and help his mother. The hand holding the dandy brush paused in midair. Remembering what had happened next was too painful. Danny whinnied, showing signs of impatience. Laying the brush down, Reese reached for a pick to clean the hooves. He examined one hoof, pushing the more hurtful memories aside.

"Think we can stay a whole year, boy?"

The horse nuzzled Reese's pocket, looking for the bit of carrot or apple sometimes lodged there. Reese walked over to the feed bin, mixing a hearty portion of oats in with the winter grain, then rubbed the paint's sleek flanks as he chewed on the feed.

"Think of what we can do with the money. We've gotta move fast if we're gonna make a go of the freighting business. But think about it. No more orders. We can take up and go whenever we want." Reese's face set in a deep frown. "Not like this. I don't know about you, boy, but I'm not so sure I can last a year."

Giving Danny a final pat, Reese turned to take care of the tack, not seeing the figure that slipped from the stall at the end of the barn and into the inky darkness.

Chapter
9

Reese slammed his hat down on the desk, but this time Jem refused to show any emotion.

"Why do you want Orton so badly?" Reese demanded.

She avoided his question, instead countering with one of her own. "Why do you want Harris? Everyone knows his reputation, his—"

But Reese refused to be sidetracked. "What aren't you telling me about Orton?" A niggling in the back of his mind tugged at him.

Jem brushed the hair away from her face, trying to secure the escaping strands with a loose hairpin, a maneuver designed to avoid Reese's gaze. But as she glanced up, she saw his eyes narrow and recognized the light of dawning awareness.

"This has something to do with Charles Sawyer, doesn't it?"

Jem didn't intend to discuss her feelings for Charles with Reese. Since he'd brought his name up a month ago, she'd avoided the subject. Perhaps a fraction of the truth would serve her purpose.

"Charles did place a great deal of faith in Grady. I see no reason to doubt him."

"If Charles Sawyer is so loyal and trustworthy, why isn't he here now?"

Jem turned away to hide the sudden stab of pain at Reese's question. It was one she'd asked herself a thou-

68

sand times since Charles had left. But, as Charles had convinced her, it was the only way. He couldn't stay under the cloud of the Bar-W and he had promised to come back and marry her. The Bar-W's survival had altered that plan.

She made her voice deliberately harsh. "That's none of your concern."

"Who we hire is my concern, and we can't put off a decision any longer."

Suddenly drained, Jem didn't want to continue the fight. It dredged up too many memories, too many unanswered questions.

"Fine, hire Boyd Harris." Reese's face reflected surprise that she'd given in. "But hire Grady as well."

"I don't need Grady Orton."

"As far as I'm concerned, we don't need Boyd Harris. Both or neither."

Knowing how badly Harris needed the job, Reese hated to slam the door on her offer. His better instincts told him to avoid Orton, but he knew Harris was counting on him for the job. By damn he was going to remember who Charles Sawyer was if it killed him.

"All right. But Harris is going to be assistant foreman."

Jem didn't have much fight left in her, but she salvaged as much of her spirit as possible. "That's not settled yet."

They both turned as they heard Della's chair squeaking as she maneuvered the corner and entered the study. "I'm sorry. I thought Jem was here alone."

"No trouble, Della, I was about finished."

"I'll just be a minute. Would shortbread be all right for Saturday night?"

Reese rolled his eyes and snorted his opinion.

"Don't like shortbread, Mr. McIntire?"

"Reese," he corrected automatically. "It's not the shortbread."

"Must be the social," Della surmised accurately. Although she thought Jem needed some enjoyment, the social sounded like a bunch of silliness. She and Mary had enough work to do without preparing for this party.

"Once was enough," he said succinctly.

Della glanced between them and decided it was time to exit. Whatever was gnawing at them had made the air in the house tenser than a first-time father waiting for a ten-month baby.

After she'd wheeled out, Jem backed away from the desk, hoping for a quick escape. Then she saw it again, that look in Reese's eyes—the one that made her want to bolt and stay at the same time.

Once was enough. Enough to know what it felt like to be crushed tighter together than she'd known was possible. Enough to wonder why his nearness had affected her so. More so than Charles ever had, her ruthless conscience reminded her.

Across the room Reese watched her, saw the sudden acceleration of her pulse, the shift in her stance, the awareness in her eyes. It had been an uneasy week. Like wary combatants they had stalked one another, avoided one another, but even more so, had been aware of one another.

Reese didn't understand his feelings. The restlessness he recognized, but had attributed it to knowing he had to stay in one place for longer than he wanted. But the rest . . .

Jem walked across the room, and unconsciously Reese's eyes traveled over her body. Tall and long-limbed, she was as lean as he remembered, but the feel of her breast in his hand was a warm memory that denied she was shapeless beneath her ugly clothes.

"I don't want to argue anymore, McIntire." Close up he saw the signs of weariness he'd recognized once before. Glancing down before he thought, Reese found himself searching for the glint of her locket, imagining where it lay. But the oversized shirt she wore concealed anything and everything.

Catching the direction of his eyes, Jem stopped speaking. For long moments he held her gaze, then turned away. Hearing the echo of his boots against the wooden planking of the floor as he walked away, Jem reached for the locket that swung between her breasts. Clasping the warmed metal, she wondered if she'd just imagined the unspoken message in Reese's expression.

Jem stared at Boyd Harris with ill-concealed distaste. She admitted he was an attractive sort—tall and dark, with even features and deep blue eyes. She swallowed her bitterness at not being able to bend Reese to her way of thinking. Boyd tipped his hat in her direction, and Jem acknowledged the gesture with the barest of nods. It was bad enough the man was beneath contempt, but to have him crammed down her throat made him even more unacceptable.

She wondered if Harris was plotting, as he worked, on how to steal her best horse stock. The fact that he'd never been convicted or strung up was inconsequential. He'd been entrusted to run a ranch while the owner was gone, and during that time better than half the stock had disappeared. True, the ranch had run smoothly for over two years, but the rustling in the last six months of its operation had effectively ruined that record. It was as though he'd carefully plotted and then collected on that plan. Lack of proof had kept him out of jail, but not off the blacklist.

Shading her eyes, Jem watched the rising dust of an approaching rider, and her already displeased expression turned dour. There was no mistaking Randolph Cushman on his distinctive palomino. Unconsciously she adopted a battle stance, her gaze narrowing as he closed the distance to the corral. Before he could speak, she challenged him, her voice a surly growl.

"What are you doing here?"

"I'm fine, thanks," he replied.

"State your business or leave."

He sighed audibly and eased off the mount. "There's an association meeting next Wednesday. I think you ought to be there."

She laughed without humor. "I see. You couldn't force my father to go along with your tactics, so now you think you'll get me to your lynching parties?"

"James Whitaker was a shortsighted man. Never did have the sense to know what was best for the range."

"He got in your way, and you killed him."

"I see you're not only as stubborn as your father, you're just as addled."

"Get off my property. Now."

"You'd better think over who you're riling." Cushman's pale, piercing gaze held Jem's. She trembled with pent-up frustration and anger, her hands twitching with the desire to end his life as he'd so callously done to her father's. Her eyes traveled over to the shotgun slung in the scabbard of her saddle. When she looked up, she saw that Cushman's gaze had followed hers and correctly surmised her thoughts.

"You're a foolish woman, Jem."

Boyd Harris's voice startled them both. "No need to talk to Miz McIntire like that. I believe the lady asked you to leave."

Jem didn't know which man she wished to throttle more. Her voice gritted out between nearly clenched teeth, "I don't need your help, Harris."

"So it's true." Cushman shot a calculating glance at Boyd Harris. "You do have a bunch of misfits running the place. Your father'd turn over in his grave."

"The one you put him in!"

Cushman merely shook his head in reply as he mounted the horse, the saddle creaking under his weight. "Instead of running me off, you'd best think about your own interests. Whether you like it or not, the range wars are getting worse. You're sticking your neck out and you'll be all alone when someone goes to chop it off."

"Threats don't mean any more to me than they did to my father."

"And look where that got him." Cushman dug his spurs in the horse's side and trotted off before Jem could form a reply.

Boyd's voice was awkward and hesitant. "Don't pay him no mind."

All of Jem's bottled-up frustration poured out. "I don't need your advice or help."

"Yes, ma'am."

Great waves of fury still swirled, just waiting for release. Boyd Harris seemed to be a convenient receptacle. "I didn't want to hire you." Her voice rose. "I don't trust you."

"Yes, ma'am. I know that." He removed his creased Stetson.

Jem stared at him, slightly appalled. Reese had told the man her objections?

"I know what people say about me, but I aim to show 'em it ain't true. And I thank you for the chance to prove myself."

The last of Jem's anger seeped through. "You needn't thank me. It was all Mr. McIntire's doing. If he was wrong, this time you won't get away without a rope around your neck."

Boyd turned the hat in his hands, but met her gaze steadily. "It's a hard thing for people to change what they believe. My situation's not all that different from your pa's. The ranch I was running got hit by rustlers, too. The owner'd been gone for better than two years. That's why—"

"You're nothing like my father!"

Boyd held her gaze for long moments that crackled with untold tension. His voice was emotionless as he answered evenly, "No, ma'am."

Jem's anger was now ebbing, and she realized with a touch of shame that Boyd had not deserved her full wrath. She turned away to face the mountains looming behind the corral. "You'd best get back to work."

"Yes, ma'am." Without a backward glance, Boyd headed toward the corral.

"Oh, Harris."

"Yes, ma'am?"

"Do you know where Grady Orton is?"

Jem wondered if she imagined the peculiar expression

that darted across Boyd Harris's face. He pointed toward the east. "I saw him ride out with a few other liners this morning."

So Reese had sent Orton out to eat dust while Boyd worked the best horseflesh on the ranch. The wood splintered beneath her hands as she clenched the corral railing. The men crowding her thoughts all infuriated her. From Cushman to Harris to Reese.

"What the hell is she thinking?" Pete's voice bounced off the walls of the kitchen.

"Ssh. Jem'll hear you." Della dumped the potato peelings into a bucket.

"I hope so. Hiring Orton and Harris."

Della defended Jem. "She didn't want Harris."

"That was obvious. Only reason she fought so hard for Orton was 'cause she thinks he can lead her to Charles Sawyer."

"You believe so?"

"Yep, and it's time she gave up. Sawyer's gone for good."

"It isn't always that easy to let go." Della's voice was thoughtful, almost distant. Pete turned and watched his wife, his gaze lowering to the lifeless legs resting in the chair. It had been ten years since the crippling accident, but the scars were still visible, the memories painful.

Pete's voice was low as he spoke. "It does get better though, doesn't it?"

They both knew that they no longer spoke of Jem. Della reached out and clasped his hand.

"Yes, it does, with the right person at your side."

Pete closed his eyes briefly, thankful once again for this woman.

"You really think Jem hired Orton just because of Sawyer?" Della questioned.

Grateful for the change in subject, Pete released Della's hand and retrieved the large pot to boil the potatoes in. "Why else?"

"I don't know. You think Grady's up to something?"

Pete shrugged. "He hasn't got enough sense to be up to much. Probably just wanted an easy ride and didn't figure on Reese showing up and making him work."

"Jem's not over Charles, you know." Della's fingers moved expertly between the cornmeal and egg, forming a well in which to mix the ingredients.

Pete paused before the open pantry door. "Reese ain't the kind of man to hold still for that."

Della raised surprised eyes to meet Pete's gaze. "But their marriage—"

"Might not have started out like a regular marriage, but Sawyer better not mess with Reese."

"Charles is probably a thousand miles away by now. He was always talking about heading toward Texas." Della's voice was even as she checked the temperature of the oven.

"If we're lucky."

She closed the oven door and wheeled around toward her husband. "Why do you suppose he carried on so about Jem if he was going to up and leave like he did?"

"Hard to figure. Probably got cold feet, figured it was a good time to get out."

"She was talking about him the other day."

"Uh-huh." Pete's voice was even.

"You don't sound surprised."

"Nope. She and Reese come back from that social like two cats, spitting and scratching. Stands to reason she'd be wondering about Charles about now."

"You're a very smart man, Pete Johnson."

"If that's so, why am I burning an empty pan?"

Della cocked her head, considering as Pete grabbed a towel and removed the smoking skillet. But before she could reply, he turned, a serious expression enveloping his face.

"Cushman came by today."

"Jem still convinced he killed her father?"

"Seems so."

Della wheeled her chair about, reaching for the baking powder. "Won't do her any good to keep hating Cushman."

"Maybe not, but somebody killed the old man."

Della looked troubled, her normally busy hands stilled. "She's taking on a lot."

"And you're worried."

"She and Reese look fair ready to explode."

Pete issued a hearty hmft. "There's nothing wrong with them that a good roll—"

"Shush. What if somebody hears you?"

"If it's the somebody I have in mind, maybe it'd do 'em good to hear."

Della tossed him an onion. "Will you chop this?"

"Why, we making another pecan pie?"

Chapter
10

The massive furniture of the handsome ranch house gleamed with lemon oil and beeswax. New wicks in freshly cleaned lamps illuminated the spotless front room, and the windows were thrown open to allow the early-summer air to circulate through the house. The oak-planked floor shone with new polish that Mary had painstakingly applied. Under Della's direction, the entire house had been spit-shined.

Strains of violin and harmonica music filtered through the hum of voices, and sporadic bursts of laughter punctuated the air as pungently as the apple cider that brewed in the kitchen.

Jem glanced about the room, nervously checking her guests. They seemed to be having a good time.

"Relax!" Abigail's words just behind her had the opposite effect. Jem jumped, and Abigail steadied the tray in her hands. "Everyone's having a wonderful time, and you should be, too. Pretty soon all this will be painless."

"That's what Doc Riley said when he set my broken arm when I was ten."

"And it healed, too, didn't it?"

"Guess so."

"Trust me, this will, too."

"Thanks, Abigail—for everything."

Abigail had arrived two hours early to help arrange and see to last-minute details. Her practiced touch lent grace to the table, and Jem was beginning to realize how much she'd lost out on by snubbing the friendship of other women all these years.

"I enjoyed it," Abigail replied. "Now, I think I'll find my husband."

As she moved away, Reese walked up, holding a platter. "You're running out of cookies."

"Didn't know you liked sweets."

"Somebody does," he replied as Jem glanced down at the platter she'd recently refilled. It was almost empty.

"I'll get some more. Della was just baking another batch." But as she turned, Reese took the platter from her hands.

"You'd best entertain your guests."

Jem slanted a glance upward. "You don't want to stay in there, either."

Reese cocked his head and thought a moment. "Nope."

"You're honest about it."

"Why not? A bunch of prisses with nothing better to do than sit around, drink cider, and play stupid games."

Considering she completely shared his opinion, Jem let this pass. "I'll help you," she added, retrieving another empty platter that had contained moist slices of lemon cake and now only held crumbs.

They headed together toward the kitchen, and Reese quietly swung open the big door that led to the inner room. As abruptly as they'd entered, both halted. Pete sat in one of the wide kitchen chairs holding Della in his lap, kissing her thoroughly.

Backing out hastily, Reese and Jem gazed at one another in the hall for an endless moment. Their own tension of the past week reared its head. They both started to speak at once, laughing awkwardly, and then let the laughter die.

"Jem, Reese! Where you hiding?" Several voices reached their ears. "Newlyweds ducking out, I bet!"

Suddenly crimson, Jem smoothed an imaginary wrinkle in her skirt.

"This is what you want, isn't it? For everyone to believe

we're so taken with one another we got lost on the way from the kitchen?" Reese's voice was low and close to her ears. His breath sent shivers up her spine that had nothing to do with embarrassment.

She hesitated, unwilling to reveal how his nearness affected her. "Of course it is."

"Nothing you can't handle."

Jem's eyes flickered in indecision.

"Come on, your guests are waiting."

Jem stepped forward, her foot catching on the hem of the skirt she was unaccustomed to wearing. Feeling ungainly and at least seven feet tall, she held back, wishing she'd never agreed to this damned social.

"Come on, no more kissing in the hall, or our guests will think we've deserted them." Reese's voice was loud enough to be heard in the next room. As he spoke one of his eyes dropped in a deliberate wink.

Drawn into the group, Jem accepted their teasing with relatively good grace. Catching Abigail's eye, the other woman nodded her approval, and Jem breathed a little easier.

Even so, when the hue and cry for games arose, Jem felt her stomach churn. Clasping her damp palms together, she noticed one other person in the room acting equally uncomfortable. Reese, resembling a prisoner on the gallows, looked ready to escape.

If she had to suffer, so did he. Unobtrusively she rose and blocked his path.

"I was just going to—"

"Abigail was kind enough to suggest that when we were ready for games, she'd tell you which ones would be good to lead off with."

"I don't suppose she had any games you could be in charge of?"

Jem shook her head in mock regret. "Afraid not."

The gleam in Reese's eye told her he'd get even at the first possible chance. Jem stood to the side, checking the refreshment tables as the others launched into the first game. Unobserved, she watched Reese, noticing the way his eyes crinkled as he laughed at Mabel's antics, and the ease with which he bantered with the ladies. Her hands stilled; she was aware of how his tall frame dominated the room, making the other men seem to diminish in comparison. Although she tried to keep her attention away from him, her gaze slid repeatedly in his direction.

At the conclusion of the game Reese produced a fluffy feather, and laughter broke out. What now? When Reese strode purposefully in her direction, Jem had little doubt she was going to be a participant. Nervously she ran her hands down the length of her skirt, trying to appear composed. Damn, she wished she'd never agreed to this social.

After the chairs had been drawn into a close circle, Reese threw the feather in the air and then blew on it to keep it upright. It floated in Michael's path, and he blew on it also. It seemed the most ridiculous game yet, but those in the circle were dissolving in helpless laughter as the fool feather floated over their heads.

When the feather landed on Abigail, Mabel shrieked forfeit in a voice loud enough to be heard in town. Remembering the result of her last forfeit, Jem dug in, determined to keep the feather off her person.

Seated next to Reese, Jem watched as he blew the feather her way. Straining upward, she nearly met him eye to eye as they pursued the airbound bit of fluff. It occurred to her suddenly that her body was a hand span from his, that her breasts were within inches of his chest. All the effort she had put into keeping the feather aloft she now rechanneled into keeping her equilibrium.

Trying to ease away, she didn't calculate Reese's complete absorption in the game. Just as she turned aside to escape their closeness, Reese spun to chase the feather. The breath of air he had intended to direct toward the feather grazed her ear and traveled down her neck. The warmth he caused shot through her body.

Knowing she should get up and move away, Jem remained paralyzed, her eyes fastened on the face so close to hers. Her chest rose with the increased effort of breathing, and she saw that the pulse at the base of Reese's throat matched her own ragged beat. The cause of every petty argument the last week was suddenly clear, irreversibly visible.

Reese lost track of the game and the people surrounding them. A strong memory of Jem's body crushed close to his at the last social overtook any other thought. And now she was only inches from his touch. A flashing memory of her long legs as she rode her wild stallion emerged. His hand reached out just as he heard an ear-piercing shriek.

"Forfeit! Forfeit!" Mabel Deems chortled as the others laughed. Jem and Reese looked upward. The elusive feather rested where their heads joined together. Drawing shakily apart, each tried to appear composed, unaffected. Reese noticed that Jem even managed a smile for Mabel's benefit. But the rapid rise and fall of her breathing spoke otherwise.

As the game progressed most of the players received a forfeit before collapsing into laughter at the ridiculous positions they had landed in.

"Jem, what kind of forfeits do you have planned?" Lorraine asked as the game ended.

"I thought that came at the end of the evening," Jem replied, stalling. Was she supposed to have thought up forfeits?

"Not with this many," Mabel intervened.

"Don't tell me you didn't think up any new forfeits?" Lorraine's voice was rich with disappointment.

Abigail said, "Jem thought you were all so clever she wouldn't need any forfeits."

Appreciative laughter sounded around the room, and Jem looked up gratefully. Abigail cauterized every wound, splinted every fractured rule of etiquette.

Michael Fairchild's eyes were trained on his wife. "We could ask for a favor or a kiss."

Abigail blushed as she smiled, and the others responded with glee. As the forfeits were paid, Jem squirmed nervously in her chair. Reese leaned close so that only she could hear his words. "Will it be a kiss, or do you agree to let Boyd be the assistant foreman?"

"Isn't that a waste of your forfeit?" she hissed, realizing she'd just lost another battle. Damn him, before long he'd have everything at the Bar-W under his control.

Michael Fairchild claimed his forfeit, and Abigail finally had to break his embrace with a playful swat on the arm. Jem's eyes collided with Reese's, and they held the gaze, each remembering their own embrace. Jem turned away first, unwilling to accept what she saw.

Too soon it was Reese's turn to extract his forfeit. She gazed at him, fully expecting his favor. "I'll have a kiss for my forfeit," he announced. Jem's jaw sagged slightly. Before she could think further, Reese's lips covered her own. They felt as she remembered, only better. Just when she felt as though she'd slide off the chair into a boneless puddle, Reese drew away. The taunts of the others finally reached her.

"No more kissing forfeits with newlyweds!"

"We'll be gone in a few hours, son!"

Crimson with embarrassment, Jem wished for a large hole in which to swallow her when Mabel leaned closer. "He's certainly taken with you, dear. I'm just green with envy—such a love match."

Awash in unfamiliar emotions, Jem could only smile uncertainly. Her lips still tingled with the imprint of Reese's, but her mind reeled with the possibilities. Why hadn't he asked for the favor that was so important to him? Why had he chosen instead to kiss her?

Shaken and uncertain, Jem rose and excused herself from the next game, pleading the need to refill the cider bowl and refreshment table. She needed some time to consider Reese's motives and her own reactions to his kiss.

Knowing her heart belonged to another, Jem couldn't understand her response to Reese. Love was something sacred, to be treasured, not a mating of two bodies like animals. There was no explanation for her behavior. She was dismayed to realize she still tingled just at the thought of his nearness. It made no sense. Charles Sawyer was the man of her dreams—sensitive, caring, thoughtful. Yet she'd never felt this way with him.

Suddenly it hit her. Charles had been a true gentleman, never pressing himself against her, restraining his passion. Of course, that explained it. If they'd had the chance to be alone together, lie in the same bed, the same fire would have been ignited. She was sure of it. Still, she paused as she reentered the parlor. Standing back, she observed Reese, trying to understand how he could affect her so.

The next game was beginning. Through all the posturing of the players, Jem found her gaze stealing toward Reese, examining his handsome face, the way his full mustache settled over even white teeth that flashed when he smiled. What with his natural leadership, which caused him to butt heads with her over every detail, he was winning the friendship of her fellow ranchers.

Jem could also see the other women preen for him. While she'd acknowledged his handsomeness, she hadn't counted on its effect on the rest of the female population.

Seemingly oblivious, Reese paid equal attention to the men and women in the room. Jem found it impossible to grasp, having been all too aware of her own inadequate appearance her entire life. That made Reese's reaction to her even harder to understand. Perhaps he considered her a challenge, to make the skinny ranch owner swoon in his arms with a look, a touch.

Laughter broke out, and Jem jerked her attention back to her guests. A new game had begun. Mabel and Lorraine rapidly lined up several chairs and pushed a few of the hesitating men into them, among them a reluctant Reese. As the game unraveled, Jem watched in disbelief as the women took turns kissing the men they wanted. When it appeared that Reese was the star attraction, some of the confusion in her was replaced by the growing seeds of undeniable envy.

Although she laughed and reacted graciously to the

game, Jem found herself wanting to demand that it end. Her eyes fastened on the compelling features of Reese's face, his strong, lean body. When Beatrice laid a playful hand on his dark curls, Jem moved forward without thinking. She opened her mouth to protest when Reese stood up abruptly. The game was over, but the tightening in her chest told her the reactions it had caused were far from gone.

"Statues next," Reese announced in a tight voice, sounding uncomfortable. "But that'll be the last one of the evening."

There were a few groans of disappointment, but mostly sounds of agreement. It was a long ride home to their ranches. Jem joined in the seemingly harmless game as the music began. She watched the others dance with great and somewhat silly abandon across the room.

"Want to be my partner?"

Jem gazed into Reese's face, wondering why he hadn't chosen one of the pretty ladies to hold in his arms. Nodding in agreement, she held out her hand. Reese led them across the room, his tall frame making hers seem less so by comparison. Unable to understand the feelings gripping her, Jem met his eyes and read the challenge there. It flared as strong as it had been before.

When the music stopped abruptly, Reese had to grab her to keep them both upright. Suddenly they were face-to-face, chest to chest. Holding their immobile positions, Jem noticed the nearness of his jawline, the faint lines that traced a path away from the dark lashes shadowing his eyes. Eyes that questioned, demanded.

The music started again as abruptly as it had stopped before. Long moments passed as they alone continued to stand still, before easing over the dance floor in unison.

Reese led them mindlessly, knowing each step was bringing them closer to the destination that had kept them apart all week. When the last note of music died, the warmth of their hands clasped together was searing.

Michael Fairchild cleared his throat directly behind

them. "Abigail and I will be going now. It was a fine evening."

Turning to acknowledge them, Jem realized with a start that the room was clearing rapidly as couples retrieved coats and cloaks and were preparing to leave.

The door shut behind the last guest, Jem and Reese were left in the deserted parlor. Party evidence lingered like forgotten friends. Limp decorations, dirty dishes, and half-eaten refreshments cast a pall over the room. She reached for the cider bowl at the same time Reese did. Their hands collided, and Jem stared at Reese's hand as it touched hers. Startled, she drew away.

"I think I'll wait till morning to clean up," Jem muttered.

"I'm going to have a smoke." Reese turned abruptly and headed out the door.

Not certain why, she felt slightly deflated as he left. She dragged her feet as she walked up the stairs and into her bedroom. Taking the hairpins from her coronet, she shook her hair free, relieved as always to escape the confining feeling. She kicked off the silly slippers that accompanied the silk dress, pulled off her stockings, and then reached around to unfasten the row of buttons down the length of her back.

Twisting awkwardly, she realized they were impossible to reach. Della had helped her dress, and she hadn't thought about unfastening them. It was so late, she was certain Della was in bed by now, and she didn't want to disturb her for something so inconsequential.

Still trying to stretch toward the buttons, she paused as the door to their room opened. She hadn't moved to the alcove as she normally would, expecting Reese to remain outside with his cigarette. Their gazes met as he entered and then stopped abruptly.

"I can't seem to reach my buttons," she explained.

His long legs covered the distance between them, and her mouth grew dry at the desire in his face. When his hands touched her shoulders, she wasn't certain what to expect. He turned her around, and she felt a whooshing in her stomach. Relief? Disappointment?

Feeling his fingers moving down her back, Jem tried to push aside the craving his touch caused. When his fingers reached the last button, she felt them pause and linger. The dress drooped forward a bit, pulling away from her shoulders. When Reese turned her around again, she felt exposed, vulnerable. Every uncertainty in her past emerged, and she glanced up at him, expecting to see derision, dismissal. Instead the challenge that had simmered between them was visible, demanding.

She straightened up proudly, allowing the dress to fall even farther. When Reese's hand reached forward, she didn't shy away as he grasped the back of her head and pulled her forward. The taste of his lips was a shock despite the intent on his face. His tongue explored, and she stiffened at first, then accepted the invading warmth. Her lips firmed under his, tasting, discovering.

The unfamiliar sensations overwhelmed her, and she felt her strength diminish and seep away. When Reese's hands pushed her dress away, she couldn't even protest. Stepping out of the silken puddle, she backed away until she reached the bed. As though paralyzed, she watched Reese shed his own clothes and then advance. The sight of his powerful, unclothed body filled her chest with an emotion she despaired of understanding.

When he reached her side, she wasn't sure what to expect, but the incredible gentleness of his kiss overwhelmed her. The press of the mattress against her back was proof that she'd moved, but no memory of the motion lingered. Instead she was consumed by the feel of Reese's hand as he pressed it against her breast. The warmth traveled through her body, unleashing unknown feelings. Tentatively she reached out a hand and touched his chest, surprised that it quivered under the heat of her fingers.

Emboldened, she ran her hands over his shoulders, touching the hard muscles that had intrigued her for so many nights. He responded by gently untying her camisole. When her breasts spilled free, she heard him suck in his breath.

Gratified, she pressed close to him and felt his shuddering response. When he pulled away, she felt a sharp pang of disappointment until he brought his head down and pressed his lips against her breast, taking her nipple in his mouth. Arching upward, Jem felt the last of her reason slip away.

Unable to resist any longer, Reese tugged impatiently at the pantalets concealing her long limbs. The vision of how they would look had driven him mad for days, but when he pulled the material free, he knew it had been worth the wait. Her limbs, sleek and long, were more enticing than anything he could have imagined. He palmed her calf, feeling the strength, appreciating the curves that led upward, over her strong thighs.

The tangle of golden curls that met the juncture of her thighs intrigued him. Sensing her panic, he sought her lips again.

This time when his hands reached for her, she opened up to him, and he knew she was ready. No words had been spoken, no promises given, yet he had to ask, for he was sure this was her first time.

"Jem?"

"Yes," she murmured.

"Are you sure?"

"Yes, Charles, I'm sure."

Reese froze. Every cell of his body fused. Disentangling his hands, he used them to prop himself over her.

His voice was little more than a feral growl. "What?"

Jem shook her head, disoriented, not certain why he was angry. "I said I was sure."

"No, you didn't, *Mrs. McIntire*. You said you were ready for Charles."

"No, I—"

"Save it. But next time you pay a cowboy to marry you, you better tell him who you've been bedding."

Reese rose from the bed, snatched up his denims, and yanked them on.

"Reese—"

"At least you got the name right that time." He stalked out the door, slamming it hard enough to shake the surrounding walls. The door swung pathetically in the dim light of the hall.

Jem sat up in the bed, clutching the sheet to cover herself. Swallowing the suddenly huge lump in her throat, she realized the nakedness that couldn't be concealed was in her soul.

Chapter
11

Reese rode the land with an intensity not lost on his companions. The cloudless azure sky was awash with sunshine, heating the land and everything on it. Even the aspen withered under the midday sun, drooping along the blue-green line of juniper trees. Dust swirled in the windless sky, promising no relief to the dusty, heat-soaked cowboys.

Sensing Reese's prickly mood, Pete and Boyd had kept their silence while they'd ridden the fences and checkpointed the herd. Attempts at conversation had been met with short, barked answers that didn't invite more of the same. While neither Pete nor Boyd knew the reason for Reese's foul mood, both were itching to get away from him.

Spotting the chuck wagon ahead, they glanced at one another in agreement. Spurring their horses on, they reached the camp quickly and dismounted, leaving Reese to his own devices. Not unaware of his bad temper, Reese chose a solitary spot, took a cup of bracing coffee, and swallowed the bitter liquid gratefully. It was the first thing to hit his belly all day. After nursing bourbon through the night, Reese had refused breakfast and tried to ride off some of the anger boiling inside him. It hadn't worked.

So he was sharing Charles Sawyer's leftovers. Distaste left an ugly curling sensation in his gut. While the marriage hadn't been in his plans or desires, he'd at least respected Jem. Now even that was gone. The disappointment he felt was too familiar. It seemed he'd never learn.

Taking another swallow of coffee, Reese dumped the rest on the ground. The acid was threatening to eat a hole right through him. Certain he'd given Pete and Boyd time enough to eat, he went in search of them. He could hear their voices before he could see them.

". . . pale eyes that could look right through you. Always gave me the creeps," Boyd said.

"You're right—hadn't thought about that in a spell. Peculiar color or something. Didn't seem natural," Pete agreed.

Reese felt as though a fist had been smashed through his already overwrought insides. "Who you talking about?"

Pete and Boyd looked up in surprise at Reese's presence. Pete hesitated, but Boyd spoke up. "Charles Sawyer, the old foreman."

"I thought so." It came back to him in a rush. Charles Sawyer was someone he'd had good reason to forget. The many years since Reese had last seen him had almost accomplished that. But the man whose eyes seemed to hold no color or emotion wasn't someone who could stay forgotten. Their brief association dated back to the first days of the war and wasn't one he remembered with a shred of fondness. The buried memories surfaced with all too much clarity. The man was a snake and a turncoat. And he'd bedded Jem.

"You knew him?" Pete asked.

"You could say that," Reese hedged, knowing Pete's loyalty to Jem.

"You two friends?" Pete persisted.

"Nope."

"Good."

Reese regarded Pete with surprise. So he and Jem didn't agree on everything. That was good to know. He'd made Pete foreman and didn't need for the man to be Jem's ear.

"How long's he been gone?" Reese questioned, wondering if he sounded casual, deciding he didn't care.

"Since Jem's father was killed," Pete replied.

"So he didn't stick around?"

It was Peter's turn to be taciturn. "Nope."

Enough said. So the man hadn't changed his stripes since the war. That was no surprise. But, hell, he'd have thought better of Jem. Sawyer was a smooth talker, but holy ... Reese glanced up and saw that both Pete and Boyd were staring at him.

"Time to hit the trail. You two had your fill?" Reese asked.

"Yep. How 'bout you?" Boyd questioned.

"I've had more than my fill."

The land sloped away from the rising foothills, demanding attention as the jagged mountains thrust forward. Reese ignored his rumbling stomach as he pressed on, seeking the far reaches of the ranch's borders. Unable to accept the day's revelations, he concentrated instead on the landscape that refused to be ignored.

The clip-clop of hooves was the only sound that carried over the plateau. A light breeze eased through the heat-filled day, bringing some relief. Pete and Boyd had fallen into an uneasy silence, no doubt wishing Reese would either spit out what was bothering him or let them escape his ire. Instead the trio traveled forward, disturbing nothing more than the loose rocks and wild grass beneath them.

"Who's that?" Reese's voice startled his companions, and they all strained to see what he was pointing at.

"One of Cushman's hands," Pete answered.

"Cushman?"

"Owns the ranch over the next border."

"He's the one Miz McIntire don't like," Boyd commented.

"Oh?" Reese wondered what else Boyd knew about his wife that he didn't. Bitterly he realized there was a lot he had to learn.

"Came by the other day. She was madder'n a hornet."

Reese stared at the strange hand who was rounding up several strays. "Those Cushman's cattle, Pete?"

"I reckon so. Never knew him to rustle any cattle."

Reese watched a few moments longer. "You know why Jem doesn't cotton to him, Pete?" Hearing Pete's sigh, he narrowed his gaze.

"Hell, she thinks he was the one who killed her old man."

Surprise flickered in Reese's eyes. "I thought a rustler killed him."

"That's what the law said. But Jem's sure it was Cushman. There was bad blood between 'em for years."

Reese digested this, gripping the reins a bit tighter. "What do you think?"

"I dunno."

Reese repeated Pete's own words to Della only days before. "But somebody killed him."

"Yep."

"What kind of bad blood?"

"Cushman's head of the cattle association. Thinks the ranchers who got here first have claim to all the land. Doesn't think any newcomers do."

Reese stared at Pete for a moment. "That mean he was willing to do anything to keep the newcomers away?"

Pete nodded. "Guess you could say that was so. Old man Whitaker said it was all a bunch of piss."

"What about the law? Was Cushman right about the land belonging to who got here first?" Reese questioned, absently patting Danny's neck.

"Whitaker said it was claptrap, that the land was public property."

"Who owns the biggest spreads?"

"Cushman and Whitaker." Pete spat out the juice of his chew after he spoke.

"Probably made Cushman madder than hell when Whitaker took the other side," Reese observed, suddenly seeing the picture Jem had excluded him from.

"They fought till the day the old man died."

"Sounded like he wanted to carry on the fight with Miz McIntire," Boyd added.

Reese didn't comment, but instead turned the paint back toward the ranch house, remembering his thoughts earlier in the day. Having reminded himself of why he'd taken on this venture, he knew that one thing had been clarified. If his goal was to be accomplished, so was Jem's.

In the early morning hours he'd contemplated firing all the hands and then walking out, leaving Jem to find another way to fill her army contract. But the stark truth was that he wanted what she had to offer. He intended to start his own freighting business, but wagons and drivers cost money, Jem's money. That would be his opportunity to be his own man, never to take orders again. If it meant furthering her cause by helping the ranch, then by God he would.

If the cattle association was vital to the Bar-W's existence, then Reese intended to get involved. Jem wasn't to be trusted, and he certainly didn't intend to lay both their futures in her hands.

Chapter 12

Jem wound her way down the path to the Fairchild home, glancing up at the sky, which provided an endless canopy for the craggy, cloud-high peaks. Far-flung grasslands stretched into the timbered hills and juniper-bordered fields decorated the dirt-packed road, but she didn't notice their beauty. Her mind was too occupied for her to do more than amble down the trail.

Her eyes burned, and she couldn't be sure if it was from the dust rising from the trail or the sting of tears she'd fought all night. After the interminable night had ended, Jem had risen and gone to speak to Della. Her hand had been on the kitchen door to push it open, but she had stopped short at the sound of Della's voice. Both she and Pete were concerned about Reese, his haggard appearance and unusually bad temper. Realizing that they had grown fond of Reese, Jem knew she couldn't confide her awful secret to Della. Despite knowing their allegiance was hers, Jem wanted a neutral sounding board.

So she'd found herself heading toward the Fairchild ranch, hoping to find Abigail home. Approaching the immaculate structure, Jem scanned the yard, seeing only the neat rows of flowers that flourished beneath the spreading limbs of an ancient oak.

Tying her horse to the hitching rail, she approached the front door. She paused, then lifted the knocker, hearing the sound reverberate throughout the house. A moment passed, and then Abigail opened the door in a rush. Her initial look of surprise was replaced by a delighted smile.

"Jem, come on in. You're just the breath of fresh air I needed. Tell me I shouldn't be inside planning to bake cinnamon rolls on this gorgeous day."

"All right," Jem obliged.

"Good. I do have some lemonade made. Sit down on the swing, and I'll bring it out."

Jem had barely settled in the swing when Abigail bustled out with a pitcher and glasses on a tray. "I needed an excuse to get out. I've been wanting to play hooky all day," Abigail confided.

When Abigail kicked off her perky slippers and tucked her legs beside her on the swing, Jem was surprised. Never having gone visiting or spent endless hours over gossip, Jem didn't realize the normality of Abigail's action.

Taking a long drink of the cool lemonade, Abigail leaned back in the swing. "What brings you out today?"

Jem fiddled with her hands, then started to speak, but nothing came out. Abigail sensed Jem's nervousness and abandoned her relaxed position. "Something wrong?"

Jem picked at a spot on her finger and tried to decide how to answer. When she managed to tear the cuticle from one finger, Abigail spoke up. "Whatever it is, ripping your fingernails to shreds won't help."

"Abigail, has everything always been like it is now between you and Michael?"

"Do you mean being happy?" Jem nodded, and Abigail looked thoughtful for a moment. "Michael and I have had a good marriage from the start. To be honest, I don't know what I'd ever do without him." Her voice turned quiet. "I love him more than I ever thought was possible. Why do you ask?"

Jem got up and paced the length of the porch. "Was it ever, well, awkward?"

She laughed. "Of course. Every marriage has its awkward moments. But you get through them. Just being a newlywed can be quite unsettling."

"It's not so much that."

Abigail smiled, a light of understanding dawning. "The happiest couples disagree, argue. It's all part of it."

"This isn't exactly a disagreement," Jem hedged.

"Do you want to tell me what it is?"

Jem wasn't certain she wanted to share this embarrassing and painful episode with anyone, but she was at a loss as to how to deal with Reese now. In as few words as she could manage, she imparted the evening's disastrous ending. Abigail didn't answer immediately, but sat thoughtfully, absorbing Jem's words.

"What do you want to do now?" Abigail finally asked.

"I guess that's why I'm here. I don't know."

"Do you care about Reese's feelings?"

Jem paused, realizing that her caring was why she was here. It was her own fault that things had gotten so far out of hand. She had decided when she married Reese that she would bear with her marital duties, but she hadn't counted on being such an active participant in the lovemaking. It wasn't Reese's fault she'd reacted so shamelessly. She still didn't know why she'd allowed things to get so out of hand, and her voice was hesitant as she answered, "I didn't intend to hurt his feelings or make him feel, well, unmanly."

Abigail swallowed her dismay. Jem's lack of knowledge about men was no less than mammoth. It would help to get to the gist of the problem. "Do you still love Charles Sawyer?"

"Of course." The words rushed out of Jem. There was no question, no debate. Her heart belonged irretrievably to Charles. It always would.

Abigail sighed. "Then you do have a problem. If the slip had been made, and you didn't really mean it . . ." She paused, wondering how to phrase her next words delicately. "From what I've seen of Reese, I can't see him accepting the situation."

"You're probably right." Jem stared into the horizon, uncharacteristically quiet.

"Jem, why ever did you marry Reese if you still loved Charles?"

Having come this far, Jem saw no reason to hide the rest. When she finished telling Abigail the true reason for their marriage, the other woman sounded appalled. "Oh, Jem."

"I know. It's a terrible thing to have done."

"You've made a great sacrifice, but to give up love for a ranch. I just don't know." Abigail shook her head in dismay.

"And now I don't know what to do about Reese." Jem rose and paced the length of the porch, remembering his anger, her own shame.

"Understandably. He doesn't seem like the sort of man to accept this."

"Judging from the way he acted, I'd say not." Jem stopped pacing, picturing Reese's face when she'd realized she'd called him by Charles's name.

Abigail chose her next words carefully. "It would seem that Reese is a reasonably virile man. . . ." She would have continued, but the look on Jem's face stopped her. "Jem?"

But she couldn't answer. A tantalizing image of Reese's sleek, muscled body rose in her mind. She felt a lump in her throat—there was no doubt he was virile. While her heart didn't belong to him, the response she'd given him was proof that her body could easily have been his, increasing her guilt.

"Jem?" Abigail asked again, worry in her eyes.

"Is it possible to feel . . ." Jem floundered, remembering the heat of Reese's touch on her flesh, the overwhelming desire she had to continue the journey they'd started.

Abigail had seen them at both socials, and it was obvious what Jem could not put into words. Reese had certainly been attracted to his wife. Knowing how reticent Jem was, Abigail was touched at her confidence. Still she was at a loss as to what to advise since her own experience with Michael was so different. She'd loved him almost from the first moment she'd set eyes on him. While she craved his touch, she also yearned for the man he was, strong, caring. What could she tell Jem about this kind of love?

As she studied Jem's troubled face Abigail wondered how she could express her belief that Reese was not the sort of man to accept his wife's continued love for another man. Jem was stubborn, always convinced she was right. How could she tell her that this was one time she would have to bend to another's will?

"Jem, what did Reese say?"

"Nothing really." His hateful words surfaced for a moment, and she deliberately shook them away. "He just got up and stormed out."

"And this morning?"

"He was gone when I got up."

"So you haven't talked to him at all?" Abigail wasn't able to completely disguise the dismay in her voice.

Jem remembered the nearly empty flask of bourbon she'd found on the kitchen sideboard. "I think he drank quite a bit last night."

Abigail recalled the few occasions she'd observed Reese drinking. At the wedding and socials he'd imbibed freely enough, but hadn't seemed like the type to get mean. But then he hadn't had this reason at any of those occasions. She chose her next words even more carefully. "Jem, I think you'd better be careful."

"Me? I can take care of myself. I can outshoot—"

"What I'm thinking about doesn't concern guns."

"But . . ." Jem paused. "You don't think Reese . . ." She couldn't complete the thought. Remembering the intent on his face last night, she looked at Abigail in consternation. "You think Reese could really be that angry?"

It was obviously time to be blunt. "You cut him off at the knees, Jem."

"Oh, I see." Jem's voice was quieter than Abigail had ever heard, and she sensed that Jem was beginning to realize the implications of her actions. Always headstrong and stubborn, she wasn't used to faltering or dealing with the consequences of her mistakes. Perhaps today was a beginning.

But even as Abigail anticipated her remorse Jem surprised her once again. "I should have kept the relationship strictly business. When Reese knew I was boss, he wouldn't have dared lay a finger on me."

"But didn't you—"

"Turn to undercooked jelly? Yes, but it won't happen again. I've got a ranch to get back on its feet."

"Do you really think it will be that easy?"

"If he wants his money."

Abigail shook her head in dismay. Everything was so black and white for Jem, no confusing shades of gray. Still it was evident she couldn't say anything to change Jem's mind.

"Please be cautious, Jem."

"I just told you I could take care of myself."

"That's not what I mean. The hurt I'm thinking of isn't physical."

Abigail refilled their glasses. Jem accepted the drink, a thoughtful expression crossing her face as she lifted the glass to her lips. "I'll just let him get it over with and make sure I don't call him by Charles's name."

The lemonade flew out of Abigail's mouth in a splutter. She coughed and choked on the liquid. Jem slapped her heartily on the back and nearly knocked her off the swing. When Abigail could speak, her voice was laced with exasperation. "Jem, I hardly think that's the attitude to take."

"Don't worry—no more silly, sappy stuff for me." Jem drew herself up to her full height, remembering the challenge in Reese's eyes. This time he wouldn't win. "I'll just keep in mind what happened before and make sure it doesn't happen again."

"I don't want to offend you, but sometimes you have a way of taking something by the horns and not letting go.

It can be quite upsetting for a man, especially in a delicate situation."

"I can't back down. I need Reese's name attached to the Bar-W. If it means bedding him, I will. He'll forget about my slip about Charles."

"I don't mean to play the devil's advocate, but just how do you intend to manage that?"

Jem drew herself up. "Why, I'm a Whitaker, of course."

"Don't you mean a McIntire?"

Some of the air seemed to leave Jem's puffed-up posture. "Once we're back to the right relationship, it won't matter." She ignored the niggling reminder that they'd crossed a line that could not be recrossed.

"You're going to be the boss who just happens to sleep with the man running your ranch?"

Jem cocked her head, surprised at the tone she'd never heard sweet Abigail use. "You think I'm wrong?"

"I believe you've never admitted to being wrong, so you wouldn't know how it feels."

Jem narrowed her eyes, considering Abigail's words. Nonsense, just because her vision was clear and certain didn't mean she couldn't acknowledge a mistake. "I've never heard you talk like this, Abigail."

"That's because we haven't talked much before. I do know a little more about life than quilting and planning socials."

Jem considered this, knowing Abigail was probably right. But she had a ranch and a number of people counting on her. She couldn't abandon her purpose or doubt her own decisions. Too much was at stake, and she had only herself to depend on. "I appreciate your advice and for listening to me."

"I may not agree with your methods, but for your sake I hope they work."

Jem stared at the swiftly gathering cumulus clouds that clung to the snowy peaks of the mountains. Rising to her feet, she replaced her glass. Abigail walked with her to the end of the porch. Jem hesitated at the last step and turned. "I'd be grateful if you didn't tell anybody about this."

Abigail looked shocked. "Of course. I never repeat a confidence."

"I didn't think you'd say anything about last night. But I mean the other—about why I married Reese. If people find out, I'm finished."

"You needn't worry. I won't say anything."

Satisfied, Jem turned away. Her words were thrown back over her shoulder as she mounted her barely tamed stallion. "Thanks, Abby."

A slow smile formed on Abigail's face. Jem hadn't called her Abby since they were kids. The smile on her face broadened as she saw Michael's horse approaching. Sweeping down the porch, she waved at her husband. Right now an affirmation of love seemed most appropriate.

Jem could scarcely believe her ears. Of all the subjects she'd expected to be discussing with Reese, the last would have been Randolph Cushman. She'd prepared herself to confront him about last night, but he hadn't given her time to begin, instead talking about her father's worst enemy. Reese's next words caught her like a steel barb in the heart.

"I think we should be at that next meeting."

"What?" Jem jumped to her feet. "Are you crazy?" Not allowing him to answer, she continued as she paced the length of the study. "What makes you think I'd even consider such a thing?"

"Because we need to know what's going on in the association."

"My father refused to go along with Cushman, and I plan to do the same thing."

"At the expense of the Bar-W?"

"What does that have to do with it?"

Reese started to uncork the bourbon and then replaced the stopper. The distant ache in his head along with the burning in his stomach warned him to refrain from another alcohol-soaked night. Instead he sank into a soft leather chair.

"Everything," he answered succinctly.

She threw her hands in the air in disgust.

"Do you want this ranch to succeed?" he demanded.

Jem stared at him down the length of her nose. "Of course."

"The Bar-W and Cushman's spread are the biggest ranches in these parts, right?"

Thrown off track, she answered warily, "So?"

"Stands to reason if we're going to make a go of this, we need to be one step ahead, not behind."

"I'm not pandering to Cushman."

Reese rose from the depths of the chair to face her. "If you don't take a stand at the association, you won't need to."

"That man killed my father."

Jem expected the declaration to wipe the determined look off Reese's face. Instead not even a trace of emotion flickered across his features. "I intend to collect my money, and if this ranch doesn't succeed, I won't," he stated flatly.

Jem's face slackened in amazement at his callous statement. She was speechless as she watched him utter his final shot. "I'm going, with or without you."

The echo of his boots filled the air in the otherwise silent house. Jem swallowed an unexpected lump in her throat. No one knew how she missed her father. He had been everything to her since she was a child. While she hadn't expected Reese to hover over her with concern, she hadn't expected his total disregard.

"Jem?" Della's soft voice drifted through the open doorway.

Jem composed her face and turned. "Yes?"

"Are you all right?"

"Of course, why shouldn't I be?"

"Pete and I were going through the hall . . ."

"And you heard everything."

"I'm afraid so."

"Well, this time I've really gotten myself into a pickle." Jem walked to the windows and stared at the slate-blue mountains that rose in the dusk.

Della shook her head as she watched Jem's profile. For once she had to agree.

Reese stalked into the barn, shaking off the anger that had accompanied him. He found a lamp and struck a match, filling the closed space with the flare of sulfur. Seeking Danny's stall, he picked up a carrot from the bucket near the feed bin. Danny's whinny told him that the pony had caught his scent. Unlatching the stall gate, Reese led the paint out. Predictably Danny nosed around for the carrot Reese held.

Reese held out the carrot, and Danny munched it appreciatively. The calm of the barn felt soothing, but when the door opened abruptly, he sensed that calm would disappear.

Pete's face as he entered was determined.

"Pete," Reese acknowledged.

"Reese."

Formalities aside, the two men stared at one another. Pete broke the silence. "Don't you think you were a little hard on her?"

"Isn't anything around here private?"

"Nope."

Point taken, Reese rubbed the paint's flanks. "I got a stake in making sure this ranch stays going."

"We all do."

Reese raised his head in surprise. He hadn't really considered that aspect before. Pete, Della, the collection of old hands—they were all depending on the success of the Bar-W. "I wasn't any rougher on Jem than I had to be. She's stubborner than a mule headed for water."

Pete nodded his agreement. "I 'spect she is. But it seems maybe you are, too."

"Me?" Reese asked in surprise.

"You seem hell-bent on collecting your money. What're you plannin' to do with it?"

Reese considered telling Pete. It had been a long time since he'd settled in a place long enough to make friends he could confide in. Pete had proven himself to be honest and reliable. He'd never rubbed it in about the marriage, his own knowledge of Reese's role in the farce. "You'll probably think it's a damn fool idea."

Pete cocked his head. "I'd have to hear it first."

This was the tough part. He'd never told anyone but his horse, and fortunately Danny couldn't talk back and tell him what a fool he sounded like. His words were slow, almost halting. "I been thinking this over for a long time. Seems what the territory needs is a freighting company."

Pete was silent for several moments, and Reese wished he'd kept the information to himself. Then Pete spoke, obviously having turned over the idea. "But what about the railroads?"

Reese hunkered into the subject that had held him captive since the idea had sprouted. "Railroad's good for some of the territory, but it doesn't hit the remote areas."

Pete nodded as he listened. "That's true."

Warmed up, Reese launched into his theory. "Lot of ranchers have to send their own men and wagons to the nearest railroad—costs 'em good hands, time. They'd be willing to pay to have someone else do the hauling just to keep from having their own hands gone so much."

Pete scratched his chin and reflected. "I think you got something there. Never thought too much about getting supplies from the railhead, but it makes sense."

Reese rubbed the paint's nose as he spoke. "Thing is I got to have enough money to buy wagons and horses and to hire drivers."

"Probably take a good piece."

"That's why Jem's offer . . ." Reese paused, finding it difficult to explain to the other man why he'd sold his pride.

"Seems like you two needed each other about the same time."

So they had. Reese hadn't thought about it in that light before. He turned aside, then stared directly at Pete. "You still think I was too rough on Jem?"

Pete's gaze was steady. "I believe that's one you'll have to decide for yourself."

Saying no more, Pete left the dusky confines of the barn. Reese's eyes dropped to the floor, then he looked out the door to the wide, beckoning range. Pete had left him with even more to consider, and the twist in his gut told him it would be another long night.

Chapter 13

Boyd Harris spotted the chuck wagon and dug in his heels. It had been a hot, dry morning, and his stomach rumbled, reminding him of the hours since breakfast. Dismounting, he tied his horse to a sapling and headed toward the wagon. He stretched his long legs, glad to be out of the saddle. Accepting a steaming plate of beans and corn bread and a cup of muddy-looking coffee, he searched for a place to settle. A soft, grassy knoll looked inviting. Head bent, Boyd attacked his lunch. Concentrating on his food, he didn't hear the other man's approach.

"You eatin' with the common hands?"

Boyd glanced up as he heard Grady Orton's voice. It was no secret that Orton resented being overlooked for the assistant foreman job.

He wasn't the only one. Boyd knew that a lot of the hands had been reluctant to accept him as a leader. Nodding, he kept his attention on his plate.

"You can ignore me now, but when we're in town, McIntire won't be protecting you."

"You got something to say, spit it out. Otherwise get back to work and let me eat."

"That an order? Around this ranch that don't mean much, does it? Already got a woman and her pretty boy giving the rest of the orders."

Boyd laid his plate down and rose to his considerable

height. "I don't know who put a burr up your ass, Orton, but it ends here."

"What'd you promise McIntire to get the job?" Grady taunted.

"I could ask you the same thing. The boss didn't want to hire you. If it weren't for Miz McIntire—"

"Whitaker, you fool. She owns the ranch. McIntire will be gone before long, and we'll see who's giving orders then."

"If you don't get your lazy ass back to work, I'll kick it clear off the ranch."

Orton's face opened in a snarl, but before he could retort, Pete's voice bellowed between them. "I been lookin' all over for you, Boyd. We need to check the railing on the north end."

Grady digested Pete's words, and the expression on his face was transparent. It was apparent he thought Boyd had been ducking both his work and the foreman. Boyd ignored Grady and quickly disposed of his cookware before joining Pete.

"What's Reese got Orton doing?" Pete asked as they rode away.

"He didn't tell me."

Pete glanced at Boyd's closed face, wondering about him again. It had looked like he and Orton were about to come to blows when he'd ridden up. "Time to check in with Reese, anyhow." They rode quietly toward the north, stopping to check the railing, but saw no sign of Reese.

Reese had deviated from the path and had ridden up past the foothills and into the mountains. Sloping away from the immense granite crags, the valleys rolled into fields where the grass grew so high it brushed against a rider's stirrups. An occasional cluster of wildflowers dotted the landscape, breaking the illusion of unending green.

Reese pulled up at the crest and surveyed the land that fell away from the ridge. The towering mountains that loomed across the valley mocked the notion that he was at the top of the world, but from his vantage point he could see for miles. It was a view that took away a man's breath. It was hard to believe all this land belonged to the Bar-W and the woman he was married to.

Reese had deliberately shut Jem out of his mind for the last several weeks. Remembering both her actions and Pete's words, he'd known a confusion that was both unfamiliar and disturbing.

Sweet gusts of wind teased the air about him, bringing the scents of pine and wild grass. The land pulled at him in a way it never had before. The timbered hills and fallow fields drew him as no other place had. Intertwined with this unaccustomed feeling were his thoughts of Jem. It had occurred to him as he had tried to repair his shattered ego that perhaps Jem really loved Charles Sawyer. Knowing what he did about the man, this, too, filled him with disgust. He looked out again at the landscape that called to him. The answers he sought were still elusive, but the questions refused to go away.

Jem waited anxiously in the bed, twisting her fingers in agitation. She had watched Reese eat his dinner, but scarcely touched her own. Any appetite she'd had disappeared at the thought of the evening ahead. Much like an army general, she had plotted out her course. It seemed logical, but then logic had not been her strongest suit the last few weeks.

She hadn't yet found the courage to try the plan she'd discussed with Abigail, instead retreating each night to the study to sleep on the settee. But after weeks of wrestling with her conscience, she was convinced she had to try. Reese's callous attitude was proof she had to attempt a truce. Deliberately she turned her back on the desire he'd brought out in her. This was a business deal, pure and simple.

Reese's heavy footsteps sounded in the hall outside their room, and she froze. Trying to relax, she attempted to look casual as he entered. Not sparing her a glance, he walked to the chair and perched on its edge to pull off his boots. This accomplished, he shed his denims and shirt. Jem tried not to stare as he slid his muscled body beneath the quilt.

She opened her mouth to speak when Reese lifted the globe from the lamp and blew it out. Feeling a bit ridiculous sitting up straight in the darkness, she tried to slip unobtrusively beneath the down coverlet. This accomplished, she waited several long minutes, expecting him to make some sort of move, since this was the first night she'd occupied their bed since that disastrous night.

When that didn't happen, she tapped his back tentatively. He jerked and twisted around as though she'd jabbed him with a red-hot poker. "What?" he demanded.

"I . . ." Her voice sounded high-pitched and wavering. Clearing her throat, she tried again. "I thought about the night of our social, and I've decided I was wrong. It seems I led you on and gave you the wrong idea."

Reese stared at her as though she'd grown horns. "So?"

She took a deep breath. "I've decided that I will accept my marital duties and not involve myself like I did before. You may . . . do what you like. I will not protest."

The anger in Reese's eyes was frightening. "You're telling me you're going to lay there like a dead fish while I get my fill?"

Jem flinched. Both his voice and words were ugly, and suddenly she felt ugly, too.

"Thanks, but no thanks. When I'm that desperate, I'll ride into town and find one of the saloon gals. I'll get more honesty from them." He raked his eyes contemptuously down the length of her plain cotton gown. "God knows I'll enjoy it more." Automatically she drew up the quilt to cover her exposed gown. He laughed bitterly. "Don't worry. I don't plan to avail myself of your offer. It's not like you'd tempt a man." Turning over, he presented her with the flat length of his back.

Swallowing the huge lump in her throat, Jem clutched the coverlet, hearing his mocking words reverberate in the stillness of the room. Suddenly all the taunts of her youth returned in full force. She had never fit in, never been accepted. Only Charles Sawyer had seen beyond her plain, awkward, skinny frame. And he was gone.

Loneliness crowded her as it never had before. First her father's death and then Charles's departure. Glancing over at Reese's unwavering stance, she sensed an even greater rejection. Passing a hand over her unbound hair, Jem wondered what he saw when he looked at her. Every unflattering image she'd ever known rose to torment her. And it was scarce comfort to realize that the curl of desire in her stomach when he'd disrobed had begun the same trail of fire it had the night of the social.

Abigail twisted her gloves nervously as she reached for the knocker. She wasn't sure if Jem was even at home, but somehow she suspected she wouldn't be riding the same ranges as Reese.

When Della unlatched the door, Abigail smiled at the older woman. Della's answering smile was mixed with relief. "I'm glad you're here, Miz Fairchild. Jem's not been herself the last few weeks."

That was what she'd been afraid of. "I hope I can help."

"She won't talk to me," Della stated bluntly. "It's not like her."

Abigail sensed some of the hurt underlying Della's words. Obviously she felt left out. "I imagine Jem feels torn. I'm sure you've grown fond of Reese by now. Perhaps she'll find it easier to talk to me since I'm not family."

Della considered her words. Apparently mollified, she agreed. "Makes sense. Pete and I have taken a liking to Reese. But Jem knows she can count on us."

"Of course she does. Perhaps that's why it's so difficult to talk right now."

"Well, I'm glad you're here. She needs to talk to somebody." Della had ushered Abigail to the door of Jem's study. "She's holed up in there. Won't come out for nothing."

Abigail reached a tentative hand toward the door and rapped on the cedar panel. Della was already wheeling away as she heard Jem bid her to come in. Opening the door hesitantly, Abigail poked her head in first, surprised to see Jem staring out the window.

"Jem?"

At Abigail's voice, Jem turned. "Come in."

Entering, she sensed the quandary Jem was in. "If I've come at a bad time . . ."

"No." Jem's sigh was heavy. "I'm glad you're here."

Abigail saw no need to mince words. "Have you talked this out with Reese yet?"

"No." Jem turned away, remembering her ridiculous decision to let Reese have his way with her. The following nights he had merely presented his back without conversation. Realizing Abigail was waiting for some sort of explanation, Jem faltered. "I don't think there's anything to discuss."

"You're wrong there. This is worse than a festering sore."

Jem fiddled with the heavy paperweight on her desk. "My plan didn't exactly work."

"Oh, Jem."

"You were right, I don't know anything about men. I was always so awkward—never knew what to say or do." Staring out the window, Jem remembered her painful youth, the agony of not belonging. She'd covered it up well by being tough, emulating her father and turning her back on anything feminine. But the scars were there. Turning back to Abigail, she continued, "Until Charles, that is. He was the only one who ever treated me, well, special." She laughed bitterly. "He even made me feel pretty."

The compassion on Abigail's face stopped her flow of words. "Jem, you *are* pretty." She held up a hand to stem Jem's protests. "Maybe not in the same way other women are, but that's because you don't allow yourself to be. But in a marriage there are much more important things. Respect, caring, trust. That's what takes you through the worst times."

Trust. Jem remembered Reese's words. Somehow she doubted trust and respect were among the attributes he thought she possessed. His comment about her lack of honesty had stung as much as his others.

"Jem." Abigail's voice was urgent. "At all costs you must speak to Reese and resolve this. You can't let this continue."

"He said some very unkind things to me."

"That was his wounded ego speaking. First you called him by another man's name and then offered to submit yourself as though you could bear his touch only because of the bargain you'd made. He was striking back, trying to hurt you as much as you'd hurt him."

Jem's voice was halting. "I suppose that could be true."

"Of course it is. It's imperative that you settle this. Apologize for your actions, and the rest will work itself out. If you can't bring yourself to tell him about Charles, at least let him know that you're sorry for the botched attempt at fixing things."

Jem nodded her agreement, wondering how she could begin to broach the subject. Even as she thought of asking Abigail the other woman rose, preparing to leave. "Michael will be home soon, so I must go. But please promise me you'll speak to Reese."

Jem's words were dredged up painfully. "I'll try."

Knowing this was the best she could hope for, Abigail left, sensing Jem's presence as the other woman stared out the huge windows of her study. Suddenly she was impatient to be home, to be held by Michael. Glancing back at Jem's shadow in the window, she was inordinately glad not to be in her shoes.

Chapter
14

"If you really want to apologize, you'll go to the meeting tonight." Reese stared at her, his gaze even, unblinking.

The heavy weight in Jem's chest deepened. She'd mulled over Abigail's words, dredged up an apology, but now she was stymied. What he was asking violated all of her principles. "But—"

"I didn't think you were serious."

Raising troubled eyes to meet his, Jem countered, "Why the association? Anything else—"

"Wouldn't matter. Well?"

She swallowed. "I'll go."

Expecting a favorable reaction, she was surprised when Reese only replied, "We have to be there at seven."

The ride to town was interminable. Jem doubted they exchanged a half-dozen words. As much as she dreaded the meeting, she was loath to spend another moment in the wagon with Reese.

She waited until Reese helped her down, but this time he didn't offer his arm, instead walking at her side as they entered the church, which doubled as a meeting hall.

The ranchers scattered around the room stared at her in surprise when she was recognized. It was well-known that the Whitakers never attended association meetings. Feeling as though she were betraying her father in the face of his enemies, Jem scrunched down in the seat. Desolation clawed at her, making her feel alone in the crowded room. Meeting Reese's eyes, she saw no sympathy there. Resolutely she inched her chin up.

At first the meeting progressed without incident. Then Cushman took the floor. Jem sensed her hackles rising. Anger slowly replaced the despair she was feeling as he leveled his pale gaze around the room, his silvery blond hair glinting in the lamplight.

"We all know why we're here. There's a new bunch of homesteaders who've settled up north," Cushman began. A chorus of agreement greeted this announcement. Glancing around the room, Jem recognized the seeds of discontent, the unfounded bluster of the smaller ranchers who were ill-equipped to fight their own battles. Their stand depended on Cushman's army of cowhands to carry out the threats they were making. "And we all know what more sodbusters are going to mean."

More rumbles of agreement punctuated the room.

Jem stood up. "And just how are you planning to keep these farmers away? You going to kill everybody that stands in your way?"

Cushman's face was smug, gloating. "So, you showed up after all."

"Somebody has to keep you in line." Jem couldn't restrain the challenge in her voice. She doubted an army of marshals could force Cushman to be honest.

"And you think you're going to do the job?" He dropped any pretense of friendliness, his heavy-jowled face contorting into a snarl.

Jem squared off. "Why else would I be here? You don't think your sugarcoated invitation did the trick?"

"You'd have to be at least part female for that to work."

Jem blanched. The memory of her last fumbled attempts at being womanly were too new, too raw.

"Cushman, I've got a good mind to take you outside and whip you into the ground." Reese's voice from beside her was feral. "But I don't knock around my elders."

For once Randolph Cushman was speechless. Reese

gripped Jem's arm, preparing to walk away. He delivered one parting shot. "Talk to my wife like that again, and I'll forget just how old you are."

He half dragged Jem out the door and to the wagon. When they were out of hearing distance, he pulled the wagon over, his tone nearly startling her off the seat. "Just couldn't keep quiet, could you?"

"Me? He was the one who—"

"I heard it, but you egged him on."

"Then why did you defend my honor?"

He laughed, but there was no humor in the sound. "What honor?"

Jem's eyes widened. He had heaped one hurt on another. The wound that Abigail had called festering was now raw and bleeding. Jem wasn't sure what Reese meant, but the derision in his eyes was clear.

"You don't understand."

"I understand all I need to." He flicked the reins, and the horses started forward. Jem stared ahead, and Reese spared her one glance. What he saw almost made him stop. In the darkness it looked as though two tears trembled on her lashes. He shook his head to clear the fanciful notion. His tough wife wouldn't give in to tears. It must have been a trick of the moonlight. He snapped the reins, and the wagon moved forward. She was more likely to blow his head off than start crying.

The moon was high overhead by the time they reached the gate to the ranch. The darkened house loomed ahead. Jem dragged herself down from the wagon without waiting to see if Reese would offer his assistance. Emotionally battered, she didn't think she could cope with any more hostility.

She didn't bother to light any lamps as she entered the main hall. Della had left one small globe burning, and Jem used its dim light to guide her up the familiar stairwell, not waiting to hear whether Reese followed her. It didn't really matter.

For the first time in months, she crossed to the small

wooden box that held her few treasures and pulled out the bandanna she'd lovingly placed within its depths. She held the rough material to her cheek, remembering the day Charles had used it as a ground covering for her to sit upon. He had treated her like a fine lady as he swept the ground clear and offered his hand and later his heart. She had kept the memento of that day, their enchanted picnic and the promises he had made.

Standing alone in the dark, Jem wondered what had happened to Charles, if he missed her as much as she had missed him. She breathed in the scent of the bandanna, remembering it as it lay against his fair skin. As she leaned forward to replace the bandanna her locket swayed between her breasts, the smooth metal igniting another pain.

The mockery of its presence was a sore reminder. She reached to pull the offending trinket off when Reese's voice bellowed through the doorway, "Are you trying to kill me? Why didn't you light the lamp?"

Jem's hand fell away as she turned toward him. "There's a match in the box by the door." She heard him fumble for a moment, then the quick hiss of the match as it ignited. The tinkle of the glass cover followed as it was removed and then replaced. She winced as the light enveloped the room.

"Why were you standing in the dark?"

She pointed toward the window. "There was enough moonlight to see by."

"For bats, maybe." His disgruntled voice floated past as he sat on the chair and pulled off his boots.

"Hmm." She stared at his back as he peeled off his denims and shirt. His muscles rippled as he neatly hung up his clothes.

Catching her gaze, he narrowed his eyes. "What?"

"Nothing."

Shaking his head, he turned away, and Jem watched him settle in.

"Are you coming to bed? We wasted enough time tonight. Don't need to get a late start tomorrow."

The arrow pierced her heart again. "No, we don't." She moved to the lamp and blew out the flame. Gathering her nightgown, she withdrew to the small alcove off the bedroom. Sitting in the dark, she tugged at her boots, hearing them thud in the stillness as each was removed. Taking off her clothes, she stared down at her lean frame before pulling on her nightgown. She could understand Reese's rejection and wondered again about Charles. What had he seen when he looked at her? Did he recognize the woman she was underneath or just see the scrawny length that showed?

With a heavy heart, she folded her clothes and made her way toward the bed. Making sure to stay far to the edge, she climbed on the mattress, pulling the coverlet up. It caught on one of Reese's arms, which lay over the quilt rather than under it. For a long moment she stared, mesmerized by the muscled biceps and forearm before he turned, allowing her to smooth out the quilt.

The familiar recesses of the room were bathed in the silver glow of the moon, and her eyes, accustomed to the dark, were able to see each shape clearly. Cautiously easing on her side, Jem faced Reese's back, seeing the smooth flesh that covered his broad shoulders. Impulsively she reached out, but stilled the motion before it was completed. The ache in her heart was proof that she could not bear one more rejection.

Chapter
15

The following days passed in a painlessly uneventful fashion except for Cushman's repeated visits, which ended in heated, unresolved arguments. Another vote had been taken, and the association was deadlocked. Furious, Cushman blamed Jem and Michael Fairchild, feeling they represented the resistance.

Reese spent his time on whatever range Jem wasn't near. She had tried to avoid being in the same area until today, realizing she could no more stop being herself than she could stop breathing. Headstrong, opinionated, unfeminine; that was what she was. And she wasn't going to tuck her tail and hide on her own land.

Dressed in her oldest and baggiest clothes, she had spotted Grady and asked him to ride with her in search of the chuck wagon. She hadn't questioned her choice of clothes, refusing to admit it was a defense mechanism.

Retrieving her horse, she saw Boyd Harris hanging around the corral. Feeling a bit of her spirit return, she called to him, "Head on over to the herd, you can help with the branding."

"But, Reese—"

"This is my ranch. You have any trouble following my orders, you can leave."

"No, ma'am. I'll get right to it."

"See that you do."

He saddled a horse, and she watched as he headed out

in the direction she had ordered. Grady joined her, and they rode in the same direction, her stallion gaiting nervously. She wanted to make sure Harris really showed up at the branding camp. Her mount continued its thrashing, and Jem attributed it to the days she hadn't ridden him while hiding out from Reese.

When she arrived, Boyd was gesturing as he spoke to Reese. Both men turned as she pulled up on her horse.

Reese stalked over to her. "What the hell do you mean giving the men different orders?"

"There's too much work at this ranch for one man to lollygag—"

"There's also too much work for me to assign a man a task and have you come along and undo it. If I'd have needed Boyd on the branding, he'd be here. He was supposed to be checking on the men riding fences and this one"—he pointed to Grady—"is supposed to be fixing the corral railing."

"This is still my ranch."

"It won't be for long if we don't fill the contract. And this is the kind of damn fool thing that'll keep us from it. These men need to be doing what I told them, not catering to your whims."

Jem leaned forward, her legs clenching the horse's sides. "Whims!" But even as she spoke the stallion reared, its great eyes rolling. Always able to control the beast, Jem was taken by surprise when he bucked from side to side. Unable to secure a grip on the reins, she reached for a fistful of the stallion's mane, but he bucked even more furiously, sending her flying from his back. She felt herself being flung through the air, and when she landed, she heard a bone-crushing crack. Mercifully darkness took over.

Reese shouted for Pete to control the horse and then dropped to her side. He turned her toward him, but her head dangled limply. Her unnaturally pale skin now looked almost translucent in the glare of the midday sun.

Trying not to panic, he rubbed her hands in his, but still she didn't respond.

Without wasting more time, he scooped her up in his arms. Striding forward amid the unnatural silence of the hands, he laid her in the back of the chuck wagon and mounted the wagon seat. Flicking the reins, he stood upright, driving the team quickly toward the ranch house.

Minutes later, after he had calmed the stallion, Pete stared after the retreating wagon. He had removed the saddle and blanket. A silver spike had been embedded into both the saddle and the horse, and fresh blood spotted the animal's back. Pete turned back toward the men, his face grim as he stared at Boyd Harris and Grady Orton. The suspicions forming in his mind were ugly, but then so was murder.

Reese was shouting as he came through the door. Mary came running, and the *whoosh* of Della's chair was only seconds behind.

"What . . . ? Jem!"

"Her horse threw her." Reese stared at the still face cradled in his arms. She hadn't moved. Only the ragged pulse beating at her throat proclaimed she was alive.

"Take her upstairs, and then come get me," Della ordered.

"But—"

"Do as I say. I'll be gathering what I need and send it up with Mary, but I can't get upstairs by myself."

Following her instructions, Reese carried Jem up the stairs and into their bedroom. Easing her onto the mattress, he removed her bandanna and tossed it aside. Long, dark lashes swept over her cheeks. He'd never seen her so pale. Her skin was always the shade of honey from the long hours she spent outside. It occurred to him that she'd spent an inordinate amount of time inside that week.

Seeing the dark shadows beneath her eyes, Reese remembered the last words they'd exchanged. He'd not realized he possessed such venom—and seeing her help-lessness, he didn't know he could feel such remorse.

Della's voice floated up the stairway, urgency laced through her words. "Reese? Can you come get me?"

Releasing Jem's hand, Reese ran down the stairs. Awk-wardly at first, he managed to lift Della's insignificant weight from the chair. When they reached Jem's room, she instructed him calmly: "Put me in that chair, and then go get mine." He hesitated for a moment. "Hurry."

Glancing at Jem's still form, he obeyed. Within mo-ments Della was mobile in her chair, her competent hands examining Jem. Reese paced as she carefully checked Jem's head and then her limbs.

"She's got a nasty crack on her head," Della finally pro-nounced. Ringing out a wet towel, she bathed Jem's face.

"And?"

"And we'll have to wait until she wakes up. There isn't anything else we can do. There aren't any broken bones."

"What about a doctor?"

"Doc Riley's over a hundred miles away. Won't be back for better than a week."

Reese slammed his hand against the frame of the win-dowpane. "Damn!"

"I've put a cool cloth on her head, but you'll need to get her into her gown." Della glanced up and saw the un-certainty on Reese's face. "No need to be embarrassed. You're wed, for heaven's sake."

"Of course," he murmured.

"I'd help you, but to be honest I'm not strong enough, and Mary's gone for more cool water."

They both turned when they heard Pete's voice. "She all right?"

Della wheeled close to the doorway. "She's still out. We won't know for sure until she wakes up. Right now I should get downstairs and make a poultice for that bump on her head."

"Reese, you need us?" Pete asked.

But Della answered instead. "No, he can handle this. I want to get started on that poultice."

Pete bent to lift Della and take her downstairs, and Reese was left alone with Jem. She was so terribly still. He reached out hesitantly to touch her face, but pulled back before the contact was made. Instead he bent over to pull off her boots. Those and her stockings out of the way, he eased off the huge duster that all but swallowed her. Uncinching her belt, he then unfastened the buttons to her breeches and removed them also. Freeing the last of the shirt from her shoulders, he was struck by her thinness. While he'd always been aware that she was lean, he knew that this fragility was new.

Dispensing with her undergarments, he swallowed at the sight of her breasts when he removed her camisole. Slipping the cambric gown on, he quickly concealed her exposed flesh. It seemed somehow indecent to be able to observe her when she was unaware, vulnerable.

Pulling the coverlet up to rest beneath her arms, Reese picked up one of her hands. The question that had haunted him the past week rose again. Had she really loved that renegade Sawyer? And if she had, could he live with the knowledge?

Reese remembered his own hateful words, recalling them with chilling clarity. He imagined a woman like Jem had felt the brunt of being different all her life. He wondered what his reaffirmation of that difference had meant to her. He'd deliberately let her know that her father's killer hadn't mattered to him, that her apology wasn't good enough. Worse, he'd zeroed in on her weakness and let the shots fly.

Only her even breathing was a sure sign that she hadn't slipped away. Sighing, Reese dropped his head in his hands. The quiet creak of Della's chair told him she had returned.

"She'll be all right, Reese."

"How can you be so sure?"

"Because she's a fighter. Jem never gives up—right or wrong. She won't now."

Recalling the tortured look on Jem's face this last week, Reese fervently hoped Della was right.

"Why don't you go downstairs and have a drink. I can sit with her," Della offered.

"No, I'll stay here."

Della glanced at his set face and apparently decided it was useless to argue. She applied the poultice to the angry crack on Jem's head, carefully binding it with a clean cloth. Reese watched her ministrations, waiting until she finished to speak.

"Why do you suppose she hasn't come to yet?"

Della stared at Jem's still countenance. "Sometimes it's just nature's way of healing. Nothing will help like sleep." Straightening up, she wheeled back a bit. "What about you, Reese. Can I fix you some lunch?"

"No." He didn't move from his chair. "Thanks," he added distractedly. "I'll just stay here."

The hours passed slowly. An untouched tray that Della had sent up with Pete still sat on the dresser. The sun's bright rays faded into twilight, the spectacular sunset went unnoticed, and dusk was past.

Rumination and regret were poor companions, Reese decided. He wished he could recall the ugly words he'd issued. Seeing the pale blue smudges beneath her eyes, he fervently hoped his words weren't the last she was to hear. Hell, a woman like her couldn't have been around many men before. If she had been duped by Charles Sawyer, she wouldn't have been the first person to fall into his snare. And judging from her uncertain responses to his touch, Sawyer couldn't have been much of a lover.

Reese still didn't know what possessed Jem to make such a damn fool offer to accept her marital duties, but it occurred to him that in her own fashion she'd meant to do the right thing.

His deep sigh filled the room as he shifted his position in the hard chair. He didn't recall ever sitting still for so long. The long shadows of dusk deepened and then passed into night. Pete came and lit a lamp, removed the tray, and brought a flask of whiskey. It, too, lay untouched. Prevailing upon Mary to crank the dumbwaiter every hour, Della had checked on Jem constantly, but there was no change.

And for the last several hours Reese had talked. About everything and nothing. He even confided his dreams for the freighting business and the strange territorial attachment he'd developed toward the Bar-W. Jem's even breathing was the only response he received.

Then he lapsed into talking about the past he never mentioned to anyone. He told her about his mother's struggle to keep their family together after his father's death. The words slowed and almost halted as he completed the story. The memory was as clear as if it had happened yesterday.

Fifteen-year-old Reese pocketed his pay and headed toward home. He knew he had to stop and pick up some stew meat for dinner first. He started to cross the street to the butcher's when the saloon door next to him swung open. Intrigued, he watched as the painted ladies at the bar simpered and the men ordered drinks. He leaned so far inside to see that one of the ladies at the bar noticed him. Taking a shine to him, she bought him a sarsaparilla and told him how handsome he was. Puffed up with pride, he wasted better than an hour before he realized he still had to buy the family's dinner.

Finally disengaging himself from the fascinating woman, he hurriedly bought the stew meat and then walked home. When he turned the corner toward his house, his skin turned cold, and his heart tried to claw its way through his chest. The house, their house was on fire! His mother, the kids! He ran with a desperation born of sure futility. The part of the house that still stood was consumed in flames.

Panicked, he looked from face to face. One at a time the neighbors and boarders each gazed downward when he questioned them, none eager to tell him the awful truth.

None of the boarders had been home, only his mother and the kids. One of the neighbors finally told him he thought his mother could have made it out alive, but she was trying to save all the children—an impossible task alone. While he'd sat and flirted with the saloon gal, his mother and brothers and sisters had burned to death. Everyone told him it hadn't been his fault, there was no reason to feel responsible. But the guilt had never faded.

Watching Jem's unresponsive face, he recounted the guilt. It was almost a relief to pour out the story. Nineteen years had passed since he'd told another human being about what had happened. One thing was certain, Jem wouldn't judge him, because she hadn't heard him. Pulling up his chair, he reached out to touch the hair that tumbled down her shoulders.

Soft and golden, it glowed in the lamplight. His hand moved down the length of her face, feeling the softness, sensing the weakness.

The voice had been gentle, soothing, but now she sensed the agony, the despair. The light of the room hurt her eyes, teased the pain in her head, but still she struggled to return to consciousness. The boy needed help. Wouldn't anyone help him?

Her eyelids fluttered, trying to open, but the enormous weight that lay across the bed held her captive. Soft whisper strokes touched her cheeks, her hair, her hand, yet she couldn't move.

The words continued to flow around her, creating a cocoon of warmth. A sigh escaped her lips, and the words stopped. The brush of a whiskery cheek touched hers as she sensed another face close to hers.

Reese held his breath as he listened. Unable to tell for certain, he held his head close to hers. The pattern of her breathing had changed, He blinked, then looked again. Her eyelashes fluttered, then drooped back in place. Torn between shouting for Della and remaining utterly still to watch Jem, he chose the latter.

Her face was still pale, but it seemed as though a touch

of color tinged her lips now. His hand went to her brow, and he smoothed the line of worry in her forehead. He wondered what nightmares were raging in her troubled sleep.

But the eyes that finally opened were clear as they gazed at him. Her voice emerged as little better than a croak, however. "Reese?"

"Yes."

"Have I been asleep?"

His hand continued to stroke her forehead. "For a little while."

"Why am I asleep in the middle of the day?"

Reese glanced about the semidarkened room, partially lit by a small lamp. Only the quarter moon saved the night from pitch darkness. "You needed your rest."

"Oh." Her eyelids fluttered shut. The danger she'd sensed must be slipping away.

Watching her, Reese took one hand in his, keeping it warm. She was strong, more so than he'd realized. But the slender fingers entwined with his reminded him she wasn't invincible. Her vulnerability, seldom shown, was very real. He vowed to find out what Charles Sawyer had promised her and make sure she wasn't duped again. This iron maiden possessed delicate webbing, and he didn't intend for it to be crushed again. Obviously she carried loyalty far beyond its limits and had sadly misplaced her trust.

The creak of Della's wheels as she wheeled in from her room interrupted his thoughts. His voice was quiet in the shuttered room. "She woke up."

Della nodded. "Good. Did she say anything?"

"Just gibberish."

"That's normal. She may be addled for a day or so. I can sit with her for a while if you want to get some sleep."

"Nah, I'll stay around for a while." He pointed to the softer chair next to the window. "That'll be fine for me."

The next hour he dozed fitfully in the chair, wakening often to check on Jem. The last time, finding no change, he returned to his cramped chair, pulled off his boots, and closed his eyes. He started to drift off when a cry awakened him.

As she thrashed in her sleep Jem's cries were plaintive. Instinctively he climbed on the bed, gathering her in his arms, soothing her nightmares. Jem's body shook violently, and Reese ran his hands down her back, comforting and cradling her.

When the shaking subsided, he started to draw away, but she tightened her tenuous grip. "You're all right now," he murmured.

"Stay." Her voice, still weak, drifted through the silent room. As though clutching a lifeline, she clung to him, and he could not distance himself. Remembering the others he couldn't save, Reese held her close. His eyes wide open, he stared into the inky darkness, knowing sleep would not come for him that night.

Chapter 16

Jem's head throbbed as the morning light filtered through the drapes and lace panels covering the window. She reached up a weak hand to touch the source of pain and felt the bandage Della had applied. What in the world?

Before she could complete the thought, Della wheeled into her room. "Looks like you're going to live."

"What happened?" Jem was surprised at the weakness of her own voice.

"Horse threw you. Got a nasty bump on your head."

"Oh." Jem raised her head gingerly and gazed around.

"Reese is downstairs eating."

"Wouldn't want to inconvenience him."

Della's voice was sharp. "I think sitting up all night watching you was inconvenient enough."

Jem's voice faltered. "Reese sat up with me?"

"We offered to take turns, but he wouldn't hear of it. Even after you woke up, he stayed. Didn't leave until I made him eat some breakfast. Didn't touch a lick of food I brought in here yesterday before you woke up."

Jem picked at the coverlet and didn't meet Della's eyes. "He really did that?"

"Yes, he did."

Jem thought over this information. "Why ever do you suppose he wanted to?"

Della stilled her hands. "I'd say you're the only one who'd know that."

Jem's eyes widened as she absorbed Della's words. A rap on the door announced Pete's presence with a breakfast tray.

"You feel up to eatin'?" he asked, bringing in a delectable tray full of food. All of her favorites had been prepared, and the tray had been set with her mother's best china. A small cut-crystal vase overflowed with fragrant tansybush blooms and delicate pale blue wild iris.

She managed a tremulous smile. "You're both too good to me."

"Probably," Pete responded as he set the tray down. "But it was a group effort. Della cooked, I fixed the tray, and Reese found the flowers."

The delicate flowers reminded her of the ones Reese had painstakingly picked for their wedding day. A lump almost too large to swallow materialized in her throat. A second rap on the door sent her heart pounding.

Della and Pete started to leave. "You don't have to go. . . ." Jem began. The glance Della shot her quelled the rest of her sentence. As they exited, Reese entered awkwardly.

"Did you eat your breakfast?"

"Not yet." She gestured to the tray Pete had left. Ducking her head, she mumbled, "The flowers—thank you."

"Sure." He walked around the room, aimlessly picking up a brush, then a comb, and laying them down just as quickly.

"You didn't have to sit with me all night." His gaze sharpened in surprise and met hers. "Della told me," she explained lamely.

"Oh."

"But it was nice," she managed.

He shrugged, obviously as ill at ease as she was. "How's your head?"

Her hand went automatically to the bump. "Sore."

He managed a smile. "I'll bet."

She stared down again at the coverlet, plucking at invisible threads. "You're probably pretty tired."

"I've had more restful nights."

Jem wished she could form the words that hovered so close to the surface. She wanted to thank him for . . . for being there. A distant memory of her mother sitting with her when she was sick was the only time she remembered being nurtured. Her father, as much as she'd loved him, hadn't known how to treat a young girl when she fell ill. And there was the expression on Reese's face. He no longer acted angry and disgusted.

"Well, I'd better go check on the hands."

"Can't Pete do that?" she asked quickly.

Surprised, he nodded. "I guess so."

She scratched her head and looked anywhere but at him. "Maybe you could get some rest, stay with me for a while."

The moment lengthened. "Sure."

The day passed quietly. She dozed much of the time and began to feel rested, renewed. When she tried to read, however, the pain in her head intensified, and Reese took the book from her hands. His deep, rich voice filled the room, and Jem experienced unfamiliar contentment as he took her to the faraway land of Germany. Closing her eyes, she visualized the castles he read about and felt the brush of the lush green land the words described.

After a leisurely lunch and nap, he returned to the book, and Jem savored each full moment. When the shadows lengthened, Reese lit the lamps and then returned to her side.

"You look tired," Jem commented.

"Guess I am," he admitted.

She patted the bed beside her. "Then you'd better get some rest."

"But your—"

"I'm fine." He started to protest, but she continued. "Or I will be soon. It's your turn."

Reese sat down heavily and removed his boots, unable to repress a sigh as he leaned back. Watching him, Jem noticed the fine lines that were etched in his weary face. The night stretched ahead. For the first time in weeks the night wasn't to be dreaded, but anticipated.

Jem awoke with a start, the morning light startling her. She reached out beside her, but touched only a soft feather pillow. She'd barely dozed off for a moment. Or so she thought. The evidence of an empty bed proved she had given in to the overwhelming need to sleep. She wondered where Reese was. Already yesterday seemed like a dream.

Sitting up carefully, she reached gingerly toward the bandage around her head. While still very tender, it wasn't as painful as the day before. She glanced around the room, seeing the familiar furnishings in the early sun-washed light. Yesterday the room seemed to have taken on a magical quality while closeting Reese and Jem in its space.

The creak of Della's chair rounded the corner and paused in her doorway. "You awake?"

"Yes, and you don't have to whisper."

"Cranky. Good, you're back to yourself. You hungry?"

"I'm not sure yet. Is Reese downstairs eating?"

Della straightened the dresser as she answered, "He left hours ago."

"Oh." Jem couldn't keep the disappointment from her voice.

"Good," Della mumbled under her breath.

"What was that?" Jem strained to hear, wondering if the fall had affected her hearing also.

"Nothing. I'll send up a tray. Just something light."

"Whatever you say."

"Now that's something you don't hear every day," Della muttered.

"I didn't hear you." Jem shook her head slightly to one side.

"As soon as it warms up, we'll get you out into the sunshine and you'll feel better."

"Fine." Jem's tone was disinterested.

Della plumped her pillows, and Jem leaned back to stare out the window, missing Della's broad smile as she left the room.

Reese's face was grim as he palmed the incriminating length of silver.

"It wasn't any accident." Pete's voice was blunt.

"You got any ideas?"

Pete shook his head slowly. "I don't know, but . . ."

"What?"

"Jem always claimed a rustler didn't kill her pa."

"And you're thinkin' now she's right?"

Pete scratched his chin and stared at the slice of silver. "All I know is that barb didn't get underneath her saddle by itself."

"Why didn't you tell me about this yesterday?"

Pete ducked his head to hide a wry smile. "You seemed kind of busy."

Reese hitched up his gun belt self-consciously and glanced away. "Guess I was."

"How much do you know about Boyd Harris?"

Surprised, Reese searched Pete's face. "Enough."

"Enough to know whether he could have a hand in this?"

"What makes you think he did?" Reese couldn't keep the exasperation out of his voice.

"I'm not saying he was the one, but he was around when Jem's horse was saddled."

"Seems like Grady Orton was working on the corral about the same time," Reese challenged.

"So he was." Pete's quiet voice was more effective than a dousing of cold water. It could be either of them.

"We'll have to watch out for Jem. She won't like it, but we'd better make sure she's not alone."

"Yep," Pete answered. Reese turned away to mount his horse, but Pete's voice halted him. "You too."

Reese turned around slowly. "Me?"

"If whoever did this is after the owners of the Bar-W, it seems you could be next in line."

Chapter
17

A day of rest and sunshine had improved both Jem's disposition and her color. A long, hot bath in some of Abigail's bath crystals had relaxed her bruised muscles and restored some of her energy. Spending an inordinate amount of time fussing with her hair and gown, she looked as radiant as a woman who'd just missed a brush with death could.

Turning the lamplight down, she had asked Della to have Pete bring up two trays for dinner so that Reese could share a quiet supper with her. Not without effort, she had unearthed some floral talc and sprinkled it on the clean sheets. The fragrance teased the air, mixing with the scent of the wildflowers.

When Jem heard Reese's footsteps in the hall, she straightened up in the bed, trying to still the sudden beating of her heart. The door opened, and she glanced up with a welcoming smile.

Her smile faltered somewhat when Reese dropped his hat directly on the trays of food that were covered with spotless white linen.

"Reese?"

"Hmm," Reese answered without sparing her a glance.

"Your hat." She pointed to the Stetson.

"Oh, sorry." Removing the hat, he tossed it on the empty side of the bed. She stared at the hat and then at

Reese. Unless he planned to sit on the hat, they weren't going to have quite the cozy supper she'd envisioned.

She smiled brightly again. "Della prepared a very special supper."

"Oh, yeah. She said it was up here. Told her Mary didn't need to be hauling two trays. I'm not that hungry anyway."

Slightly deflated, Jem cleared her throat and tried to rally. "Why don't you just try something light?"

He shrugged and walked over to the trays. Pulling off the linen cover, he speared a roll and began munching on it. Allowing a decent time to pass, Jem tried again, determined to be cheerful. "We could eat together."

"Oh, you hungry?" He glanced down at the two trays. Having stood and eaten the rolls from both, he now picked up one tray and headed her way. Depositing it in her lap, he sniffed and walked over to the window. Parting the drapes, he opened the window. "Smells funny in here."

Jem glanced over at the talc on the sheets and discreetly pulled the quilt up toward the pillow, covering the fragrant dust. Managing a half smile, she watched as he returned to the dresser and continued to snack from the remaining tray in an absentminded fashion.

Eating silently, Jem wondered at his preoccupation as she finished what little food appealed to her and tried once more. "I'm through now, Reese."

Coming to life, he retrieved the tray and then started with it through the doorway.

"Reese, you don't have to take that down. In the morning Mary can—"

"No bother. I'm going down anyway."

Helplessly Jem watched as Reese departed. Fully deflated, she leaned back against the headboard of the bed with a sigh. From the corner of her eye she spotted Reese's hat. Plucking the Stetson from the talc-scented sheets, she twirled it slowly in her hands, determined to wait for his return.

When at least an hour had passed, she carefully replaced

the hat and then hunkered down under the quilt, feeling the loneliness of the bed. One hand smoothed the empty sheets before she closed her eyes.

Still preoccupied, Reese swore as the match he'd ignited burned his hand. Tossing the offending stick into the fireplace, he reached again into the matchbox. Lighting the lamp in the study, he adjusted the wick to provide a bright glow.

His mind flew among the possibilities. Had it been someone other than the rustler who had killed Jem's father? And why?

Restlessly roaming the room, he pushed open the window and stared into the darkness. No answers there. The peace that blanketed the dark, star-filled landscape was at odds with the turmoil within the house. Whispered conversations buzzed behind closed doors. He and Pete had decided not to tell Jem what had caused her accident, knowing it was essential that she rest in order to recuperate. If she knew the truth, she'd be up in a moment, guns in hand.

Conspirators in the mistress's home, he thought ironically. But at least these confederates were conspiring to help her.

The knock at the study door was a welcome interruption since his own thoughts were a merciless adversary. "Come in."

Pete entered. Taking one look at his face, Reese poured him a tumbler of whiskey and gestured to the two wing chairs that faced one another. Pete passed a weary hand over his face after he had accepted the drink and taken a long swallow.

"You find out anything?" Reese questioned.

"Plenty. We got more suspects than victims."

Reese raised his eyebrows.

"Hell, Boyd Harris, Grady Orton, and a half-dozen other men were near the corral that morning," Pete continued in disgust.

"Who could've got to the horse?"

"Any of them." Pete took another swallow of his drink. "I talked to Della. Jem went out and saddled her horse, then came back in to get her bandanna. Anybody could've done it while she was inside."

"And probably only the guilty man was watching the others," Reese said, still pacing the confines of the room.

"More than likely."

"Which gets us nowhere," Reese concluded grimly. "You'll both have to stick close to the house, stay out of range of—"

"No. That's exactly what we're not going to do." Reese gripped the whiskey decanter until his knuckles were white. "Hiding out will tip off the killer that we're on to him." He released the crystal slowly. "No, we'll be very visible."

Pete protested. "I thought you said Jem couldn't be left alone."

"I plan to stick closer than fleas on a dog. You don't flush out a poacher by hiding away."

"But this isn't a poacher."

Reese tipped the drink to his lips, his face grim. "An even better reason to uncover him."

"Are you sure you're feeling all right?" Abigail asked in concern.

Jem leaned back in the wing chair, enjoying the tea Della had prepared. "Absolutely. I started my regular routine a few days ago."

"Oh, is that safe? I mean riding alone—"

Jem laughed softly. "Well, I'm not exactly alone."

Abigail raised her eyebrows. "No?"

Jem concentrated on the blue delft pattern of the cup and saucer in her hand. "Reese has been riding with me every day." Her other hand strayed to her now healed head. "Just to be on the safe side."

"Of course."

"It's a precaution in case I get dizzy," Jem protested.

Abigail laughed. "It sounds like you managed to talk out your problems and find a solution."

Jem shoved the cup and saucer on the table and stood. Walking over to the window, she gazed out at the cloud-covered mountains rather than at Abigail. "Not exactly."

"Oh, Jem." The dismay in Abigail's voice was apparent.

Defensively, Jem turned to face Abigail. "It just never seemed to be the right time." Her face softened. "And after my fall, Reese was so kind and concerned. It was as though the other had never happened."

"But, Jem, you can't just leave it like that."

"Why not? Reese has put it behind him. Why shouldn't I?"

"You need to talk over this misunderstanding."

Jem turned back to the wide window and braced her hands on the wall beside it. "It's the strangest thing. Before I woke up, I had the feeling we had discussed everything."

"That doesn't make a lot of sense."

Jem turned around slowly. Assessing Abigail's expression, she could see that the other woman thought the effects of the fall were not completely gone. "I know. But when I woke up I felt as though a lot of that had been settled."

"For your sake, I hope it has been." Abigail hesitated. "Has this changed your feelings about Charles?"

"Why should it?"

"Sometimes our first love is built up in our memories as something more special than it really was." Abigail chose her words carefully, as though she trod on eggshells.

"Is that how you feel about Michael?"

"No, it's not."

"I can't explain about Charles," Jem mused, her face transfixed with earnestness. "But I was always on the outside looking in—wanting to be like other women." Her expression turned wistful. "But I was too tall, gawky. A skinny bag of bones is what the boys used to call me." A smile replaced her look of pain as she reminisced. "And then there was Charles. He courted me. Brought flowers and silly little presents." Jem's eyes connected with Abigail's. "And he never made me feel I wasn't feminine enough to deserve his attention."

"Oh, Jem." Abigail's voice filled with sympathy and distress.

"But all that makes me even more confused about Reese."

"What do you mean?"

Jem glanced away, somewhat embarrassed. "I have, well, feelings, about Reese."

"That's good," Abigail encouraged.

"I'm not sure it is."

Puzzled, Abigail cocked her head. "I don't understand."

"I was trying to explain the other day—I'm attracted to Reese in a different sort of way." She gestured aimlessly with her hands.

"Different?" Abigail's face suddenly creased with dawning awareness. "You mean . . ."

"Yes, and I never thought I was that sort of person. It's nothing like the pure love I feel for Charles. It's more, well, basic."

So that was how it was. "Uh-huh."

"I knew you'd think I was terrible."

"Not at all. A physical attraction is often the first thing that brings two people together."

"I just want to survive this year and make sure we fill the army contract. When it's over, we can even part friends." Jem turned, not seeing the disbelief darting across Abigail's face. "Can't I have these more base feelings for Reese while I still love Charles?"

Hesitating, Abigail finally answered, "I suppose so."

"Is it too awful to not want to be at war with Reese the whole time?"

"Hardly. But I see now why you were so willing to fulfill your marital duties."

Jem protested. "It's not—"

But the other woman's laughter drowned out her words.

Gasping, Abigail spoke before Jem could. "Your secret's safe with me."

"You have this all wrong, Abby."

"Um-hmm. I promise not to interfere again."

Jem stubbed her boot into the tapestry of the rug covering the wooden floor. "I don't mind." She paused. "Actually I guess I kind of like it. Before, all my problems centered around the ranch, and I had my father to discuss them with. But this is all so . . ."

"I think I understand. I'm here to nose into your business whenever you want."

"Thanks. I used to think women were so foolish." Jem flushed, realizing what she'd said included Abigail. "I don't mean—"

"It's all right. You didn't have the opportunity to know me before. It is nice to have women friends."

"One, maybe." Jem's voice was blunt. She thought of Della. "Or, two. But I don't know how you put up with Lorraine and Mabel."

Abigail laughed. "I don't."

Jem looked puzzled.

"I'm polite to them at social occasions. It's not quite the same as being friends."

Jem's face was thoughtful. "No, I don't suppose it is." Apparently it was much more. She lifted her head, seeing that Abigail was gathering her gloves. "Reese and I are planning to go to the dance next week."

"Good, in the meantime I hope to see you at church Sunday." She started out the door and then turned back. "I'm very glad to see that things are working out so well, Jem. You deserve to be happy."

Abigail's shoes tapped lightly as she walked through the entry and out the door. Turning back the curtain at the window, Jem watched her climb into the buggy and flick the reins. Happy? It was something she had never considered.

Chapter 18

Jem was surprised when Reese agreed so readily to go to church with her. He hadn't accompanied her to church before, but today he had risen and dressed for the services without hesitation. Although he had never told her about his background, she sensed that he had wandered for so many years that he hadn't bothered to go to church or fit into a community.

"How long does this go on?" Reese muttered next to her ear.

Glancing up, she saw the people in the room through his eyes. Neighbors from outlying ranches, eager for gossip, were abuzz. Mabel Deems was pounding loudly on the piano in direct competition with the growing noise of the crowd. Considering the piano was one they wheeled over every Sunday from the saloon, its sound was hardly what one might expect to hear in church. A tinny rendition of "Sweet Hour of Prayer" was being laboriously cranked from the ancient instrument.

"Don't care for our local church?" she asked, seeing how uncomfortable he was.

Reese straightened up for the dozenth time. "It's different."

"From what?"

"Oh, churches I've been to before."

Surprised, she studied his expression. "In what way?"

He glanced around the plain, functional room. "Looks

141

different." He paused, staring at Mabel, who appeared to be trying to transport the entire congregation to heaven by the sole means of her offkey but spirited music. "Sounds different."

"Ranches you worked at were near big, fancy churches?"

"Not ranches," he muttered, seeming even more uncomfortable.

"Where then?"

"Back East."

Jem couldn't contain her surprise. "East? You?"

"It was a long time ago." Reese's expression closed, and she watched him move restlessly on the pew.

But Jem refused to let the subject rest. "Are you from the East? Is that where your family is?"

The lines next to Reese's mouth tightened, and she wondered at the flicker in his eyes before he answered shortly, "I was born in Chicago."

She wanted to ask more, how he had come to be living in the West, where he had learned to be an outstanding cowhand. But not only had Reese's manner become forbidding, Reverend Filcher was standing at the front of the room, trying to quiet the congregation. Hard-of-hearing, he bellowed, his voice echoing in the small, crowded room.

"Brothers and sisters, welcome." The old preacher continued his greeting, but Jem didn't hear his words, instead concentrating on Reese. She would never have guessed he wasn't born and reared in the West. His natural abilities and affinity with the land were rarely seen in dudes who came from the East.

A niggling of something that should fit into this puzzle teased her, but she couldn't grasp it. Reese's ramrod posture convinced her this wasn't a subject he would easily discuss.

They stood for the opening song, and when Reese stared ahead without singing, Jem nudged him with the hymnal, offering to share it with him. Accepting the book reluctantly, Reese gazed at the pages before adding his voice to the growing sound.

The last time Reese had sung in church, he had been standing beside his mother, his still-changing voice joining in with her strong, sweet notes. The memory gripped him painfully. He had deliberately stayed away from church since then, finding it hard to forgive God for allowing his family to die.

Only his vow to remain by Jem's side to protect her had prompted him to attend the service today. When the song and prayer were finished, they sat back down on the hard pew, and Reese tried to relax. Instead his body was uncomfortably rigid, his hands knotted tensely. When Jem's tentative touch grazed his arm, he jerked, turning his head to stare at her. She smiled in return, and he accepted the gentle pressure of her hand on his arm, the comforting gesture rescuing him from the memories that were washing over him.

Calming down, he focused on the preacher's words, realizing they held no threat. Brought back to the present, he enjoyed the touch of Jem's fingers against his arm, grateful for her insight, yet also surprised.

As the minutes passed he also became aware of the closeness of Jem next to him and how right that felt. He relaxed as the minister's voice droned on, surprised to see the service nearing its conclusion.

As they stood again for another hymn Reese reached for the book at the same time Jem did. Their hands collided, but this time she didn't draw away. Lingering over the pages, their fingers grazed one another's.

Drawn to her, Reese felt the connection as they stood side by side. The long legs he remembered so well were next to his, hidden by layers of skirt and petticoats, but still he felt the firm pressure as he deliberately leaned closer. Her eyes widened in surprise, yet he didn't pull back.

Reese joined in the singing, surprised when Jem's rich voice warbled a bit. Meeting her eyes, he realized that she wasn't totally unaffected by his hand touching hers, his body pressed beside her.

Satisfaction seeped into his voice as he sang a bit louder. Jem's head tipped back, and he was gratified to see her consternation.

The song ended, and the preacher launched into a long, closing prayer. Trying not to fidget, Reese instead chose to focus on Jem. Her elbow was bent outward and within his reach. He drew his fingers lightly over the soft flesh and was pleased to feel her jump and then shoot him a quelling glare.

Smiling innocently, he tucked the same arm to his side as the preacher issued a final "amen" and released the congregation.

People poured out of the stuffy room, breaking into conversation as soon as they exited. Children flew outside, and games of tag immediately ensued. Mothers made half-hearted attempts to control them but were too interested in catching up on gossip to do more than make a few obligatory reprimands and then sink into their own conversations.

"You two are staying for the picnic, aren't you?" Abigail asked as they stepped down onto the packed dirt of the street.

Jem gazed helplessly at Reese, not certain if he wanted to attend the weekly outing.

"We didn't bring any food," Reese explained.

"Abby brought enough to feed a dozen," Michael interjected. "You're welcome to eat with us."

Jem held her breath, hoping Reese wouldn't snub their overture. She needn't have worried. "If Miss Abigail cooked, then I'd be a fool to say no."

Reese took Jem's elbow once again, and she tried to ignore the shiver his touch induced. Away from the swirling dust of the town's only street, a stretch of field carpeted with wild grass provided a perfect picnic area. Michael and Reese stretched a soft quilt under the branches of a tall aspen while Abigail and Jem unpacked the sturdy basket. Other families did the same, and soon the meadow was awash with running children and the hum of voices.

In little time Abigail's lunch was consumed. All that remained was a pile of chicken bones and an empty jar of lemonade. Jem finished her slice of chocolate cake, sighing as she speared the final crumbs. Replete, they all sat without speaking, listening to the sounds of the surrounding families.

Michael was the first to move. He rose and then offered his hand to his wife, pulling her up. He patted his stomach as he spoke. "Let's take a walk, Abby. I ate too much lunch." They took a few steps. "Besides, I'd like to get you alone."

"Michael!" Abigail's embarrassed whisper drifted back to Jem and Reese, who listened to her weak protest.

Watching until they were out of sight, Jem finally turned back to Reese, avoiding his gaze as she repacked the plates and silverware. Self-consciously she straightened the barely rumpled quilt.

"You could unpack the basket and then repack it," Reese suggested from beneath the brim of his Stetson as he watched her nervous flurry. He had stretched out on the quilt, his supine body a study in relaxation.

"I think I'll go see if the reverend needs anything—"

Jem's words were cut short when Reese's arm snaked out and pulled her down to his side. "I don't think he needs you as much as I do."

The breath whooshed from Jem at Reese's words. Not daring to put too much meaning in them, she lay still in the circle of his arms. Surprising her again, he rolled over, propping his weight on his forearms as he pinned her beneath his gaze. While still maintaining propriety, she was uncomfortably aware of their closeness.

His leg burned next to hers, and she wished she had doubled the amount of petticoats beneath her calico dress. When the curve of his rib cage pressed against hers, she wasn't sure a thousand yards of material would have served the purpose.

Trying to remain composed, she clamped her lips shut

when his fingers trailed lazily up and down the length of her arm, dwelling near the sensitive flesh of her elbow.

"You've lived here most of your life, haven't you?" he asked, startling her.

"I was born here," she answered, wondering at the direction of his questioning.

"Never had an itch to go somewhere else?"

"Not really. Everything I need is right here. When Pa was alive, I had my family. Now there's Della and Pete, the hands. And of course the Bar-W."

"Land has a way of eatin' at you, doesn't it?"

Jem tried to wiggle away from Reese, afraid that the pressure of his body near hers would cause her to lose control. "I guess so."

Reese clamped an arm over hers, thwarting her escape. Suddenly the meaning of his words penetrated, and she gave up the struggle. "You getting attached to the Bar-W?"

"Didn't say that. A smart man doesn't get attached to anything."

Jem's heart sank at his words. "Anything?" she questioned softly.

Reese searched her eyes, his gaze flickering over the length of her face. Long moments passed as the sunshine warmed their bodies and the calls of children playing drowned out the singing of the birds. One finger brushed the softness of her lips before he answered regretfully, "Nope, not anything."

Chapter
19

The week before the dance passed as Jem reveled in Reese's constant attention. Even now he was solicitous as he escorted her into the livery that housed the dance. Greeting her neighbors, Jem glanced around the converted barn, appreciating the smell of the freshly brewed cider and ginger cookies. Reese took her crocheted shawl and put it with the other wraps. When he returned, he held two cups of cider in his hands and offered her one.

Accepting the drink, she stood next to Reese as they both watched the dancers as first one and then several other songs followed. Abigail and Michael glided by, but both were too wrapped up in each other to notice anyone else.

Self-consciously Jem and Reese smiled at one another. The Fairchilds could be an advertisement for the perfect marriage. Glancing at their empty cups, Reese spoke. "More cider?"

"I don't think so," she replied, setting her cup on the table.

The silence stretched between them for several long moments. "You want to dance, then?"

Knowing how awkward she was, Jem automatically started to refuse, but then a memory of their last dance surfaced. "I think I'd like that very much."

The first dance was a lively polka, and Jem moved easily in Reese's arms. After a resounding finish they both applauded and waited for the next song. The fiddles warmed up and glided into a soft waltz. Reese's eyes questioned her, and she held out a hand in reply. Drawing close, they moved to the haunting melody.

The invisible, self-conscious cloak she always wore slipped away as they rounded the makeshift dance floor. The gathering of people in the room even seemed to diminish as Jem moved to Reese's lead.

Fitting her body close to his, she felt the strength of his thighs next to hers, the lean length of his body. She turned in his arms, her locket swaying as she did. As they moved to avoid another couple the tips of her breasts grazed his chest, startling them both.

The music ended, and the Fairchilds approached them. Abigail's face was wreathed in smiles, and Michael appeared equally happy. Abigail spoke first. "Are you two having a good time?"

Still flushed from the dance, Jem managed to smile and nod.

Michael chuckled and spoke to Abigail as he tucked her arm in his. "They still have the look."

"The look?" Jem questioned.

"Newlyweds," Michael replied. "Of course, I don't know if this dance is as much fun for you as the last one we saw you do."

A sudden memory of their double forfeit, the Blind Man's Waltz, and its subsequent conclusion struck them both.

Abigail tugged at Michael's arm. "They're playing one of my favorites." As they turned away, Abigail sent Jem a pleading glance as though to apologize for Michael's remark.

But his words had started a reaction that was impossible to ignore. Reese held out a hand, and Jem moved into his arms. Each nuance of his body was engraved in her heightened senses. The music continued to play on, but Jem wasn't sure she heard a note. The tension that had been buried after her accident rose up, assaulting her in waves. Rearing her head back, Jem clearly read what was written in Reese's gaze. The memory of their last dance together was a tangible, burning reminder between them.

The waltz ended, and the caller announced a round dance. Jem and Reese moved blindly into step. Passing from partner to partner, their eyes returned continuously to one another. The crackling in the air had nothing to do with the spring storm brewing outside.

When the round brought them together, their hands met, the contact searing and much too brief. Even as they passed away from one another the caller announced a square. Bowing to one another, they were both aware of the tiny space, barely a footfall, that separated them; then they were engulfed by the others as the caller continued the square. When a loud crack of thunder split the air outside, their eyes met. The challenge had returned, the tension escalated. Mercifully the square ended.

Mabel Deems giggled next to them. "Ladies' choice, and I choose you, Reese McIntire."

Helplessly Jem watched as Reese moved off with Mabel in tow. His eyes signaled his frustration, but Jem barely had time to register this as she turned to Mabel's waiting husband. Plastering a smile on her face, she moved into his overenthusiastic embrace to endure a polka in which she was steered about like a foundering ship.

When the dance was completed, the music softened once again. Not taking any chances, Reese reclaimed Jem, tucking her close to his side. The next three dances were all waltzes, and Jem and Reese didn't leave the dance floor, barely separating as one song ended and another started. The buzz of the room faded, the presence of everyone else in the room dimmed.

As though flung on a deserted patch of the earth, far away from prying eyes and concerns, Jem and Reese swayed to the music. Jem felt the ragged beat of her own pulse and saw that Reese's matched hers. Her eyes followed the path from that pulse beat down the opening of his cambric shirt to the tufts of hair that escaped its top button. Clearly remembering Reese's naked chest, Jem's mouth went dry in moments.

Reese managed to dodge the other dancers through sheer luck only. His concentration was focused on only one thing. While part of him tried to remember the result the last time they'd trod this path, a warm memory of her flesh against his was foremost in his mind. When the musicians took a break for refreshments, Reese and Jem drew away from one another raggedly.

"Do you want to stay for the next set?" Reese's voice was low, thick with passion.

"It has been a long night," Jem hedged, unwilling to vocalize her desires.

"It could be longer," Reese promised. Gulping, Jem followed blindly as Reese retrieved her shawl and then led them out the door.

Knowing that Della and Pete had remained at the dance only intensified their hurry to reach home. Lightning flashed through the slate sky, and only moments later the clouds opened up, dumping torrents of rain. As they huddled together the heat from their bodies warmed them more than the cool night should have allowed.

This time when the empty house loomed in the darkness, both were eager to see the welcoming structure. The wagon stopped, and despite the rain Jem waited until Reese crossed to her side. He lifted her, and she savored the sensuous journey as her body slid down the length of his. Not waiting until they were encased within the house's walls, Reese tipped her head back and devoured her mouth with his own. She welcomed the first thrust of his tongue, recognizing the slow curl of fire that traveled first from the pit of her stomach down to the weakness of her knees.

When his hand boldly cupped her breast, she gasped in pure pleasure, feeling an expected warmth shooting through her loins. Their rain-slickened bodies strained toward one another, and the water sluiced down their cheeks, wetting their lips.

Tugging her moist lips gently with his teeth, he felt her

sigh in pleasure. The rain beat down around them, drenching their clothes. He wondered if the heat from their bodies was causing a cloud of steam.

"Inside," he growled. "Now."

Obeying blindly, Jem walked with him to the door, but he stopped her. Sweeping her into his arms, he put his lips near her ear. "This time we're going to do it right."

Effortlessly he carried her through the doorway, up the staircase, and to their room. When he kicked open the door, Jem felt only overwhelming anticipation. As he put her down she swayed a moment, feeling the sodden garments that dragged at her limbs.

Della had left a fire burning in the fireplace. Although it had burned down, it still cast a glow over the room. Reese took a moment to throw a few more logs on the fire. A few sparks jumped as he turned back to her, matching the feelings he'd ignited within her.

Not sure what to expect, she allowed him to draw her close to the growing warmth of the fire. She was certain her shivering had nothing to do with the temperature in the room, however.

When Reese lowered her to the soft mattress, she closed her eyes a moment, unwilling to let him see the passion reflected there. When his lips met hers, they warmed her in a way she'd not thought possible. And when he drew away, she experienced a fleeting pang of disappointment. But his hands were tugging at her ruined slippers and cotton hose.

When she felt his hands at her back, she sighed in sheer pleasure as he unbuttoned the row of tiny buttons holding her dress together. Slipping the wet garment off, he tossed it aside and brought his body back to hers. Tasting the fresh scent of rain on his lips and face, she arched her back in delight when one thumb flickered over the wet fabric of her camisole. He found the aching nipple, and she was amazed at the sensations his fingers, combined with the wettened material, were arousing.

Surprising him, she grasped his clothes in a frenzied attempt to feel his naked flesh against hers. Allowing her to pull open his shirt, he reveled in the feel of her pushing the shirt off his shoulders and tugging it free of his denims. When those same long, slim fingers slid over his chest and traveled down his sides to rest on his hips, he felt his control slip.

Turning on his side abruptly, he stilled her protests with his lips while sliding his hand over her camisole once again. He heard her moan against him, and intensified his search. Impatiently he tugged at the ribbons fastening the undergarment, catching his breath as the remembered rosy peaks tumbled into view. Trailing his hand down the smooth line of honey-colored flesh, he allowed his fingers to caress the length between her breasts and the waistband of her pantalets. Hesitating only a moment, he hooked his fingers under the waistband and peeled her remaining garment away.

Once again her long, graceful legs took his breath away. Like a fine-limbed filly, she stretched beneath his touch and arched toward his hands.

When her fingers rested on the fastenings of his breeches, he strained toward her touch. Hesitantly she unbuttoned his denims, gasping as she encountered the evidence of his desire. Unwilling to wait, he slipped out of the rest of his clothes, joining her again.

The firelight flickered over the droplets of moisture that still clung to their bodies. Breathless with anticipation, Jem savored the feel of their bodies touching one another. His smooth flesh was finer than velvet as he draped one muscled leg between hers.

She swallowed as she felt the nudging of his knee contacting with her womanhood. When his fingers journeyed to the same destination, she instinctively moved closer.

Reese smoothed his other hand down her hips, feeling the strength of her lean body as well as the softness she offered to him. Leaning forward to graze her breast with his lips, he gloried in the blatant pleasure of her response. But this time he had to be sure.

"Jem." His voice was low, urgent.

Her eyes were clear, knowing. "Yes, Reese."

No more words were needed as he captured her lips again, probing her other sweet flesh until she writhed under his touch. Shifting, he poised himself over her, searching her eyes once more. The first thrust filled her, and wonder dominated her eyes. The hesitant response of her body increased with his thrusts. Her lean hips and long legs met each move, matched each stroke.

Feeling the fine film of perspiration breaking out on his skin, Reese luxuriated in the slickness of their bodies as they met one another.

Devouring her lips, Reese washed the recesses of her mouth, feeling the tiny tugs of her teeth as she nipped him gently. Inflamed, he increased his strokes, feeling the thunder that raged both outside their room and in his blood.

When an all-consuming shudder shook him, he felt Jem's answering response. Her breasts crushed into his chest, and her ragged breathing matched his own.

Drawing his head back, he was unprepared for the gentleness in her eyes, the tranquillity in her face. He reached out to smooth the damp hair from her forehead and traced a path to her lips, easing his thumb over their fullness. Her luminous eyes were the color of aged whiskey, framed by incredibly dark lashes. Gazing into their depths, he wondered how he could ever have thought they were merely brown.

Hungrily his eyes roved over her gleaming body once more. The golden locket between her breasts winked at him in the firelight. Washed by the glow of the fire, he met the question in those captivating eyes by covering her body with his own once more.

Chapter 20

The softness of the mattress enveloped their bodies as Jem stretched, surprised at the unexpected soreness in her limbs. As she gradually awakened, a smile spread across her face and she remembered the reason for her mild discomfort.

The early-morning sun filtered through the drapes, giving evidence that the storm had washed the air and left it fragrant and fresh.

She glanced across the bed at Reese's slumbering form, her expression soft as she thought of the previous evening. Leaning forward quietly, Jem retrieved her wrapper. She wanted to take advantage of this time to wash up before he awoke. Sliding gently from the bed, she walked to the alcove, pouring fresh water from the pitcher into the bowl.

Her quiet movements awakened Reese, who stared around in confusion for a moment. Hearing the normal sounds of Jem's preparations, he leaned back in satisfaction. Running a hand over the whiskers on his face, Reese decided he could use some washing up himself.

Turning back the quilt, he started to rise from the bed. What he saw stopped him. Staring at the sheets, he felt a mixture of surprise and guilt. The evidence of the virginity he was so sure Jem had given to Charles Sawyer mocked him. Why hadn't she told him? Because she assumed he knew, he thought in disgust. Glancing up, he stared in the direction of the alcove. The quiet sounds of water splashing and clothes rustling still filtered into the room. His mind reeled. Had he hurt her?

Shame filled him as he started to walk toward the alcove. But Jem emerged before he could approach her.

"You're awake." She smiled, refusing to give in to her initial feelings of awkwardness.

"Why didn't you tell me?"

Seeing no returning smile, Jem faltered for a moment. "Tell you what?"

She followed his eyes to the bed. Her face flushed with embarrassment. She hadn't thought about the bed linens.

He repeated the question. "Why didn't you tell me?"

"You mean . . ." She paused, realizing what he meant. "I just thought you knew."

"But what about . . ." He almost said Charles Sawyer. What about him? "Did I hurt you?"

An unexpected softness lit her features. "Everything was just as it should be, Reese."

Knowing she hadn't answered his question, he was still disturbed. Had he been wrong about her devotion to Charles Sawyer? If so, what made this woman tick?

"I can bring up some trays for breakfast while you shave," she offered.

"No need," he replied brusquely. "I'll grab something quick downstairs. Got to see to the herd."

Jem glanced away from the rumpled bed, her hopes dashed. "Of course."

Despondent, she moved toward the window. Early-morning rays warmed the day, outlining the hills that sloped toward the infinite range of mountains.

She kept her attention focused outside as she heard Reese gather his clothes, wondering if his attention of the past few days would disappear also. Had all that been a ruse to bring her to life in the bedroom? Inching her chin upward, she vowed not to show how this affected her.

Taking her time, Jem dressed in her usual baggy attire. She made her way slowly down the stairs and into the dining room. Expecting the room to be empty, she stopped at the entry, surprised to see Reese still seated at the table. He shoved back his chair and rose. "You'd better hurry. We need to get out to the herd."

Surprised, she merely stared at him. She had assumed he'd left much earlier, along with his solicitous attention.

He frowned as he appraised her features. "Unless you don't feel like going out today."

"No!" Her voice cracked on the word, and she swallowed before continuing. "I do plan to ride the herd."

"Good, but you'd better hurry. We let a good part of the day go by."

"All right," she replied in a daze, moving toward the sideboard.

As he left, Della wheeled in with a fresh plate of scrambled eggs.

"Della?"

As Della arranged the platter on the sideboard her back was to Jem as she answered. "Uh-hum."

"Do you understand men?"

Della spun her chair around quickly as though this was a question worthy of her full interest. "Why?"

"It's just that I can't seem to keep up from minute to minute. First Reese is angry because"—she looked up and amended her words—"of something I said. Then he's mad when I offer myself to him." Della's eyes widened in surprise, and Jem rushed on. "I know how it sounds. But things seemed to have gotten better." She paused, remembering the night before. "Much, much better. And now he seems angry because I didn't tell him I was a virgin."

Della's mouth succeeded in completely dropping open.

"Was I supposed to tell him?" Jem questioned earnestly.

Della's voice was slightly strangulated as she tried to answer. "Was there any reason for him to believe otherwise?"

Jem considered this, remembering how she'd called him by Charles's name. Had he thought they'd made love? She dodged Della's question with one of her own. "Would he have been nice just so that I would sleep with him?"

"You don't need a little information, you need a whole library." How had Jem grown to womanhood so ignorant of the opposite sex?

"You're probably right." Jem fiddled with her silverwear, not quite meeting Della's eyes. "Was Pete the first man you loved?"

An inkling of the problem between Jem and Reese surfaced. Della took care with her answer. "Loved? Yes, but he wasn't the first man I cared for or who courted me."

Jem pulled her chair closer to Della. "Did you have lots of suitors?"

Della remembered herself as a young girl with flying feet and midnight-colored hair. "I had my share."

"Then how did you know you loved Pete?"

"There was a specialness to him, a gentleness." She laughed. "And a strength."

Jem thought of Charles Sawyer and the special place he held in her heart. Unbidden, an image of Reese's strength as he took her, and his gentleness afterward, flashed in her mind. She swallowed in discomfort. "Did you ever have feelings for two men at once?"

Della answered honestly. "No, child, I didn't. I'm not saying love is crystal clear, but once I knew, there wasn't any place in my heart for another."

"Oh." Jem's voice was uncharacteristically small.

"Jem?"

"Yes?"

Della took Jem's hand in her own. "You didn't take the time to have a lot of suitors when you were younger."

"Be honest, Della. No one came to call."

"Either way, you didn't go through what a lot of women do. Knowing the attention of different men, understanding that despite their sweet words, we don't love them all."

"Don't beat about the bush, Della."

"Charles Sawyer may have been the first man to take notice of you, but that doesn't mean he's worthy of you."

"But Reese is?" Unjustified anger rose in Jem, and she snatched her hand back. "The foreman's not an appropriate choice for the owner's daughter, but a man who'd sell his soul for a pot of gold is?"

"Please don't take what I've said the wrong way, Jem. I'm only concerned for your welfare—"

"I know, Della. I've been a misfit all my life, and you think I lost my head because Charles paid attention to me. Have you ever considered he did it because he loved me, or is that too farfetched?" Jem rose and shoved her chair back. "You're right about one thing. Reese is open about what he wants—the money."

Della watched helplessly as Jem stormed from the room. For such a smart woman, she was acting impossibly dense.

"I was expecting more than this," the man complained, counting the bills in his hand.

"And I was expecting more than a bungled mess."

"Wasn't my fault she didn't ride out like she usually does. Hell, she'd been holed up in the house for a week. I was lucky she even saddled the horse."

"Some luck. Now she's onto us."

The first man scratched his whiskers on his face. "I don't think so. They're trying to keep her from finding out it wasn't an accident."

"How do you know that?"

"Heard Pete telling that cripple wife of his."

The second man digested this information. "Then it's even more important to keep her away from McIntire."

"Now, that might be pretty hard."

The other man's voice was hard. "Why is that?"

"Saw 'em last night outside the big house. The way they was kissing . . ." The first man chuckled obscenely.

The second man nearly broke the quirt he held in his gloved hand. "Find out what'll break that up and do it. Now. Otherwise we'll have to get rid of him, too."

"There's no need to get so heat up."

"Don't be a fool. I've waited far too long for this already. I won't have everything ruined now."

The first man responded to his companion's anger. "Sure. You can count on me."

"I'd better, or you'll end up like old man Whitaker."

Chapter 21

Jem stared over the rim of the cup, gulping down the water with distinctively unladylike gusto. The shouts of the men drowned out the most persistent of the women who were grouped around the table.

"You really shouldn't be working like the men," Abigail fussed at her side.

Staring up at the barn they were erecting, Jem bit back an honest reply. It seemed the other women were merely in the way. She'd rather be pounding in nails than standing around fixing plates of chicken and pouring punch.

"Really, Jem."

"Why in the world shouldn't I be helping?"

"It's not . . ." Abigail hesitated. "Well, not very lady-like."

Jem rolled her eyes. "That's never been a big concern of mine."

"I guess you know best." Abigail threw up her hands and turned back to the table as Jem wandered among the people, taking a breather. The large oak that shaded the area looked inviting. She slid to the ground and leaned against the rough bark, allowing the soft breeze to cool her gradually. Hearing approaching voices, she sighed. She had no patience for these people.

Relieved, she recognized Pete and Della's voices and started to rise when Della's words stopped her. "You've got to stay closer to Jem. All these people around, it could be any of them."

"I'm doing the best I can."

"I thought Reese was going to stick to her like tar," Della complained.

"He has been, but it's kind of rough when she's climbing all over the walls like a monkey. He's practically been her shadow the last two weeks."

"Pete, I still can't imagine anyone wanting her dead."

"This is probably how Jem felt when her father was killed," Pete mused.

Della's voice broke a bit. "We can't let the same thing happen to Jem."

"We won't." Pete's voice was soothing. "We'll find out who rigged her saddle. It's just a matter of time before the culprit trips himself up."

"As long as either you or Reese are around to make sure he doesn't succeed." Della's voice was filled with concern.

"We will be, don't worry. Now, are you hungry?"

"I'm supposed to be asking you that," Della chided.

Pete began to push her chair away, and only some of their words floated back. Jem's throat constricted with emotion. Fear had spread its wicked tentacles while Della's concern had touched her. Realizing the three of them had kept her ignorant of a murder attempt infuriated her almost as much as Reese's faked concern. No wonder he'd been so solicitous. She didn't doubt the reason behind his actions—if she died, there'd be no payoff. She wondered bitterly if his concern had led him straight to her bedroom.

Seeing that Della and Pete were out of earshot, she jumped up and went in search of Reese. Fortunately he was alone, working on a bent piece of the barn frame.

He looked up when he saw her. "Hey, you're pretty hard to keep track of."

She kept her voice low, but the venom in it was obvious. "It was your turn to keep up with me, wasn't it?"

His jaw dropped open.

She continued relentlessly. "Don't worry, you don't have to bother. I can take care of myself."

"But how did you—"

"I'm not as easily duped as you seem to think. Did it ever occur to you I could take better care of myself if I knew what was going on?"

"We wanted you to get better. It seemed like the right thing at the time."

"Don't presume to think for me again, Reese McIntire. And drop the fake concern right now. I don't need it." She stalked away, found her horse, and mounted quickly.

Reese threw down the piece of framing. Damn woman, didn't she realize the jeopardy she was putting herself in? He took a fleeting moment to explain what had happened to Pete and Della, assuring them he would go after Jem and that they should stay at the raising. Locating his own horse, Reese took off after her, but she remained ahead of him until they reached the ranch house.

The dust of her stallion's hooves filled the air as he dismounted and threw the reins over the hitching rail. Striding inside, he found her in her father's study, looking much as she had the first time he'd set eyes on her. Only now there was a difference, even if she refused to admit it.

"That was a damn fool thing to do," he stated bluntly.

Her voice dripped with sarcasm. "Your concern is so touching."

"You aren't going to run off alone again," he warned.

"I think you're forgetting something, McIntire. I'm the boss here and I'll give the orders."

He closed the distance between them, grabbing her shoulders when he reached her. "Do you want to prove that?"

She shrugged away, refusing to give in to the challenge in his eyes. "Must have been a real chore for you, sticking to my side all day and then having to climb into my bed."

Reese saw red, pulling her close enough to face him again. "Is that what it was for you? A chore, something you had to submit to?"

"Yes!" she bit out hatefully.

The lips that covered hers were relentless, devouring. She fought the invasion of his tongue, felt his arms close about her like steel bands, fitting their bodies together. Her mind screamed at her to resist the challenge, the attraction that clawed at her, as she tried to remember why she shouldn't be giving in to the passion, to him.

Her hands struggled against his chest for a few moments before sliding into the opening of his shirt. It was as though her touch sent off a lightning storm of gigantic proportions. Frenzied, they tore at one another's clothes.

Sinking together to the rug, their movements were in no way controlled. Jem didn't know or care how their clothes were removed as long as their bodies could fit together, as long as she could feel his naked length over hers.

This time there was no gentleness, no languid teasing. Poised over her, Reese barely paused before thrusting and filling her. The shock of his strength subsided, and Jem wrapped her legs around him, pulling him close, demanding every stroke.

The exertion of their efforts made their bodies slick, enticing. The fullness she felt always surprised her, ignited her. She arched toward him, greedily accepting each movement. When she shook with completion, she felt his answering shudder.

Spent, he drew away, searching her face. Not allowing her to speak, he rolled over and drew her close to his side. When she started to speak, he placed a finger over her lips. Cradling her head in his hands he compelled her to look him squarely in the eye. "Don't ever call our love-making a chore again."

Once again she tried to speak. He stopped her, not with a kiss but with his eyes. The gentle message conveyed itself to Jem, and she felt her anger drain away.

Now that their frenzy was spent, he allowed himself to roam over her body. The strength of her long limbs always amazed and aroused him. He slid a hand from her face, to travel the delectable journey down the hollows of her throat, to tease the plumpness of her breasts. His hand continued down her smooth flesh to rest on the curls between her legs. At his insistent touch, she opened up to him like a flower. Hesitant at first, then dewy with growing delight.

When she shuddered beneath his hands, he covered her lips with his, delighting in the sigh that echoed between them.

Watching the softness of her face, he was struck again by the same emotion that had plagued him since her fall. He truly cared for this woman. He no longer saw the brown wren who issued orders like an army general. He saw the determined woman who refused to lose her family home and who took under her wing every misfit who fell into her path. Her misplaced bluster was only a disguise for the endless cache of emotions she kept buried.

He reached a hand up to smooth back the golden hair framing her face while covering their bodies with the huge bearskin rug that lay upon the floor. Settling beside her beneath the warm covering, he also saw a woman of hidden passion and boundless pride. Bittersweet regret tore at him. How had she given her love to someone like Charles Sawyer? Purposefully he closed the pathways to his own heart. If she couldn't care for him, he was going to make sure that Charles Sawyer didn't hurt her again.

They lay together peacefully under the covering of the rug as the shadows outside the window lengthened. The hours passed, and as darkness descended a single shadow approached the window and stood out among the others. Minutes later the same shadow moved away and mounted the horse tied to the railing. The lone rider disappeared along with the sun setting over the mountains.

Chapter
22

The next month was a magical interlude. Despite Jem's insistence that she could take care of herself, Reese still continued to dog her every move by day, not allowing her to be more than a section away. By night they discovered wells of passion neither could have imagined.

Staring across the expanse of land at the branding, Jem frowned, realizing their main source of contention still existed. Both Boyd Harris and Grady Orton could ignite an argument simply by being on the same piece of ground.

Grady Orton spotted Jem and headed in her direction. "Miz Whi— McIntire."

"Everything all right, Grady?"

"Yes, ma'am." He looked back at his adversary. "Least what I can get done without interference."

She frowned. "What's the problem?"

"I ain't one to spread rumors, you know that. But I have trouble working with a man I can't trust."

This was exactly what Jem had feared would happen. With time clicking by till the contract had to be filled, she knew they had to put their fragmented herd back together. They couldn't afford to lose any beef or time because men fought with each other. "I would appreciate your trying, Grady."

"Oh, yes'm, I'll try." He twisted his hat in his hands. "If it gets too bad, I can leave so there's no trouble."

"But I don't want you to," she protested.

"Me neither, ma'am, but I wouldn't want to be the cause of trouble."

Jem stared in distaste at Boyd Harris. "I don't think you're the cause."

He shrugged. "I can always go to work for Cushman."

Her head snapped up sharply and her voice was low, almost trembling with suppressed anger. "Cushman?"

Grady looked uncomfortable as he answered. "He offered all the hands a raise to go work for him. Said the Bar-W's about to go under, and we could all get out before it does."

The fury she had tried to suppress surfaced again, but she managed to keep her voice under control. "Are you planning to accept his offer?"

"I don't want to, ma'am, unless you'd rather I would."

"No, I don't. You're a good man, and I need you here."

"That's all you have to say, ma'am." He glanced over at Boyd Harris. "For me, anyway."

Jem followed the direction of his eyes, her frown deepening as she watched Boyd Harris. With his hat flung off, his chestnut-colored hair shone in the sunshine while rivulets of sweat lined his face. It appeared as though he was working hard, but she knew appearances could be deceiving.

Riding the fence line, Jem searched for Pete. She found him close by with Reese, but as she pulled up, her burgeoning anger spilled over. They were pulling a stump, and Pete was straining as though he could lift the massive piece of wood by himself. Knowing the state of his health, Jem wanted to smash both of them. She'd believed that making Pete foreman would force him to take it easy. More jobs like this, and they'd be burying him.

Dismounting, she strode to Pete's side. "Pete, I need you."

Reese, his face covered in the perspiration from their efforts, looked at her as though she was crazy. "We're kind of busy here, Jem."

Her voice took on the authoritative tone Reese recognized as her boss-lady self. "I said I need Pete now."

Reese's reply was sarcastic. "I could pull the stump by myself."

"I guess you could. Come on, Pete."

Pete tried to protest. "But, Jem, we'll be finished in a—"

"I'll send one of the hands to help Reese." Jem turned to her horse, ignoring Reese's obvious anger.

"But—" Pete tried to protest again.

"You'd better listen to the boss lady," Reese bit out.

Jem hid her regret. She didn't want to anger Reese, but if Pete knew the reason for her treating him differently from the other hands, he'd never put up with it.

They rode back toward the far side of the section, and Pete studied Jem's expression. "What was so all-fired important?"

Jem pulled her horse up, easily controlling his pawing. "Has Boyd Harris been doing his share of the work?"

"You couldn't ask me that back there and let me get back to helping Reese?"

"You know how Reese feels about Boyd."

Pete rolled his eyes. "You two are something." He stared out at the men in the distance. "Yeah, Boyd's a good worker. Better than a lot of others I've seen."

"Why do you suppose it was so important for him to get on at the Bar-W?"

Pete pushed his hat back and looked at her as though she was crazy. "It was important for him to get on somewhere, Jem, anywhere. No one was hiring him."

"For good reason."

"Right now I'd better get back and help Reese." He started to pull his horse around.

"No, I'd rather you kept an eye on the men. Send one of the other hands to help Reese."

"Damn fool nonsense . . ." Pete started to mutter.

"I've got my reasons, Pete. Somebody put that spike

167

under my saddle, and I think you'd better keep an eye on the suspects."

"You mean Boyd? But what would he get out of having you hurt? He already knows he's got a job here."

"Maybe he's not working alone."

"But who—"

"Cushman won't rest till the Bar-W falls in with his plans. He probably thought killing Pa would scare me into voting his way, but none of the votes have gone his way yet."

Pete's voice was slow as he answered. "And you think Boyd's working for him?"

"He sure had some itch to get on here."

Pete pushed back his hat, scratching his head absently. "Word was nobody else would hire him."

Jem laughed mirthlessly. "Which certainly makes us smart."

Reese stalked into the house, slamming his Stetson on the hall tree. A day of recalling Jem's lady-of-the-manor voice had set him on a vicious edge. Watching her head back to the ranch house alone, he planned to confront her, having had his fill of her high-handed behavior. And, damn it, she wasn't supposed to take off alone.

Hearing voices, he headed toward the kitchen. But he paused as he heard Jem's voice clearly through the door.

"You should have seen him, Della. Pulling on that stump like a twenty-year-old."

"What am I going to do with him?" Della's voice was full of concern.

"I don't now, but we've got to stop him or the next time Doc Riley won't be able to dust him off and let him walk away."

"Jem, I've done everything I can think of to get him to slow down. He still thinks he can do everything he could twenty-five years ago." Della's voice broke. "I don't know what I'd do if anything ever happened to him."

"Nothing's going to happen to him." Jem's voice was strident, the reassurance sounding forced.

"You heard what Pete told Doc Riley when he said it was his heart. Refused to listen then, what's going to make him start now?"

Jem seemed to hesitate before replying, "I'll talk to Reese. He can make sure he doesn't give him any more jobs like today. I never told Reese about Pete's heart 'cause I didn't want to be talking about him behind his back. Hell, you know how Pete would feel about that."

"Do you think Reese will help us?"

There was no doubt in Jem's voice as she answered. "Of course he will." Her voice softened. "Don't worry, Della. I only told you so you could get Pete to bed early. We're supposed to go to another one of those damned association meetings. Tell Pete you need some rest while we're gone."

"I will, Jem, and thank you."

"Thank me by making him rest. And try not to look so gorgeous, or he'll decide you want him to get to bed early for other reasons."

Della laughed softly, and Reese eased away from the door, wondering what else in her nature Jem had kept hidden from him. Today had convinced him she'd only pretended to drop her determination to be in total control. Now he wasn't so sure. It seemed she adopted her bosslady demeanor when it suited her purposes, as though no route but her own should be taken. No twisting, winding paths, only a straight corridor.

The layers she kept hidden fascinated him more than he cared to admit. It was as though every day a new edge was honed, another facet gleamed.

His booted feet trod quietly up the carpeted stairs. His bargain with Jem was growing more complex each day, and it scared the hell out of him.

Chapter
23

Jem poured another cup of coffee, savoring its fresh aroma as the steam curled from the thick porcelain mug. Piles of freshly prepared eggs, steak, and buttermilk biscuits lay on the platters that covered the table. She chose a biscuit and reached for the honey while watching Reese enjoy a steak. Feeling satisfied from the previous night, she was enjoying this unusually quiet interlude.

Reese's companionship was growing more than acceptable, and she had come to anticipate their time together. His suggestions about the ranch were both well thought out and valuable, and she regretted that her father had not lived to meet him. The implication of her thought struck her as she raised startled eyes to view his relaxed face. Had her father lived, she would have never have had the opportunity to know Reese. He would have drifted through the town, unknown to her, and she would most likely be seated across from her father and Charles Sawyer.

A frown replaced her look of contemplation. James Whitaker would never have easily accepted her alliance with the foreman. Marriage to him would probably have meant she would have had to leave the Bar-W. Since her relationship with Charles had not developed that far, she'd never really envisioned all the consequences.

When Della entered with a fresh dish of eggs, Reese stopped eating and spoke to her, startling Jem out of her eye-opening thoughts. "Pete still around?"

Della's hands froze as she held the platter toward the table. Jem unobtrusively took the dish from her hand and placed it on the table.

"I believe so."

"Could you ask him to come in?" Reese took another biscuit. "Need to talk to him."

Della nodded, her eyes worried as she glanced at Jem before wheeling out. Reese turned his attention back to his breakfast, and Jem regretted not already having spoken to him. She should have told him last night. A warm blush reminded her that Pete hadn't even strayed into her thoughts.

"Reese, I need—"

The door to the kitchen swung open, and Pete entered.

"You lookin' for me, Reese?"

"Sit down and have some coffee." Pete obliged, pulling up a chair and pouring a cup. "We need to rethink who we've got assigned to the range."

Pete's forehead puckered, and he glanced at Jem. Not knowing what Reese had in mind, Jem looked genuinely surprised and remained silent while Pete questioned him. "What do you have in mind?"

"I've been thinkin' that we're not using the men we have the best way. I'd like you to scout the eastern range, find the best grasslands, and decide which part of the herd needs to be moved."

"What about the fence line? I'm not near finished."

Reese shrugged. "You got too much experience to waste your time doin' that. Assign Grady Orton and one of the other men to the fences."

"If that's what you think's best."

"Pete, I need you to be overseein' the work. I can't do it all alone."

Pete stiffened, his hand falling away from the coffee cup. "I never meant to slack off."

"That's just it—you and me been workin' hard, not smart. It's not slackin' off we got to worry about, it's

171

thinkin' it out, puttin' the right men in the right places. I'd like you to take Boyd with you, train him right."

Mollified, Pete reached for his coffee and took another sip before answering. "Guess I have learned a bit over the years."

"That's worth more on this ranch than ridin' fences and branding. We can train a greenhorn to do that stuff. I'm countin' on you, Pete. Between us, we can oversee everything, make sure it gets done."

Jem clutched her biscuit, tempted to pinch herself to see if she was dreaming. What a perfect solution—and Reese had thought of it on his own. Pete wouldn't be pulling stumps if he was busy overseeing the other men.

Staring across the table, she watched as Reese lifted his head and granted her a slow, knowing smile. If she didn't know better, she'd have believed he'd read her mind, known her dilemma, and solved it for her.

Pete drained his cup and replaced it on the table. Shoving back his chair, he rose. "I'd best go round up Boyd." He hesitated a moment, then his voice strengthened with unaccustomed self-consciousness. "And give the other hands their assignments."

Reese calmly cut another piece of steak as he answered. "Right. I'll be out on the range later, and you can fill me in."

As Pete departed Jem stared between them.

"Something wrong?" Reese asked innocently.

Distracted, she replied, "No, I can't seem to find the jelly."

He pointed to the cut-crystal dish directly in front of her.

Her brow furrowed as she stared at the sweet substance. "It's not chokecherry. I'll be right back."

She failed to see his amused smile as she bolted from the table and through the swinging door.

"Della, did you tell Reese?"

"Tell him what?"

"About Pete. You know. Yesterday, the stumps."

"Of course not. You said you'd talk to him."

The tips of Jem's ears flamed. Last night she'd forgotten everything but her name in Reese's arms.

"Is there a problem?" Della questioned anxiously.

Jem's voice was slow as she replied, "No, not at all. Everything's been taken care of."

Everything.

The sun overhead promised another day of Indian summer even though autumn was relentlessly marching forward. Because of the heat, bog holes had become a problem. Jem and Reese rode the range, knowing most of the spots, checking them for stranded cattle that had sought the muddy areas for water or an escape from swarming blowflies.

This was the part of ranch life Jem enjoyed most, riding under the far-reaching canopy of blue skies. She looked up, seeing an occasional puff of cloud drift by. Sheltered by the mountains, Jem knew no finer land existed. Seeing the peace on Reese's face, she wondered just how much he had grown to appreciate the land.

"Look there." His voice was enthusiastic as he pointed toward a stand of trees. Several elk stared at them before moving off majestically across the foothills. No fear painted their faces. It was all too clear who had claimed this land first. "Gets to me sometimes."

"The animals?" Jem questioned, watching the footing of her mount as they approached the next bog hole.

"No, it's this land. Never seen anything so changeable, but . . ." He paused, then ended his sentence with an embarrassed laugh.

"Unchanging?" she completed his thought.

Surprise lit his features. "Exactly."

"Most of us feel that way. I could never leave this place."

"Don't you ever have a hankering to see more, just take off when you want?" He thought of his own dreams to roam free.

173

Her face was thoughtful as she answered. "No, I never did." His face started to close again, but his expression brightened as she continued. "I can understand it happening, though. Not everybody in my family always felt the same about the land." She shrugged. "I guess it's something you either feel or you don't. You can't make someone want to stay."

He wondered if she referred to Charles Sawyer. Had she tried to make him stay? "And not everybody's cut out to wander."

"That's a fact," she agreed. She cocked her head and then glanced at Reese. They'd both heard the frantic cries of a stranded animal.

Reaching the bog hole, they confirmed their suspicions. Fortunately it was a young steer they could probably release successfully. The old cows were usually too weak to stand, making them almost impossible to rescue.

Coordinating their efforts, they roped the steer and then used their horses to pull it to safety. Reese turned away to loop his rope and return it to the saddle. Unfortunately the steer was full of anger at being trapped, and started to charge. In a flash Jem saw that Reese hadn't noticed; without thinking, she pushed him out of the way and then ran out of the animal's path herself. The only place for Reese to land was in the bog.

"What the hell?" his angry voice bellowed through the air. Seeing that the bull still headed in her direction, Jem dodged. When the steer continued running, she walked back to the bog, reaching a hand down to Reese.

A wicked grin lit his face, and Jem barely had time to register it before he yanked her into the muddy mess with him.

"Why'd you do that?"' she demanded angrily, looking in dismay at the muck covering her breeches.

"Same thing I asked myself."

"I was trying to save your stupid hide," she retorted, unsuccessfully trying to shake the stuff from her hands.

"Why, ma'am, I didn't know you cared."

Refusing to answer, she reached out for a handhold and let out a huge whoosh when Reese grabbed her from behind, making her sink even deeper in the mud.

Furious, she let fly with a handful of the mud. Horrified, she stared at his face, which she had plastered with a great glob of the gray stuff.

He didn't speak for long moments while the mud oozed down his cheek, dripping a path to his neck. In the distance she heard the caw of a bird as time seemed to stop. Her eyes widened; she expected the ire she knew he could easily uncork. For a split second she thought his reaction would be just that. "This means war," he returned. *He wouldn't!* The blob of mud running down her chin was apparent proof that he would.

Without thinking, she scooped up handfuls, flinging mud and dodging his volleys. Moving around the sticky stuff was next to impossible, but the both tried as they jockeyed for position.

Jem scored a direct hit between Reese's eyes and laughed in glee at his surprise. Her laughter turned to shrieks when he returned her fire, barely missing her open mouth. She recovered quickly and threw a huge glob, splattering his face again.

When Jem saw Reese advancing, she was too consumed with laughter to move. "Think you're pretty funny, huh?" The mock anger in Reese's voice only made her laugh harder.

"You should see your face," she said, gasping.

"What do you think you look like?"

She reached up a hand to her mud-encrusted hair. He took advantage of the movement to capture her arms. "Dangerous weapons," he muttered.

Staring at his dirty face, she dissolved into uncontrollable giggles with an abandon she hadn't indulged in since she was eight years old. His laughter joined hers and echoed over the plain. The steer that ran free snorted in disdain and trotted away.

"Is there a creek or a pond around here anywhere

close?" Reese asked when he'd regained his breath. Their clothes and bodies were covered with the goop and they were miles from the ranch.

"Not too far."

Reese pulled himself out and then turned and tugged her up with him. Jem led the way and they found the pond, surrounded by a grove of tall aspen. They pulled off their boots and socks on the bank, and Reese lost no time wading into the water, fully clothed. Following his example, Jem braced herself for the chill and walked in also. When they were near shoulder-deep in the water, Reese turned around, his mischievous smile returning as he dunked her thoroughly in the water.

Sputtering and spitting, she emerged and demanded, "Why'd you do that?"

"I couldn't stand seeing your dirty face anymore."

She took his grinning statement to heart. "You know, you're right." Using the element of surprise, she dove down and yanked his legs, upending him in the water. When his freshly washed face emerged, she smiled coyly. "Yes, absolutely. We both look much better clean."

The expression on his face was absolutely wicked, and Jem swam away, surprised as the pond deepened abruptly. Treading water, she moved backward until her feet touched bottom again, and waited for his next move.

He came closer, staring at her shirt intently. She glanced down. "What?"

"I just thought of something else that would make you look much better."

"Oh?"

He reached forward, unbuttoning her shirt as he spoke. "Reese, no, someone might see!"

Not stopping, he slid the shirt from her shoulders as he gazed around. "Who? There's no one out here for miles."

"I don't know, someone could ride by and . . ."

Her words trailed off as Reese clasped his hands around her breasts, bringing them to life. The cool water rushed over her nipples, creating an incredible sensation. He bent his head to suckle one breast. Fire shot through her, igniting every nerve in her body. He removed one hand to put it around her waist and pull her to shallower water. Her feet were able to reach the bottom now, but when he removed the rest of her clothing, she felt as though she were floating.

Urgency gripped her, and she tore at his shirt, ripping off the buttons in her haste. When his clothes, too, were gone, she transmitted her frantic desire to Reese.

Wrapping her legs around his torso, buoyed by the water, she craved the feel of his naked flesh against hers. His hands sought her out, found the tousled curls and the tight wetness waiting for him. The pad of his thumb circled against the soft spot radiating that moisture. She arched and cried out, her voice startling the birds that flitted in the trees. Reese parted the soft folds of flesh and plunged two fingers inside her, and Jem gyrated against them, unable to believe her abandon, unable to believe the sensations he created.

Her heated skin defied the cool water sluicing over them both. Wantonly her hands moved over the cords of his shoulders, digging in, demanding. Knowing she was ready, he thrust inside her, filling her completely. Her back was shoved against the back of the tiny pond, and she responded to each stroke with a ferocity she didn't know she possessed. His hands grasped her buttocks, each squeeze bringing even closer contact.

When the overpowering climax shook them, Jem found herself clutching Reese. Sated, they stared at each other. The animal hunger hadn't faded and was clearly outlined in both their faces.

No longer greedily desperate, he let go of her. They both let out a little whoosh as they parted, neither wishing the contact to end. He scooped her legs around and into his arms as he walked them up the bank. Her arms crept on their own to clasp together behind his neck near the dark curls.

He laid her down on the carpet of wild grass as gently

as if she were delicate porcelain. The kisses they hadn't had the patience to explore now tasted sweeter for the waiting. Their lips, cool from the water, warmed each other as they met. The fire had not been extinguished, but burned quietly as each explored as they never had before. His tongue questioned, hers answered. His hand moved down the velvet length of her cheek, easing over the hollows of her neck, resting on the pulse beat that sent out a staccato of desire.

Not yet replete, they stared at each other. Reese pushed the length of gold hair away from her brow, trying to search the secrets of her soul as he did so. Despite his insistence not to, he felt his heart tug, squeezing the fragile walls that had been hurt so badly before. When his lips gently touched hers, the questions only grew more difficult.

Closing his eyes to the emotions he saw in Jem's gaze, he knew with a certainty he could no longer close his heart.

Chapter 24

As the next month passed, the memory of Jem's fall from her horse faded. No more attempts on her life had been made, and the danger seemed to have passed. She rode the land freely, but was always glad to have Reese at her side. She showed him parts of the Bar-W that took his breath away—a hidden waterfall, a point that looked out over hundreds of miles in every direction, and a field blanketed with waist-high grass and carpeted with untouched flowers that grew as wild as the rugged mountains surrounding them. The trees on the hillsides had turned to vivid gold, burnt umber, and startling orange, providing a backdrop to the magnificent evergreens.

Reese's interest in the ranch bordered on the proprietary. While his dream of the freighting company still intrigued him, he spent long hours drawing up plans for the Bar-W that extended far beyond the year he'd promised to stay. In quiet moments he admitted that the land drew him like nothing else ever had. He wanted to discover its secrets, as he did Jem's. Like a kaleidoscope that never failed to produce a new effect, the land beckoned to him, revealing new facets, new fascinations.

During his solitary time, he tried not to dwell too much on Jem. He'd discreetly sent some letters, trying to find out the whereabouts of Charles Sawyer, but so far had come up empty. Despite the brevity of their association in the war, Reese was certain Charles could not have changed into the white knight Jem believed him to be. He'd been unscrupulous, almost cold-blooded in his dealings, willing to sell out his comrades for a pittance.

Treating Charles like the better-known outlaws of the time, Reese had given him wide berth, not wanting to end up with a knife in his gut or a bullet in his back. Reese remembered Charles's departure from the army. Even though he'd only known the man a few weeks, he wasn't shocked when Sheridan had booted him out of their outfit, suspecting his traitorous activities. Sawyer had been careful to cover his tracks, but Sheridan, not willing to tolerate his cowardly, underhanded ways, had sent him packing.

Reese intended to make sure Sawyer didn't turn up to undo all the good they'd accomplished on the Bar-W. A possessive attitude seized him whenever he thought of the man. Reese didn't want Charles to control the Bar-W or, more important, Jem. Beyond that, he refused to dwell on why he cared so much about her future.

Glancing at Jem's set face, he knew he still hadn't convinced her these association meetings were a good thing. She'd come only because she'd wanted to maintain the delicate balance of peace. The meeting was winding to an end, and so far the only surprise of the evening was Cushman's absence.

Jem tapped her foot impatiently, eager to leave the confines of the room. She almost regretted Cushman's absence. Like a snake who could slither through the knee-high grass and bite without warning, Cushman was less venomous when out in the open. It would be highly satisfying to chop him to bits like a rattler with a fine-edged hoe.

When Reese's knee nudged hers, she felt the familiar thrill of his touch and harrumphed to make him stop. He complied, instead picking up her hand, edging his thumb up the length of her arm from her bare wrist to her elbow. The swirling motions reminded her of more intimate things, and she felt her cheeks flame.

Daring a glance at Reese, she saw that he'd read her

mind. Trying to hide her transparent reactions, she stared straight ahead as Reese pressed the long length of his leg against hers, rotating it ever so slightly. The impression he left on her leg burned even as she jerked away. She tried to sit up straighter and discovered that if she perched any more forward on the chair, she would fall off.

Glaring at him in her most intimidating manner, she wasn't surprised when he answered her with a long, lazy grin that left little doubt as to the direction of his thoughts. She pursed her lips sternly, and his eyes zeroed in on them while he quirked his eyebrows. Then his eyes lowered, settling on the gold of her locket twinkling between her breasts. She didn't have to look to know his gaze had aroused her breasts. Her nipples ached, and the heat intensified between her thighs.

Completely immersed in her own thoughts, she didn't see fellow rancher Ralph Drummond slip down the aisle, and was startled when he stopped at Reese's side and whispered quietly to him.

Reese leaned over toward Jem. "Be right back."

Before she could ask any questions, he disappeared. Refusing to sit still any longer than she had to in the stuffy room, aching with untold desires, Jem waited only a moment before she followed Reese.

His tall form made a distinctive silhouette as he crossed the street toward the saloon. Intrigued, she started to follow him. So, these meetings were so important he could abandon them to go to the saloon, she thought huffily. Actually she could scarcely believe he'd light a match under her and then desert the kindling when it caught fire.

As she left she encountered Cushman entering, a scowl covering his face. He held a crumpled note in his hand. "You responsible for this, missy?"

"What are you talking about?"

"Sending me on a wild-goose chase so I'd miss the meeting. Don't play innocent, missy. It's just the sort of trick you'd pull." The men sitting at the back of the room had turned around and were listening avidly.

181

"And you called my father crazy."

"That what you trying to do? Make me think I'm crazy? Well, it won't work."

Refusing to argue with him further, she drew to the side, pulled past him and out into the fresh air.

Striding across the street, she paused at the low-slung doors of the saloon, her eyes riveting on the two brawling figures Reese was trying to separate. Boyd Harris and Grady Orton barely let a foot of space between them as they threw punches designed to kill. The sickening sound of hardened fists landing on flesh filled the air. Even the shouts of the men who stood alongside yelling encouragement couldn't drown out the horrible thud of bruising blows.

Sickened, Jem watched as Reese pulled them apart momentarily. Within seconds Boyd was back at Grady's throat, more vicious than before. It was true—Boyd Harris was the disgusting animal she'd feared he was. Fighting for all he was worth, he'd bloodied Grady's nose and split his lip. She wasn't sure, but it looked as though he'd knocked a few teeth loose.

Ralph Drummond grabbed Grady at the same time Reese captured Boyd's arms. Together they were able to wrest the men apart. Panting, sweat and blood coursing down their faces, the two glared at each other. Their hate was a tangible force in the air.

"I don't know what this is all about, but if it happens again, you'll both be fired," Reese declared, panting a bit from the exertion of separating the combatants. "The men of the Bar-W have to be on the same side all of the time. You don't have to like each other, but I'll be damned if you'll fight each other. When you're at each other's throats, you're not watching out for the best interests of the ranch."

Boyd and Grady stared at one another as though itching to get back in the fray, but Reese's words kept them in check, barely. Jem took umbrage at those same words. She didn't want Grady fired. As far as she was concerned,

Boyd had shown his true colors and should be shipped out immediately.

Jem pushed open the doors of the saloon and approached the odd trio. All heads swung her way. A lady never entered the saloon, not even one dressed in pants as Jem was.

Reese stepped away from Boyd and Grady, gripping Jem's arm. "What are you doing here?"

"The same thing you are. And I don't agree with what you told them."

Reese dragged her away from the interested patrons, who were taking in every word. "Not here, Jem. Go back to the meeting and wait for me there."

Not used to being dismissed, Jem dug in her heels. "No. My place is here. These are my men."

His voice was low, his face butted against hers. "No. They're mine. That happened when you married me, remember?"

"In name only," she hissed.

The fire in his eyes made her pause. "Not quite, madam." He turned back to the men. "Harris, Orton, get back to the Bar-W. Now." Both men heard the anger in his voice and stooped to pick up their hats. Brushing them off, they headed out the doors. Reese watched until they separated in the street and headed for their horses. Then he pulled her out the door. He didn't slow down until he reached the next building, out of earshot of anyone who might still be around.

"What was that all about?" he demanded.

"I don't want Grady Orton fired."

"Because he can lead you to Charles Sawyer?"

Her head snapped up, surprise filling her face. "Charles?" she questioned weakly.

"Don't take me for a fool, Jem. Why else would you want Orton around? He's worthless as tits on a bull."

She searched for a reasonable answer, but her mind was blank except for the truth.

"Can't think of an answer?" His laugh was bitter.

"That's no surprise. But don't make the mistake again of trying to turn me into Mr. Whitaker."

"Reese, I—"

"Save the explanation. You're chasing enough ghosts to fill a cemetery."

"You don't understand about Charles."

"I understand everything I want to. Now let's go home."

Jem followed without argument, her head sunk in dejection. Awash with unwanted feelings, she didn't notice the shadow that slipped from the back of the alley and into the concealing darkness.

Climbing into the wagon in silence, she and Reese both stared ahead as he snapped the reins and headed toward the ranch. Their uncomfortable silence lengthened as the wagon jutted over the holes in the road, bouncing Jem and Reese from side to side. They were almost home when Jem tried to make amends.

She cleared her throat and spoke hesitantly. "I'm sorry about saying what I did in front of the others. I'm not used to worrying about somebody else's feelings. It's just that I've been in charge of the Bar-W for quite a while." She shrugged as she stared into the cold night. "Well, I'm not used to answering to anyone."

Reese slowed the wagon down to a walk. The silence stretched out again before he replied. "You're a different sort of woman, and I keep forgetting that." She grimaced at his choice of words, and he continued. "Not different bad, just different. Guess I'm not used to that, either."

She nodded in the darkness, glad they'd settled into a somewhat easy truce, when the wagon lurched abruptly. She thought fleetingly that they'd hit a hole the size of Texas when the seat started to crack loudly, splintering as it released from the bows. Feeling her footing disappear beneath her, she realized with horror that the wagon was splitting apart.

The horses, panicked, tried to run from the debris falling on them. Reese held on to the reins, the muscles in his arms bulging beneath his shirt as he attempted to keep the team steady, but they were out of control. Grim lines of determination etched themselves in his face as he wrestled with the reins and the weight of the foundering wagon. Despite his efforts, the vehicle ran off the road, and the wagon split at the bed and fell sideways, plunging its passengers into the outlying field.

Stunned, Jem lay where she was flung when they left the road. She didn't feel any immediate pain but lay still, taking stock. Hearing a movement from the wagon, she raised her head and saw Reese emerge, crawling over to her.

"Jem." He opened her coat and ran his hands over her arms and legs, and although she didn't think anything was broken, she let him feel at will, enjoying his touch. "Can you sit up?"

"I think so." She tried, and her body cooperated nicely. "Just knocked the breath out of me."

"Me too. Damn good thing we weren't going faster."

Jem gulped. What if she hadn't spoken? They'd have been clipping along at a pace fast enough to kill them. A second thought struck with equal clarity. If she hadn't started such a ruckus back at the saloon, they wouldn't have been rushing home at such a fast rate in the first place.

"I'll see to the horses," Reese said as he rose. She heard his calming voice and the stamping, anxious reactions of the horses.

Getting to her feet, Jem walked closer to the wreckage. The wagon looked almost indecent, split like a chicken to be roasted on a spit. Bending close to the area that had given way, Jem ran her hand lightly over the splintered wood. She paused as she continued her examination. Next to the bows the wood was not fractured—it had separated smoothly, as though it had been cut.

Unable to believe what she'd felt, Jem pulled at the seat so that she could see how the damage was done. Her stomach turned as she saw the evidence. The distinctive grain of newly sawed wood stared back at her. She reached out

185

to touch the cross-cut pattern. It had only been partially sawed through. The bouncing of the wagon in the jutted road had completed the job. Sickened, she wondered who could have done such a thing. The possibilities sifted through her mind. Boyd Harris had been in town, obviously very angry.

Her hand stilled over the ambushed wagon. Cushman! As far as she knew, he hadn't missed a single meeting since he'd established the association. Where had he been tonight? It seemed far too coincidental that he'd been absent the same night only to come up with a phony excuse about a note.

Reese was returning with the horses, still speaking to the agitated animals in a soothing voice.

"I want you to see this." Jem beckoned to him.

He made the same examination Jem had. Angry now, he raised his eyes to hers. "Obviously this was no accident, either."

Either. She hadn't connected this sabotage to her fall. But he was right. Both incidents had been attempts to kill her.

Her voice was blunt. "I think it was Cushman."

Reese pushed his hat back on his head. "How'd you come up with that?"

She recounted the thoughts that brought her to that conclusion.

"Just because Cushman wasn't at the meeting doesn't mean he did it."

"No, but don't you think it's funny that this is the first meeting he's ever missed?"

"Yeah," he admitted. "But it doesn't prove anything. Why would he want you dead?"

"The same reason he wanted to be rid of my father. He needs all the big spreads to join together on the association vote and he knows I'll never change my mind. Besides, if he's rid of me, the cattle will run loose, and the land will be his to claim."

Reese shook his head in denial. "Everybody would

know he was guilty if you were killed and he started taking over your land."

"Not if it looked like an accident," she reminded him grimly. He stared silently at the wreckage as she paced restlessly.

"Your mistake is in assuming Cushman is the only suspect."

"Well, Boyd Harris was in town, too."

His head snapped back. "When are you going to let the man alone? He hasn't done a thing wrong since he started at the Bar-W."

"Could be he's working for Cushman." The thought had just popped into her mind, but it made sense. He could easily have been planted by the powerful rancher, a traitor in her midst.

"If we're throwing wild accusations around, what about Grady Orton?"

Her stance became defensive. "What about him?"

"Just because he was Sawyer's lackey doesn't make him an angel."

She deliberately ignored his reference to Charles Sawyer. "So you're telling me not one but three people want me dead?"

He shook his head and rolled his eyes heavenward. "You've got a hell of a way of looking at things."

She stared at the wreckage that could easily have been their coffin. "I'd say I have good reason."

Chapter 25

The lamplight was dim, the covers turned down on the bed. Della sat on the bench in front of the mirror, brushing her long, black hair while Pete looked out the window. The quiet from the empty ranch stared back at him. Jem and Reese had left again for the night, despite the danger Pete sensed since their wagon had been sabotaged two weeks ago.

"Jem told me they're going to the shoot and quilting tomorrow," Della murmured as she pulled the brush through her hair. "I thought you were going to try and talk them into staying close to the ranch."

"Did a lot of good tonight," Pete replied bitterly, knowing they'd taken off to another association meeting determined to find out who was behind their "accidents."

"I know how stubborn Jem is, but what about Reese?"

"I tried to tell him." Pete fiddled with the drape at the window, then dropped it as he stared into the darkness. "Almost every day since the wagon was cut apart. Reese won't believe me or doesn't want to." Pete turned away from the window, the worry on his face evident in the creases that lined his mouth. "Thing is, Reese never owned anything worth killing over. He's sure no one's after him, only Jem." He paused. "He can't get it through his head that he's legally part owner of the Bar-W now." Pete shook his head. "You should have seen that wagon. It's a wonder they weren't killed."

"You're really worried about him, aren't you?"

"Him and Jem are too stubborn to worry about themselves."

Della turned toward him. "Sounds like you've grown kind of fond of him."

"He's a good man, Della. Most of the time Jem pert near shoves him up to the edge of a cliff, but he still hangs on."

"Did you talk to her?" Della questioned.

Pete shrugged. "For what it's worth. She was so busy grilling Grady Orton she didn't pay me any mind."

"Again?" Della's worry transmitted itself to Pete.

"Every chance she gets. 'Course he told her he thought Cushman was behind both accidents." He walked closer, pausing as he stood behind her.

Della's hand stilled. Pete took the brush and drew it through the long, glistening strands. Her voice was disturbed. "As though Grady would know anything about Cushman. The only reason Jem believes him is because she thinks he can lead her to Charles Sawyer. When is she going to come to her senses about him?"

"Not anytime soon, it looks like."

"Reese and Jem are both pretty thickheaded," Della stated, but there was no satisfaction in her words.

"Yep. Whoever's behind this had a wide-open shot at them because of it."

Della reached her hand back to touch Pete's. "But who would want them dead?"

Pete's eyes met hers in the mirror above the vanity, his voice grim. "Somebody who can walk in here and take over the Bar-W. Men will kill for a lot less."

Cushman cornered Michael Fairchild as they lined up the next shot. "You in on the vote, Fairchild?"

Not taking his eye away from the sight, Michael cocked the rifle, found his target, and pulled the trigger. Lowering the gun, he replied, "Just like I've always been."

"Don't be a fool. Even the smallest ranchers see there's no other way to keep the range intact."

"There's always a better way than to terrorize families and drive them out of their homes," Michael replied.

"You're as crazy as that Whitaker woman," Cushman said in disgust.

"McIntire," Michael corrected.

"I didn't think even you believed that horseshit. He's no more married to her than I am."

Michael smiled knowingly, the recipient of Abigail's confidences. "I wouldn't count on that."

"There's a meeting next week. We're either going to stick together, or there's going to be trouble."

Michael leveled his gaze. "Then I guess you're going to have trouble."

Cushman left abruptly, snorting in disgust as he walked toward the house where the women sewed on their quilts. Swallowing his frown, Michael turned back to his sport, refusing to give credence to the man's notions.

Inside, Jem tried to poke a resisting needle through the material, but it stubbornly refused to cooperate. She glanced at the other ladies' stitches. They all lay neat and even. Dismally she stared at her own crooked, oversized ones that resembled chicken scratch. She glanced at Abigail, who sat next to her, chatting easily as she stitched.

Frankly Jem couldn't see what the appeal was. This was about as exciting as coddling eggs. But the other women were animated as they worked on the quilt, gossiping about their spouses and children. One more story about colic and she'd start to howl herself.

Hearing the men coming in, she sighed in relief. At least they talked about things she could relate to—the condition of the ranges, a new breed of cattle. Reese walked to her side, staring over her shoulder at her efforts. Embarrassed, she smiled weakly. "I'm not very good at this sort of thing."

He leaned even closer so that his words reached only

her ears. "That's all right. You have other talents that more than make up for it."

Cheeks flaming, she tried to give him a look of stern reproach. Instead her expression emerged as mostly conspiratorial.

"Are you two going to behave?" Abigail admonished with mock severity. "Or do I have to rap your knuckles?"

"Probably." Reese's grin was wicked.

Abigail pretended concentration in the stitches she was taking. "I hear there's punch in the kitchen."

Needing no further encouragement, Jem and Reese left the circle of chatty women. Like children escaping grownups at Sunday dinner, they darted into the kitchen, laughing as the door swung shut behind them.

"Oh, look at these," Jem exclaimed, eyeing a big plate of rich, heavily frosted cookies. Reese looked doubtful, and she picked one up, playfully waving it near his mouth. "Just one little taste."

"I don't know. . . ." he said. "They look awful gooey—" Jem took advantage of his open mouth to slip the cookie between his lips.

Although he chewed and swallowed the cookie, the glimmer in his eye promised revenge. He scanned the room and found just the right thing. Following his gaze, she spotted the custard-filled ladyfingers at the same time. Backing up, she waved her hands in front of her. "No, I was just playing around." He kept advancing. "Reese!"

He plucked a ladyfinger from the plate and turned toward her. Jem kept backing up until she reached the solid bulk of the wall. Facing him, she clamped her lips shut.

"Playing dirty, huh?" he quizzed.

Refusing to answer, she merely stared at him, challenge written in her changeable brown eyes. Before she could realize his intent, he dove for her ribs, tickling her mercilessly.

"Don't—" she started to squeal, but the gooey custard confection obliterated the rest of her words. The custard dribbled over her lips and down her chin.

"That is messy," he sympathized. Unable to answer, she merely glared as she was forced to chew the dessert and swallow it. When she was through, he leaned closer. "Let me help." His tongue reached out lazily to lap the custard from her chin. Her body stilled as his movements extended to her lips, licking the sweet dessert clean. His voice was low as he spoke. "See, I told you you have hidden talents."

The heat that blazed within her had nothing to do with the warm stove in the corner of the room. Her voice was husky in return. "I do?"

He pulled her body close, feeling her breasts rub against his chest, the long length of her legs pressed against his own. He nudged a knee between them, bringing her even closer. "Absolutely."

She shuddered, wishing they were home in the privacy of their own bedroom. The sensations he was causing with his leg made her want to fling aside any conventions and feel him inside her. When she pulled back, her thoughts were written clearly on her face.

Reese felt the same heat and answered her with a deep kiss, his tongue thrusting sensuously, convincing her of his intent.

Neither heard the door open, only Abigail's embarrassed apology. "I'm sorry, I didn't think . . ." She paused, flustered while Jem and Reese sprang apart.

Reese recovered first, hoping the straining bulge in his denims wasn't visible. "Just stealing a kiss in the kitchen."

"I was only coming in to get the refreshments started," Abigail explained weakly, obviously wishing she hadn't disturbed them.

"I know I'm hungry," Reese replied, watching Jem blush at his words. He picked up one of the gooey cookies she had shoved in his mouth. "I'll leave you two to that." He put the cookie in his mouth and bit off a small piece as Jem watched it slide between his lips, fascinated. "These are better than I thought they'd be." He winked at Jem as he left.

The door swung shut behind him, and Abigail turned to Jem. "I am sorry, I didn't even think."

"It's all right. We just got kind of carried away...." Jem's voice trailed off.

Abigail couldn't keep the smile from her face. "Apparently things are much better now."

Jem stared intently at a plate of very plain butter cookies, as though they were highly intriguing. "Oh, well, yes."

Abigail laughed. "Is that all you can say? The last couple I saw who was that enamored at a social was Pete and Della."

"Pete and Della?" Jem couldn't keep the amazement from her voice.

"I was about eighteen," Abigail reminisced. "It was at the July Fourth picnic. Everyone else had gone on to the dance. I went back to get my basket and saw them. They were so wrapped up in each other they never even noticed me." Abigail gave a small laugh, which turned into a sigh. "I'd never seen anyone so much in love." Remembering Jem, she shook her head. "Until now, perhaps."

"What?"

"You and Reese. It's just as obvious."

Jem swallowed in confusion. What she and Reese shared was a passion she'd learned to acknowledge and a grudging amount of respect, but love? Love was the chaste, longing adoration on Charles's face as he treated her like a delicate rose. He'd made her feel pretty and soft. Hardly the same feelings Reese inspired. No, her thoughts toward Reese generally led them straight to the bedroom. She was sure it wasn't the same thing.

Abigail stared at the locket that lay on the outside of Jem's dress. "It looks like two hearts truly are one."

Jem reached blindly for the locket, remembering Abigail's sentiment on her wedding day. The rush of emotions stunned her.

But Abigail had turned away, retrieving two platters of cookies. "Shall we?"

Automatically following Abigail's lead, Jem carried refreshments into the other room, helping to arrange the table. The rest of the evening passed in the same blur. The quilting continued, a harmonica and fiddle emerged, and they danced, but it was all lost on Jem.

When she and Reese finally climbed in the wagon to return home, Jem was unusually quiet, thoughtful.

The sky was lit by a carpet of stars and the deep yellow of the half-moon. For some time only the clip-clop of the horses' hooves stood out among the quiet song of the crickets and the cry of an occasional hoot owl. The familiar night sounds were soothing, almost lulling. When Reese's voice broke the silence, it wasn't startling, only another chord in the night symphony.

"You haven't been this quiet in all the time I've known you." He glanced aside at her, expecting a responding smile. Instead the furrow between her brows deepened.

"What do you think of Pete and Della?"

Her question surprised him, but he thought for a moment before answering. "Pete's probably the straightest guy I know—fair, honest, loyal. And Della's"—he paused, smiling—"Della."

"That's not what I mean. Do you think they're really in love?"

Reese replied without hesitation. "Of course. A man doesn't stand by a woman who can't walk if he doesn't love her." He thought of the tender embraces he'd accidentally seen, all of their exchanges that demonstrated an abiding love. "That's not all, it's just . . ." The explanation eluded him as he tried to describe the type of relationship he'd never experienced, but recognized as very special.

Jem's concentration seemed to deepen, the expression on her face growing more thoughtful. "Abigail said something strange tonight."

"Oh?" He glanced at the horses then back at Jem.

"She said we reminded her of Pete and Della."

Words failed him. There were few people in the world he allowed himself to grow fond of. Pete and Della were the first ones in a long time who had broken the barriers he automatically erected. Pete had offered nonjudgmental friendship, and Reese had accepted it.

Abigail, in her own way, was another. He'd seen how she had befriended Jem, and her caring touched him. He was stunned to think Abigail likened his relationship with Jem to that of Pete and Della's. While they no longer scrapped at every available opportunity, they hardly had the same kind of love he saw between Pete and Della.

Often he'd observed them, their gazes connected, their emotions open, loving. Not exactly comparable to his and Jem's uneasy truce. The only time they agreed on anything was when their bodies took over and left their minds behind.

He glanced over at Jem's face, seeing the same thoughtful expression lingering there. If anything, he'd grown protective, determined to keep Charles Sawyer from hurting her. He shook his head. No, it wasn't the same thing. Her heart belonged to another, and he wasn't going to foolishly allow himself to care, only to lose yet another loved one. The tentacles that gripped his heart told another story, but he closed himself to the haunting thought. A love like Pete and Della's? It was something he would never even dare hope to have.

Chapter 26

Pounding hooves and great swirls of dirt filled the cold air. Bent low over their horses, the men rode with intensity, their yells and whistles punctuating the dirty, noisy confusion. The wall of the box canyon loomed ahead, inviting the wild horses to its barriers.

Snorting, long graceful necks arched, white froth escaping from their mouths, the horses ran, their sides heaving as they tried to escape their captors. The massive stallion that led the herd valiantly tried to elude the cowhands, but the loyal mares dogged his every move, making a getaway impossible.

As the herd burst forward several cowhands rode ahead to unleash the gate they'd erected at the narrow point of the canyon.

Reese and Jem rode the rear, watching for trouble. If a man went down amid the flying hooves, he had little chance of survival. But as they neared the canyon entrance all went smoothly. The gates were flung open, and after the horses had charged through, the barriers were fastened shut, securing the beasts.

Shading their faces from the wind, Jem and Reese pulled up on their horses, watching the operation. Reese's eyes were filled with longing. Puzzled, she prodded him. "Reese?"

Not moving his gaze from the trapped horses, he spoke. "I know we have to round 'em up for the contract, but God, I hate to see them cooped up like that."

"You knew that was the plan."

He didn't argue. "It's just that they were so free. Only thing that stallion had to worry about before today was where to take his harem next. Had the whole world to choose from."

Just like Reese had, Jem thought soberly. Did he miss his own freedom as badly? Ever since they'd bought Wisner's bull, she'd realized she had unmanned him by purchasing his name. But his freedom? She'd never given it a thought.

"Maybe the stallion will like settling down, knowing he's got a warm place to sleep and fresh oats to eat."

Reese shook his head. "That won't make up for what he has to give up to get them."

Swallowing unexpectedly, Jem let her gaze travel over Reese's face. Was the same true of him? Could he never settle down and be happy? Would the wanderlust in his soul forever entrap him? He'd confided to her that this was the longest he'd ever stayed in one place. She'd been shocked. Having been born and raised on the Bar-W, she didn't understand the desire to roam free, to never be content to stay in one place for long. To her, the length and breadth of the Bar-W were all she had ever needed. The love of the land had been as much a part of her as the brown eyes that glowed as she studied Reese's face.

"Pete's taken right well to being foreman," Reese observed. She agreed, watching him handle the men, wondering for the thousandth time why she'd been blinded to this perfect solution.

But as she was completing the thought, her smile turned into a distinctive frown as she watched Boyd Harris. He leaped to the gate, shoving aside one of the other men standing there.

The man fell to the ground, and Jem opened her mouth to remark on his rudeness, when the distinctive clang of the gate being fastened rang through the air.

Straining forward, she could see that Boyd had noticed the loose fastening that no one else had. If the stallion had charged the gate, better than a dozen men could have been hurt or killed in the ensuing stampede.

Why had he taken such a chance?

She and Reese rode toward the now secured gate.

"Fast thinking, Boyd." Reese's praise was unreserved.

"You put yourself right in the stallion's way," Jem said, more as a question than a compliment.

"Somebody had to, ma'am."

"Why you?" she asked bluntly.

Boyd ran his hand down the well-muscled length of one leg. "Maybe 'cause I got less to lose."

Jem's expression alone continued to challenge him.

He started to turn away, then paused, meeting her gaze. "It's not like a lot of people would miss me, ma'am."

Jem stared at his retreating back, still wondering at the enigma Boyd had proved to be.

"Yep, most everybody's working out," Reese remarked, unable to keep the smugness from his voice as he referred to Boyd.

She ignored his remark, mentally counting the horses they'd captured today. "We're way short of what we need for the army contract."

"I think we ought to break this bunch before we corral any more. It'll be hard on the men to deal with more than this many at a time."

In the past her father had done most all of the rounding up at one time before going to the breaking. She looked into the blustery wind. They'd also gotten the job done much earlier in the year. But then her father had had more hands to complete the job. Few men had been willing to risk associating with a blacklisted ranch. The better hands from her father's day had all left for jobs far from the dark cloud that hovered over their ranch. Their crew was lean, barely sufficient. "I guess we could try it that way," she said reluctantly.

"You did it different before, I take it."

"We can always try it a new way."

"Don't want to go to war on this one?" he parried.

"No, but since I'm going to bust my tail out there with the rest of the guys, I hope you're right." She was watching the men corral the horses and didn't see the mounting disbelief and anger on Reese's face.

"You're going to be doing *what*?"

"I always ride. My father didn't like it too much, but he realized after a while I wasn't giving up." Her grin grew cocky. "Then he saw how good I was and didn't want to talk me out of it."

"There's no need for you to be part of busting the broncs." Reese's tone was no-nonsense, devoid of any humor.

The smile drained from Jem's face. "But it's something I enjoy."

"Not while you're my wife," Reese declared.

The red cloud obscuring her vision wasn't coming from any abnormal weather formation. "If you think you can tell me what to do, mister, you're sadly mistaken."

"You've almost been killed twice. Anybody could get to the unbroke broncs before you do. A sharp spike under one of those saddles, and you'll be dead before anybody can blink."

"Why don't I believe you're concerned only about my welfare?" Jem's eyes narrowed. "Or are you afraid that people will say your wife can outride you?"

"Why can't you just act like a normal woman for once? Do you think Abigail Fairchild would be out riding the broncs with the men? Hell, you've been wearing those pants for so long you've forgotten what's supposed to be under them!"

Huge pools of deep amber shimmered at him beneath her long lashes. Her gaze conveyed disbelief, hurt, and worst of all betrayal. She whirled her horse about before Reese could speak.

Wishing he could retract the words, knowing he couldn't, Reese followed her. The path she took wasn't one he knew. Her horse fairly flew over the rough ground. She was bent low to the animal, her hair streaming out behind her hat. When he finally caught up with her, she'd tied her horse to a pine tree in a shaded grove and lay in the withered grass.

He walked quietly through the trees, afraid to disturb her, not certain what to say. He dropped to his haunches and reached out a tentative hand. She pushed his hand away, scrabbling away in the grass.

"Wait, Jem." He finally reached out and planted both arms beside her hips to keep her from escaping.

"Leave me alone," she gritted out between clenched teeth.

"Not till you let me tell you how sorry I am."

"So you're sorry. Now let me up." She still refused to look at him.

"Not till you forgive me."

"You haven't got that long," she bit back, the sting of his hateful words still echoing.

He lifted his hands in a shrug. "What else do you want me to say?" She took advantage of being unpinned to whip around and sit up. He met her face-to-face. "Do you want to hear how the sight of those long legs sets me on fire?"

"Not especially."

He pulled his hat off and dropped it on the ground. "You make me crazy, Jem. No other woman's ever done that. Just when I think I got you half figured out, you turn faster than a hummingbird in spring. Hell, I don't want you to act like Abigail Fairchild. But the thing is I never know how you are gonna act. I don't want you busting broncs with the men. And I don't want somebody trying to kill you. But every time I try to protect you, I'm useless. Damn it, Jem, you're cutting off my—"

"I can't help it if I don't act like other women. I probably never will," she said bluntly, wiping suspiciously at her eyes.

"Oh, Jem." Despite her protests, he swept her into his embrace, cradling her back and running a smoothing hand over her hair. "I didn't mean that either. I know your pa raised you like a son, even gave you a boy's name."

"Not exactly," Jem mumbled.

"Isn't Jem supposed to sound like his name, James?"

"No."

"I never heard the name Jem before."

Her face pinkened slightly. "It's short for Jemima."

He rolled the name off his tongue, enjoying the sound. "Don't believe I've ever heard it before."

"It's from the Hebrew, meaning dove. It was the name of one of Job's daughters."

"Very poetic for a rancher," Reese observed.

Jem pinkened further. "He and my mother said I reminded them of a beautiful young dove." She laughed self-consciously. "Goes to show parents don't always know best."

Reese gazed into the depths of her amber eyes, marveling again at how her features he'd once thought so plain now seemed so much more appealing than the overblown beauty of other women. Her long, trim frame was infinitely more exciting than the lush curves he used to desire. "Then again, maybe it shows they knew just what they were doing."

"You're just saying that so I don't set the bed on fire tonight with you in it."

He cocked his head, considering. "You've got a point there." Then his expression turned serious. "You just don't realize it, do you, Jem? What you've got is more special than any woman I've ever known."

His words struck them both at the same time. Disbelief warred with wonder. Jem's answer stuck in her throat, refusing to go beyond the huge lump forming there. Reese searched his soul for the reason he'd uttered the words. Doggedly he continued, "Don't sell yourself short, Jem."

Surprised, she searched his face for the meaning of those last words. His hands continued to cradle her, and she allowed herself the luxury of relaxing against his strength. Not for the first time since she'd instigated the arrangement, she wondered if she could carry it through.

Chapter 27

The voice kept calling to her. The distress was urgent.
She had to get to him, he needed help. No one would help
him! She felt him grab her shoulder as he reached out for
help. The boy's face was clear. It was Reese, and he was
in such pain, so lonely.

"Jem, wake up, you're having a nightmare." Reese's
voice pulled her into the present.

Shaking, she sat up, pressing her fingers to her mouth in
agitation.

"What is it? You were thrashing all over and crying out
loud enough to wake the dead."

"It was you," she said slowly. "In such pain."

"Me?" he asked blankly.

"No one would help you or answer your questions."

His face closed abruptly, remembering what he'd confided to her when she'd lain unconscious after her fall.
"It's just a dream." His voice was curt, dismissive.

"The same one I had when I fell," she said in wonder.
"When you sat and talked to me all night."

"You were addled when you fell. Don't tell me you
know what I said when you hadn't come to yet."

"You told me what had happened to you," she stated
with certainty.

"People remember things all crazy when they've had a
fall," Reese argued.

"No, this is quite clear." So was the gaze she pinned Reese with.

"Don't you know dreams aren't real?"

"This dream is about what you told me," she insisted.

"Just 'cause you dreamed about a kid doesn't mean I'm the kid."

Her face was thoughtful, knowing, as she answered, "Then how did you know I dreamed about a child?"

"You must have told me."

"No," she stated succinctly. "I didn't. The only way you could know that is because you're the child who was in pain."

"I thought you were named for one of Job's daughters, not Joseph's. Don't try to read me into your dreams."

"You're there, whether I want you to be or not." She straightened the crumpled coverlet, not quite meeting his eyes. "You know it helps sometimes to have someone to confide in."

"I'll let you know if I want to spill my guts. Right now I gotta get some sleep." He hunkered down under the quilt, scrunched his eyes shut, and deliberately ignored her compelling gaze. One of Jem's hands reached out gently to touch the curly hair near his temples. When he didn't move away, she continued the quiet strokes until he unclenched his jaw muscles and began to relax.

Whatever he'd confided to her that day had disturbed him greatly. The gentle wash of the moonlight danced over the strong jaw and jutting planes of his face. When the soft sigh of his breathing convinced her he was asleep, she removed her hand from his brow. As she started to turn on her side he pulled her close, as though trying to seal their bodies together in a protective spoon position. Willingly she snuggled back against him, offering him her strength for the night. It seemed an equal exchange.

"I'm telling you we're missing better than two hundred head." Pete's voice was sharp with concern. Concern Reese was beginning to share.

"Did you count the ones we cut out to be dehorned?" Boyd questioned.

"Trying to cover up something, Harris?" Grady Orton taunted.

"Only thing I'd like to cover up is you—in dirt, about six feet deep." Boyd had held his temper in check for weeks, and it seemed ready to boil over.

"Both of you, stop it. I meant what I said. You're either on the same side or you're out." It was clear from Reese's voice that he brooked no argument.

"Pete, we generally don't keep a close count. How'd you notice so many were missing?" Jem was worried. They'd barely be able to fill the contract as it was. If they lost many head, besides the ones that normally fell to disease and predators, they would fail. All their efforts to keep the Bar-W afloat would have been for nothing.

Pete gestured as he spoke. "Moved about four hundred head to better grasslands up north. They were puny, wanted to fatten them up. Went to check on them, and only half of them are left."

"Aren't those the fences you ride, Boyd?" Grady's question hung in the air, like the smell of overripe cheese on a hot summer day.

Boyd kept his face even, his temper in check. Only the angry light in his eyes betrayed his feelings. "Yeah, they're mine. You want to make something of it?"

"Just seems strange your bunch is the only one with heads missing." Grady's voice was insinuating.

Reese was thinking the same thing. Not that he suspected Boyd, but it was awful strange that only those cows were missing. Even if he didn't have a shared history with the man, knew him to be loyal and honest, one fact was glaring. Boyd Harris was no fool. And he'd have to be one to steal the cattle he was in charge of. Reese's eyes narrowed at Grady Orton. He'd never gotten over his dislike or distrust of the man. And right now he was mouthier than Reese had ever seen him. Why?

"You got anything you want to tell us, Boyd?" Jem's voice interrupted his roving thoughts.

"No, ma'am." Boyd's voice was controlled as he answered, but the tic near his mouth was working. "I don't."

"Hell, Jem—" Reese began.

"I was just asking, Reese. No one accused him of anything." Considering her earlier reactions to Boyd, this one was rather controlled. Despite having awakened to find her plastered to him as close as his own skin, Reese didn't believe she'd done a complete about-face.

"No one here suspects you, Boyd," Reese assured the man. Boyd's face stayed even, but years of abuse lurked in his eyes.

"If anyone's asking my opinion," Pete interrupted before Boyd could respond, "I don't believe I ever said it could be Boyd."

"And you are the foreman." Jem seemed to remember that fact a tad late.

"That's what I was told." Pete's voice was filled with irony. Jem hunkered down in her coat, as much to escape the expressions on the men's faces as to shut out the cold wind.

Boyd nodded to both Reese and Pete, tipped the brim of his hat to Jem without smiling, and ignored Grady Orton completely. "I'd best see about the cattle that are left."

"You do that," Pete answered for them all.

"Looks like that Cushman fellow's really serious about stakin' his claim, startin' with your cattle," Grady commented.

Reese's head jerked up sharply, distaste coating his words. "Time for you to be back at work, too, Orton."

"Oh, sure, Mr. McIntire. Pete, Miz McIntire." He smiled at them all, also tipping his hat to Jem before ambling off.

"I don't trust him," Reese said bluntly.

"And a lot of people don't trust Boyd Harris. So where does that leave us?" Jem questioned.

"In a nest of vipers."

* * *

Emotions still ran high as they prepared for dinner. Pots clanked together and dishes rattled in the kitchen as Della scooped up the vegetables. Pete picked up the pans on the back burner that were out of her reach while Mary carried a huge platter of beef through the swinging door.

"Have you covered all the far country yet? Maybe the cattle wandered off farther than you think." Della spoke over the steam escaping from the boiling potatoes.

"I haven't had time to check everywhere. But it's just like last time." Pete frowned, remembering. It had started out with the winter calves. They'd lost every one, but had chalked it up to a bad winter. Then in the spring more beef had started to disappear. A few at first, then enough to show that a rustler was at work.

"Those two still at it?" Della asked, referring to Jem and Reese, who had stomped in before dinner. The only words Della had heard them exchange hadn't been particularly pleasant.

"They're never going to agree on Harris and Orton. They're probably having it out right now."

Upstairs, Jem's behavior belied Pete's words. She sat on the vanity bench, clad in a thin wrapper and little else, and was slowly easing a pair of thin stockings up her legs. Calculating the time of Reese's reappearance, she held one leg up, critically assessing the stocking as he walked back into the room from the washstand in the alcove. The towel dropped away from his freshly washed face as he stared at her in surprise.

Apparently after the day they'd had, he hardly expected to see her flashing her legs like delectable tidbits directly in his line of vision.

Focusing on his widely staring eyes, she smiled in a way she'd been practicing in the mirror for the last few days. She was delighted to see it had just the effect she wanted. With studied, casual movements, she pulled another stocking on as slowly as humanly possible. Fastening the garter with hands that only shook slightly, she completed the task and stood up slowly. Taking a deep breath, she untied the sash to her wrapper and let it fall away.

The whoosh of Reese's breath was pleasing. Trying to still the pounding of her own heart, hoping she didn't appear unbelievably foolish, she continued her charade. Leaning over the dresser, she bent down to retrieve her corset, letting her breasts fall forward. The garment in place, she laced it up slowly. Then, pretending confusion, she looked about for her camisole. Spying it across the room, she walked in front of Reese, only an arm's span away from him. Darting a glance at him, she was pleased to see his mouth drop open.

Lacing up the camisole, she paused midway up. Walking back in front of Reese, she retrieved her pantalets and stepped into them slowly. Tying them lightly at the waist, she allowed her fingers to trail down her hips and over her thighs. To her delight, Reese still hadn't moved, struck by her performance. When she moved to complete the fastening of her camisole, he finally came to life. His voice was low, husky, as he spoke. "There's no hurry about that."

She laughed lightly, wondering if she sounded as foolish to his ears as she did to her own. "Whatever do you mean?"

Reese stared at her in puzzlement. "Huh?"

This was harder than she thought. "Did you forget about dinner, Reese?"

"I'm hungry, but not for food." Once again he advanced, and she tried to flit over to the other side of the room the same way she'd seen other women do it.

Even more puzzled, he stared at her peculiar movements. "You hurt your leg today?"

Exasperated, she gave up the attempt at a sultry walk. "No, I didn't hurt my leg. We simply have to finish dressing for dinner."

"I'd rather undress and have mine here." There was no doubt to the meaning of his words, but Jem wanted to play her hand awhile longer. She was determined to make him see she could act feminine, like other women. Despite his apology, Reese's words from a few days ago still stung. She reached into the chifforobe and selected her best day dress, a beautiful silk that Abigail had insisted on ordering from *Godey's*. Since their friendship had deepened, Jem's wardrobe had improved considerably.

She stepped into the dress and then glanced up to see the confusion on Reese's face. "What was all that about?" he demanded.

"All what?" she answered, deciding that Abigail was right. Using her womanly wiles wasn't an entirely bad idea.

"You know what."

She finished fastening her dress and then smoothed the material down over her hips. "I'm sure I don't know what you mean, but you'd better hurry. I believe Della has dinner ready."

"Oh, no, you don't." He started to lunge toward her, but she slipped out the door, and unless he wanted to follow her into the hallway clad only in his long johns, he was stuck.

She awarded him another sultry smile. "Try to hurry, Reese. I'd hate to see everything cool off. It's so much better when it's hot." When it appeared he was willing to follow her out into the hall despite his half-clothed state, she fled down the stairs.

Exhilarated, she entered the dining room. Her visit with Abigail the other day had been worth every moment. Jem had confided Reese's hurtful words and Abigail had offered comfort but an equal amount of sage advice as well. She'd told Jem that Reese's reactions were normal. Most men were protective about their wives and would be outraged at the danger she was putting herself in. She had also said that his hateful words had been unthinking, just an attempt to lash back at her stubbornness. But Jem had felt the grain of truth in what he'd said. Sensing this, Abigail had given Jem a few ideas, one of which she'd just used upstairs with Reese.

Jem had discarded Abigail's advice at first, but then it

took root. Like a seed in fertile ground, the thought had sprouted. Feeling like a prize fool, she'd rehearsed what she planned to do in her mind a dozen times before she'd found the courage to try it tonight.

A smug smile crept to her lips. It had actually worked. Hearing the tread of Reese's bootsteps on the stairs, she froze, then scurried into the kitchen. Della and Pete glanced up and then gaped in surprise. She never dressed for dinner. Smiling weakly, she tried to act relaxed.

"You going somewhere?" Della asked.

"No, why?"

They both stared mutely at the dress.

"Oh, this? Just thought I'd wear something different." Jem studied the table when they didn't comment. "No fresh bread?"

Pete pointed to the rolls that were within her reach. "Right there."

"Oh, of course. I'll just take them in."

Pete and Della didn't answer, but Jem could hear their muffled snickers as she swung through the door into the dining room. She stopped abruptly. Reese, dressed in fresh clothes and a string tie, stood at the end of the table, waiting.

"Dinner's about ready," she announced unnecessarily.

"Good, because I'm not sure how much longer I can wait."

She gulped. Perhaps she should have taken more instruction before she'd embarked on this course.

Reese advanced in a determined manner, and she found herself starting to back away. When he reached her side, he paused, staring at her without flinching. Abruptly he pulled her chair out. Dumbfounded, she stared at the piece of furniture. Realizing his intent, she dropped into the chair and watched while he crossed the table and took the seat opposite her.

She reached for her napkin, but her hand stopped when she saw that Reese was following her every movement. Self-consciously she shook out the napkin and smoothed it onto her lap. As they politely passed the serving dishes back and forth, Jem noticed that Reese took only small portions while never missing one of her moves. Her throat had constricted so badly she wondered if she'd be able to force any food down at all.

"Wine?" Her voice cracked, and she swallowed.

His answer was lazy. "Please."

She poured, hoping the shaking of her hand wasn't visible. Picking up her own glass, she placed it against her mouth and started to swallow. Reese's concentration on her lips was unnerving. She gulped the wine down, praying fervently she didn't choke. Searching the table for something more neutral, she seized on the steaming gravy boat that sat next to her plate. "This is too hot. If you'll give me your plate, I'll serve you some." Without comment, he passed her the dish. She ladled some gravy on his potatoes and then glanced up. "Is this enough for you?"

"I can never get enough."

Almost dropping the plate, she recovered when his strong arm shot out to steady hers. Determined not to let him turn the tables, she drew a deep, calming breath. *Remember what Abigail said!*

Jem tried to resurrect her coy look from upstairs. Apparently it succeeded, because the pulse at Reese's throat beat suddenly faster. Her gaze trailed down his rugged shoulders to the enticing broad chest that she knew tapered down to lean hips and powerful legs.

His mouth started to work and failed. Standing up abruptly, he crossed to her side of the table.

"What—"

Without explanation he took her hand and pulled her from the chair.

"Reese!"

Ignoring her words, he swept her from the dining room and toward the stairs. At the stairwell she balked, and he stared at her without relenting. "This is one game you're gonna finish."

She made a pretense of protest, but actually his words

211

fired her equally. Without waiting for her answer, he picked her up and carried her up the stairs. He barely paused at the doorway of their bedroom, only stopping long enough to push the door shut with his booted foot.

There was no gentleness in his motions, only hunger. Insatiable, undeniable hunger. She threw off her cloak of coyness and joined him in his quest, her hands tugging at his shirt, as she strove to fit her hands against his chest. Reaching for the fastening to his denims, she gasped at the hardness that met her hands. She tugged at his denims, her hands sliding down his sleek hips.

His hands, equally impatient, bunched her skirts up, searching for the fastening to her pantalets. Finding it, he untied the bow quickly, pushing the garment down and out of his way.

Jem started to unfasten her dress, but Reese could wait no longer. Instead he lifted her to impale her on his waiting shaft. She gasped at first, but soon her warmth accepted him, reveling in the fullness. Wrapping her legs around him, she allowed the pantalets to drop to the floor, unnoticed.

The strength of her legs gripping his torso inflamed him further. His hands clasped her firm buttocks, squeezing them as she rode him like a young bronc refusing to be broken. Her hands dug into the curls of hair that fell over his collar and then moved to clasp his shoulders. When she rotated against him, he nearly lost control, feeling the wetness, the shudders enveloping her body.

The feelings ran unchecked—hot and wild. The primal dance continued, skin abrasing skin, flesh igniting flesh. When he emptied into her waiting womb, she milked him greedily.

Gasping, they drew back. They assessed each other, their expressions hovering between guarded and amazed. As he eased her slowly to the floor they both breathed raggedly. Dropping their foreheads together, they rested against each other for a moment. Gradually the familiar sounds and sights of the night penetrated once more. The moonlight bathed them through the open drapes as they pulled apart again.

"You're something, Jem."

And so are you, Reese McIntire. She couldn't say the words aloud, but the thought remained, refusing to be dismissed.

She glanced down, suddenly absurdly self-conscious. His hand was gentle as he tipped her chin back up. He lowered her head slowly, and when his lips met hers, they were tender, undemanding. Her eyelids dropped shut under the gentleness of his kiss, and her heart reacted as well. For the first time fear licked the same path as pleasure had. The grip on her control had slipped, and she didn't know if it could ever be regained.

Chapter 28

The churchyard was filled with running children, glad to be released from the confining two-hour service. Braids and hats flying, they scampered in pursuit of marbles, sling-shots, and friends, despite the cold weather. A few parents made halfhearted attempts to control them, but were equally glad to be free. People who hadn't seen each other in weeks, or perhaps months, caught up with the gossip.

The holidays were approaching, and the festive nature of the season was contagious. Jem glanced at Reese's face and saw the same expression it always held when Christmas was mentioned. The expression in his eyes grew hard, revealing nothing, and his mouth drew into a thin, uncompromising line.

Remembering his pain when he'd talked about his child-hood, she doubted he had many good memories of Christmas.

"What about you, Jem?" Abigail asked. "What are you doing for the holidays?"

Jem glanced at Reese's set face. "I imagine we'll have a quiet dinner with just Pete and Della. Nothing too fancy."

Abigail gazed wistfully at the playful children darting among the adults, their carefree faces exuberant. "What Christmas needs is children."

It had never occurred to Jem to ask why Abigail and Michael hadn't had any children yet. She watched Abigail's fingers tighten on her husband's arm.

Catching Jem's watchful expression, the other woman managed a smile. "Maybe next year."

Smiling back, Jem wanted to comfort Abigail. It seemed to be a subject of concern and apparently pain. But she regretfully acknowledged that she didn't know how to comfort. Another thought struck her. "We'd love to have you join us for dinner on Christmas, wouldn't we, Reese?"

"Huh?" Collecting himself, Reese replied, "Sure, that'd be right fine."

Abigail and Michael exchanged a glance. "Thank you for the invitation, but we wouldn't want to intrude," Abigail said.

"You won't be," Jem assured them.

Michael and Abigail exchanged another glance. "We'd love to, then," Michael replied. Another couple jostled between them, and smiling, they moved away, the cool wind tugging at their coats.

"Reese, do you mind if they join us for Christmas?"

"Doesn't matter to me," he muttered.

Jem wanted to ask him if he had any good childhood memories of the season, but his closed face stopped her. She remembered her mother, filling the house with fragrant boughs, baking incessantly until the very eaves seemed to blossom with the fresh smell of cinnamon and nutmeg. Pulling back into her own childhood memories, she decided to re-create one of those magical holidays for Reese.

All the way home, she hummed snatches of Christmas carols while planning. Barely allowing Reese to help her out of the wagon, she raced into the house to dig through her mother's recipes.

Della found her poring over a pile of handwritten scraps of paper when she returned from church. Her mother's fragile, elegant handwriting gave her a pang, but instead of flinching from the memories, Jem embraced them.

"You look busy," Della commented as she rolled through the room.

"I am." Quickly she confided her plan to Della. "So, will you help me?"

"Of course. When haven't I baked a houseful of goodies at Christmas?" Della's voice held a note of reproach.

"Oh, it's always wonderful, Della. But this year everything has to be bigger, better. I want the tallest fir, the most fragrant cookies, the—"

Della laughed. "I see. We'll have to get one of the hands to collect the boughs, but I'll talk Pete into finding the best tree. Mary can get a start on sprucing up the house tomorrow." She rolled her chair closer. "Now, we'd better take a look at those recipes and get to work."

Reese poked his head in a few times, amazed to see Jem donning an apron, covered with smudges of flour. She'd always maintained a disdainful attitude toward such domesticity. Sleeves rolled up, Jem was clearly serious about the task, even though her cookies appeared a bit uneven and lumpy. He wandered away, uncomfortable about Christmas as always.

The next few days followed the same pattern. Leaving the majority of the operation of the ranch to Reese, Jem spent hours unearthing Christmas decorations and ancient cookie cutters. She and Della wove a gigantic wreath for the front door from pine boughs and tied a huge bow on it before hanging it on the front door.

One cowhand was drafted to collect mountains of pine boughs, which Jem used to drape down the huge banister of the staircase and over the mantels of the fireplaces. Soon there wasn't a square inch of the ranch that wasn't permeated by the delightful smells of pine, fir, and aromatic spices. Tins of shortbread, pfeffernusse, linzer bars, and leckerle cookies were stacked in the kitchen. Gingerbread boys were baked, decorated, and strung with ribbon for hanging on the tree.

As Christmas Eve approached, piles of popcorn and cranberries were strung. Since Jem knew that Reese would be unreceptive to choosing a tree, Pete was pressed into service, as Della had promised. When the giant fir was placed in the front room, its perfectly formed branches filled the space beautifully. Jem hung all the carefully cleaned glass-blown ornaments on the tree. Much like a painter studying his canvas, she arranged the glass balls, cookies, garlands, and candles. Her heart caught as she placed the star upon the top. When her mother had been alive, her parents had always performed that final touch together. Their last Christmas together had been when Jem was twelve. The next spring her mother had died, and the holiday had never been the same.

Stepping back to survey the results, she felt a warm glow and was sure her mother would approve. Hearing Reese's boots clatter into the hall, she couldn't wait another moment.

"In here, Reese." She waited in excited anticipation for his reaction to the tree. He walked in, stopped as he stared at the giant confection, and didn't speak. "Well?" she prompted.

"It's nice."

Her jaw almost dropped. *Nice!* It was magnificent! She drew a deep breath. This Christmas wasn't about her, it was about Reese. She had her store of good memories, while apparently he didn't. Recovering, she answered, "Yes, it is. When you're ready, I believe Della has dinner ready."

"Good." Without further words, he left to go upstairs. Sagging slightly, Jem watched until he disappeared from sight.

Inside the bedroom, Reese dropped onto the bed, holding his face in his steepled hands. The shock of the tree had almost done him in. He'd never expected Jem to be so crazy about Christmas. Hell, considering her character, he wouldn't have been surprised if she'd ignored it altogether so they could get more work done. But instead she'd turned the house into a cookie factory and managed to bring almost as much pine inside as she'd left out on the trees.

It had been a lifetime since he'd thought about celebrating the holiday. Usually he found a bottle of whiskey and slept it off until Christmas had passed and all the memories with it. But Jem had resurrected them. The loneliness bit into him, keener than ever before.

He lifted his head and walked over to the bureau drawer. Opening it, he stared for a moment at the brown box that held his few belongings. Since their bargain had been struck, Jem had paid Reese a salary each month. When he'd questioned the first payment, she'd gaped at him. She hadn't expected him to go the entire year without pay, she'd explained, but his bonus would be paid only if the contract was fulfilled.

Except for a paltry amount, he'd saved every bit of his pay. He stared at it now. Combined with his own nest egg, he'd accumulated a fair amount. Certainly not enough for the freighting company, but still a goodly sum. He blinked, remembering the peddler in town who'd charmed most of the other ranch hands out of their pay for some trinket or another for Christmas. He sighed deeply, thinking of the elaborate tree gracing the parlor. Jem would no doubt put presents underneath it, and for the first time in years he knew he wouldn't escape Christmas.

Downstairs, Jem, too, was thinking of presents. One in particular. It had to be special. A man who'd known no Christmas would have to have something out of the ordinary. A smile lit her face. She knew just the thing.

The days flew until Christmas Eve. Abigail and Michael had agreed to come to dinner on Christmas Day, but Jem and Reese would celebrate this evening alone. Their work done, Jem carried out her father's tradition with the hands. Having explained it beforehand to Reese, they acted together.

Each hand was given a month's salary in gold along with a silver knife bearing the Bar-W insignia. Then a huge dinner that had been prepared by the cook was laid out. Wild turkey roasted to perfection, huge hams, and the inevitable slab of beef battled with platters of vegetables, stuffing, cranberries, and fresh rolls for a place on the table. Della's contribution of mincemeat and chess pies, currant cakes, and rum-raisin pudding lined the tables, also.

It warmed Jem's heart to see many of the hands who had no family share the holiday together. Mary and her husband, one of the retired hands, sat with the single cowboys. Their children had long since grown and left the ranch. Jem knew most of the ranchers felt it was up to the cowboys to celebrate on their own, but her father had always felt a responsibility for his men.

She and Reese departed once the others started their dinner. While a huge meal was planned tomorrow to include Pete, Della, Abigail, and Michael, tonight dinner was for two.

Reese looked in surprise at the dinner table, set with only two places, but Jem smiled. "I promise not to burst into Christmas song. I thought perhaps a quiet dinner tonight might be nice."

Gratitude flickered over his face. The strain of the holidays showed in his expression, and Jem hoped her efforts hadn't been misdirected.

Once dinner was past, Jem led Reese into the parlor, where the fire flickered, casting a glow over the shining tree. She walked over to the window as Reese poured their drinks. "I wish it would snow."

"Never thought you'd be so sentimental."

She kept her voice light. "I'm not always, you know."

"No? And here I thought you were the female Saint Nick."

"Just got to considering how lucky I am. When my mother was alive, this house glowed at Christmas. She and my father . . ." Jem paused, remembering their loving ways.

"That's the way it usually is."

"Is that how you remember Christmas?" Jem asked softly.

He stood up, walking back to the sideboard and pouring another drink. "My memories of Christmas are a pretty mixed-up mess."

"Perhaps we can create some new ones." He turned at her words and watched her approach. Hesitantly she reached out and touched his face. He stilled as her fingers trailed over his skin.

There was one special gift she wanted to give him before morning. But she was not demanding. Kissing the sensitive skin of his neck, she sighed against him as his arms crept around her. Together they sank to the rug in front of the fire. As she remembered their last time in this room, her eyes promised a gentler time. Her hands were not frantic, but giving as they stroked him. The firelight flickered over their faces, outlining his strongly etched features, revealing the hidden pain in his eyes.

Determinedly she worked to erase that pain. Feeling as though she had all the tomorrows in the world before her, she felt no haste, no greed.

And it was the giving that was Reese's undoing. Painted across her face, it humbled him. Wanting to give back, he knew only that his soul held great emptiness—a void that had been waiting to be filled all his life. For the moment he forgot that Jem's heart belonged to Charles Sawyer, and pretended that it was his.

When they finally came together, he knew for a certainty that no two people had ever fitted more perfectly or belonged together with such rightness. In many ways his pain deepened, knowing as he did that this present was one he couldn't put on a shelf to take down and treasure forever. Because in three months this giving woman would no longer be beneath him, offering herself. But gazing into her amber eyes, he was certain she would still hold his heart. Her head dropped to his shoulder, and he glanced out the huge window. The snow she'd wished for fell softly in huge, downy flakes, blanketing them in a winter wonderland. At that moment he was convinced it, too, fell at her will.

Christmas morning dawned in the best possible fashion. The beautiful snow of the evening before still fell—big, fat puffy flakes carpeted the ranch and lent magic to the landscape.

Like a child on her first holiday, Jem bolted from the bed. When Reese tried to remain securely under the warm cocoon of the quilt, she was merciless. "Oh, no, you don't, sleepyhead." With a huge yank, she pulled the quilt off the bed.

"Didn't you ever grow up?"

"No. Did you have to?"

He sighed with great patience. "You're not going to leave me alone until we go downstairs, are you?"

"Nope."

He rose and reached for his denims. "I want coffee," he warned in his most intimidating manner while digging in his bureau drawer.

"As soon as we see what's in our socks."

He groaned as she led the way downstairs. Not deigning to dress, she'd pulled a wrapper on over her gown, content to celebrate in the fashion she best remembered from her childhood.

As he'd expected, the tree was surrounded by gaily wrapped presents. "Aren't you gonna wait for Pete and Della?" he asked, hoping for a reprieve.

"Nope." She grinned again.

She shook the presents she found with her name on them and then put them back reluctantly. "I have to wait for Pete and Della to open these," she admitted ruefully. "Otherwise they'll probably make me give them back."

"Then let's get some coffee."

"Not so fast." She dug around amid the packages till she found the one she wanted. He observed her suspiciously as she unearthed the tiny gift and handed it to him. Untying the ribbon with apprehension, he wondered what the small box held. When he opened it, he stared at the contents, stunned.

"A lump of sugar?"

She laughed. "I didn't think you'd remember to get Danny anything."

"So you got him a lump of sugar and wrapped it?"

"Let's go give it to him."

"Now? Before my coffee?"

"Of course. Animals have feelings, too." She dragged him unwillingly to the barn. The dusky interior held the pungent aroma of new hay and well-groomed horses.

His steps were reluctant as he followed her. "This is ridiculous, Jem. I'd never have expected you to act so silly and sentimental over a horse. What'd you get your stal . . ." His voice trailed off as he watched Jem lead Danny out of the stall. On the horse's back was the most beautiful saddle he'd ever set eyes on. Tentatively he reached out and ran his hands over the well-tooled leather, pausing over the fine detailing on the fenders and skirt.

Grasping the horn, he spoke with wonder. "It's the finest thing I've ever seen." He examined the magnificent piece of work. The buckles of the cinch were made of pure silver, and he knew it must have cost a good six months' wages. "Jem?"

She shrugged, self-conscious now that she'd presented him with her surprise. "Your old one was looking a bit ragged." His eyes widened, but he refrained from commenting on the obvious. She could have bought a perfectly good, serviceable saddle for a fraction of the cost. She hurried on. "And I wanted this Christmas to be special for you."

His eyes narrowed suspiciously. "Do you usually go to all this fuss at Christmas?"

"Most of the time."

He didn't answer, his gaze unrelenting.

"Sometimes."

Still he didn't speak.

"Okay, never. Not since my parents were alive."

"You did all this for me?"

She turned away, fidgeting with the stall door. "Of course not. After all, it is Christmas." He stared at her again without speaking. "All right, yes. I thought it might make up for some of the ones you've missed."

Watching him swallow, Jem wondered what his reaction would be. His eyes were somber as he answered, "It has."

She breathed a sigh of relief and started to turn toward the door.

"Wait, Jem." She turned in question as he reached into his pocket. "I have something for you, too."

"But you didn't have to get me anything."

He cocked his head in the direction of the saddle. "Obviously gifts don't mean anything to you."

She flushed, realizing the futility of arguing, and remained silent as he handed her a small box. "I didn't wrap it," he apologized.

For some inane reason her hands shook as she lifted the lid. Gifts from men were not something she was accustomed to. She gasped as she saw the contents. It was a small daguerreotype of Reese.

When she didn't speak or move, he took the picture from the box. "I was in town, and a peddler had a camera. I thought you could put it in that locket of yours you always wear." *To remember me by.*

Jem's throat constricted, and she was horrified that she might burst into tears. *No one's ever done anything like this for me before.*

His hand found her locket and opened it. "Need some help?" She nodded mutely while he arranged the picture for her and then snapped the locket shut. "Merry Christmas, Jem."

The words struggled past the emotions locked in her throat as she replied, "Merry Christmas, Reese."

Chapter
29

The noise and bustle of the kitchen was typical of Christmas morning, but Reese didn't know that. When he and Jem entered, he thought he'd wandered into a hornet's nest. It looked like every pot and pan they owned was out and overflowing with one ingredient or another. Pete, Della, and Mary were working with great concentration.

Trying to unearth a cup for coffee, Reese joked with the foreman. "Thought you were still in bed."

"On Christmas morning? Della and me have been up for hours. Who'd you think saddled Danny?"

Good point. Although Reese wouldn't have been surprised if Jem had employed an elf to do the job. Instead of answering, he asked instead, "You want some coffee?"

"I've already had half a gallon, and if I slow down for a minute, Della will have my hide," Pete replied as Della turned to give him a frown. "Won't you, darlin'?"

"Don't 'darlin'' me. I need those breadcrumbs over here."

"See what I mean?" Pete's expression was tolerant, though, as he handed her the bowl, stealing a quick kiss before she could protest. Reese watched as she turned a faint shade of pink and tried unconvincingly to reprimand her husband. He wondered how anyone stayed together as long as they had, through Della's crippling accident, and still be so taken with one another.

The rest of the day passed in the same disorganized fashion. Neighboring ranchers stopped by with gifts and home-baked goodies. Around three o'clock Abigail and Michael arrived, laden with gifts and an equal share of merriment. Both of them looked positively ready to explode, and Jem finally turned to Abigail in exasperation. "Whatever is the matter with you two?"

Abigail glanced at Michael, her expression both loving and mischievous. "Shall we tell them?"

"Any way I could stop you?" Michael answered, but his protest was halfhearted. Reese and Jem glanced at each other, mystified.

"This is our last Christmas alone," she announced. "Next year we'll have a little Fairchild running about."

Jem hugged her impulsively while Reese pumped Michael's hand. "Abigail, that's wonderful. A baby!" Jem responded joyously.

"He'll look like Michael," Abigail responded confidently. "I had hoped, prayed. It's been a Christmas of miracles."

Reese met Jem's eyes and sent her a silent message of agreement. Overcome with emotion, Jem bustled about, pouring eggnog and wassail.

Abigail trod quietly to Reese's side, and he smiled at her. "We're happy about your news, Abigail."

"Thank you, Reese. It looks as though we all have something to celebrate." Her eyes lighted on Jem's flushed, happy face, and Reese followed her gaze. "The promise of her locket seems to have come true."

"Her locket?"

Abigail glanced at him in surprise. "You know, from the wedding. Two hearts becoming one." When he didn't speak, she placed a hand on his arm. "I hope I haven't spoken out of turn."

Shaken, he collected himself. "Not at all, Abby."

From their wedding day? The image shook him with more intensity than he thought possible.

* * *

After they'd settled at the table, everyone agreed that the food smelled delicious. Hardly an inch of the table was left bare. Having coaxed Reese to tell her all his favorites weeks before, Jem and Della had conspired to fill the meal with his choices.

Reese began carving the turkey, a bit self-conscious at the head of the table, when the doorknocker sounded through the house. Jem started to put down the platter she was holding for Reese. "I'll get it, Della. Mary's swamped in the kitchen."

"No, you two stay put. My hands are free," Abigail offered, going to the door. Reese continued carving, and Jem paid little attention to Abigail's excited cry of welcome since the house hadn't stopped stirring with guests since morning. Abigail reentered the dining room, bringing someone with her.

"Look who's here!" she announced in an excited flourish.

All heads swung in Abigail's direction, their faces an arresting array of responses. Reese appeared curious but appreciative, Pete and Della welcoming, but Jem's face was a picture of shock. The beautiful blond woman smiled at Jem, her huge blue eyes full of mischief. Her curvaceous, petite body was poised at the threshold of the dining room, giving the effect of a staged entrance.

"Lily?" Jem found her voice quavering with disbelief.

"Merry Christmas, sis!" Lily rushed forward to give Jem a hug."

Sis? Reese stared at Jem questioningly as she embraced her sister. Jem's face reflected confusion and, more surprisingly, displeasure.

Pulling back, Lily gazed around the table. "I thought I'd surprise you."

Jem found her voice. "That you did."

While Lily hugged Della, the latter proclaimed wryly, "You always did have a way of turning the cart upside down."

"And on her head," Pete finished for her.

Lily's melodic laugh tinkled through the dining room. "You're too kind." She glanced down the length of the table, pausing when she encountered Reese's frank regard. "I know everybody here"—her voice lowered in appreciation—"except you."

"That makes two of us," Reese replied evenly.

"I'm sorry," Jem muttered. "Reese, this is my sister, Lily. Lily, this is Reese, my husband." If she stumbled a bit over the last two words, it was lost in her sister's reaction.

"Why, Jem, however could you have kept a secret like this from me?" Jem shrugged helplessly as she watched Lily go into action. "And such a handsome fellow, too. I am quite furious that I wasn't invited to the wedding, but I'll forgive you if you'll get me a glass of sherry."

Lily winked coyly at Reese, and Jem scrabbled to answer. "I couldn't find you to let you know about the wedding. You hardly ever stay in one place long enough to have an address."

"Too true," Lily agreed with a smile. "But then, I didn't know you'd have something this good to write me about."

Jem glanced between her beautiful sister and Reese, feeling her stomach sink like a stone. She went to get the sherry, feeling as she always did around Lily—awkward and ugly. When she returned, Michael was complimenting Lily. Watching all the admiring eyes trained on her sister, Jem felt all of her old insecurities rise up to haunt her. She handed her sister the glass of sherry and stood hesitantly next to Abigail.

She felt Abigail clasp her hand, its reassuring squeeze a reminder of the many changes in her life. Still, as the dinner and evening progressed, Jem wished for the millionth time that she'd inherited some of their mother's looks and grace.

Intensely feminine, Lily had commanded attention since she was born. She and Jem had been different from the start. The more Jem yearned to learn about the ranch, the less Lily was able to tolerate the isolation. At her first chance she'd left for finishing school and had rarely graced the portals of the Bar-W since.

Jem hadn't seen Lily since her father's death, and then she'd only breezed in long enough for the funeral before she was off again, determined not to be tied to the loneliness of the ranch.

As the evening came to an end Jem and Reese closed the door behind the Fairchilds, and Lily yawned hugely. "Thanks, sis," she murmured against Jem's hair. "I needed to be home for Christmas." Jem returned the hug, battling the conflicting emotions she'd always felt for her sister.

Once inside the privacy of their room, Reese turned to Jem. "Any special reason you didn't tell me you had a sister?"

Of course. She's beautiful, and I'm not! "No," she said aloud. "It just never occurred to me." Shrugging, she went to the window and stared into the inky darkness. "She rarely visits anymore, and I figured with Pa dead . . ." Her voice trailed off. With their father's death, Jem had assumed Lily would grace the continent instead of the home she'd always battled to be free of.

"So you had family for Christmas after all."

Jem collected herself. "Yes, that always makes it special." She laughed lightly, remembering the long-ago Christmases she hadn't thought of in years. "When Lily was little, she would get up and dig through all the socks and take out what she wanted. Then she'd put the presents that she didn't want into mine in exchange for what she'd taken. She never could figure out how Mama and Pa knew."

Reese came up behind her, embracing her from behind. "I guess you're right. Memories are meant to be changed. I bet she wouldn't dare fight you for your sock now."

The feel of Reese's arms around her were comforting, but a cold chill formed nonetheless. Perhaps Lily wouldn't fight over trinkets, but would she like to garner Reese for her own? Charles certainly hadn't been immune to Lily's charms at her father's funeral. It had occurred to Jem that if Charles and Lily hadn't taken off in different directions, she might have had a battle then. But she hadn't blamed Charles. Lily had always had the pick of all the men and one who was inaccessible became even more appealing.

When Reese turned her gently in his arms, she sought reassurance rather than passion. She knew it shouldn't matter. Her arrangement with Reese was purely business. The hand stroking her hair in comfort belied the thought, but she knew it was true. In three months he would ride out of her life to the freedom he craved, and she could devote her thoughts to Charles and the life they once intended to create. She tucked her head more securely into Reese's shoulder, wondering at the stab of pain her thoughts had produced.

Apparently Lily could stir up hurt simply by appearing, making her difference from her sister stark. Lily was a picture-perfect replica of their mother. She had always been the beautiful one, the sought-after one. Jem remembered countless nights when she'd lain on her bed, face buried in her pillow, while she recounted Lily's successes and her own failures.

It took some probing, but she also recalled Lily's attempts to draw her into her social circle and her own determined efforts to remain aloof, pretending her unpopularity meant nothing. It had been a slap in the face when her younger sister had inherited not only her mother's grace and appearance, but her ability to draw others to her as well.

If Reese's head was turned by Lily's beauty, so be it. When he left the Bar-W, he would be able to pursue whatever women he chose. Her throat constricted tightly as she tried to remember that meant she could also pursue Charles. For some reason, the thought of Reese in another woman's arms was far more disturbing. She allowed Reese to continue comforting her, refusing to consider what it would be like when he was no longer there to do so.

* * *

The next few days passed in a whirlwind of activity. In her usual fashion, Lily dominated the household, turning the most routine tasks into dramatic events. She insisted on planning a huge party for the new year, declaring the house to be a mausoleum—a tomb, in fact—which she intended to liven up.

Jem pored over the account books in the study, hoping to escape Lily's relentless activity. When the door burst open, she had little doubt who it would be.

"What are you doing all shut up in this stuffy room?" Lily demanded.

"Working." The implication was lost on Lily, who perched on the leather chair and opened the box on the side table, disappointed to find only cigars.

"No chocolates?"

"I believe Della made some."

Lily waved a hand in dismissal. "Hardly what I'm used to." Jem's eyebrows rose. "Never mind. I want to know what you're wearing tomorrow night."

"I hadn't thought about it. A dress, I suppose." After Lily's arrival, Jem had returned strictly to her wardrobe of pants and shirts, not wanting to emphasize the comparison between herself and her curvaceous sister.

"You suppose? I would think with that handsome husband of yours you'd have improved your wardrobe." Lily's gaze raked over Jem's outfit critically. "I remember what you're wearing from five years ago. Trust me, it didn't flatter you then either."

Jem flinched but tried not to let it show. "My work isn't cut out for frilly dresses and parasols."

"With all the men around, why do you insist on doing all that ranch business?" Lily's tone indicated that to her, Jem's work was on the level of shoveling dung.

"Because I enjoy it, Lily. Something you never understood and probably never will."

Lily bent forward. "You know, Jem, there are other things—operas, plays, shopping. A whole other world you've never even tried."

"I'm happy with the one I live in."

Lily let the subject go with typical abandon. "It's your life. But you do have to find something to wear tomorrow to knock the eyes out of that gorgeous husband."

Uncomfortable, Jem rose from the desk and retrieved her coffee. "Our relationship isn't exactly what you seem to think it is."

"Because you hooked such a wonderful man? I'm impressed—"

"Don't be. Our arrangement is only to ensure the future of the ranch."

"Arrangement?"

"Yes. Reese agreed to marry me in order to end the blacklisting. After Pa died, people believed he was the one responsible for the rustling. Figured he was double-crossed by his accomplice and shot. The only way to keep the Bar-W was to change the owner's name."

"But why would Reese agree to such a thing?"

"For the money, of course."

Lily's eyes narrowed. Despite her reputation as a featherbrain, she was no fool. She'd seen her sister and new brother-in-law together. Jem could protest all she wanted, but what Lily saw was no business arrangement. "And you don't plan to try to make the marriage work?"

Jem replaced the coffee cup on the table with a definitive hand. "It's not an option. Reese wants his freedom, and I promised to wait for Charles."

Lily's voice held disbelief. "You're not still carrying a torch for that foreman, are you?"

Jem remained stubborn, forcing herself to believe the words she uttered. "Is that so hard to believe? I love Charles."

Lily blinked. Either her sister was capable of loving two men or she'd purposely blinded herself to the truth. "What about Reese?"

"Reese is very nice."

"Rice pudding is very nice, but I'd hardly use the same

words to describe your husband. And the way you look at him, I know you know what I mean."

"There's an attraction, I'll admit that."

Lily wondered if her sister was purposely being dense. "So you don't have any real feelings for Reese, only Charles?"

Jem hedged. "That's right." She ignored the multitude of feelings Reese had aroused in her, the passion she'd felt only in his arms.

"You're a fool," Lily stated bluntly, rising from her chair. Jem stared at her without answering. "You're afraid to admit that you love Reese because you've got some ridiculous notion that Charles's is your first and only love. If he loved you, why didn't he come back and marry you like he promised?"

Jem had no answer.

"Well, sister dear, love doesn't always work out the way we want." Jem wondered at the shaft of pain crossing her sister's face, but Lily didn't give her time to reflect on anything other than her words. "If you're too stupid to know a good thing when you've got it, don't be surprised if someone comes along and snatches it right out of your arms."

"In three months he'll be free to choose whatever woman he wants," Jem said quietly, refusing to acknowledge the steel band closing around her heart.

"If not sooner," Lily's cryptic words echoed through the room as she turned on her heel and marched out of the study. With a sinking feeling, Jem realized she was looking at the person who could fulfill that prophecy.

The night of the party, Jem fretted over what to wear, realizing her sister was right. Her wardrobe was inadequate, unflattering. Reese had strolled in, and his eyes had widened when he'd seen the bed piled with the clothes she'd pulled from the chifforobe and discarded.

This was ridiculous, she told herself. Why was she fussing so? If Reese took a fancy to her sister, then so be it.

She leaned close to the cheval mirror, the locket between her breasts swinging forward as she did. Straightening up slowly, she reached for the gold metal and opened the clasp, staring at the picture of Reese. The peddler had captured the remarkable look of Reese's eyes. Her finger reached out tentatively, drawing over the planes and valleys of the face that had become so familiar over the past months.

When she emerged from their room sometime later, she wore the white evening dress of *poult-d-soie* shot with *glace de blanc* found in her mother's trunk. She'd unearthed white satin shoes as well and with Della's help had ironed the dress until it draped perfectly. When Della had questioned her unusual choice, Jem had responded that her own dresses were not appropriate. Della had kindly kept her own counsel as she helped arrange Jem's hair. As she'd started to leave the room Della had hugged her and told her to believe in herself.

Now, as she walked down the staircase, Jem hoped fervently that she didn't appear as foolish as she felt. She took a deep breath, silently mouthing Della's words, *Believe in yourself.*

If she'd expected a reaction to her descent, it wasn't forthcoming. Lily was holding court at one end of the great hall, and all the men were giving her their attention. Slightly deflated, Jem gazed around for a familiar face. Abigail's was reassuringly friendly.

"Why, Jem, you look lovely. Almost as pretty as on your wedding day."

Jem glanced self-consciously at the elaborate gown. "Do I look like a peacock during molting season?"

"Hardly." She examined Jem's appearance with a critical eye. "I wouldn't change a thing."

"Thanks, Abby."

"Just because Lily's here doesn't mean you won't still shine, Jem."

"I don't know what you mean."

"I mean that Reese still has eyes only for you. Don't

forget that. You and your sister are different. While you may not flutter around the room like a butterfly during mating season, she doesn't have your strengths either. Remember that."

Jem tried to, but when her sister coaxed Reese into the first dance of the evening, it was damnably hard. Seeing her float around the room, a vision in pale blue silk that matched her huge cornflower eyes, Jem fought to keep her envy at bay with little success. Jem thought nastily that Lily seemed to be batting her lashes at the speed of a hummingbird's wings. When Lily arched her long, graceful neck back in an amused laugh, Jem found her nails digging into her palms.

Reese was attentive as he swirled Lily across the room, and Jem's stomach knotted in apprehension. What was wrong with her? In a few months he could squire around anyone he chose. For some reason that thought made her stomach hurt even worse. Standing on the sidelines, dejection a ready companion, she tried to envision the years ahead, waiting for Charles to return.

As the dance ended she noticed that Lily refused to let Reese go, her arm entwined with his, her smile full. Her attention riveted, she acted as though she wished she could melt right into him. Reese moved away from Lily, smiling as he disengaged his arm and headed toward Jem.

When he approached and asked for the next dance, she found her movements awkward, their conversation strained. He pulled back, trying to read her expression. "Something wrong, Jem?"

"No, I just want to make sure everybody's having a good time."

"I thought you'd put your sister in charge of that." Jem stiffened in his arms, and he continued. "She's been entertaining ever since she came downstairs."

No doubt. Why had she ever thought she could compete with her beautiful sister? Their differences had been clear since childhood. Adulthood only intensified the comparison.

"Where are you, Jem?" Seeing the puzzled expression on Reese's face, she realized he must have been talking while she was lost in her thoughts.

"Lily's very beautiful, isn't she?"

Reese led her around the room, passing other couples. "I suppose so."

"I'm not surprised you noticed," Jem answered somewhat nastily.

"You asked. What did you want me to say—that she's ugly?" Jem held her temper in check, wishing the evening was over, that she could run and hide. "That why you never told me you had a sister?"

Jem wanted to bluff, but the words failed to come to her.

They turned slowly to the music, and Reese didn't press for an answer. "Yep, your sister's not ugly," he repeated. "You, on the other hand, have never looked more beautiful."

Her lips trembled as one of his fingers reached out to still them. Refusing to think further, Jem sank against his chest as he led them slowly across the floor.

The rest of the evening, Jem held her head high, ignoring her sister, concentrating on her husband. When Michael Fairchild complimented her, she took it in stride, for the first time not assuming he spoke only out of kindness.

Refusing to dwell on her reasoning, she positioned herself to dance every dance with Reese. Once, when she glanced at Lily, she thought her face gleamed with satisfaction and victory. But that hardly made sense. Reese was in her arms, not her sister's.

Holding Jem carefully, Reese swirled around the floor, wondering again about this unfathomable woman. She was secure enough to issue orders to a hundred men, but her esteem disappeared around her sister. And he had the feeling Lily knew the effect she had on Jem and was prodding her with the knowledge. He wasn't sure quite why, but as Jem settled closer into his arms he chose not to question her.

What had seemed so simple months ago was now incredibly complex. How was he going to ride away from this woman? His expression sobered, the fine lines around his mouth tensing. Worse, how could he stay and live under the shadow of another man? Jem tipped her head back, and Reese stared into the bottomless depths of her eyes. It was a fanciful notion, the hired help married to the owner. Theirs was an intolerable situation and one that had no solution. After the year ended, he had to leave. When Jem's eyes softened, his chest echoed with the pain; he knew not all of him would go. His heart would be splintered to remain with her.

Chapter 30

Jem stared with distaste at the retreating back of Cushman's horse. Yet another unexpected visit. He'd hoped to force her vote at the association again.

"He giving you trouble, Miz McIntire?" Grady Orton asked, his dark eyes shifting toward the trail Cushman left behind.

"Not any more than usual," she responded, grateful for his instant understanding. "Have you ridden the line today?"

He shook his head. "No, ma'am. Pete's got me mending the corral. He assigned the outposts, and I have to be out there tomorrow."

Jem acknowledged his words and then headed toward the outposts on the northern boundary that flanked the Fairchild ranch, thinking she might extend her ride to see Abigail.

When she spotted the men, however, she judged from their expressions that something was very wrong. Boyd Harris had been assigned the outpost they stood at and was gesturing as she rode up. "What's wrong?"

"We're missing a hell of a lot of cattle," Reese answered grimly.

"Michael Fairchild just left. Said he's lost better than five hundred head," Pete added.

Jem seldom felt fear, but now it flickered through her body as she remembered how the same string of events had led to her father's death. "Does he know any more than we do?"

"No, but he asked us all to show up at the association meeting this week. Thinks we all need to stick together and flush out the rustler." Reese drew up the cinch under Danny's saddle, smoothing the leather.

"Cushman won't cooperate."

"You don't know that," Reese argued.

Jem didn't continue the argument, knowing Reese would have to see for himself. She pulled up her horse and turned toward the Fairchild ranch. The meeting was in two days, and she had no doubt Cushman would act in his usual fashion.

It took little time to determine that Jem was right. Cushman had argued for better than an hour of the meeting that the sodbusters were the ones to worry about, not some two-bit rustlers.

"You wouldn't say that if they were stealing your cattle," Michael Fairchild finally shouted in exasperation.

Jem stood up, realization hitting her with numbing force. "And why is that, Cushman? Everybody in the valley's been hit but you."

Mutterings started around the room, an ugly force of suspicion. "Yeah, why is that, Cushman?" a rancher in the back yelled out.

Cushman's face purpled in anger. "Don't you see what she's trying to do? Her father was a thief, and now she's accusing me to throw the suspicion off her."

Jem remained standing, meeting Cushman eye to eye. "And why would I need to do that? My father's dead. He wasn't a thief when he was alive, and I think we can all agree he hasn't come back from the grave to start rustling."

"Only reason you're stirring this up is to keep us from voting on the sodbusters," Cushman snarled, his pale eyes flashing with anger.

"I'm the one who brought it up," Michael reminded

him. "You tell me where I can find my missing beef, and I'll let you vote all you want."

"You finally ready to change your vote and keep the homesteaders out?" Cushman demanded.

"Hell, no. And you can count on that till one of us is dead." Michael's threat hung in the silent air for long suspended moments. Then the meeting broke into shouts and arguments as the men left their seats and swarmed across the room.

"Let's get out of here." Reese spoke close to her ear.

"But—" she protested, not willing to give up the fight.

"We're not going to accomplish anything here. We'll talk to Michael tomorrow and decide what we want to do. I'd sooner band together with a nest of rattlesnakes than this bunch."

Agreeing, Jem allowed him to lead her out of the crowded, noisy room into the star-filled night. The silence was startling after the hour of shouting and accusations. Although the cold bit into their faces, their heavy wool coats kept them warm. Jem watched as Reese smoothed the close-fitting leather gloves on his hands. Even though she'd seen him perform the task hundreds of times, it had never brought a lump of emotion to her throat. His fingers, long and full of strength, fit sensuously in the smooth leather. Remembering their touch on her own skin, she shivered despite her warm clothing.

"Jem?"

She jerked her distracted thoughts back to the present.

"So we agree, we'll talk to Michael tomorrow?"

"Yes," she said in a husky voice. At that moment she supposed she'd have agreed to anything.

They spent the long ride home in companionable silence as they remained wrapped up in their own thoughts. Reese had spread a warm blanket over both their laps, and his strong leg was pressed next to hers, offering its warmth.

A memory of the first meeting they'd attended together washed over her, startling in its difference. Tonight they'd stood together, firmly on the same side, sharing the same views.

Despite the cold wind howling on the prairie, Jem felt warm and safe, a feeling she'd gotten from Reese. As the wagon lurched toward home she was unaccountably glad for his presence. Snuggling even closer to his side, she glanced up long enough to see the surprise register on his face, to be replaced by pleasure. Jem's eyes flickered shut briefly. Tomorrow they would have to confront the rustlers and their threat, but tonight all was right in the world.

"I still say setting a trap's the best way," Michael insisted. A week and four meetings later, they still couldn't decide on a plan of action.

"And dangerous." Reese was right, and Jem met his eyes in agreement. Michael's plan would put them in the direct path of the rustlers, provided the outlaws kept using the same pattern they had so far. Trying to trap them on the outposts would be tricky. The outposts on the Bar-W were situated ten to twelve miles apart around the perimeter. Those on the Fairchild ranch were somewhat closer together since Michael's men didn't have as much land to patrol. In either case, a man would be exposed to ambush.

"What's Harris doing?" Jem asked, noting Boyd's deserted outpost. How strange. He knew they were to meet there.

"Cutting for sign. Thinks the strays are headed that way." Pete gestured toward the south.

"If the rustlers didn't get them," Jem pointed out.

"Whoever's doing this has the"—Michael paused, glanced at Jem, considered his choice of words, and continued—"nerve to go brass-band stealing. He's likely to pull anything."

The overt stock raiding Michael referred to did take a lot of guts. And so did his plan. The strategy was to set traps for the rustlers on the most deserted borders of his ranch. By putting his best guns on those strategic outposts and doubling the manpower, Michael intended to take the thieves by surprise. His plan would leave a few men in vulnerable positions, but the risk would be worth it.

"Let's find Boyd and ask if he's seen anything out of the ordinary." Reese mounted his horse as he spoke. The line riders rode between their posts, forming a living fence around the ranch, watching for anything out of the ordinary. If someone had stolen the cattle from his area, Boyd should know.

When they spotted Boyd, he had met up with Grady Orton, the next line rider out. The cow Grady had lassoed stood between the scowling men.

"What's the problem, boys?" Reese asked as they rode up.

"Look at this brand, Mr. McIntire." Grady pushed the cow forward eagerly.

"Any fool can see what a botched-up job this is," Boyd protested.

Jem dismounted to examine the cow. She quickly determined that the Whitaker brand had been altered to look like Cushman's. Boyd was right—it was a bad attempt.

"Probably got loose before they could get it right." Grady ran his fingers over the brand.

"Or somebody wants to make it look that way," Boyd insisted.

"What're you chewing on, Boyd?" Pete asked.

"Maybe somebody wants us to think Cushman's the rustler. Hell, why else is this one cow loose on our range?"

"Could be it got left behind in the raid," Michael offered. He shoved his hat back on his forehead. "It is a damn fool thing to do, though."

"Cushman doesn't strike me as a fool," Reese stated.

"He's every inch that and more." Jem was furious. Here was proof that Cushman was behind the raids—just as she was certain he'd been the culprit who'd killed her father. And Reese and Michael were willing to dismiss his guilt because of Boyd Harris's assertions.

"Hold on, Jem," Pete interrupted. "Why don't we take this cow back and corral it? Then, if we find more, you'll have some proof." He ran his fingers over the distorted brand. "This one cow's not enough to go gunning for Cushman."

Glancing up, Jem caught Boyd Harris staring at her. He dropped his eyes after a moment, but she couldn't dispel the notion that he was glad there wasn't enough proof.

"Good idea, Pete," she finally answered. "I'm going to ride over to see Abigail. You coming, Michael?"

"No, I need to get on over and set up the trap, but give her my love."

Jem turned her horse about before she gave in to the temptation to question Boyd Harris, knowing how little Reese would appreciate her distrust of his man.

After she and Michael rode off in separate directions, Reese examined the cow again. "Thanks for the support, Pete."

"Only said what I thought was right." Pete watched as Boyd Harris entered the outpost for some rope. "Why do you suppose Harris was so quick to stick up for Cushman?"

Reese frowned. "Been wondering about that myself."

"I figure if you think he's a good man, he must be all right, but he sure has some funny ways."

"Between the war and then being accused of stealing . . ." Reese shook his head. "He's not the same man I knew, but I still believe he's honest."

Watching Boyd emerge from the lean-to, Pete dug his boot into the snowbank. "I hope to hell you're right."

Jem approached the Bar-W, her depression lifting as she spotted Abigail's wagon in front. No wonder she hadn't found her at the Fairchild ranch. Eagerly she dismounted, tying her horse to the rail before running up the steps to the porch. Shrugging out of her heavy woolen poncho and hat, she tossed them on the oak tree and walked to the parlor to find Abigail.

Her steps halted as she stepped over the threshold. Abigail was there, but so was Lily. Jem's stomach sank—the

242

reason she had sought Abigail out was to talk about her sister.

Lily spotted her first. "Why are you hanging out there in the hall?"

Abigail stood up and turned toward the doorway. "Jem, do come in. Lily and I were having a nice chat, but I'd hoped to see you."

"You're lucky she pried herself away from her horse," Lily remarked as she slid back in her chair, crossing her ankles.

"I always consider myself fortunate when Jem has time to visit." Abigail's voice was a gentle reminder that the two were friends. "After all, she has a ranch to run."

Lily rose abruptly. "You needn't get into a snit. I happen to like Jem myself."

Jem froze as she was about to sit down, her face registering shock.

"Oh, stop it. We don't see eye to eye on everything but we are sisters, after all."

Jem slanted Abigail an incredulous look. "Yes, we've always been very close."

"Jem's all put out because I tried to flirt with Reese," Lily announced as Abigail gasped and then covered her mouth with her hand. Lily waved her hand in dismissal. "Oh, pooh. He wouldn't flirt back. I tried to tell Jem he only had eyes for her, but she wouldn't listen." Abigail stuttered, but nothing recognizable emerged as Lily continued. "I did everything I could to make him notice me, and do you know what he did?"

Abigail nodded mutely.

"Nothing. Absolutely nothing. And does Jem believe he's crazy about her? Oh, no." Lily imitated a dramatic swoon. "Of course, her heart belongs to Charles Sawyer."

Abigail's look of reproach made Jem lower her head uncomfortably.

Lily swooshed her skirts as she walked toward the doorway, leaving a trail of her distinctive perfume. "If that gorgeous man belonged to me, I'd damned well fight for him and I sure wouldn't be mooning about some nit like Charles. But can you tell Jem anything?"

Abigail only stared at Lily without speaking. The latter shrugged her shoulders. "It seems the women around here are incredibly slow-witted." She started to leave the room, then turned, delivering one last blow. "On second thought, Jem, maybe I'll try harder to win him, since you obviously don't want him." She left, swinging her curvaceous hips as she walked up the staircase.

Jem and Abigail craned their heads to watch her performance, and Jem nearly jumped when Abigail spoke. "You're not still carrying on about Charles, are you?"

When she didn't answer, Abigail pressed. "Jem?"

Exasperated, Jem rose and paced the room. "I don't know what to think, Abigail." Her words were halting. "I do care for Reese, but I promised Charles I'd wait."

"Forever? How do you know he's not in Mexico with some little señorita on his lap?"

"Abigail!"

"Jem, you're a smart woman. No man leaves the woman he loves for nearly a year without any word." Jem didn't answer, the hurt on her face visible. "And Reese is a wonderful man. I don't believe you've ever considered how much he means to you. What if Lily did manage to win him away because you let her?"

Jem stared ahead, aware of Abigail's concern, even more aware of the conflicting emotions battling inside. What would she do if Reese rode away tomorrow and never came back? Her words were halting as she glanced at her friend. "I don't think I know, Abby." She turned away, hiding the consternation in her face. "I'm so confused lately. When Lily danced with Reese at the party, I wanted to scratch her eyes out."

"That's healthy."

"No, it's not. He'll be free in a few months to go wherever he wants." Her voice slowed, almost halted. "To anyone he wants."

"Have you thought about convincing him to stay?"

"To give up his dreams, his freedom? That's the only reason he agreed to this marriage, to have enough money to never answer to anyone else."

"Maybe it's time to let him know that if he stays, he won't have to answer to anyone."

Bitterness crept into Jem's voice. "I'd sooner skin a cow from the inside out."

"I didn't say it would be easy, but most everything worth getting is worth fighting for."

"What if Charles comes back?" Jem couldn't hide the anguish in her voice.

Abigail's voice was steady, her gaze level. "Yes, Jem, what about that?"

"I don't know."

"It's time to decide, Jem. What if you knew Reese would be gone tomorrow and you'd never see him again? How do you think you'd feel?"

The constriction in Jem's throat overwhelmed her at the stark thought. She dropped her chin to her chest, an unexpected sign of defeat. "I can only pray I don't have to find out."

Chapter
31

The body was cold, as cold as the frozen tundra he lay upon. His hat obscured much of his face, as did the newly fallen snow that nearly hid his corpse from discovery.

Jem swallowed with difficulty as Michael started to turn him over. Her eyes skipped over his weathered body, the bloody hole in the back of his coat standing out as Michael eased him around. It was the Fairchilds' missing cowhand, Daniel Tondo. Since the raids had intensified, everyone had been on alert, but apparently that hadn't saved Daniel.

"Michael, it wasn't your fault," Jem reminded him.

"Tell that to his family." Bitterness was etched in Michael's weary features. His ranch had been hit particularly hard since he'd stood up to Cushman. Each association meeting had dissolved into little more than a bitter verbal battle and standoff. And now this.

"Jem's right, Michael. It could've happened to any of us," Reese added.

"Cowardly bastards, shooting him in the back," Pete stated, staring in remorse at the fallen man.

The fear Jem had been feeling for the past week intensified. Michael's plan was both daring and dangerous. Remembering her father's fate, Jem had been reluctant for any of them to take part. Her eyes lifted, scanning the location. Had Daniel known his killers? Sweeping the area, she paused when she saw Boyd Harris. Kneeling on the ground, he held something in his hands, something he appeared to be concealing.

Making little noise, she approached him. "What have you got there, Boyd?"

Startled, he acted almost guilty.

When he didn't speak, she squatted down and took the iron from his hand. Cushman's branding iron! "What was your excuse for finding this here going to be?"

"Jem?" Reese's voice behind her brought her to her feet as she whirled around.

"Boyd was trying to hide this!" she accused.

Reese took the incriminating iron from her hands and turned it over slowly. "Boyd?"

"I just now found it."

Reese kept examining the iron as Pete and Michael joined them.

Boyd averted his face from Jem's accusing glare and appealed to Reese. "Hell, you don't think Cushman's stupid enough to leave his own iron here, do you?"

"What I'd like to know is why you keep defending him," Jem demanded.

"I'm not defending him, ma'am. Seems to me like someone's trying to frame him."

"Who would do that?"

Boyd's voice was stubborn. "The rustlers."

Jem's eyes narrowed. "What stake do you have in this? Did Cushman hire you to work from the inside, throw us off the track?"

Boyd met her gaze steadily. "No, I just don't believe in letting anybody get framed."

"Maybe you're looking out for a fellow thief!"

Her accusation rang in the air.

"Jem!" Reese yanked her arm and brought her away from Boyd's face. "Watch what you say to my men."

"Your men? Who's paying their salaries?"

The others standing around them seemed to take a collective breath of disbelief. Reese's fury was visible, a tangible force reverberating in the air.

"You are, boss, but if your high-handed tactics cause us to lose any more cattle, there won't be money for *anyone's* salary."

"I won't have a traitor under my own roof," she retorted.

Reese's voice was low and full of anger. "You keep this up and you won't have me under your roof, either."

As he swung onto his horse Reese's gaze was withering, and Jem swallowed at the threat in his eyes. All of Abigail and Lily's words came back to haunt her. Was she about to learn how she would feel if Reese carried out his threat?

The next few days resembled a state of undeclared war. Jem's anger gradually turned into a sickening mixture of fear and envy. Reese changed from a polite brother-in-law into a charming and attentive companion for Lily.

Jem couldn't understand the talons of jealousy that clawed at her when she saw them together, laughing, seemingly carefree. After all, she reminded herself somewhat futilely, she'd known Reese would leave in a short time, and besides, her love had been promised to Charles.

That promise had started to fray at the edges. Abigail's conjecture had taken root, and Jem tried to sort out her feelings for Charles. What stood out the most was his sweetness and how special he had made her feel. One thing was certain, her relationship with Reese could never be considered sweet. And right now, at one of the dances Lily had insisted on attending, she felt about as special as yesterday's leftovers.

Brooding, Jem stared across the room at Reese and Lily.

"You going to just sit back and watch?" Abigail asked.

"What do you suggest? Should I go rip Lily's hair out and tell her to leave Reese alone?"

"No, but you might start treating Reese like a husband."

"What do you mean?"

"Michael told me what happened when you found Daniel's body. I thought you'd gotten over this boss business."

Jem stared again across the room. "At this rate Reese

may stay in my family, but it doesn't look like it'll be as my husband."

"You're behaving like a fool." Jem's head jerked upright at Abigail's words. "You threw him at Lily. First you told him he wasn't a man and then gave him the opportunity to prove he was."

Jem stuttered, but Abigail didn't give her a chance to rebut her words.

"Thing is, I really believe Lily's only playing along to wake you up. But you'd better do something now, or there won't be anything left to salvage."

Abigail rejoined Michael as Jem continued to observe Reese and Lily. Girding her courage, she approached them. Lily's smile was even, revealing nothing.

"Your husband is wonderfully witty," Lily proclaimed, not removing her hand from his arm.

"He keeps me in stitches all the time," Jem replied without even a flicker of a smile.

Lily's eyebrows raised. "Yes, I can see that."

Jem turned to Reese. "Would you dance with me?"

"Is that an order?"

Color high, Jem stood her ground. "Does it have to be?"

Reese disengaged his arm and stood up. "Whatever you say."

As he led them across the room Jem remembered the last time they'd danced together, their hearts beating wildly, their shared passion. The stiffness with which Reese held her brought a lump to her throat. He didn't meet her eyes, instead gazing over her head to scan the other dancers.

When they turned the corner of the room, Jem felt the cold metal of her locket against her skin, remembering the picture Reese had placed there, the sentiment behind the gesture.

His silence unnerved her, and she even wished they were battling rather than politely waltzing like strangers. "Reese?"

"Yes?"

She swallowed. This was more difficult than she had supposed. "Has Lily told you what her plans are?"

"No. I didn't know that was one of my assignments."

His bitterness stung. "It wasn't. I just thought she might have confided in you."

"In a mere ranch hand?"

Jem's voice grated over clenched teeth. "You know you're not a mere hand."

"I do?" He twirled them around the room smoothly.

"I just can't understand why you stand up for that man."

"Boyd? Could be I know more about him than you do."

"Did it ever occur to you that I might know more about the rustling than you do? After all, that is how my father was killed."

"If you weren't so quick to throw your weight around, a body might learn what's really happening. Instead you want us to waste time on a wild-goose chase."

She was suspicious. "What do you mean?"

"Just what I said. If someone planted that iron so we'd go after Cushman, that'd leave the rest of the herd wide open. If you weren't so all-fired sure that Boyd was behind this, you'd listen to him and realize he makes sense."

"And if you're wrong?"

"Then you'd be right, which would make you happy."

The pain was increasing. He made her sound so small and mean. Suddenly she couldn't stand the pretense of socializing. "I believe I want to go home now."

"Whatever you say, boss."

He started to walk with her, and she halted. "Where are you going?"

"To take you home, of course."

"What about Lily?"

"I imagine she'll ride home with Pete and Della."

"I can find my own way home."

His voice grated. "Is that an order?"

She swallowed, biting her lips in agitation. "Of course not, I just thought—"

"I'm ready to go home. I don't have any stomach for more partying."

The silent ride home stretched out interminably. Jem attributed the heat behind her eyelids to the strain of the evening, refusing to consider the possibility of tears. She was not like her sister, giving in to every weak emotion that flitted by. Watching Reese's set face, she was certain he could point out their differences even more clearly.

When they reached the dark house, only the sound of the winter wind permeated the air. Snow had begun falling on them shortly after they'd started home, and now it blanketed the dark sky. Caught up in her own problems, Jem hadn't realized the severity of the approaching storm.

"I hope the others get home before the storm gets really bad, or else they stay put," Jem fretted.

"Pete's got good sense. He won't take the women out in a blizzard."

"I know, but—"

They reached the barn, and Reese turned to her in exasperation. "For hell's sake, Jem, let people do their own thinking. You can't be running everybody all the time. Way you act you'd think the world would stop if you weren't there to direct every move."

Jem jumped down from the wagon, moving aside as Reese began to unhitch the horses. "You don't mean everyone, you're talking about yourself. I happen to know that Pete and Della appreciate my concern."

"Did you ever ask them?"

"I don't have to," she replied, finding the lantern and lighting the wick.

Reese led the horses inside, muttering as he stabled the beasts. "Of course not, I forgot for a moment that you know everything, that you're in charge of everybody."

Jem paused as she was closing the doors to the blowing snow. The hurt sliced through her at his callous words.

She'd only taken charge when she had to. Because it was in her nature, she had always led. Why did Reese make that sound so terrible? "Not quite everything," she replied in a low tone.

Exasperated, Reese slammed the stall door shut. "Why do you do it, Jem?" He raked his hands through steel black curls. "You make me act like a crazy person. First you act like you have more balls than I do." She issued a sharp gasp. "Then you get all sappy and sentimental over Christmas. Then you decide you want the balls back. And now you're throwing your idiotic sister at me."

"Idiotic?"

Reese grasped her arms and shook her slightly. "Didn't you hear what I said?"

"Yes, you said she was idiotic."

Reese's hands relaxed somewhat, running up the length of her arms. "You're only hearing what you want to."

Her arms crept up around his neck to rest in the curls behind his neck. "Don't you like being around Lily?"

"She reminds me of syrup on a stack of hotcakes. Too sweet, too sticky, and her mouth's always running."

Jem laughed, imagining how Lily would react if she heard the comparison. When Reese's eyes met hers, her laughter faltered. "I can't change, Reese. I'll never be like Lily or Abigail, and I don't know if I'll ever stop wanting to be in charge."

The fire in her eyes was one he remembered well. She was the most stubborn, muleheaded woman he'd ever known. When her hand reached out tentatively to touch his cheek, he recognized that she also held the key to every emotion he'd kept firmly locked inside.

Their lips touched questioningly, offering apologies, new beginnings. The sweetness intrigued him, the taste of her mouth inflamed him.

He pulled off her heavy woolen coat and then drew her close to nuzzle her long neck. The fresh scent of her skin always drew him to her. Deigning to employ sachets and perfumes, she smelled of the soap and scented shampoo she used. When he nipped lightly on the soft skin behind her ears, she moaned against him.

The abstinence of the past few days struck them both. As though months instead of days had gone by, they clung together, their bodies signaling desire.

"We're in the barn," Jem muttered against Reese's lips.

"I don't care," he responded, closing the gate to sanity. Their room in the house might well have been miles away, so great was their impatience.

Jem's hands slid beneath his coat, pushing it back, trapping his arms as she devoured him with her lips. She inhaled his unique aroma, aroused as she always was by the feel of his velvety skin. Shrugging free of his coat, he captured her, extracting a sigh as he cupped her breasts through the confining material.

When she reached boldly to cup his manhood, she felt him strain against her hand. A sense of power filled her as she realized the effect she had upon him. It took only seconds for him to reciprocate, his hand reaching through the layers of material to palm her heated mound.

The frustrating barrier of clothes was soon removed, and Jem reveled in the feel of his skin against hers. As always, Reese marveled at her long-limbed beauty. Like a fine filly, her shapely legs glowed in the dim lantern light. Her breasts, high and firm, beckoned as he bent his head to taste them.

A pile of clean straw welcomed them, its softness more inviting than a feather mattress.

As though possessed, Jem couldn't touch enough of him. Each strong muscle, each sensitive spot appealed to her. Replacing her hands with her lips, she kissed him feverishly, relishing his clean taste, welcoming each new inch of skin. When she came to his legs, her lips crept along his inner thighs, imitating the actions he'd practiced before on her. He shuddered beneath her ministrations. When her lips grazed the stubby hair on his groin and

253

touched the length of his manhood, he pulled her up, settling her on his chest, fitting his hips to hers.

When he placed her warmth over his waiting hardness,
she gasped aloud, surprised anew at the pleasure she
felt.

Her breasts swayed close to him, grazing the nubby
hardness of his nipples with her own. She looked down,
overwhelmed by the fit of their bodies together.

Reese clasped his arms around her, reversing their positions without losing contact. Her hips came off the floor as
his thrusts deepened as though seeking the center of her
being. Panting, she met each stroke, using the strength of
her legs to entice him.

"Which one of us is the boss?" he demanded, his breath
short, his strength filling her.

She shook her head from side to side, evading him. He
stopped her not with a kiss, but with his eyes. "Who?"

Her body rocked with the sensations he was creating,
still she couldn't bend to his will. Her lips sought his, her
tongue washing the recesses of his mouth, hoping to stop
his questions. When he broke free, the question still hovered on his lips. "Who, Jem?"

"No one," she finally conceded, unwilling to submit to
his mastery, yet unwilling to have him leave her insatiated
body.

His hips ground against hers, and she reached as close
to him as possible, her own hipbones outlined against
him.

When he felt her body jerk in a spasmodic reaction to
his movements, he penetrated even deeper, finally joining
her in completion. When he would have rolled off, she
stilled him. "Stay."

He plucked the strands of hair from her face, reveling in
the dewy glow he saw in her eyes. "Why?"

She grew unaccountably shy. "This part is almost the
best. I always hate to let you go."

Reese answered her with a soul-searching kiss. The tenderness flowed through to Jem, rendering her heart a lethal blow. "I'll always stay for you, Jem."

Her eyes closed, hiding the heat of unbidden tears. What would she do without this man? The pain that threatened to overwhelm her was proof she couldn't bear to find out.

Chapter 32

The clank of shovels hitting the door woke Reese and Jem with a start. Disoriented, they struggled to free themselves from the pile of straw Reese had covered them with during the night. The snug barn had been reinforced by the bales of hay he had stacked in front of the double doors, blocking the drafts from the blizzard that howled through the night.

When they'd discovered the blinding snow that obscured the ranch house, both had decided it was foolhardy to venture into the storm. Too many people had gotten lost a dozen yards from their destination in such blizzards only to die a few feet from safety.

Between their sturdy coats and the straw they'd used for insulation, they'd remained warm through the night. They thought they'd be able to maintain their dignity, however, and slip unnoticed into the house in the morning.

The scrabbling and clinking of shovels dispelled that notion. Jumping to their feet, Jem and Reese tried to brush the straw from their clothes as the sound of voices got nearer.

When the door flung open, they stopped their frantic motions as Pete and Lily burst through.

"Thank God you're all right!" Lily rushed forward and hugged her sister, tears shimmering in her eyes. "When you weren't in the house, we were afraid you'd been lost in the storm. I wanted to go back and look, but Pete made us check in here first."

"Hell, we didn't want to make anybody worry," Reese answered for them both. "By the time we got the horses stabled, we couldn't see to make it to the house. How'd you get home?"

"We stayed the night and rode home this morning after it cleared. Only a fool would go out in a blizzard like that," Pete replied.

"That so?" Reese's words were for Jem's benefit, and she knew it.

Clearing her throat, Jem tried to ignore Reese's superior smile. "Thanks for digging us out. We're starving."

Lily examined them critically. "You look like you just woke up." Another light dawned in her eyes—this time it was one of understanding. "Let's go tell Della you're safe. She's worrying herself sick."

Lily led the procession as they emerged from the barn. In the aftermath of the storm, the snow glistened in the cold air like so many diamonds sprinkled carelessly from the heavens above. The bright blue of the sky, obliterated only by the powerful thrust of the mountain crags, denied any memory of the harsh night before.

After breakfast, Jem sought out Lily and found her in her room. A satchel lay open on the bed, half-filled with clothes. "Lily?"

Her sister turned and smiled as she carried another handful of garments to the case. "It's time for me to be moving on."

"But why? You've only been here a short time. We've hardly had time to catch up."

"It's been long enough." Lily stopped folding the clothes for a moment. Then she turned to the bureau to busy herself with the toiletries laid out there. "You know me, I need to keep moving."

"But we haven't had much of a visit yet," Jem protested.

"I think you've had about as much of me as you can tolerate."

"Oh, Lily. I'm sorry if I haven't been kind to you." Jem paced the room. "I've been kind of confused about a lot of things and—"

"There's no need to explain. Newlyweds need time alone. Besides, I'm ready to roam." Lily's voice regained its normal blitheness.

Jem shed her usual reserve and took the things from Lily's hands, setting them aside and then hugging her sister fiercely. "I don't want you to leave. Give me a chance to start over again, please."

The unexpected entreaty was Lily's undoing. "But, Jem . . ." She faltered in light of the plea on Jem's face.

"It would mean so much to me."

Lily was lost and she knew it. She doubted that Jem had asked a single thing of her in twenty years. "I'll stay if you let me get something off my chest."

Jem nodded.

"Forget about Charles. What you feel for him is an illusion, an overinflated memory. If he'd loved you, he would have stayed by your side. What you have with Reese is real. Don't lose it."

Jem stared silently at her sister for several long moments. "I'll think about what you've said." She turned and walked to the door, pausing as she fiddled with the doorhandle. "Thanks for staying. This is your home, too."

Lily smiled briefly and watched as Jem closed the door behind her. In the quiet of the room, her smile dissolved. "Not anymore, Jem. Not anymore."

The altered brands on the hides seemed to be irrefutable proof.

"You going to tell me this is my imagination? Or another attempt to frame Cushman?" Jem demanded, her expression as grave as the others' with her.

"Most of us know better than to try and tell you anything," Reese replied, but there was no rancor in his tone.

"I say we move our men to Cushman's border. It's the only way to make sure we catch him in the act," Michael insisted.

"I think we ought to confront him right now." Jem was stubborn.

"We haven't got the power to do that," Reese reminded her. "Cushman's got the other ranchers stirred up about that new bunch of sodbusters. And in case you've forgotten, he's got more hands than all of us put together. We get into a range war with him and all we'll wind up with is a ranch full of graves."

One grave in particular stood out starkly in Jem's mind. Her father, vital and full of life, lay in the cold ground as the result of this cowardly thief. She didn't intend to let anyone else she cared for come to such an end.

"Then what do you suggest?" Jem asked finally.

"Michael's onto the right idea. Only thing is, I think I ought to take on that section. Otherwise his whole western flank is open."

Fear clutched at Jem. "What about all the men we employ? You said you trusted Boyd Harris. Why can't he ride that area?"

"Because I need him in place." Reese still didn't trust Grady Orton, and he was assigned to the post closest to Boyd's. Reese didn't want the man roaming free. His unprotected back itched at the very thought.

"Let's wait to decide," Jem hedged. She glanced up at Pete, who had been silent during the entire exchange. With a start, she realized his face was a pale shade of gray. "Pete? You all right?"

"Sure, just a little tired."

"I need you to head back to the house with me anyway to check the winter feed. Want to make sure we have enough to last a few more months. Otherwise we'll have to send someone to the railhead and buy more."

"Jem, we need to finish up out here."

"I'd rather not ride alone, if you don't mind, Pete."

Reese glanced up sharply, saw Pete's waning color, and

didn't comment. When Pete didn't argue further, Jem sensed he hadn't the strength to do so. Arriving back at the ranch, she spotted a strange horse at the railing. Hesitantly she hitched her own horse.

"I'll see who's here. Why don't you have some lunch, and then we'll head over to the barn together." She watched him with a worried frown as he agreed tiredly and headed toward the kitchen.

When Jem stepped in the parlor, however, she wasn't sure who might faint first. The familiar outline of the body leaning toward the roaring fire brought her to a halt. It couldn't be!

"Jem?" He stepped forward. "It is you. You've changed so much I wasn't sure. You're more beautiful than I remembered."

Her voice was little more than a croak as it emerged. "Charles?" She stood woodenly as he crossed the space, handing her an immense box of chocolates before engulfing her in a huge embrace. "Where . . . I mean . . . when did you get here?"

He laughed, the hearty sound she'd always loved. "I'm not a ghost, if that's what you mean. Word's up the Snake River and back about the trouble here." Releasing her, he stepped away, his gaze raking over her appreciatively, a low whistle emerging.

She blushed. "Charles!"

He brought her close again. "I've felt like such a coward since I left you the last time to face everything on your own. I just couldn't do it again."

His boyish face was earnest, the pale, almost colorless blue of his eyes shimmering in sincerity. This was the man she'd pledged to wait for till eternity. How could she tell him she'd married another?

Charles embraced her again, tilting her head back for a kiss. When his lips touched hers, the butterflies she'd always experienced stayed in their cocoons. Slightly deflated, she pulled away, wondering where the excitement of his kisses had gone.

Seeing the joy in his eyes, Jem knew she had to tell him and knew no other way than to simply blurt out the truth. "Things aren't quite the same as when you left, Charles."

"I know that, Jem. That's one of the reasons I came back. If things don't turn around, you'll lose the Bar-W."

"That's not all." His appealing face angled toward hers in question, and Jem drew a deep breath. "The thing is . . ." She paused, hardly able to utter the words. "That is, since you left, I got married."

His smile didn't falter as he answered, "I know."

Chapter *33*

"You know?" The disbelief rang through Jem's thoughts and echoed in the room.

"Of course. You had to marry him to stop being black-listed."

Jem cleared her throat, trying to fight the swirl of emotions. "You knew and you didn't come back?"

"And accomplish what? You did what you had to in order to save the ranch. Did you want me to interfere, make you feel guilty, ruin all your plans?"

"Well, no. But it was you I wanted to marry, and I didn't know where you'd gone, when you'd be back."

"You'd already married McIntire, and I didn't want to confuse you. With me away, you could do what you had to. I know this cowboy can't mean anything to you." He ran a hand across her check, pausing near her lips. "Not after what we meant to each other."

Jem watched the mercurial light in Charles's eyes, re-membering how he'd hypnotized her into believing she was so special and pretty. He took her hand delicately, lowering her to a chair as though she were a porcelain doll. "I see it in your face, Jem. Your feelings haven't changed." A tiny imp inside her screamed that they had. "You need someone you can trust. I want to be that some-one for you, Jem. I failed you once. I won't do it again."

Jem allowed him to take her hand in his. "Charles, things are so different—"

"Not so different that I can't take care of you." It occurred to Jem that Reese had never felt it necessary to take care of her. "I don't want you in the middle of all this ugliness and I'm here to see you don't have to be."

"But I've always been involved in whatever happens at the Bar-W," she protested without much vehemence, remembering clearly how Charles had always made her feel protected, cossetted.

"McIntire doesn't know anything about running a ranch. I gave up my job to help you get things straightened out and I won't leave till everything's set right."

"Charles, that's not necessary. Everything is under control—"

"That's not what I hear." Charles uncorked the brandy and poured himself a generous tumbler. As he downed the liquid Jem studied him, wondering why he'd chosen now to show up. Involuntarily she compared the softness of his manner with Reese's rangy leanness, knowing the comparison didn't favor Charles. No two men could be more different. But her heartstrings tugged as Charles sat down beside her, picking up her hand and bringing it to his lips. As she always had in his presence, she forgot that she was tall and skinny. Thoughts of being an unwanted tomboy disappeared under his attention.

"Charles, I was beginning to believe you weren't ever coming back." It had been her deepest fear; now it hung between them.

"I didn't know if I was." Seeing the shock on her face, he continued rapidly. "Not because of you, Jem. I knew no one ever thought I was good enough for you." His face contorted angrily. "Foremen don't marry owners' daughters. And it was clear I could never be considered family by the ranch owners." He clenched the glass tightly in his hand and then turned aside as Jem ached at the sound of the bitterness in his voice. Not only did he consider himself inferior, now he was faced with the pain of her marriage to another. "How could you do it, Jem? How could you marry him?"

Unexpected, undeserved guilt bit into her. "I didn't know where to find you." The explanation sounded weak, apologetic.

"That won't stand between us again," he answered, firm conviction outlined on his face. "I'm back now."

"And why is that?" Reese's barely controlled voice reverberated through the room, and both Charles and Jem started at the sound.

She jumped up guiltily, removing her hand from Charles's embrace, feeling much like she had when her father had caught her smoking one of his cigars when she was eight. She seriously doubted that Reese would want her to finish what she'd started with Charles as her father had made her do with the cigar. But her stomach had the same sick feeling.

"Charles wants to help us." Even to Jem her voice sounded weak.

"You're not wanted here, Sawyer."

Jem opened her mouth to protest, saw the barely contained fury on Reese's face, and thought better of it.

"Get on your horse and don't stop riding till you hit the Dakotas." Reese's stance was proprietary, refusing to give an inch.

Charles picked up his hat from the table. "I'll leave— for now. But I'm not going far. McIntire, you're not even in charge of this ranch, much less the territory." He turned to Jem. "I'll be close enough for you to find me."

A muscle in Reese's cheek twitched as he tried to control his temper. Charles strolled out of the room and through the front door. As it closed behind him Jem implored Reese to understand. "Reese, it wasn't what you think. Charles—"

"Rode in here, and you took up where you left off. Make no mistake, Jem. While you're my wife I won't tolerate that man, under this roof or any other."

"And how much longer will that be, Reese?"

"I guess you know the answer to that better than me."

Powerful unspoken feelings reverberated through the air.

Reese raked a hand through his hair in agitation. "Can't you see what he is, Jem? I've held back from saying anything because I thought he'd tucked his tail and left your life for good." He dropped his hands. "He's flat no good, Jem."

"You don't even know him." Jem's defense was automatic.

"That's where you're wrong. I rode with him in the war. He's a liar and a thief." The accusation rang between them.

"He's no such thing!"

"He's that and more."

"You're just making wild accusations because you found him here today."

Reese picked up the elaborate box of candy Charles had left. "Sheridan only kicked one man out of his outfit—and Charles Sawyer was that man." He replaced the chocolates on the table. "One thing I don't understand. If you loved Charles, why didn't you give yourself to him?" She remained mute. "It's bothered me since the first time. Thought maybe you were playing out some elaborate act." She swallowed the thickening lump in her throat as he impaled her with his eyes. "Fact is, I'm still not sure."

His steps were heavy as he left the room, their solid sound echoing through the hall.

"You're not gonna let a good man like him get away, are you?"

Jem whirled at the sound of Della's voice. "How long have you been listening?"

"Long enough to know you're acting like a fool."

"When did Reese start getting more of your loyalty than I do?" Jem couldn't hide the hurt in her voice.

"He never did, never will. But I'm not going to watch you fall under Charles's spell again and lose the best thing that ever happened to you."

"What about my vow to wait?"

"You exchanged a few vows with Reese, too, if I recollect correctly. Seems to me they were a mite more binding than the piss water Sawyer's full of."

"Why doesn't anyone even try to understand Charles? All he wants is to help us."

"You'll have to excuse me if I don't believe a word he has to say. Slunk out of here and left you without a care when your pa died. Now that you've got a chance to hang on to the ranch, he's back."

Jem fiddled with the pillow on the settee. "Reese accused Charles of being a thief."

"Somebody's rustling the cattle."

Jem's head shot up. "Cushman all but left his signature this time, and nothing will convince me he didn't kill Pa. Charles hasn't been anywhere near here this time."

"Least that's what he wants you to think."

"Della, this is ridiculous. I would have known if Charles was close by." Jem paused. "I would have sensed it."

"Be the first thing you figured out," Della muttered under her breath.

"I thought Reese was the only one here with a hot head," Jem retorted.

Della wheeled toward the doorway. "Nope, you live here, too."

Reese slammed the barn door shut. He grabbed a bucket of oats and walked over to Danny's stall. The horse nibbled gratefully from his hand while Reese vented his frustration.

"I ought to pack up and leave right now. That woman hasn't got the sense God gave a rock." He thrust his fist angrily into the wall, not even flinching when the hard wood contacted with his hand. "Lets Sawyer waltz in here and take up with her. Any fool could see he's scum."

Even though it was late in the day, Reese led Danny from the stall and started to saddle him.

"You plannin' to take off?" Pete's voice from the back of the dusky interior startled him.

"Thinkin' about it."

"Guess I would be, too. You got your freighting company to be worrying about."

"Huh? Oh, yeah, that's right." He'd forgotten it completely. "If Sawyer's going to take over, there might not be a bonus or a freighting company."

"You gonna let him do that?"

Reese halted his movements, having smoothed the blanket on Danny's back. "You think I can stop him or Jem?"

Pete heard the bitterness and doubted it had anything to do with the gold Reese had been promised. "What happens if you don't try?"

The ranch fails and Jem belongs to Charles Sawyer. Both prospects were equally dismal. He reached for Danny's saddle, his hands connecting with the fine grade of leather. A memory of Christmas morning struck him forcefully. No one had ever tried to give him back a part of his past. He owed her to at least do the same. Remembering the memories they had created on the eve of the same holiday, he wanted even more.

Pete's voice jarred him. "You plannin' on fightin' for her?"

Reese's face was blank with surprise and Pete clapped him on the back.

"I think you'll find she's worth it."

Settling the saddle on Danny's back, Reese watched Pete leave, noticing his slow gait. Pete was wise about a lot of things, but not about his own health.

Reese cinched the saddle and led Danny from the barn. Swinging on the horse's back, he headed out toward his favorite section. The crystalline snow still glinted in the late-afternoon sun, and the purple ridges of the mountains glowed on the horizon.

Picking his way over the icy terrain, Reese found his emotions as complex as the land he rode over. A sense of pride emerged at what he and Jem had accomplished in the last several months. But it was the raw magnificence of the land that pulled at him. Climbing the crest that overlooked miles of countryside, he knew there was no place to match this one. It was as though God had poured all his best into this corner of the world.

The land alone wasn't all the good Lord had favored. Reese wasn't vain enough to believe he truly knew Jem yet, but he did know that her bluster masked compassion, and her stubbornness was born of care. If she cared less, he imagined she might be more pliant, more compromising. A vision of her sultry eyes, sleepy and satisfied after lovemaking, warmed him despite the cold, biting air. Remembering the beauty of her long limbs, he could understand Sawyer's return. A possessive streak, far stronger than any he'd ever known, seized him. He didn't intend to let those long legs stretch in ecstasy for any other man.

While he didn't want Jem hurt, he wasn't ready to give her up. Not yet. The cold wind whistled around him. Perhaps not ever.

Chapter
34

The dinner table was unusually quiet. Jem and Reese both picked at their food, neither able to muster much of an appetite. Their favorite dishes, which Della had lovingly prepared, were ignored. Finally they couldn't avoid the meal's end and their ultimate destination. Reese's boots scraped loudly against the floor as he pushed back from the table. "I'm going outside and have a smoke."

There was no relief in watching him depart. Instead the painful knot in her chest tightened like a fist. She cleared her dishes, surprising Pete and Della in the kitchen. They sat at the table, having finished their dinner, hands clasped across the table. Seeing their easy happiness was yet another blow. Remembering how Abigail had compared their relationship to her own with Reese, she wanted to give in to the agony squeezing her heart.

"You didn't have to bring these in," Della said with a smile. "Mary will be here in a few minutes to clean up."

Jem shrugged, trying to kill time before she had to face Reese in their room. "I don't mind." Della kept Pete's hand entwined in her own, and Jem suddenly remembered his pale countenance that afternoon. "Pete, would you mind keeping an eye on Milly tomorrow? I have a feeling she's going to foal any day now."

"She should be fine. I don't expect we'll see a foal for days."

"Even so, I'd feel better if you stuck around close. Do you mind?"

He scratched his head absently. "No, not if Reese doesn't have anything special lined up. But I reckon with the rustlers, he's gonna want every hand riding the line."

"I'll check with him." *And make sure he doesn't.* "Della, do you and Mary want some help with the dishes?"

"Of course not. What's wrong with you? You never—" Della stopped abruptly, and her voice changed. The inflection wasn't lost on Jem. "No, you can go on to bed. We'll take care of everything here."

Dragging her feet, Jem crossed to the stairs, climbing them with the energy of a ninety-year-old. Her hand paused on the knob of her bedroom door, and she was tempted to flee to the sanctuary of the study. Knowing avoidance wouldn't heal her aching wound, she stepped inside.

The empty room was a disappointment. Crossing to the window, she turned back the drape, easily spotting the glow of Reese's rolled cigarette in the dark, winter night. Apparently he wasn't eager to face her, either.

Changing into her gown, she discarded her clothing and searched impulsively for the lavender water Abigail had given her. But her hand fell away from the bottle. The chasm between them couldn't be crossed by toilet water.

She climbed into the cold bed and stared ahead. Bit by bit, her head angled toward the other side of the bed. Barren and lonely, the bed seemed to mock her. Her fingers crept over her lips, remembering Charles's kiss, wondering at the disappointment it had evoked. What had happened to the feelings he'd once created with only a look? Perhaps it was the shock of seeing him again so unexpectedly or the fear of discovery.

In a few short months she'd be a free woman. Free to accept Charles's caresses. The thought crowded her mind, but refused to lodge in her heart. Right now her heart was too full of pain to contemplate anything but Reese's reaction.

Had he really believed she'd only acted throughout all their lovemaking? Was their Christmas celebration special only to her?

The soft tread of Reese's boots outside their door made her freeze. Glad that she'd dimmed the lamplight, she waited in the near darkness. The rustling of his clothes as he discarded them seemed to echo in the stillness. She heard the thud of his boots, but Reese's sigh was much more distinct.

The mattress creaked under his weight, and Jem swallowed the lump in her throat, remembering the nights they'd turned eagerly to one another. Now they lay stiffly, each unwilling to bend toward the other.

She clasped her fingers around the gold locket she wore, seeking comfort from the meaning it had symbolized on their wedding day. When she felt Reese's weight shift and turn toward her, she held her breath. When he didn't draw closer, she did.

Fighting the stinging behind her eyes, she willed her heart to still its erratic beating, knowing he could feel it in the darkness. Long moments hung suspended between them when suddenly his arms came around her, crushing her close. It wasn't passion he sought, and Jem clung to him with equal fervor. No words were exchanged as he held her close, their ragged heartbeats telling their own tale.

When he finally released her, he stared at her face in the dim moonlight, eyes blazing as his hands traced the contours of her face. The pent-up emotions of the day spilled from her eyes—her pain, her indecision. Because, God help her, she still didn't know which man should have her allegiance.

Reese pulled her gown from her impatiently, but once again he only held her close as though trying to absorb every cell of her being with his. When he rolled over and rose above her, she saw the desperation in his face. Like an ancient warrior staking his claim, he sought her. There was no harshness, only a definition of purpose she'd never seen.

Soon she shared his desperation, wanting to erase her doubts, to seal him to her. He filled her suddenly, and she accepted him, shocked at the feelings he evoked. The perfect fit of their bodies further shredded her already torn emotions. When she matched her movements to his, it wasn't a physical fulfillment she craved. She couldn't bear to lose contact for a second, as though the loss would sear her very soul.

Reese moved against her, leaving his imprint as surely as a burning brand against her flesh. Each movement reminded him of the imminent loss, driving him with a force he didn't know he possessed. When he was finally spent, he lay atop her, his body heaving, his face turned from hers. He felt her fingers weave into his hair and turn his head gently toward hers. When her lips touched his, they were soft, reassuring.

He didn't move, remembering how she'd acknowledged her pleasure in having him fill her, knowing he shared the feeling. He couldn't keep her strapped to the bed, but fear clutched him as he realized her heart was for the taking, and Charles Sawyer had first claim.

He dropped his forehead to hers, closing his eyes against the pain filling them. How had this bullheaded, ornery woman captured the heart he'd kept protected all his life?

The salty taste of tears mingled between their lips, and neither could discern the beginning of the path they traced.

Chapter 35

The soft tinkling music made Jem pause on the threshold of her study. The song was one she remembered well. It was the waltz Charles had first asked her to dance to when she'd begun to fall in love with him. Where was it coming from?

With hesitant steps she moved farther into the room, gazing at her desk. Crafted of finest porcelain, the Dresden music box stood open, playing its unusual song. Charles!

Turning in a flash, she saw him. Leaning negligently against the opposite wall, he waited. Her hand crept across her heart, and he leaned forward, moving toward her. Not asking her permission, he captured her hand, then bowed in a courtly manner. Her mock curtsy followed as she fell under the spell he was weaving. As though gracing the halls of a fine court, dressed in silk and satin, instead of her habitual breeches, Jem followed his lead.

No longer tall and skinny, she was weightless as they floated around the room. Still proper, Charles didn't permit his hands to roam, instead merely guiding her in her flight. When the music wound to an end, Jem looked about in surprise. Flustered by her unusual performance, she backed away, laughing nervously. "I didn't mean to lose my head."

"I'm glad you did." Taking one of her hands in his, he led them to the settee near the fireplace. "I've missed that about you, Jem. Not many women have the confidence to be themselves."

Hardly herself, she thought. More like a stranger who possessed her body when Charles was near. "Wherever did you find a music box with that song?"

"So you do remember!"

"Of course." Jem's voice was soft, but regret tinged its edges. "How could I forget?"

"I was afraid you'd lost sight of what we meant to each other. When McIntire walked in yesterday, it was as though you erased everything that came before."

Jem read the entreaty in his face, her indecision multiplying.

"I want to help you, Jem. You can't give Cushman another chance to ruin you."

Surprise lit her features. "Then you believe . . ."

"Who else? First your father—"

Relief blossomed in her face. "You're the only one who believes me, Charles. Everyone else thinks I'm crazy."

"Not you, sweet Jem."

Without thinking about the gesture, Jem withdrew her hands, adding their movements to her agitated speech. "I can't tell you how frustrating it is to know the truth and not have anyone believe me."

Charles's reply was measured. "I think I know that better than anyone."

Her breath released in a whoosh, and she cocked her head to study his face. "You've always been my champion, haven't you?"

"Seems sometimes you needed one."

"That hasn't changed. Cushman's acting even crazier than he ever has."

"What do you mean by that?" The light in Charles's eyes had changed, gleaming with speculation.

"Just something my pa used to say. That after Cushman's family died, he was never the same. He seemed ready to fight everyone on the range—like a crazy man.

Couldn't stand the thought of anything of his being taken away."

"He's always taken what's not his." Charles did not give any further explanation to this cryptic statement. His expression seemed far away, distant. "I was friends with Douglas, you know."

"Douglas?"

"Cushman's son."

"I didn't know his family well. I was only about ten when they died." Charles was eighteen at the time, and Jem hadn't known him either. He'd left Wyoming Territory a few years later, joined the army, and stayed away. It was years later that he returned to become her father's foreman and her first beau.

"Sometimes I even forgot I didn't belong in the big house with the family," Charles continued.

Jem's heart went out to the boy he'd been—the unfairness of being treated differently because his mother was the housekeeper. A sense of kinship surfaced—she remembered clearly how it felt to be the outcast. Her voice caught as she answered. "You've overcome the past, Charles. You can take your place anywhere you want now."

He laughed, but there was no mirth in the sound.

Jem searched his face, wondering at his past, the one they'd never discussed. "Did you and Cushman have a falling out? Is that why you left after your mother died?"

Charles's almost colorless eyes fixed on her, his expression rigid as he reached out to clasp her hand again. She tried to read the look on his face as he stroked her hand. "You're a lot like my mother, you know."

Startled, she almost pulled her hand away.

"Is something wrong?"

Jem shook away the uneasiness that gripped her. "I've never heard you talk about your family before."

The light in Charles's eyes flickered, then died away. "There's never been much to tell."

Jem searched his face, then spoke gently. "Why did you come back now?"

His face seemed blank, almost drained. "I told you yesterday."

Jem stood up abruptly, pacing the floor in front of the settee. "This is so hard." She paused, trying to find the right words. "You've come back at a very difficult time."

"Difficult?"

Jem waved her hands distractedly as though trying to explain. The complexity of the situation overwhelmed her. "Reese would be very upset if he found you here. And that complicates—"

"Why are you so worried about McIntire? You sound as though he's your main concern."

"It's just that we're in this together. I've made promises—"

"To him?"

"He is my husband."

"And so that makes it all right? You promised to wait for me, or did you forget?"

"Of course not. It's just that—"

"You know, you're not like my mother at all. You're really more like my father."

Surprised by this sudden turn in the conversation, Jem tried to assess his expression. "I didn't know your father."

Charles's lips tightened abruptly, the fine lines tracing his cheeks deepened. "That's just as well."

"I'm confused about you, and about Reese. I'll be the first to admit that. But I'm committed to the Bar-W. It's only a month until the army contract will be filled. Perhaps then we can talk and—"

"In other words, you want me to walk away and leave the entire burden to you?" Charles clasped her hands and drew her back on the settee. "No, my dear, this time I'm seeing things through to the end."

"But—"

"I won't leave this time, Jem, not until everything's finished."

Chapter 36

The morning sun poked through the drapes insistently, and Jem buried her head under the covers to escape its rays. Abruptly she sat up straight. What was she doing in bed this late on a workday?

Hastily washing and dressing, she tore down the stairs, passing Mary, whose hands were full of fresh linens, and burst into the kitchen. Della was stoically kneading bread, but she was alone.

"Where's everyone?"

"On the range." Della's voice was taut.

"Why didn't anyone wake me up?" Jem poured some coffee, cupping her hands around the mug, savoring its warmth.

"They didn't want you to know what they're up to."

"What?" The coffee forgotten, Jem turned Della's chair around, frightened by the tone of her voice. "Tell me, Della."

Her voice quavering, Della broke down and told Jem of the men's plan to set a trap for the rustlers. Michael Fairchild had ridden in early to meet Reese. It was the most daring plan they'd thought of so far, and Reese hadn't wanted Jem involved because of the danger. He had decided to take the spot most likely to be hit because he refused to ask a hand to assume the risk. Stunned, Jem stared at Della in horror as the older woman's voice broke. "Pete's out there, too, Jem."

Remembering how pale and gray he'd looked the past few days, Jem was horrified. Even more so when she realized she'd completely forgotten to warn Reese about the danger to Pete's health. What if, caught up in her own concerns, she'd allowed Reese to send Pete to his death? Or to his own? Taking time only to find out which range they were on, Jem sped out to the barn and quickly saddled her horse.

She rode mercilessly, fear clutching at her. Why had Reese purposely put himself in the path of the most danger? Had that been the reason for his desperation in their lovemaking the past few nights?

Digging her heels in, she urged the horse on, terrified of what she'd find. Cresting the butte, Jem saw a cluster of horses and knew she'd found them. The horses were not manned, their reins trailing in the snow. Her heart stood still as she realized one man lay on the ground, unmoving.

Blindly she made her way down the incline, dismounting and running into the backs of the men who stood in a circle around the body. Her fists beat furiously against one back and the man turned in surprise. Boyd Harris stared at her blankly as she shoved him aside. Strong arms reached out to grab her, and she fought them away. But he held on fast and forced her to look upward. Relief coursed through her at the sight of Reese's drawn face. Sagging briefly in his arms, she thanked God for the life she felt beating against her own chest.

But her relief was short-lived. Pete! Pulling back, she dodged Reese's grasp as she pushed toward the body, determined to see who it was. Shock was colder than the winter of the ragged mountain range. Michael Fairchild's lifeless body stared back at her. Horrified, she covered her mouth to prevent the cry that threatened to escape.

Not Michael! What would Abigail do without him? Remembering her many kindnesses, her joy at Christmas when she'd confided that they hoped to have a child by

the next Christmas, Jem was filled with agony for her
friend.

Dimly she felt Reese pull her back, his arm circling her,
shielding her as the other men picked Michael up and laid
him across his horse.

"Jem." She didn't answer, the image of Michael's
body paralyzing her. "Listen to me. The men will take
Michael to the ranch and get a wagon. Abigail can't see
him like this." Tears filled Jem's eyes at the mention of
her friend. Abigail didn't deserve this. She should live
happily ever after with her husband and the child they expected.

Reese turned Jem toward him gently. "We have to tell
her." Denial seized her, and Jem shook her head, trying to escape Reese's firm grasp. "She's your friend,
Jem. It would be better hearing it from you than anyone
else."

Jem gave in to the pain and the weakness, sinking her
head against Reese's shoulder for support, seeking his
strength instead of her own. He cradled her for a while and
then drew back and looked firmly in her eyes. "You have
to be strong for Abigail. She'll need you."

Nodding, Jem swiped at the tears that still seeped from
her eyes and picked up her discarded hat. When she had
composed herself, he led her to her horse and assisted her
as she swung into the saddle. His concern was tangible,
but Jem felt frozen inside at the horror she'd just witnessed.

On the ride to the ranch, Reese filled in the details.
Michael's plan had not gone awry; the rustlers had taken
another tack. But Reese was filled with overwhelming
guilt because he and Michael had exchanged places. Reese
had felt Michael's spot was the most dangerous and had
insisted on taking the position. Michael had been shot in
his place.

Reese was grim as he surmised that their actions had
forced the rustlers out. Now they would either have to

reveal their identities or do something even more desperate to reduce the ranchers' resistance.

Jem could scarcely digest this even more appalling discovery as they collected the wagon containing Michael's body and headed toward the Fairchild ranch. She scarcely noticed that Boyd Harris drove the wagon.

It was both the longest and shortest ride she'd ever taken. It seemed to stretch out forever, the sound of the wagon grating over slush-filled ruts ringing in the clear winter air. At the same time, the Fairchild ranch loomed into sight far too soon.

Abigail came to the door, her attention riveted to their horses and the wagon. Boyd climbed down from the wagon seat quickly. As their mounts came to a stop no words were necessary as Abigail met them. The beginning of her smile faltered and then fell away as she gauged their expressions. Jem's eyes brimmed with tears as Abigail flew to the wagon, her plaintive cry filling the air.

As though a dim cloud filled her brain, Jem watched Boyd catch Abigail before she crumpled, carrying her up the steps and into the house. Jem trailed behind, feeling useless, numbed by the pain she knew consumed her friend. Entering the parlor, she dropped to the floor by the settee Boyd had laid Abigail on. Taking one of her limp hands, Jem rubbed desperately, wishing she could infuse some of that same life into Michael's still body.

Abigail clung to Jem's hand, surprising her with the strength of her grip. "Why, Jem?"

The same question had haunted Jem throughout the painful ride. "He cared so much for you," she answered instead.

Abigail's eyes flickered shut briefly, and Jem sensed she'd said the right thing. Crooning words of comfort spilled out, even though she wasn't sure what to say. She gripped Abigail's hand, offering reassurance.

She glanced up, surprised to see Boyd's concerned face, wondering why he was still there. He had brought a quilt and offered it to Jem. Not questioning him, she merely smoothed it over Abigail's shaking body.

He left, and as the numbing time passed, Jem heard Reese's departure also, knowing he was leaving to take care of Michael, grateful for him in a way she'd never believed possible.

Chapter
37

The day of Michael's funeral the weather was unrelenting, the biting cold of the wind stinging their faces. Jem's lips felt raw where she'd bitten them, and she was certain her face was red from the merciless cold. Glancing at Abigail's face, Jem knew the redness she saw there was from the many tears she had shed. Ravaged, she looked defenseless, without Michael's constant support.

Spadefuls of frozen dirt hit the pine coffin as the mourners each took their turns, covering the solitary box. Lily picked up the shovel, closed her eyes briefly, and tossed the dirt into the open grave. Unusually solemn, Lily had shown more sensitivity to Abigail than Jem had witnessed in all their years growing up together. As the assembled neighbors and ranch hands took turns, the obscene white of the freshly cut pine began to disappear.

"Ashes to ashes, dust to dust . . ." Reverend Filcher intoned.

The sorrow and futility of Michael's death overwhelmed Jem, making it almost impossible to lift the spade. Reese's hands closed over hers, steadying her. She managed to toss a shovelful of dirt into the grave, blindly handing over the spade and then turning away.

Ragged strains of "The Old Rugged Cross" emerged from the grieving group. Michael Fairchild was not only loved by his wife, he was liked and respected throughout the territory. Jem remembered his kind smiling face in the

Fairchild home as he'd openly declared his love for his wife, his teasing as they played parlor games. She could scarcely believe he was dead. Having seen his murdered body didn't make it any easier to accept the dreadful reality.

Neither Michael nor Abigail had any family in the area. Other relatives lived far away. Jem imagined the loneliness Abigail would now experience—climbing into a barren bed made so much larger and emptier by Michael's absence, sitting down to a table set for one, reaching out in the night to find only emptiness, starting to speak only to find no one there to share her thoughts, her dreams.

Darling Abigail, always thinking of others. Who would now consider her first? Love and cherish her as Michael had? Jem's heart ached at the thought, and guilt filled her when she remembered how glad she'd been that the dead man wasn't Reese. Remembering, too, her dread when she thought she'd lost him, she sought his hand, feeling the warmth through their gloves, both of them sharing the empty void she knew Abigail must be feeling.

Once the mound of dirt had been built over the grave, the beautiful cross Reese had carved was placed at the forefront. There were no flowers blooming in the harsh winter weather, no decoration for the lonely grave.

Tears seeped from many sets of eyes at the final gesture. Reese released Jem's hand and walked over to Abigail. "Please come home with us, Abigail."

"I don't know. . . ." Like a lost child, she didn't know in which direction to turn. Michael had been her source of guidance, and now she was pitifully uncertain.

"For a few days at least," Jem urged, wishing she could smooth the lines of pain from her friend's face.

Abigail's head bent in agreement, and Reese and Jem each took one of her arms, feeling her fragility as they moved toward the wagon. Abigail stopped suddenly and looked back, new tears shimmering in her eyes, her voice barely a whisper. "I never got to say good-bye."

Jem's heart ached, and as her eyes met Reese's pain-filled ones she knew he shared some of her agony.

Lily remained quiet as they rode home, speaking softly only to Abigail, her solicitousness comforting. Arriving at the ranch, Jem insisted that Abigail lie down, and Lily offered to sit with her. Taking her place in the rocker, she wouldn't budge, surprising Jem once again.

When dinner was ready, Jem checked on them and found Abigail asleep and Lily's vigil still steadfast. Motioning Lily out into the hall, she tried to persuade her sister to eat some supper, but Lily refused.

"If she wakes up, it's important that someone be there." Lily's actions were instinctive, almost as if she'd known the same experience, held the same expectations. Jem had never questioned her beautiful sister's life outside the ranch, but now she wondered. Had she lost someone special at one time that Jem didn't know about?

"Lily—"

"Don't ask, Jem. I just know. I'm not hungry, but thanks for asking." Closing the door on any further interrogation, Lily reclaimed her place by Abigail's side.

Jem and Lily remained with Abigail for the next few days, finally convincing her to eat by reminding her of the precious baby she carried. Any mention of her child brought a disturbing mixture of pain and joy, but propelled her on.

In the days that followed, Jem could not shake the grief that plagued her. Michael's funeral emphasized the horror, the loss. But fear was also a constant companion. In the light of Michael's death, Reese felt it was his responsibility to smoke out the rustlers. It was like a cause, a crusade he wouldn't abandon. Worried about his safety, Jem found she couldn't concentrate.

Hearing the doorknocker, Jem glanced around and saw the hall was empty. When she opened the door, Charles's concerned face gazed at her.

He offered a small package and she looked at it in question. "Just something to help perk you up."

"Charles, you shouldn't have."

"I know how softhearted you are. You're taking on Abigail's grief like your own. Somebody needs to cheer you up."

A soft smile creased Jem's worried face as she led them into the parlor. Charles—always thoughtful, sensitive. As she unwrapped the gift her smile deepened as she saw that it was perfume, the same fragrance he'd given her on her birthday the year they courted.

"Your smile's sweeter than all the perfume in the world," he said as she blushed.

Unused to such flowery compliments, she ducked her head a bit. "Thank you, Charles. I appreciate the gesture." She sat the bottle down on the marble-topped table, watching the sun glint off the glass container. "But until I've resolved everything with Reese, I'm not sure I should take any more gifts."

Charles's ready smile faltered. "You have less than a month to worry about him. From what you've told me, his contract was for a year, then he'll be gone."

"It's not quite that simple." Jem fiddled with the bottle, then rose and walked to the window. "When Michael died, I realized how I would have felt if it had been Reese."

"What are you saying, Jem?"

Her sigh filled the air as her chin sank to her chest. "Only that I'm not ready to say good-bye to him yet."

"So your promise to me meant nothing?" The fury in his voice was barely contained.

"Of course it was important. I just didn't know how complicated my life would become. Right now I'm concerned about Reese's safety, about Abigail—"

"About everyone except me."

"No. That's why I'm so confused. I've held your promise dear ever since you left."

"Not so dear that you didn't sell out at the first opportunity."

"You weren't here! I didn't have any other choice!"

"We all have choices, Jem. But you want to take the easy way out."

"Nothing about this is easy." Jem ached with the knowledge of how difficult everything had become. She'd thought when the Bar-W's existence had been threatened that she'd known the full extent of pain. Bitterly she realized that she'd only touched on the edges.

"You could make it easy. It's your decision." His voice was unrelenting.

Jem flinched, realizing that Charles didn't understand, that he might never fathom the depth of her dilemma. "But not one I'm ready to make."

Uncharacteristic venom laced his words. "I think you've already made your choice."

Startled, Jem backed away. "I told you—"

The gleam in his pale eyes unnerved her. "I thought once that you were different, Jem." His gaze swept over her, a combination of regret and anger filling his expression. "But you're just like the rest, aren't you?"

"Charles, I don't understand. Who are you talking about?"

But he stalked from the room without answering. The terrible sense of foreboding she'd felt over Michael's death now intensified. The last thing she needed right now was another enemy.

Chapter
38

Reese's departing back was a stark silhouette on the horizon. Jem threw the quirt to the ground, damning his stubbornness. Taking the brunt of the responsibility for Michael's death, he still took the most chances, putting himself in danger every day. The ranchers had banded together, forming vigilante patrols, determined to stop the attacks on their cattle and, more important, on their men.

Reese headed their group, a distinct departure from Cushman's usual leadership. Still convinced that her father's old enemy was responsible, Jem balked at Cushman's inclusion in the ranchers' patrol. But no other proof had been uncovered, and the other ranchers were slow to believe her assertions of his guilt.

Jem stared in the direction Reese had ridden. She knew his destination—the Fairchild ranch. Abigail had finally insisted on returning home despite their protests. Jem and Lily alternated visiting her, worried about her health in view of her pregnancy, but Reese had made it his priority to check on her every day.

His figure had left her line of vision, and Jem turned wearily and entered the house, nodding to Della. Seeking refuge in her study, Jem acknowledged that her own priorities had changed dramatically.

Her sleep had soon filled with nightmares. Waking breathless, she would see corpses on the ground, but the faces all belonged to Reese. Agitated, she would turn to

Reese, seeking reassurance, taking the sustenance of his comforting arms as he cradled her in her sleep, soothing away the demons that haunted her.

Realizing that Reese could well have been killed instead of Michael, Jem felt the foggy layers of her emotions try to stabilize. Charles's constant presence wore on her nerves. He'd apologized for losing his temper and sought to remind her of her promise to wait. Even as he pleaded his case she tried to visualize her life without Reese and how she would have felt if he had been the one killed instead of Michael.

An hour later a knock on the door disturbed her thoughts. Mary stuck her pert face into the room. "Della thought you might like some tea, Miss Jem."

"Thanks, Mary."

She brought in the cup of tea that Jem recognized as soothing camomile.

"Is Della still in the kitchen, Mary?"

"No, she's right here." Della's voice answered instead.

Jem hadn't heard her come in, but looked up in relief at her familiar face. "Good."

"Maybe not."

Jem cocked her head in question.

"Sawyer's here," Della said, and Jem made a moue of dismay. "Exactly what I thought. He's in the parlor."

Jem dropped her head wearily in her hands. She simply did not want to deal with him. His daily visits were draining.

"You want me to tell him to go away?"

Knowing how that would delight Della, Jem resisted the urge, instead rising and walking around her desk. She gave the soothing tea a regretful glance as she passed it by and headed toward the parlor.

"Jem." Charles's voice was bright despite the gloom of the winter day outside.

"This really isn't a good time, Charles."

He frowned. "It never seems to be anymore."

"My life is very complicated right now. People need

me." She thought of Abigail, the hours they'd spent together, the grief she was trying to help her friend through.

"What about me, Jem? What about my needs?"

Jem sighed heavily. Even though Reese could well ride out of her life in less than a month, her responsibility was firmly entwined with him. "I'm sorry, Charles, but right now I have to focus on the survival of my family and this ranch."

Charles's lips drew into a thin line. "So that's it? You're shutting me out like a stranger."

"Not a stranger, Charles. But I do have a husband, and my ultimate responsibility is to him."

"I thought this marriage was a sham." Jem's head flew up in surprise. "Why else would you marry someone you found in a jail?"

Jem hadn't thought of her beginnings with Reese in a long time. Those details hardly seemed significant now. She fleetingly wondered how Charles knew about their deal, but instead said, "I don't expect you to understand, Charles. I can't say I do myself."

"Jem, does he make you feel as special as I have, as cherished?"

She shook her head as though to clear it. No, Reese didn't treat her like fragile Dresden, but he provided her with a sense of her true self. One she'd been missing all her life. Sadly she gazed at Charles's beseeching expression. What he offered no longer consumed her as it once had. She wanted a partner in life, not a protector. The indecision and regret in her eyes must have transmitted themselves to Charles because he pulled back abruptly.

Picking up his hat, he walked toward the doorway. "I won't give up, Jem. Don't expect me to."

She watched him through the curtains as he rode away. These days she never knew what to expect.

Chapter 39

Walking wearily toward the barn, Jem lamented the events of the past days. Head down, she didn't see the shadowy figure that melted into the darkness.

Despite her gloomy countenance, she smiled unexpectedly when she opened the door. Reese was hunkered down near the mare she'd come to check on. His long fingers stroked the horse's swollen abdomen, and she marveled at his gentleness, his natural affinity for animals. "How's she doing?"

Reese raised his head, answering her smile. "Won't be long now. She's ready to be a mama." He dipped his hands in a bucket of clean water and washed them before wiping them dry on a rough towel.

Jem dropped to the hay next to Reese's side, snuggling tiredly beneath the arm that draped over her shoulders. "I wonder if Abigail still is."

"I reckon so. That baby's part of Michael. Only bit she has left."

"His death seems so senseless." Jem plucked at the straw next to her, thinking of their fallen friend.

"Murder generally is. That's why we've got to stop the rustlers, Jem."

His reminder wasn't lost on her. In the days since Michael's death, there had been two more deaths, one of their hands and the Fairchilds' foreman. Fear of discovery and the last aborted attempt had driven the rustlers to lie low. But no one could expect the uneasy truce to last long.

"You can't stop them single-handedly, Reese. You've put yourself on the line a dozen times. It's a miracle you weren't one of the men killed."

Reese stroked her hair, loosening the pins as he did so. "Don't worry about me." He thought of his family's death, how close he'd come to being included in their numbers. "I've got nine lives." She didn't answer, only settling deeper against him. "Unless I miss my guess, Della ought to be having supper soon."

"Uh-hum."

"I could use some," he reminded her gently.

"Oh, I'm sorry." She disengaged herself. "I'll see what I can scavenge."

"Better not let Della hear you talk like that."

"You trying to tell me no one around here takes me seriously as boss?"

"You could say that."

She swatted him playfully and then rose, glad for his teasing, which lifted her sagging spirits. Glancing back at his now familiar form, she smiled as she left.

Entering the kitchen, she found Pete and Della involved in one of their rare squabbles. It didn't take long to get to the root of the problem. Della was worried about Pete's health, and he was tired of her fussing. Stepping delicately around them, Jem tried to gather Reese's supper, found her hand thwacked by Della's, and decided it was best to wait until she prepared a tray.

Jem made the mistake of drumming her fingers on the table, received a quelling glare, and retreated to the pantry to study its less-than-fascinating contents.

"I haven't got all night. This tray's ready." Della's voice penetrated the wall of the pantry, and Jem backed out hastily.

Deciding Della was in no mood for teasing, Jem took the tray and escaped. She hummed as she strolled to the barn, the first time she'd felt any such inclination in the last week.

The angry flames licking at the barn stopped all sound, all motion, all thought. Terror seizing her, Jem dropped the tray and ran forward. Nearing the door, she stared in disbelief at the wooden bar dropped in place, locking Reese into the growing inferno. She reached forward to lift the bar when two strong arms grabbed her. Trying to fling them aside, she turned, shocked as she stared into Charles's face.

"Thank God you're here! Reese is in there. He'll be burned to death!"

"I know," he replied as Jem stared at him blankly. "I just can't figure out why you're out here instead of in there with him."

"What?" Disbelief and fear warred across her face. "I need your help."

"And you think I'm going to give it to you?"

Jem stepped away from him, unable to believe the expression on his face. His hand reached out to stroke her cheek and she flinched. "Sweet Jem, you still don't understand, do you?"

Numbly she shook her head, intensely aware of the growing heat of the barn, wondering how to stop Charles's flow of words and let Reese out of the death trap.

The heat from the fire washed over their bodies, obliterating the winter cold as Jem inched away from him.

"You just couldn't give up, could you? I thought after your pa was dead, you'd leave. But you had to keep on."

"Why are you doing this?" Her cry was frantic as she became more and more horrified by the growing flames.

"Because Cushman wanted your land, and I had to beat him to it. The old man spent his whole life trying to get the place away from your father. He never could. That's why I have to."

"I don't understand." Jem reached blindly behind her, trying to connect with the bar that held the door shut.

"No, you don't, do you, Jem?" His face grew strangely intense, frightening. "Cushman took what was mine. I have to get what he wants the most. He has to suffer, and nothing could be sweeter than taking the Bar-W."

Desperation laced her words, knowing she had to free Reese. "What did he take of yours?"

"My birthright." Jem stared at him blankly, wondering if he were truly crazy as he continued. "I'm his bastard, Jem. Not a very pretty word, is it?" She backed up, away from his fearful presence. "He kept my mother in bondage, while his wife and son were treated like royalty."

"Cushman's your father?" The words edged past her smoke-clogged throat as she tried to inch nearer the door. His pale eyes and silver hair gleamed in the darkness, and Jem recoiled as she realized the resemblance he bore to Cushman.

"I tried to outrun him, outsteal him, but it didn't work. Now I'll have the Bar-W, and he'll never get over that."

"But you could have had it all if we'd been married. Why did you have to kill my father?" Jem reached for the bar, but Charles jerked her forward, pulling her away from the door.

"No. The ranch has to be mine. Not yours. The old man wouldn't suffer enough unless he knew it was me who beat him." His voice softened, his pale eyes glistening as he stared at her. "It never was you, Jem. You were just in the way."

"The hides? The murders? You were framing your own father?"

Charles's voice was so soft it crawled through the night. "You helped set him up, Jem. You were so ready to believe he was guilty, the rest was incredibly easy."

The crackling roar of the fire penetrated the air. A vision of Reese trapped inside terrified her. "You don't have any reason to hurt Reese. Let him go, please."

"Don't you see? It has to be this way." The grip on her arms tightened painfully, even though the expression on his face was regretful. "When you married Reese, you signed his execution order. I can't take over the ranch if any of the owners are alive." He stroked her cheek again, the macabre sensation chilling her flesh. The soft touch deepened, gouging her instead, as his mood changed once again. "You're like him, you know. Treacherous. That's why when you rejected me, I knew there was no other way."

"But all your courting?"

"How else could I have free rein with everything on your ranch?"

Fingers of fire burst over the roof of the barn as Jem struggled to free herself. The sickness of deceit clawed at her as Charles's accomplice darted into view. Boyd Harris came closer, raising his gun, and she braced herself to feel its cold metal piercing her flesh.

The gun arched high in the sky, the metal gleaming in the light of the fire before landing firmly on Charles's temple. He slumped forward, almost crushing her beneath his weight. Boyd pulled her out and she stared at him for a brief second before screaming Reese's name.

It took him only moments to see the bar locking the barn closed. Pulling at the stubborn wood board, he tried to open the doors. As he did so Grady Orton ran from behind the barn, and Jem sagged forward in relief. "Grady," she started to shout. Boyd turned quickly just as the other man pulled his gun.

"No! Reese is trapped inside. Boyd's trying to get him out."

Grady didn't lower his gun, instead leveling it in Jem's direction. "Now that's a real dilemma. Which one of you to shoot first."

Jem gaped at Grady, unable to believe what she was hearing. This was the man she'd befriended, taken into her home. She walked toward him, disregarding the weapon in his hand. "Put that gun down."

"Back up, missy. I've had enough of you telling me what to do. Lording it over everyone, putting a thief like Harris in charge. Charles was right. You wouldn't ever have given us a fair chance if we let you live." His gun wavered between them as Grady laughed in the acrid air. Sickened, she watched as he cocked the trigger.

The gun roared, but the bullet plowed aimlessly into the sky as Boyd tackled the other man. Running to the door, Jem pulled uselessly at the wooden bar that had been shoved in at an angle to prevent its removal. Boyd and Grady grappled desperately, and when the gun fired again, Jem turned in terror, holding her breath until Grady's body slumped to the ground.

Not wasting any precious time, Boyd ran to the side of the barn, grabbed a pitchfork, and pried the bar up. He yanked open the barn doors and ducked his head before they both entered the smoke-filled building. The sound of horses screaming in terror paralyzed Jem for a moment as she searched the barn for Reese.

Boyd found him first. There was an ugly gash across his forehead, and his body was terribly still. "Get help," Boyd yelled over the noise of the fire and the screams of the horses.

Tears threatened, but Jem shook her head, still stubborn. "Not until we get Reese out." He had to be alive, he just had to.

Realizing the futility of arguing, Boyd took one arm and lifted Reese under one shoulder while Jem took the other. She sagged momentarily and then dredged up strength she didn't know she possessed. Together they dragged Reese through the choking air. A flaming beam split, its cracking sound warning them as it crashed to the floor inches from their feet. Doggedly they continued, gulping fresh air into their lungs as they emerged from the barn.

Boyd's yells split the night, and hands stumbled from the bunkhouse as he ran back into the barn to help the trapped animals.

Jem held Reese's head in her lap, unable to see through the tears that ran unchecked. The meaning of the words he had confided in her after her fall were now clear. He was the one in pain in her dreams, the one reaching out for help. And instead of helping him, she had caused this.

Jem's eyes closed in pain as she cradled him close, unable to believe that his old enemy, fire, had finally caught up with him. And it was her fault, her own blind stupidity at believing Charles Sawyer.

Her grief intensified as she realized that she'd led him to kill her best friend's husband. Gazing in fear at Reese's still face, she only prayed he hadn't killed Reese as well.

A strong arm came down on her shoulder and she looked up through the shimmer of her tears to see Pete's reassuring face. "Oh, Pete," she sobbed.

He bent close, offering his strength. "We'd best get him inside, Jem."

"What if . . ." She couldn't finish the sentence, couldn't complete the thought. The agony was unbearable.

Pete clasped her shoulder, squeezing it firmly, lending the support she needed. "Reese is strong, but you'd better let some of the boys get him inside."

Dazed, Jem looked up into the circle of smoke-smeared faces. Glancing around, she realized the horses had been freed, and the fire had spent the worst of its fury. The windless night wasn't carrying the embers, and the barn was flanked by hands equipped with hoes and shovels to combat any errant ashes. Boyd stepped forward along with two other men, and they picked Reese up carefully.

She followed closely as they placed him in her bed. As Boyd turned to leave she placed a hand on his arm, stumbling over her words. "I don't know what to say. I—"

"Just watch over him, ma'am." His eyes were filled with a compassion he seldom let surface. She swallowed the lump in her throat, but fresh tears still spilled forward.

He left, and Jem dropped to Reese's side as the door shut behind him. Alone, Jem reached for Reese's hand, terrified at its lifeless appearance.

"You can't leave me now, Reese. I won't let you." The hand remained limp, unmoving. "That's an order, dammit!" she cried, her voice cracking as she gulped past the fear choking her.

"You can even leave in a month, if that's what you

want. Just don't die." She closed her eyes, praying desperately, promising anything in exchange for Reese's life.

"You're dripping all over me." His voice was a croak, but Jem jumped as though he'd shouted. Wiping away her tears, she touched his face as though to reassure herself she'd really heard him.

"Reese?" She gripped his fingers fiercely.

"You tryin' to break my hand?"

She laughed raggedly through the sobs that threatened her. "It is you."

"Better be, or you're in the wrong bed," he croaked again.

She couldn't laugh this time. Instead she buried her head against him and gave in to the emotions that overwhelmed her.

Chapter *40*

Pete waited in the wagon seat as Jem and Lily walked out on the porch. Recovered from a serious bout of influenza, he was back to his old self. He'd been down for several days, and although everyone had been scared, Doc Riley said his heart was no worse, even though he would have to take it easy for a while. A relieved Della had said her good-byes inside.

"I wish you'd stay longer and I really mean that," Jem implored.

"I believe you do." Lily finished smoothing her gloves and impulsively took Jem's hands. "This marriage can work, you know." Jem ducked her head, and Lily rushed on. "But it's up to you. You saw how I tried to flirt with Reese, hoping to knock some sense into that stubborn head of yours. But he wouldn't have noticed if I'd walked in the room stark naked."

"Oh, Lily."

"Now that Charles is out of your life, maybe you can see your way more clearly."

"I still don't understand how I could have been so wrong about him."

"None of us knew his connection to Cushman. He's sick, Jem. Eaten up by hate."

"Why do you suppose Cushman never did anything about him?"

Lily shrugged. "When Charles was young enough for it

to make a difference, I imagine Cushman was worried about what his family would think. When Charles's mother told him before she died, it was probably too late."

"Kind of like a festering sore," Jem mused. "I guess he always wanted to prove something to his father."

"Cushman must have felt guilty to have allowed Charles to live at his ranch all this time." They'd all been shocked to learn that Cushman had harbored Charles, even while his son plotted to frame him for the murders and rustling. Apparently he held no illusions about his illegitimate son, but couldn't bring himself to disown his only living child.

"Guilt has a way of eating at you," Jem acknowledged.

Lily ignored her sister's comment, knowing her supply of strength was endless. "What'll they do to Cushman?"

Jem shrugged. "I don't know. He did say he was leaving his spread to Abigail, though."

Lily looked surprised.

"And then I expect he'll watch Charles hang."

"There's no reason to feel bad about that."

Jem found it wasn't difficult to agree. She'd come a long way from enchantment to disillusionment to acceptance. The hard-fought path had left its scars. "You were right all along, Lily."

"Even I didn't know Charles had killed Pa. I figured you were right, that Cushman was behind it all. He stood to gain so much that it made sense."

"I spent so much time being sure I was right, I never allowed for any other explanation."

"You can take the time now. You've got a husband to think about." Lily dropped Jem's hands and adjusted her reticule.

Jem dug the toe of her boot against the snow banked near the steps. "It's not that simple. I don't know if he wants to stay."

"Then ask him. Don't throw away love, Jem." Lily's eyes darkened again in remembered pain. "Trust me, it can't always be reclaimed."

"Lily, can't you tell me—"

Lily sucked in her breath. "It was a long time ago, Jem. And you've had enough sorrow around here to last a lifetime." She straightened up and met Jem's eyes. "Go, love and be happy." Throwing her arms around her sister, Lily hugged her hard. Climbing into the wagon, she waved as Pete flicked the reins and started off.

The sound of Reese's footsteps on the porch brought Jem back to life. "She's like a whirlwind, isn't she?" he commented, waving good-bye.

Jem nodded in agreement, the lump in her throat making speech difficult. She had so much to be grateful for. They watched the wagon as it bumped its way through the archway leading away from the ranch. The last month of the year's contract was drawing to an end, and Reese and Jem were intensely aware of the clock ticking away. They'd completed the contract, and delivery was all that was left. The blacklisting had come to an end, and Reese's job was completed.

"How could I have been so wrong about everything?" Jem asked, the added guilt and pain of her many wrongs seeming to compound by the moment. She'd misjudged her own sister, loved the man who had murdered her father, and trusted Grady Orton. They had all been wrong and costly decisions.

"You did the best you could with what you knew."

"That's generous, considering I almost got you killed, too."

Reese lowered his arm and faced her. "It's just the truth, Jem. You're not the kind to back away from a fight or follow someone else's lead. But if you'd been meek and mild, Della and Pete wouldn't have a home. Your old geezers would've been turned out without a thought."

"If I hadn't been so blind about Charles, Michael would still be alive." Jem couldn't fight the guilt that engulfed her, feeling Abigail's agony as though it were her own.

"Michael's death was senseless, but even if you'd distrusted Charles, it wouldn't have stopped the killing. He was bent on getting rid of anything in his path."

"I acted like a fool, mooning over him, almost losing everything dear to me."

Reese's eyes probed hers, the questions in them searing. "You're a strong woman, Jem. Stubborn sometimes, but not always without reason." His hands gripped her shoulders, forcing her woebegone face upward. "You did what you had to. Most women would have given in, but not you." As his fingers grazed the line of her cheek, he marveled at the softness of her skin, so at odds with her strength. "Not you, Jemima."

Her name fell from his lips, magical in its resonance. She managed a small smile, knowing the scars of her bad judgment would be slow to heal, impossible to forget.

He squinted in concentration, deflecting her thoughts. "Look at that, Jem. The W is turned upside down. I'd better get someone to fix it."

"I already did," she answered quietly. He looked blank, and she prodded. "What's an upside down W, Reese?"

"An M, I suppose."

"Does that stand for anything you know?"

The light in his eyes warred with disbelief.

"Seems to me it could stand for McIntire," she continued.

"Jem, do you know what you're saying?"

She held her head up proudly, remembering her promise the evening of the fire. Even if he rejected her, she would wish him well and allow him to ride out of her life. Nothing was more important than his happiness. "Yes. I'm offering you the Bar-W for your own."

Long moments passed as the whistling wind provided the only sound. "And what about you?"

"We're a package deal."

"And who'll be the boss?"

Her heart shimmied within the constriction of her body. One step at a time, they closed the space separating them.

"No one?" she offered.

His embrace wasn't gentle as he picked her up off the porch, his lips seeking hers. A reminder of the freighting company he wouldn't be forming teased him briefly and was tossed aside as easily as the wind buffeting their bodies.

The fire had cleansed his soul, purging the guilt that had plagued him for better than half his life. For the first time he didn't want to roam, he wanted to put down roots. Roots that included the impossible woman in his arms.

The sound of someone clearing his throat in embarrassment brought him back to earth. Lowering Jem to the porch, they both turned, seeing Boyd Harris holding the reins of his horse in his hands.

"Didn't mean to disturb you. I just came to say good-bye," Boyd said, twisting the reins uncomfortably.

Shocked, they both stared at him but Jem recovered first. "Please don't go, Boyd. You haven't given us a chance to thank you—for our lives." Her voice was filled with guilt and shame over her earlier treatment of the man.

"Where you headed, Boyd?" Reese asked.

"Miz Fairchild needs a man who can run the place. What with Michael and the foreman being killed, I 'spect she's going to need some help."

"You're the man for the job," Reese offered, his gaze steady. "With your experience, she couldn't ask for a better man."

"She's going to have a baby," Jem said softly, touched at his generosity.

"Yes'm. She'll probably want to keep the ranch going for the child."

Jem lowered her head and then met Boyd's eyes. "When my father was killed, I couldn't believe that everyone would accuse him so unjustly, judging him without knowing the facts. I was guilty of doing the same thing to you, Boyd. Nothing I can say will ever make up for that, but I'll always be ashamed of it."

"It's in the past, ma'am. Trust is hard to come by. I was glad for the chance to work for you. It gave me back part of myself that's been missing for a long time." He shook Reese's hand and started to mount the horse.

"Boyd," Jem called to him. He paused, one booted foot in the stirrup. "I'm glad Abigail will be in such good hands."

He swung into the saddle, his mahogany hair gleaming in the sunlight. A rare smile tugged at his mouth, and Jem was overcome as she saw it meet his eyes. She knew she didn't deserve his easy forgiveness, and her lips trembled as she smiled in return. Tipping the brim of his hat to her, he rode off.

Together Reese and Jem entered the house, its unusual quiet a reminder of all the changes in their lives. A soft fire glowed in the study, but Jem couldn't face the reminders of the mistakes she'd made while seated behind her father's desk.

Instead she tugged hesitantly at Reese's hand. "I want to show you something."

He followed her up the stairs, pausing in front of their room, but she continued down the hall. Puzzled, he stared at her as she swung the door open, revealing a much larger room, its massive four-poster bed dominating the space. Pulling him along, they stepped inside.

"Whose room is this?" Reese asked, trailing his hand along a deep tufted leather chair that was angled next to another in front of the fireplace. Kindling had been laid, and it burned steadily, warming the room. The bureau caught his eye, and he walked closer, recognizing his own effects.

Was this her way of kicking him out of their room?

"It's the master bedroom," she replied, smoothing the plump coverlet on the bed.

"I don't understand."

"This room belongs to the master of the house. We've been living in my room."

He glanced over her shoulder and saw her hairbrush and mirror lying next to the washbowl. He tilted her chin upward, searching her eyes, finding them unmasked and clear. "Is that what turning the sign around was about?"

She nodded.

"You want me to be in charge?"

"I want you to stay." Her voice was low as she shared her deepest feelings.

"I don't know."

Her heart sank, and her eyelids flickered shut as she tried to remember the promise she'd made to let him go if he wanted to.

Curling his hand around her long strands of hair, he continued. "I'm not sure I want to be in charge."

She opened her eyes warily.

"Sharing might be a different story."

"You want to stay and share the Bar-W?"

"Bar-M," he corrected. "I've been learning from this pigheaded woman who knows how to ranch and rope and break horses. Seems we could share all that till the babies come along."

"Babies?"

"Dozens of them, with your eyes and my good sense."

"You want to stay married for real?" She couldn't vanquish the doubt or quell the hope in her question.

"Of course. You'd be in one hell of a fix with a stomach out past your toes and no real husband."

"I love you, Reese McIntire." The words burst free, and an unexpected shimmer of tears accompanied them. For a woman who had only cried twice in twenty years, the past few days had been a waterfall. Still her voice was fierce, unrelenting.

Reese found the tenderness for them both. "I knew I loved you ever since your eyes stopped being brown."

Dazzled, she stared at him in wonder. Not that she cared if he thought her eyes were purple. "What?"

"Amber. They're amber. Not brown."

She closed those eyes, her gratitude and love engulfing her. This special man was hers, not only for today, but for all the tomorrows they would share.

Another thought struck her, and she held her breath, imagining the worse. But she had to ask. "What about your freighting company?"

"That's the kind of business for a man who wants to roam."

"And you don't?"

"Nope. I want roots so deep, they'll trip over them in China. I want you, Jem, and the babies you'll carry and this crazy land I've gotten kind of attached to."

Her eyes shuttered together briefly before she gazed at him with all the love she had denied for months. When he pulled her toward the bed, she followed willingly, eagerly. She watched his strong hands as they unbuttoned her shirt, gasping as they surrounded her breasts, taking their full weight. He shrugged her shirt away, reaching for the belt that fastened her denims. His touch continued down her flesh as he pushed her pants away, cursing briefly under his breath when he encountered her boots.

"You are a difficult woman, Jem McIntire."

But soon her boots as well as his were shed. The path around the bed was scattered with the remains of their rumpled clothing. As always, the feel of his skin against hers screamed at her senses, making her want to touch every inch.

But he held her head between his hands, staring at her face as though memorizing every detail. "You were wrong, Jemima. Your parents knew what they were doing when they named you." He traced a path over her cheeks, past her lips. "You are the dove, opening like a night bloom when I touch you."

Jem remembered the bouquet of evening primrose he'd brought to their wedding. The night-blooming flower had touched her then, and its significance overwhelmed her now. Choked on the love she was just beginning to understand, Jem reached for him, pressing against him. She knew her life would never again be complete without this man. She had fought him, cursed him, and now she embraced him. Knowing she would have given over her ranch to him, she valued him that much more for not wanting her to make such a sacrifice.

He was willing to allow her to be the person she was, not the one she'd seen herself to be in Charles's eyes. She was strong, opinionated, and abrasive, and it amazed her that Reese accepted who she was with all her faults. A flash of pain assaulted her as she fully understood Abigail's loss.

As though reassuring herself of his existence, Jem touched his face, her fingers skimming over the sunburst of fine lines near his distinctive eyes.

When she reached his mouth, she replaced her fingers with her lips, tasting him greedily.

The pent-up fears of the past few days erupted as they touched one another. Slowly, sensuously, their bodies moved together, finding each other with practiced ease. Reese's head sank against Jem's shoulder briefly, his breath sighing against her as she arched toward him.

Feeling the heat pooling between her thighs, she transmitted her fire to him. His hands sloped down the breadth of her body, lingering over the curve of her hipbones and traveling down the soft path of her legs.

When his fingers explored the thatch of golden hair at the apex of her thighs, she opened herself to him, sighing in satisfaction, gasping in wonder as always. Impatient to feel him inside her, she grasped him boldly, feeling the strength grow beneath her fingers.

He shifted, his eyes meeting hers, never releasing her from his gaze as he plunged inside. The passion built until their eyes had to close from the intensity. When Reese's opened again, he pulled back for a moment, studying the fit of their bodies, reveling in its perfection.

The love Jem offered overwhelmed him; the sacrifice she had been willing to make humbled him. There were no more roads to travel in search of an end to his loneliness. This time his eyes closed to hide his gratitude.

Jem's long legs crept around his back, her incredible

strength milking him. Reese's passion conquered all else, and he thrust inside, each stroke bringing them closer.

When he brought them to a shattering climax, Jem didn't release her grip on him, not wanting to break their contact. There was an incredible satisfaction in feeling that huge strength subside to rest inside her.

He lifted his head to meet her eyes, and she felt her breath catch. She reached out a hand to run her fingers through the black hair that fell onto his forehead. The piercing blue of his eyes had softened in pleasure, and she noticed the fanning of faint lines that had been caused by countless hours in the sun. Her fingers trailed from his hair, down his cheeks to outline his mouth. If possible, the heart that touched hers as they lay together beat even faster.

Raising his head again, he stared into her eyes, compelling her to return his gaze. "You're mine now, Jem McIntire, and you'll never belong to another."

Her eyelids flickered shut only briefly, gratitude and wonder filling her. But when she opened her eyes, they were fierce with promise, tender with love. Together they'd conquered every obstacle, forging a bond she would never relinquish. "Never," she whispered in return.

The locket between her breasts glinted in agreement, both halves now united.

"Never, little dove."

Author's Note

The author welcomes mail from her readers, and you can write to her c/o the Publicity Department, the Berkley Publishing Group, 200 Madison Avenue, New York, NY 10016.